No Place too Far

ALSO BY KAY BRATT

True to Me

Wish Me Home

Dancing with the Sun

Silent Tears: A Journey of Hope in a Chinese Orphanage

Chasing China: A Daughter's Quest for Truth

Mei Li and the Wise Laoshi

Eyes Like Mine

The Bridge

A Thread Unbroken

Train to Nowhere

The Palest Ink

The Scavenger's Daughters

Tangled Vines

Bitter Winds

No Place too Far

A By the Sea Novel

KAY BRATT

LAKE UNION
PUBLISHING

Text copyright © 2020 by Kay Bratt
All rights reserved.

Published by Lake Union Publishing, Seattle

www.apub.com

Amazon, the Amazon logo, and Lake Union Publishing are trademarks of Amazon.com, Inc., or its affiliates.

ISBN-13: 9781542021012
ISBN-10: 1542021014

Cover design by Shasti O'Leary Soudant

Printed in the United States of America

To Maui

Chapter One

"Is that a search-and-rescue dog?" the old man asked, his eyes on Woodrow. He'd been staring at them for a good ten minutes before he finally spit out what he wanted to say.

Maggie wondered if the man realized that the clothes he'd picked that morning matched the black, brown, and white coat of the basset hound at his feet. If dogs tended to look like their owners, this was a prime example.

"No, he's not," Maggie answered. "Why, do I look lost? This *is* the veterinarian's office, isn't it?"

The old man seemed not to notice her sarcasm.

"Yes, it sure is. I only ask because, well, he's wearing one of them vests. Did you buy it off Amazon like my niece did? She's got a little Chihuahua she can't go nowheres without. Carries it all over town. Even takes the little shit-eater into the grocery store."

Maggie didn't take the bait. But he wasn't done with his investigation.

"What about yours? You take him into stores and to eat with ya?"

Woodrow looked up. His soulful brown eyes locked on Maggie's, instantly calming her. He had that way about him. She could feel one tiny trigger of irritation or nervousness and a look from him could dissolve it. Unless it was warranted—then he was as alert as could be. Ready to protect.

"Mine is a *real* service dog, trained by a *real* trainer to employ techniques that can aid with a *real* disability," she said politely but firmly, in a voice that didn't invite further questions. Inside, she prayed he wouldn't ask what Woodrow was trained for, not that she'd tell him if he did. It was nobody's business that because of her experience with a relentless stalker, who was thankfully now behind bars, her fear had developed into sometimes-crippling anxiety attacks.

Woodrow was unique. Not only was he there to keep her composed, but he was protective and would never allow harm to come to her on his watch. If he sensed her anxiety rising, he'd nudge her, then move on to barking if she still didn't employ her learned coping mechanisms to calm herself down. If all else failed and she went into a full-blown panic attack, he knew how to lead her out of a building if possible and could even keep people away from her until she felt safe again. He'd only had to do it once, when a crowd at a craft festival she thought she could handle overwhelmed her and she couldn't get away fast enough. That day, she'd sat down and covered her eyes, crying and shaking. Each time someone approached to help, which would've made things worse, Woodrow used his body to shield Maggie and keep strangers at bay.

When she was calm enough, he led her away from the people to a quiet area. She'd bought him a steak that night, and he ate it while she praised him and thanked the universe that her son, Charlie, hadn't been with her.

Thankfully this man wasn't going to continue his fact-finding quest, though he did keep his gaze on her in an intense way that verged on being uncomfortable.

"They sayin' that tropical storm might be headin' this way and turn into a hurricane," he said, finally finding something else to talk about.

"Oh, I hope not." She didn't mention that from what she'd seen on the news, the storm was in the Atlantic, not the Pacific.

She fidgeted in her seat, turning her body the other way, hoping he took the hint. She could feel the sweat pooling in her armpits and wished she'd worn a different-color shirt. At her feet, Woodrow shifted and leaned against her leg. He gave her a nudge of comfort, his usual reaction to the anxiety that oozed off her in waves of anticipation.

Maggie's best friend, Quinn, couldn't believe how nervous Maggie was to talk to Dr. Starr. It wasn't as though she were interviewing to be a rocket scientist. She'd been a vet tech for seven years before changing over to public relations, so she had the required certification and the experience. Still, her desperation to land the job was sending her back ten years into a fresh-out-of-college scatterbrain with no self-confidence.

The outside door swung open and a woman rushed in, obviously in a hurry. She approached the desk and slid a framed photo toward the clerk.

"I was halfway to the airport and I remembered this. I have to hurry or I'm not going to catch my flight," she exclaimed, looking at the time on the cell phone she held.

"And . . . it's for who?" the clerk asked.

"Eleanor. She's my Maltese being boarded because I can't get my no-good brother to take our father to surgery and stay with him for a few days. Now I have to fly to Ohio and do it myself," she said, pointing to the frame. "See that button? I recorded a message to Eleanor so that she will know Mommy hasn't forgotten her. Please play it at least five times a day."

The girl at the desk blinked several times at the harried woman, then nodded. "Will do."

"Thank you. And please, please make sure she has her gummy vitamin every morning. It makes her hair shine." With a whirl the woman turned and was out the door, leaving the clerk looking shell-shocked.

Maui had some interesting people, to say the least. From hippies to surfer types, classy to laid-back, millionaires to street people, all carving out a life between the hordes of oblivious tourists who came to share a piece of their island one week at a time.

Only days ago, she and Quinn had breakfast at a small café in Paia, and lo and behold, the actor Owen Wilson and his brother Luke were there, having coffee and omelets, dressed for the beach and all but unrecognizable from the characters they'd played in movies.

Then later she took her son, Charlie, to the beach and watched the surfers trying to outdo one another. Small families were camped out all along the sand, the sun-kissed children playing in the surf, not a care in the world.

Yes, she could see how living there could be addictive. And it was weird, but she felt a rare sense of safety knowing they were surrounded on all sides by water.

Quinn had finally talked her into moving to the island so they could be close again, and Maggie didn't regret it, but wow—Maui was more expensive than she'd anticipated. She'd thought rentals were crazy expensive in her hometown of Savannah, Georgia, but Maui prices made those seem cheap. She'd found a little apartment smack-dab in the middle of a strip of four other tenants, then she bought a used car that had seen better days. Between rent and groceries, her savings were depleting at a rate she could only glimpse as it swirled down the drain of reality.

Luckily, now that she had a permanent address again, Charlie's dad was sending the monthly child support they'd agreed on, but even that barely made a dent in what it cost to live in paradise. She was also thankful for the legendary Hana food trucks that could whip up a simple dinner of tacos, fish, or several other options at a price she could afford occasionally. The roadside fresh fruit stands were another good place for her to pick up snacks for Charlie and add some color to their lives and plates.

Quinn had offered to hire her part-time at the hotel, but Maggie always heard the best way to ruin a friendship was to either live together or work for each other. Still, she might have to take Quinn up on her offer if this job didn't pan out.

Moving to Maui was taking a huge financial leap of faith, but starting somewhere fresh with a built-in support network like she had in Quinn was worth the worry. Anyway, Maggie liked a challenge. She was determined to prove she could come out on top, and do it with minimal help from anyone.

So far, the morning had her digging out from the bottom. Her overly enthusiastic uterus had decided today of all days to unleash the floodgates, her air-conditioning unit stopped working when the temperature was predicted to hit a hundred degrees, and her little prince showed his disapproval of breakfast options by throwing his microwaved French toast sticks on the floor . . . after breaking them into microscopic pieces that he pretended were fish food for his imaginary piranha.

He also did the said event while belting out an unintelligible tune—one surely meant to assure Maggie that her headache from sleep deprivation could only be worse, because she was blessed with nurturing a tiny being and was justly rewarded with messy hugs and a promise that she could sleep when she was dead.

Charlie is a blessing, Charlie is a blessing, she kept reminding herself as she sped around the house tending to a million little things.

Despite never having a minute to herself and feeling like there was an endless to-do list that hovered over her head, he was her everything.

Thankfully, he always considered staying with Auntie Quinn a fun adventure, which allowed Maggie to slip out without more drama to heap on her overflowing plate. Very generous of Quinn, considering that bookings were filling up after her successful opening of the inn.

Quinn never said no. She'd pushed Maggie out the door, telling her not to worry about Charlie, that they'd be fine. Even with Quinn's help, though, Maggie was behind schedule by the time she and Woodrow left the inn and got on the road.

In her haste that morning, she should have paced herself by remembering that veterinarian waiting rooms were all about . . . waiting, even if she was slated for a job interview. She'd arrived at the clinic with only three minutes to spare, yet another ten minutes had already passed after her scheduled interview time. That left lots of opportunity for contemplation. She couldn't have picked a worse day for a job interview. But this was the day, and Quinn's boyfriend, Liam, had pulled some strings for her to get in. And honestly, how many jobs was she going to find that would allow her to keep Woodrow with her? This kind of opportunity didn't come around often, so she had to put on her big-girl panties, suck it up, and get it done.

Mommy needed cash. Stat.

The lobby was already jumping though the hour was early. She remembered that Fridays and Mondays were usually busy for vets. It never ceased to amaze her how people brought their animals in for any tiny thing, including a sniffle or a discolored pile of poo.

Yes, your dog ate rabbit droppings. Or maybe he gobbled too many Cheetos. Are you sure you aren't feeding him grapes? So many stories still in her head from previous pet patients and their well-intentioned but sometimes irresponsible parents. And it was standard for someone's cat or dog to be near death on a Saturday or Sunday, when the office was closed.

But some of these early risers were definitely warranted.

Already she'd witnessed a young couple with their Lab puppy, frantic because the dog was barely eating. They described his vomiting episodes in detail as the receptionist jotted notes. They were strapped for money, obviously, and had tried to wait it out, hoping the dog would recover, but when he stopped drinking water, they'd brought him in and he was taken directly to the back.

Listening to the communication going on around her, Maggie could feel her clinical instincts coming back, and that gave her a small burst of confidence. In this case, she would bet anything the puppy had swallowed an object that was blocking either the esophagus or intestines. Many moons ago, before she was a fancy executive public relations manager and still worked a humble, wholly fulfilling job in a veterinary hospital, Maggie had helped treat dogs with those same symptoms, and most recovered if the item was found before it perforated anything vital.

Some dogs would eat anything.

Thankfully Woodrow wasn't like most dogs. Maggie had seen the strangest things recovered from exploratory surgeries—the weirdest being a whole baked potato. The owner had expressed surprise at that, but Maggie couldn't figure out how the woman hadn't missed a whole baked potato from the dinner table. Did people just make so many extra they didn't notice when one disappeared? She wished she could be so extravagant, but then she remembered how much it pained her that Charlie had wasted his breakfast that morning, and she was struck with a new bout of anxiety over how much she needed this job.

On the other side of her, a woman and her young daughter waited with a carrier full of newborn kittens. The little girl had been sliding around on the floor, hands all over the tile, making Maggie cringe at the germs she was most likely picking up that would inevitably land in her mouth.

But she said nothing. It wasn't as if she herself would win any Mother of the Year awards. After the blatant refusal of the French toast sticks, she'd given Charlie sliced strawberries, and since they weren't organic—because who could afford organic in Hawaii?—some might say they were fruit-shaped poison bombs.

7

She also hadn't studied the fine print on the back of the accompanied juice box to see if it contained real sugar. Not to mention the fact that she'd be accused of frying his brain cells since she let him stare mindlessly at cartoons while she'd fluttered around cleaning the kitchen, putting a load of clothes into the washer, and searching through her wardrobe for an interview-appropriate outfit.

She needed this job, damn it. Charlie needed shoes. And other boy stuff. Maybe even the confidence that she could keep a roof over his head and running water. Yeah, that might be a requirement of this parenting thing she spent her days fumbling at.

One thing was for certain: being a single mom was not for the faint-hearted. She struggled to make good choices for him and guilted herself constantly. Then sometimes she remembered that she and her brothers were raised on bologna sandwiches and tap water—snatching tube time whenever they could—and they'd lived through it, so she wasn't *that* concerned if some days she failed as a modern parent.

If she could just overcome the anxiety that creeped in sometimes, reminding her that she alone had the responsibility of raising a productive, decent human being. That she'd be graded on it when he was eighteen, and not on a curve either.

The clock on the wall showed twenty minutes past her interview time. Her nails tapped against the side of her chair, almost at their own accord as though not controlled by her brain.

The tapping alerted the receptionist, who looked up from the computer. Maggie was surprised that the young woman's short blue hair and nose ring were allowed by the veterinarian. Her name tag read "Juniper." *I guess a few things have changed since I've been at it,* she thought. She had to remind herself that this was a new start in a new place, and things were a little different—a little more laid-back.

The girl gave Maggie a sympathetic smile. "He should be out any minute."

"Okay, no rush," Maggie said, stopping the tapping.

The phone rang again and Hip Receptionist picked it up.

"Dr. Starr's office, how can we help?"

She watched Juniper nod, then smile, her ear to the phone.

"I don't think you'll need an appointment, but I'll run it by Dr. Starr. If it makes you feel any better, my toxicology teacher said *Cannabis sativa* doesn't cause serious implications if digested by dogs."

Maggie was impressed by the girl's response. And her unique style.

"Furthermore," Juniper continued, her voice taking on an official tone, "it'd be best to just leave him alone—maybe in a dark, quiet place. Or turn on some Bob Marley tunes for him, set him out a plate of treats, and wait it out. No worries, he'll be back to normal in no time."

Before Maggie could even get a giggle in at that, the swinging door behind the reception desk flung open, and a man—obviously the doctor—stood there. He was tall, wearing dark-blue scrubs, but she couldn't see much more than his rumpled hair and dark eyes. He wore a face mask and plastic gloves all the way up to his elbows, and he held a small wiggling cat in his hands.

"Are you Maggie Dalton?" he said, his eyes darting around the room to ensure no one else answered. He looked quite panicked.

Maggie stood. "Yes. Is everything okay?"

He gestured for her to follow and led her through the doors into an examination room. Woodrow stayed at her heels, then sat in the corner she pointed to. The sight of the cat didn't even phase him, and he didn't break focus.

The doctor used his foot to close the door behind her and then practically dropped the cat into her arms.

"I—what do you want me to do?" she asked, looking down at the wriggling kitten. It was a calico of dark colors, but she saw that much of its hair appeared to be gone in patches across its body.

"This cat is suffering from some sort of contagious condition, but it's different from any I've seen. Just hold it while I look through my book." He turned his back to her and opened a cupboard above the sink, taking a huge textbook from it. He set it on the counter and began thumbing through the pages.

Maggie held the cat firmly, but as she stared down at it, she wished she had put her long hair up before coming. Now it was like a curtain, impossible to keep from falling over and around the cat.

She felt confused because she'd thought she was only coming to an interview. Did he want her to prove she could assist? And why had he given her the cat to hold without giving her gloves first? She felt her skin crawl, sure something was creeping off the cat, onto her hands, and up the stands of her hair, ready to burrow into her scalp and make camp.

"Shouldn't I have some gloves?" she asked, feeling self-conscious.

He waved a hand in the air, dismissing her concern. He didn't look up from the book, though he mumbled a response.

"Too late for that, but you can wash up when we put her back in her cage."

Maggie didn't reply. Over the years, the office she'd worked for had seen more than its fair share of pets with hair loss. Gloving up was the very first prevention method, and one even the greenest vet student would follow. On that note, where was the doctor's normal handler? Or his temporary vet tech? What kind of place was this Dr. Starr running?

Her thoughts ran rampant while he spent the next two minutes flipping through the book.

The cat fought to get loose, but Maggie held tight, cringing at the vision of its body now totally pressed against her middle, contaminating her clothing along with her skin. She planned to burn the shirt when she got home, and Liam was going to pay to replace it.

The door burst open and a tiny elderly woman stepped in, looking around until she noticed the cat.

"Well, I'll be," she said, closing in on Maggie's personal space. "Joe, I was looking for this little one. Why'd you bring her in here?" The doctor turned and lowered the mask. He was grinning ear to ear.

"Mother, haven't I told you not to interrupt when the door is closed?" he said, tilting his head and giving her a reprimanding look. The woman narrowed her eyes, looking from him to Maggie, then back to the cat.

"Joseph Michael Starr," she said slowly. "Is this what I think it is?"

The doctor's laughter rumbled, and the woman stepped over to him, taking the skin on his arm in what appeared to be a painful pinch. Suddenly he went from a focused doctor to a chastised little boy in 2.4 seconds.

"This is Miss Dalton, isn't it?" She looked at Maggie. "Joe! I told you to be nice—we need her. Do you think your little pranks are going to make her want to take the job?"

Maggie felt dizzy. "Pranks?"

The old woman stepped closer and took the cat from her, snuggling the cat and cooing to her a minute before looking up at Maggie. "This is Princess. Her five-year-old child companion decided to give her a haircut with her kindergarten scissors. The mom doesn't trust the grooming places, so she brought her here for us to even it up."

Maggie looked at the doctor for confirmation to help clear the confusion.

"Just a little warm-up joke," he said. "To break the ice, you know?"

Maggie's face flamed with embarrassment. She'd thought for sure the cat had ringworm and possibly even mange. Now she didn't know whether to feel relief or be mad at being the butt of his joke.

"I'm Francine," the woman said. "And if you come to work for us, I promise that at least for a little while, I'll keep Joe here in check. After that, you're just going to have to outwit him, which shouldn't be too hard."

With that she—and the patchy cat—disappeared and left Maggie standing there, looking like an idiot as the doctor watched her reaction, his face still holding a tiny smile.

"Come on, let's go to my office," he said. "I'll try to act like a grown-up."

She and Woodrow followed him and she noticed right away that though the lobby was mostly utilitarian, the furniture in the office showed some personality.

He sat in the chair behind the desk, and Maggie slid her résumé in front of him.

"Nice dog you got there," he said, watching as Woodrow settled into the small space under Maggie's chair.

"Thank you."

"Look, I'm really sorry about that little test, but I'm impressed at how cool you kept it," he said, grinning once more before turning his attention to the paper. "This place is a zoo even on a good day, and while we all take our jobs seriously, we try to have a little fun every now and then. Otherwise, you go crazy, or so I've heard . . ."

She studied him. Now that the mask was gone, she could see he was in his midthirties or so. He had a young face, even with the series of laugh lines around his eyes. At least she knew where those came from, if the first ten minutes of their meeting was any indication of his usual behavior.

Finally he looked up.

"Thank you, Dr. Starr, for bringing me in today," Maggie said.

"Call me Joe. And you don't have to thank me. Liam has become a friend of mine. He told me you could use some loosening up. So really, you can blame him for the mange scare."

Maggie didn't reply. She wasn't too thrilled that Liam was telling people—her potential new employer, no less—that she needed loosening up.

"So why did you want to become a vet tech?" he asked, his eyes still on her résumé.

"Originally I wanted to be a vet. Not a tech," Maggie said. "I really don't know why. Don't all kids want to be a veterinarian when they grow up?" She was glad to turn the subject to anything other than her sense of humor, or apparent lack thereof.

He chuckled.

She saw his face change as he read more of her résumé. "But you haven't been in animal medicine for some time."

"I—I know. I took a little detour for a while. Did some public relations. But I'm ready to come back."

"Public relations didn't work out?" He looked up at her.

Now that he was serious, she saw his eyes were the deepest pools of chocolate brown she'd ever seen.

Concentrate, Maggie, she told herself.

"Things got complicated." She thought of how being hunted like some sort of animal had forced her to pull herself and her son as far from the public eye as possible. And how it made moving to a tropical island she couldn't afford sound like a good idea. Putting an ocean between her and her biggest—yet most unwanted—fan was indeed the catalyst for her relocation to Maui.

"Things are always complicated around here. Tell me a little about what you did when you worked for your last veterinarian. Did you draw blood?"

She nodded. "Yes, I'm good at that. I also cleaned teeth. Gave medication. I had lots of duties, and the doctor I worked for piled on more responsibilities as I learned."

"You didn't mention cleaning cages," he said, looking at her intently. "Or do you consider yourself graduated from that task?"

"Absolutely not," Maggie said. "I'll clean cages, bathe the animals—whatever it takes. I'm not too proud."

He smiled slightly. "Well, tell me what all kinds of animals you've worked with, or are comfortable working with."

"Mostly small animals. Dogs and cats, the occasional wild raccoon or squirrel. Oh, and reptiles and birds. I was the one they always called when an iguana was brought in because I find them fascinating."

He raised his eyebrows in appreciation. "Iguanas are illegal to own on Maui. But so far I know you wanted to be a vet when you grew up, you tried a different career path, and now you're looking to get back in the game. Oh, and you like reptiles. Do I have that right?"

"That's right, except I don't want to be a vet anymore. I wouldn't be able to devote that kind of time to school. I'm looking for a job that's dependable and safe."

"Safe? Hmmm . . . that's interesting."

Maggie didn't take the bait, but she did wish she'd answered differently.

"What about you as a person?"

What about me? What could he be getting at? She struggled to find something interesting but . . . safe . . . to say.

"This isn't an exam, Maggie," he said. "I'm just trying to get a grasp on who you are. Any hobbies?"

Was chasing a little human around the house a hobby?

"Oh, I do yoga," she said, relieved to find a decent answer. "Or at least I did when I was on the mainland." She didn't mention that other than having Woodrow at her side, yoga was the biggest tool in keeping her anxiety at bay.

He was staring at her too intently, as though trying to analyze her. Maggie could feel her armpits getting swampy again.

"I don't believe in all that New Age stuff, but if it works for you, that's great. As for me, I've got the ocean and the jungle to keep me spiritually and physically in shape. Much easier than all that twisting, turning, and chanting in a hot room, if you ask me."

She smiled. Her brothers were the same way. They thought yoga was something that hippies did to look cool. They were too tough to get in touch with their inner peace, too, it seemed.

"What about dealing with difficult people?" he asked.

"I've got plenty of experience in that department." If only he knew. What could be more difficult than a man relentlessly pursuing you after you'd said you weren't interested, for months on end?

"With that strawberry blonde hair and pale skin, you'll find yourself a target at times."

"Excuse me?"

"Some of the oldest families are clients here—the native Hawaiian ones, not the ones who moved here later—and they aren't too happy with mainlanders or foreigners coming in and taking jobs. Usually since we work with their animals, they keep it under a tight lid, but in times of stress, it comes out. It can get ugly."

Maggie was surprised. On the surface, Hawaii seemed like such a gentle place. A happy one too.

"Don't get me wrong," he said. "They need tourists and business owners. But they don't *like* that they need it. Their attitudes are justified too. It's a result of their land being turned into some sort of Disneyland for outsiders, ruining much of the natural landscapes to make room for more resorts. And everything they once held dear has become commercialized. The grass skirts, the Hawaiian shirts, even their custom of making beautiful leis with native flowers has been insulted by the garish plastic knockoffs sold all over the world and meant to represent their home."

"I've never even considered that. It's just such a beautiful place, I assumed they were glad that other people appreciate it."

"All of those things, the items and the dancing, it's the history of their ancestors and it's their culture. The hula dances were taught to the younger generations in order to pass down stories that spoke of family morals and values. Most of that was lost during the years of oppression. The majority of visitors don't know much about Hawaiian history and don't care to learn. They're here for vacation—to escape and be pampered—not for a cultural education."

Maggie decided right then and there that she'd learn about her new home, whether he gave her the job or not. She wanted to. Out of respect. Maybe curiosity too.

"It makes me sad that their way of life is being destroyed. Of course, if that comes across as bitterness toward me, I won't take it personally."

He shook his head. "You hit the nail on the head when you said 'destroyed.' Or at least, their culture is seeing a steady decline. Long ago the Hawaiian language was banned, along with chanting, hula dancing, and many other aspects of their traditions. Even though the ban was eventually lifted, now only about a thousand native speakers are truly fluent, and they're dying out too quickly to pass it on."

"I thought you're new here too?"

"I am, but before I came, I did my research. I want my business to succeed not only for me but in the hopes that one day I can contribute to helping keep alive many of the Hawaiian traditions. That takes money for lessons, schools, and giving to foundations. I'm not there yet, but I hope to be."

Maggie considered him. He had dropped his comic side and was earnest. Caring and compassionate. She imagined he was probably a damn good veterinarian too.

"I'd like to be a part of that vision," she said.

His solemn mood changed and he smiled, then looked over at Woodrow. "I'm not going to ask you about your dog. Liam let me know that you have him and that he's a good boy. Whatever the reason you need him, it's your business and you can tell me in your own time. I think it'll be nice to have a normal-size mascot, as long as you can guarantee he'll never be aggressive."

Maggie had already started sweating bullets again as soon as his eyes had wandered to Woodrow. She breathed a sigh of relief that she wasn't going to have to explain, at least not today. Ironically, when she'd gone to find a dog at the shelter, she'd been looking for possibly a German shepherd or a Rottweiler. A dog who looked threatening. But when she'd passed him—a quiet, shaggy fellow just lying there observing everything outside of his cage as though lost in thought—they'd locked eyes and she'd melted.

Until that point, she hadn't even thought about what she'd name her new companion, but the name Woodrow popped into her head as she was signing the paperwork. He'd easily gone with her to the car and jumped up in it as though he'd been expecting a ride. He sat up in the seat, staring straight ahead with the most solemn look on his face.

She'd loved him instantly. And he couldn't have been a better fit, even if he didn't look the part of a guard dog. To cement her gut instinct, he'd sailed through his service-dog training, impressing his instructors just as much as he impressed Maggie.

"He's not aggressive. He's really a good boy and just happy to be wherever I am. He's trained to stay where I direct him, if he can't be with me. And I may not bring him to work every day. At least once I'm comfortable. I mean—if I get the job. I know you probably have other applicants to—"

"Can you start on Monday?" he interrupted, breaking her out of her pity party.

"I—I—" she stammered. "Yes. I can start."

He smiled. "Don't you want to know how much you'll be making?"

Now she felt like an idiot. What kind of grown woman didn't ask the salary, hours, or try to negotiate some employment perks?

"That was my next question," she said.

"Oh? What was your first?" He raised his eyebrows at her.

Maggie felt her face flush. Was he toying with her?

"Sorry—I thought I asked you what the hours are," she said.

"Liam said you could only do part-time for now. I've got a woman to cover the morning hours so she can get her lab hours in. Can you do noon to six?"

She nodded. Noon to six could work for now—if she really buckled down on her budget—then when Charlie started school, she'd have to figure out something for the afternoon.

From the hall they heard a laugh, then a string of orders. Maggie recognized the voice from the woman who had taken the cat.

"So your mother works for you?" she asked, the words slipping out on their own volition.

He laughed. "Not technically. But since she's the one who found me this little investment, she thinks she needs to hang around to make sure everything is running as well as her beloved Dr. Kent had it going. Most of his staff have bailed, which is why we put Juniper at the front desk. She's usually a tech too."

"Oh, your mom knew the retiring veterinarian?" Now it was making sense why he had to hire some new staff. Dr. Kent's employees probably chose to leave when the business changed hands.

"Right. Dr. Kent was the only one she trusted to treat her little yapping ankle biter. Speaking of the five-pound devil, he's running around in here somewhere." He grimaced.

"Yorkie?" Now she understood what he meant about Woodrow being a normal-size mascot.

"How'd you know?" he asked, his expression incredulous.

Yapping. Little. Ankle biter. "Just guessed."

"I suppose I should be happy that she's got him. My parents retired here a few years ago, and Dad died six months in of a massive heart attack. Her little Rudy has been the light of her life ever since. But wow—she's walking on clouds since she got me to come here. I thought I'd stay in Honolulu forever."

Maggie smiled. "I can imagine. My mom would love living near Charlie and me, but it's just too far from home for her. She has too many ties to the mainland."

The doctor nodded, then stood. "Well, I think we're done here. The pay is eighteen bucks an hour. Stop and give Juniper your email address, and I'll send over the employment offer. Just reply that you agree to the conditions and you accept the job. Oh, also ask Juniper for scrubs. I'm sure we have some that'll fit. On Monday she'll give you a key. I like all my employees to have one in case of an emergency."

"Thank you," Maggie said.

"For the key? Or the job?" he asked, his voice teasing again.

"The job," Maggie replied. "I can't wait to begin working with animals again."

And to start getting a paycheck again, she bit down to keep from adding. She didn't want to look too desperate.

"You're welcome. I'm glad to have you here. Liam has done some work for my mom without charging her an arm and a leg. She thinks he's some sort of superhero. I suppose it's hard for seniors to find someone they can trust these days, so I'm glad he called in a favor."

She laughed. "He's got a lot of fans around here."

"I hope to gain a few myself," Dr. Starr said, and Maggie wondered if he was talking about her. She liked him okay, but after his stunt with the kitten, it was going to take a while if not longer for her to become a fan of any sort. A year or two ago, she would've been more receptive, but that was before she'd learned how fast someone could intrude on your life and turn it upside down.

"Great. Thanks." She stood.

He held out a hand.

Maggie wondered if he would still hire her if she didn't take his hand. Touching strangers wasn't something she was comfortable with anymore. Was she jaded from the one blind date that had turned into a nightmare? Absolutely. She now knew how any innocent interaction with the opposite sex could be misconstrued. However, since her—and the little tornado's—future was on the line, she made herself relax enough to accept the gesture. It was strictly professional, after all. "Thank you again for hiring me. I'll be here at noon on Monday."

Dr. Starr grinned and let go. "Oh, since you're coming at noon, do you think you can stop off and bring me a poke plate for lunch?"

Chapter Two

Quinn slid the key across the counter to check in her latest guests. Emily, her front desk clerk, was working, but these were special guests. She wanted their check-in to be perfect, so she'd sent Emily on break.

Charlie was another story. Quinn kept him by her side—a three-foot assistant with big blue eyes and a never-ending string of questions that didn't even stop while he concentrated on weaving the string through the flower lei he was making.

"Whoa, real keys," the customer said. "I thought all hotels went to those magnetic key cards?"

"Not us," Quinn said. "We do things differently here at the Hana Hamoa Inn. As stated on the website, our rooms also do not have televisions, alarm clocks, or other devices. This is truly meant to be a place to unplug and unwind."

"But you do have internet access, right?"

"Yes, the rooms have Wi-Fi so you can catch up if need be. Or you can reserve our business office in one-hour increments, though we recommend you spend as much time outside as possible, enjoying the true Hawaiian experience," she said. "We've also given you the room with the best views, and it's completely wheelchair accessible. I hope you and your wife enjoy Maui, Mr. Westbrooks."

He tucked the key into his pocket and smiled sadly. "Oh, I know we will. We came here on our honeymoon sixteen years ago," the man said. "Since then we've come every year on our anniversary. For the first ten years, we stayed in Lahaina where we could be closer to everything, including the nightlife. You know when you're young and in love, you want to experience all the sights, sounds, and activities a place has to offer. The last few years we've tried some of the other parts of Maui that are popular but not as touristy as Lahaina. We chose up-country for this trip so that we could just have peace. The only show we'll be taking part in is stargazing."

"Oh. You're a fan of astronomy?"

"I am," he said. "And Hawaii is an astronomer's dream because of almost nonexistent pollution as well as access to Haleakalā. I can't wait to take my wife up there again for the sunrise preshow of stars."

"That sounds lovely," Quinn said. And it did. She was going to have to tell Liam she'd added another item to her Maui bucket list. "Please let me know when you need transportation, and we can also pack you an easy breakfast to take with you."

He smiled broadly. "That would be great. I'm so glad I found this place."

"We are too. And as for the peace you crave, that's one of the biggest perks of staying in Hana, where you're surrounded by waterfalls and other sounds of nature. There's nothing more peaceful than a rain forest. Then if you're interested in going to the beach, you can get to Hana Bay Beach from a short path off our property. Also, the Kaihalulu Red Sand Beach isn't too far away, and if you prefer to check out the more distant Hamoa Beach, we can arrange a shuttle."

He nodded. "I might take a few walks on the beach if my wife sleeps in."

"It won't beat what you see at the Haleakalā summit, but you can catch a lovely Maui sunrise there around seven," she said. She stood back and clasped her hands. "Mr. Westbrooks, I'd like to thank you for choosing to stay with us for this visit. We're thrilled to have you both. I hope you'll understand if there are a few imperfections. Since we are so new, there might be some hidden issues we need to find and address, so please point out anything you see that needs improvement."

"I doubt we'll find a thing, but thank you. I truly appreciate it."

She nodded to him, then to his wife, who sat quietly in her wheelchair just to the side. She wore a flowered scarf wrapped around her head, the bright colors a stark contrast to the paleness of her face. The circles around her eyes were dark, but her expression was patient. "Your luggage will be delivered to your room shortly, and I'll send one of the girls to unpack for you. Again, please let me know if there's anything else I can do for you. Oh, and Hasegawa General Store is only a short ride away if you need any staples for the room."

"Thanks. For starters, you can call me David. And my wife is Julianne," he said. "We're not formal people either. So it seems we'll all get along just fine."

Charlie walked around the counter and up to the wheelchair. He ran his finger along the armrest, his eyes wandering to the shiny spokes on the wheels.

"Why does your chair have wheels?" he asked Mrs. Westbrooks.

Quinn cringed. Charlie was a unique little boy. He'd never met a stranger and was inquisitive, but in a sweet way. She'd thought she had him sufficiently occupied with lei making, but she should've remembered his short attention span.

"It's so that I can go where I want to go without walking," Julianne said.

"Why can't you walk?" Charlie asked.

Quinn wanted to melt into the floor and started to interrupt, but the woman held her hand up, stopping her.

"That's a good question. I can walk, but right now it's hard for me because I haven't been feeling well. When you don't feel good, you don't like to walk around either, right? Sometimes you're just tired?"

He nodded. "Yeah. Then my mom carries me."

She laughed. "Wow. Someone must have some strong muscles because you are a really big boy."

Quinn raised her eyebrows at that. She was right. Charlie was too big to be carried, but you had to know his mom to understand. Maggie grew up the only girl in a family of boys, and despite being thin as a reed, she was strong as an ox. Stubborn as one too.

"Can I ride in your chair?" Charlie asked.

Quinn felt her face flush. "I'm so sorry. He's not good with boundaries."

"No, don't be sorry," Julianne said. She turned her attention to Charlie. "You sure can. I mean, if your mom says it's okay. I'll take you for a ride on my lap, and David can push us."

"Oh, I'm not his mom," Quinn said. "I'm just looking out for him today. And we need to let you get settled in, Mrs. West—I mean Julianne. Charlie, maybe you'll see her later after she has time to rest up from their trip."

Julianne tousled Charlie's hair and he grinned, then quickly lost interest as he remembered his project and returned to Quinn's side of the counter to tend to it.

"Thanks so much," David said. "We'll probably see you this afternoon."

He went to his wife's chair and turned it around, then headed down the hall.

Quinn watched them go. She couldn't help but feel sad for them, especially the husband. It was obvious that he loved his wife dearly and was putting on a brave face as time with her was slipping away.

A bittersweet memory flooded back. Quinn remembered the last time she'd bathed her mom—not her biological mother, but the woman who'd raised her—both of them crying silent tears that mingled with the warm water Quinn so lovingly poured over her mother's battle-worn body. Somehow they knew it would be one of the last times they'd be so physically close, and they were right. Her mom had died a few days later.

Because of that experience, people battling cancer held a special place in Quinn's heart, and this couple, even before she'd met them, made her want their visit to be memorable. She'd put a pitcher of chilled fruit-infused water and a basket of specialty cheese and crackers, as well as some of her friend Maria's famous shortbread cookies, in their room. The final touch was a comfortable recliner they'd put a rush order on just a few days ago, delivered that morning.

The recliner—along with a small table that held a book of Hawaiian inspirational quotes—was placed directly in front of the large window in the room so that Mrs. Westbrooks could lie back and have the light to read by or simply enjoy the scenery from a comfortable place.

Quinn had found a handmade shawl from a Front Street boutique. The label called it a Hawaiian Sea Glass shawl, obviously named for the soft shades of blue yarn it was made from. One touch and Quinn had to have it for Julianne. It would be perfect for cool nights on the beach or even from their private lanai.

She'd folded it on the corner of the bed and left a note next to it welcoming them to Hana. She also left coupons for complimentary breakfast sandwiches, as well as a full lunch at the hotel café each day of their stay so they wouldn't have to venture far if they didn't want to.

Quinn didn't do as much for every guest. She couldn't or they'd be bankrupt in a year, but this couple was special. When the husband had called to make last-minute reservations, he'd said it would most likely be their final trip together before his wife succumbed to her illness. She'd recently stopped chemo and other drugs, deciding on quality of life over quantity—a decision that Quinn was positive didn't come easy.

He'd told her everything in what sounded to Quinn like a practiced monotonic voice. But she was sure she'd heard a dip in his tone once or twice before he was businesslike again.

"I'm so sorry to hear that, Mr. Westbrooks," Quinn had answered, struggling for the proper response. "I'll do all that I can to make this a wonderful and comfortable stay for her."

When he'd asked for a fully handicap-accessible room, he told her his wife used to be a dancer, and that her new mobility problems had brought her to another level of resigned acceptance that the disease had won. He'd asked for ideas to cheer her up while they were in Maui.

Quinn was still thinking on that one.

"I'm back," said Emily.

"Good, it's all yours. Your next guests were supposed to arrive on the island an hour ago, so they'll be pulling up any minute. I'm taking Curious George outside for some fresh air."

"Got it, Boss," Emily said, smiling at Charlie.

"Who is Curious George?" Charlie asked. "Can I play with him?"

Quinn and Emily laughed.

"Let's go, buddy," Quinn said, giving Charlie a little nudge.

She followed him outside, keeping a close eye on him as he promptly forgot all about George and began his exploration for geckos. Quinn wouldn't let him out of her sight. There were a lot of places on the property amid the breathtaking tropical flora where a little boy could get lost.

She wasn't about to let that happen on her watch, especially after everything Maggie had been through to ensure his safety.

The hotel sat on eight acres, landscaped with gorgeous native Hawaiian plants. Then, to her delight, there was a five-acre nature reserve easement between their land and the white sand beach.

If Charlie convinced her to take him that far today—and he was a heck of a negotiator—he knew he'd be able to see a turtle or two. Maybe even a pair of nene geese, the Hawaiian state bird.

Quinn thought of the million little things on her to-do list. She really didn't have time to babysit Charlie, but Maggie needed to ace that interview for her own peace of mind, so Quinn was happy to set things aside for an hour or so to help her out.

"Charlie, no tree climbing today," she said, catching him just as he started shimmying up the low branch of a banyan tree. For four years old, he was impressively agile. "You can't get dirty. Your mom might be taking you somewhere later."

"Aww, Auntie Quinn," he whined, but quickly turned his attention elsewhere.

Quinn loved that he called her that, even though she wasn't truly his auntie. She and his mom had been best friends since childhood, so to her they were family.

She stopped to admire the tall banyan tree. The landscaping foreman had done a wonderful job of working around and protecting the trees and plants native to Maui. Her brother, Jonah, was to thank for that. It was his friend Paul they'd brought in on a trial basis and now couldn't do without.

Charlie knew not to pick any flowers, but he stopped and smelled a hibiscus.

"Tell me how they got here again, Auntie Quinn," he said.

Since she'd gotten to know Charlie, Quinn had also figured out that she had a knack for telling stories, many of them based on the Hawaiian myths or legends she'd read recently. Since meeting her biological family and learning that she was born on the island, she had felt an undeniable pull to learn as much as she could about her culture. The Hawaiian legends were her favorites out of all her research.

It made her happy that Charlie loved to hear them too.

"A long time ago," she began, "the Hawaiian islands stood alone in the Pacific, many miles from the nearest continent. The land was lifeless. It lay cracked and dry from many years of volcanic activity. That stayed true until Mother Nature took pity and sent the birds to carry seeds from far, far away. She stirred up the winds and the tides to also carry seeds from other lands until finally the trees, plants, and flowers began to bloom, making the islands into the tropical paradise they are today."

Charlie smiled. By now he could probably quote the story himself, but for some reason she thought the imagery he conjured up in his head worked best when she told it. He still had a smile of wonder as he quickly moved out of reach and on to the next thing. It was fun seeing the island through his eyes. He thought everything was wonderful.

And it was.

Quinn knew she was lucky. She wouldn't say there hadn't been some ups and downs to get where she was, and she was still trying to figure some things out, but it was all coming together much better than she could've dreamed. Her life had certainly changed in the last few months. Before she'd come to Maui, she was an orphan, no family to speak of after her mother's death. She was also engaged to a man who on paper was a great catch—but for someone else, not her. That page belonged in a different book.

However, a deathbed confession from her mother had set her on a search for her father, which in turn led her to the discovery that she wasn't who she thought she was. In Maui, there was an entire family for her to find. It hadn't all been easy, but day by day she was learning what it meant to have a big family who loved her unconditionally and wanted her to succeed.

She'd broken off her engagement, and leaving her longtime (and overbearing) fiancé thousands of miles away was the smartest decision she'd ever made.

A flicker of green caught her eye.

"Here's one, Charlie," she called out.

He ran back to her. Without hesitation he plucked the gecko off the tree and held it between his two fingers, looking straight into its face.

"I'm going to name him Gary," he said, taking care not to make his tail fall off. He'd learned that the hard way the last time he'd handled a gecko, his guilty tears moving Quinn.

Quinn laughed. "Gary the Gecko? That sounds good. But you're going to let him go, aren't you? If you take him home, Woodrow might eat him."

She watched the expressions change rapidly on Charlie's face as he went through the gamut of emotions. She understood the dilemma. What little boy didn't want to take a gecko home and keep it in his room?

"Woodrow doesn't eat geckos, but I'll let this one go back to his family," he said finally, setting the gecko back where he'd found him.

"Good decision. Let's go a little farther—then I need to get back."

He skipped ahead, the gecko already forgotten.

Quinn watched him while she mentally checked tasks off her list. There was never a shortage of those. When her grandmother Helen offered her a partnership in turning the ramshackle inn into something profitable, Quinn had no idea how many tiny details went into a challenge like that. The family had snagged the foreclosed property for a song, and now you'd never know it was anything but the quaint inn that stood before her.

She was so proud of it.

They kept it small to maintain its categorization as an inn. Only seven guest rooms, but they were spacious. In the common areas, the floor-to-ceiling windows showcased the beautiful views on all sides of the building. A few overlooked their lap pool, which was surrounded by a natural stone deck and flanked by not one but two hot tubs. All the floors were striking New Zealand hardwoods. The small café carried on the theme as the wood repeated itself in solid butcher counters for the breakfast bar and hand-carved tables. The lobby was open to allow the trade winds to enter from the outside, but it was protected against rain.

Quinn's favorite renovation was the gigantic inlaid sea turtle that stretched across the lobby floor, the different colors of marble coming together in an array of dazzling shades of green to give the *honu* the majestic presentation it deserved. In Hawaiian culture, the sea turtle was considered good luck and a guardian spirit. It also symbolized endurance and longevity, which was what Quinn hoped the inn would have.

For her personally, the *honu* represented the beginning of her story, as she'd finally worked through her dreams and shards of memory to realize how she'd survived being lost at sea as a young girl. It wasn't luck. It was her guardian *honu* who had led her to safety, and it was a story she kept close to her heart, declining to share it with anyone.

Liam had done the turtle himself, showing his artistic side. He'd ended up doing much more than he'd signed on for as a contractor. After the turtle, he'd helped redesign the guest rooms so that each had its own beautifully situated private lanai and outdoor shower. It was his idea to outfit the rooms with rattan and teak furniture, bringing the feel of the island inside. Quinn immediately agreed, and they chose the furniture together.

Working with Liam wasn't a chore either. They'd finally acknowledged the attraction they held for each other, and though they were intimate—and he was the most generous and sensual lover she'd ever known—she wasn't yet ready to talk about making things permanent.

Quinn was wary of getting in too deep with anyone or letting someone else influence who she was trying to be. She'd been down that road with her ex-fiancé and had nearly lost herself becoming the woman he wanted to marry. She never wanted that to happen again.

Liam had a past too—one that he hadn't yet shared with Quinn—making her wonder if he was as all in as he claimed to be. Only time would tell, but in this case, they weren't rushing it. Quinn was enjoying being independent for the first time in her life. Never had she known how capable she was until she'd stopped letting others do everything for her.

She had to admit: Liam did a little something to her heart every time he smiled at her. But she remembered long ago, when she and her ex-fiancé had met, he had made her feel he was smitten with her too. Then he'd systematically, over time, modeled her into someone she wasn't. Though she went along, after everything was said and done, she still wasn't good enough because he cheated on her.

Then said it meant nothing.

Well, maybe not to him. But it did to her.

Quinn was logical enough to grasp that Liam was nothing like Ethan, and she shouldn't hold someone else's past transgressions against him.

She needed to work on sorting it all out in her head.

However, there were other things requiring her attention at the moment.

This week Quinn would hopefully receive the rest of the linens she'd chosen—a blend of earth tones and turquoise for a few of the rooms and a smooth coral color for others. She and Maggie planned to go shopping for the accents soon.

The major construction was finished. They'd been able to add two new outbuildings to serve as studio apartments, and her brother, Jonah, had taken up one of them, leaving the other open for renters who wanted that extra bit of privacy. Her sister Kira had the idea to make it a honeymoon suite, and she'd had a strong hand in the design. It had really turned out special.

On the other hand, Jonah wanted his quarters sparse, and they definitely were. She'd peeked in one day, and it still appeared as if nobody was staying there. He was a minimalist, to say the least, even denying himself the joy of art on the walls. No flowery bedding either. Just a plain army blanket and one pillow. At his kitchenette, she'd spotted one cup and one plate in the dish drainer and a jar of instant coffee. She'd offered him a coffee maker, but he'd declined.

If that's what made him happy, so be it. She still couldn't help but feel like he was punishing himself for something. Hopefully in time he'd accept that he deserved more than a blanket and a cup of instant coffee lacking even a granule of sweetener.

Quinn had to admit, in the beginning, her brother had been a little difficult. They were meeting one another as adults, so there were no childhood rivalries or affections instilled to help them get through the rough patches.

Jonah was complicated. After years of living on the beach, away from the rules of society, it wasn't easy for him to move in and take on a full-time job with responsibilities. Hurdle one was her insistence that he cut his hair, shave regularly, and wear somewhat professional clothes. She needed all the staff to look the part.

Jonah was probably as shocked as she was at the good-looking fellow who'd emerged from the barbershop one morning. He'd even let her help him pick out some clothes that could double for work. All he really needed was pants, since the employees were going to get hotel shirts, but they'd clashed just a little when she'd asked him to wear khakis instead of his usual board shorts.

Just a few snafus, but so far they'd worked through them. He didn't know exactly what he wanted to do in life, and Quinn was determined to help him figure it out.

The fact that they were working together to make the inn successful meant more to her than he could know. To say she was proud of all they'd accomplished in just ten months was an understatement. And he was really good with Charlie, coming alive as he explained different things to the curious boy. She wished he was that comfortable talking to her.

Speaking of curious, Charlie was squatting near a small stump. In his hand was a tiny stick, and he was using it to create a trail around a line of carpenter ants.

"Why don't we go in and get a snack?" Quinn said.

Charlie stood instantly, a smile spreading across his face. He was always up for food, and the fact that their chef, Jean Paul, let him help in the kitchen made it even more special.

They followed the path up through the garden to the main house and onto the patio of the café garden. They were still working on getting just the right ambiance but already it was looking cozy and romantic—and would be even more so when the sun went down and the strings of lights twinkled overhead where she and Liam had hung them.

She opened the door that led to the dining room and held it for Charlie.

"Hello?" Charlie called out, hopping through first.

"Oh, I forgot. Chef's not here right now. I think he's gone shopping," Quinn said.

"Awww . . . ," Charlie groaned.

After Liam, Chef rivaled Jonah for Charlie's favorite buddy on-site. His obvious yearning for male attention made Quinn sad about the separation from his father.

"I'm sorry, but we can still fix up a good PB&J, right?"

She'd learned quickly since she met Charlie that peanut butter and jelly could fix just about anything, and the magic words had him following her to the kitchen. It was ironic that sandwiches were the go-to in the small kitchen that was meant to create upscale food, but she liked them too.

"Do I hear Little Man in the house?" a voice bellowed from behind them.

Charlie squealed in delight as Liam came around the corner.

"High five, bud." Liam held a hand over Charlie's head, making him jump in the air to slap it.

Today Liam wore his usual board shorts—just in case the ocean called to him as he was passing by it—and his T-shirt stretched over his biceps in a very tempting way.

"Hi," Quinn said with a smile, realizing that the day had suddenly turned brighter. She loved that he popped in to check on tasks or just to see how things were going.

"Hello, gorgeous," Liam said, winking at her. "Need some help?"

Every time he looked at her these days, she felt like she would melt, thinking of being in his arms again behind closed doors. Who knew that feeling butterflies was a real thing?

But now wasn't the time. She needed to focus.

"Can you? I promised him a sandwich, but I need to check my email to see if the mock-ups for the new menus have been sent over yet."

"Go. I got this." Liam reached down and grabbed Charlie, throwing him over his shoulder like a sack of potatoes. A sack that giggled incessantly.

Quinn headed for her office, hoping to accomplish a few things while Charlie was being entertained. She sat down at her desk and signed on to her computer. The graphic designer they'd hired was from somewhere in Asia, so the time difference meant his replies were usually there when Quinn awoke.

She really hoped the menus were done.

Quinn's two sisters had helped her decide on the menu. They'd spent their lives on Maui and knew what was popular—and what was overdone. Their idea was to keep it simple but classy. Together, the three of them decided that gourmet brunch dishes, as well as organic juices, smoothies, and specialty coffees, would be the café's forte.

Quinn's email popped up, and the first thing she noticed was an email from Maggie.

Urgent, read the subject line. It was dated from the day before, just before midnight.

That was odd. She'd just seen Maggie less than an hour ago and she hadn't mentioned anything urgent.

Quinn opened it, becoming irritated as she read.

Maggie had obviously been hacked. The email claimed she was stranded in Italy after her bag with all her money and bank cards was stolen. She'd had to put a freeze on her accounts and needed to borrow money to get home.

Quinn rolled her eyes. Who would fall for that anymore?

The email also said Maggie would pay the money back immediately upon her return.

Delete. Quinn quickly sent it to the trash and moved on to the next email. Just as she saw one from the graphic designer, she heard Maggie's voice echoing through the lobby.

"I'm in here," Quinn called out.

Maggie joined her, her expression triumphant as she and Woodrow came through the door.

"What? Did you get it?" Quinn said.

"Damn straight I did," Maggie said, plopping down into the chair in front of Quinn's desk and pointing at the floor for Woodrow to sit. "I start on Monday. Just need to reply to their offer letter they're sending."

"Congratulations!" Quinn was ecstatic for Maggie. Her friend needed this. Not only for the money, but for her emotional well-being. Quinn had offered to help her out financially several times over the last few months, but Maggie was just as stubborn as ever, determined to stand on her own two feet. "Charlie's in the kitchen with Liam, making sandwiches. You want to sign on here and send the reply? By the way, while you're in there, change your password. You've been hacked."

"What do you mean?" Maggie said, her expression immediately going from happy to worried.

Quinn suddenly felt bad. She should've waited to tell her.

"It's not a big deal. I got an email from you with that same *I've been stranded, send me money* email that went around last year. I've gotten them before. But you probably do need to change your password, just in case." She signed out of her own email and set the screen back to the home page. The new menu design would have to wait.

Maggie came around and Quinn got up, letting her have the chair.

"That's weird," Maggie said, her voice falling away as she concentrated on signing in.

"What's weird?"

"It won't let me sign in," Maggie said. "It says wrong password."

Kay Bratt

"Try it again." Quinn could see that Maggie was getting really agitated.

A phone rang, startling them both. It was Maggie's, and she reached into her back pocket for it.

"Hello? No, Mom . . . I didn't send you that email. I got hacked." She paused. "Oh my God. What?"

Woodrow came around and leaned against Maggie's leg, nudging her with his nose.

Quinn got an unsettling feeling in her stomach.

"What? Why would he send money?" Maggie stood up and started pacing. "I can't! It won't even let me into my email right now. It's locked me out!"

She talked a few more minutes, then hung up.

"Well, I'm screwed," she said, falling back into Quinn's chair.

"What's wrong?"

"It appears that email was sent to everyone in my contact list because people who don't have my number are calling my mom and asking if I really need money. They're worried about me and Charlie. My uncle already sent a thousand dollars through Western Union."

"Oh no," Quinn said. "Don't they know these things go around all the time?"

Maggie sighed. "He's old. He only knew I'd been traveling, so it made sense. And the message said 'Urgent,' so he sent it right away. Now I wonder who else sent money to some weirdo pretending to be me. And I can't even get in and send a retraction."

"I'm so sorry, Maggie. I'll call my tech guy right away and ask what you should do."

"Can you sign on and let me read what the email says exactly?"

Quinn came around behind Maggie and pulled up her account, then clicked on the trash folder and grabbed the email, opening it full screen.

Maggie scanned it, then gasped.

36

"What?" Quinn said.

"Look beside my signature." Maggie pointed at the screen.

Quinn felt a chill when she looked closer and saw a tiny black rose posted at the end of Maggie's name. Dread washed over her.

"Oh, Maggie," she said.

"He's looking for me again," Maggie said, her face losing all color.

Liam chose that moment to walk in, Charlie on his shoulders grinning ear to ear. He held a half-eaten sandwich in one hand, and his other arm wrapped around Liam's head to hold on.

"What's up, ladies?" Liam said.

"Hi, Mama," Charlie said.

"Hey, baby. We're having a grown-up talk. Can you go back to the kitchen and finish your sandwich? I'll be right there," Maggie said. "Take Woodrow with you."

Liam set Charlie down. "Your milk is in there anyway. Go finish, buddy."

Charlie waited for Maggie to give Woodrow the signal to go; then they took off together for the kitchen.

"Why so serious?" Liam said, taking a chair.

"Maggie's been hacked, and she can't get into her email account. We thought it was just some random weirdo phishing for money, but now we think it might be more," Quinn said.

"More how?" Liam asked.

"He put a black rose beside my signature," Maggie said.

Liam still looked perplexed.

"Her stalker's calling card was a black rose," Quinn said. "No one else would know that."

"I think I'm going to be sick," Maggie said. "What if he knows I'm here? How did he get my email address? My password? He's not even supposed to have access to a computer. It's part of his sentencing."

Liam held his hands up. "Slow down, Maggie. You don't know it's him for sure. And if it is, hacking into your email account and finding you in person are two different things. He's in prison. And even if he wasn't right now, he can't cross state lines on parole or he'll go back to jail."

Maggie was doubled over as though someone had sucker punched her. Quinn went to her, putting her arms around her shoulders.

"Stop, Maggie. Don't let your imagination run wild. We'll get someone to get you back into your account. You can change your password and send an email alert out to your contacts. Then we'll see if we can figure out how he got access to a computer from jail."

Maggie nodded, but Quinn saw she was trembling.

"Don't read any more into it than it is, Maggie," Liam said. "If he upsets your world again, he wins."

Quinn was so glad he was there. As usual, his calm demeanor and logical thinking were comforting. Or at least they were to her. And she hoped to Maggie too.

Maggie sat up and squared her shoulders, holding her head high. "I'm okay. I'll call Dr. Starr and tell him to forward the offer letter to your email. And I'll wait to jump to conclusions until we can find out more about how he got into my account. But Quinn . . ."

"What? What do you want me to do?"

"Just keep your phone close tonight in case I need you," Maggie said.

"Can't you just stay here, with me? We'll put Charlie on the couch and you can sleep with me."

"Thank you, but no. This man has made me run and hide for too long. I'm not going to start that again. Charlie needs consistency."

Quinn wanted to say more but she also knew how stubborn Maggie could be when she was angry. "Okay, but I'm here for you if you change your mind. You know that."

Chapter Three

Maggie pushed the box until it was in the corner of her small kitchen, then went to the kitchen drawer and took out a knife so large she could've used it as a machete. She'd found it at a secondhand store, in case she wanted to cut watermelon. Now it felt ridiculous in her hands.

A few quick jabs, sawing back and forth, and the box had a window. Then she squatted down and cut out a small door. She stood, folded the top flaps together to make a roof, then stepped back, feeling accomplished.

"Is it done?" Charlie asked. He stood patiently waiting, his pillow and blanket under one arm, his stuffed bear and a flashlight under the other.

Woodrow watched from under the table, his muzzle resting on the floor as he looked bored with all Maggie's hard work.

"It is done, son," she said as she made a dramatic flourish with the knife. She was thankful someone had left the dishwasher box intact at the property trash bins. After spending an hour trying to figure out how to make a miniature felt fox out of a kit bought from Amazon, Maggie had to admit defeat. Her unfinished fox looked like a lopsided carrot with the measles. She'd thought needle-felting would be therapeutic, but now all she felt was the sting coming from a dozen tiny holes in her fingers that leaked red fluid. Though she had to admit that at one point she'd taken the jabbing of the needle a little too far when her mind had wandered to her troubles.

Charlie had held her felt fox/carrot thing in his hands and looked at it as though it were a lump of the most hideous muck in the world.

"This is not a fox, Mom," he'd said, raising his eyebrows at her.

Sometimes he talked like a little professor, especially when he shortened her name to *Mom*, but how the heck did he know what a fox looked like anyway? That was her first thought, but then she remembered the box they'd passed.

Everyone knew that a box fort could make any kid happy.

And it did.

Charlie grinned, then climbed through the small door and disappeared.

"I'm sleeping in here tonight," he called out. "Come on, Woodrow."

Woodrow rose as though his bones were a million years old, but he obeyed, crossing the kitchen to head to the box, knowing it was his job to entertain his boy while at home and off duty.

"We'll see," Maggie said, feeling exhaustion settle over her. If he fell asleep, she'd lift the box off and carry him to bed. She wanted his warm little body right beside hers so that she knew he was safe every minute until morning.

"Mommy," Charlie called out.

Maggie stiffly bent again, peering into the homemade door. "What?"

"You're my favorite person," he said, giving her the soft smile that never failed to melt her heart.

"Ditto," she said, grinning at the memory of teaching him the meaning of the word. Now it was a frequent exchange between them, like Patrick Swayze's and Demi Moore's characters in *Ghost*. She wondered if she and Charlie would watch that movie together when he was a teenager, or if by then he'd outgrow nights at home with his mom. She really did cherish this time with him, when he thought she was a hero for making a cardboard box fort; it might not always be this easy, though she hoped it would be.

His voice sounded like he might be getting sleepy. It had been a long day. For both of them.

Despite the damper of the email hacking, Maggie had compartmentalized the trouble to focus on mom duty.

On the way home they'd picked up a few flower boxes, some potting soil, and the cheapest impatiens they could find. Together she and Charlie had planted them and placed them on either side of their shabby front door, centered by a five-dollar welcome mat from Walmart. It wasn't much, but she wanted to celebrate her job in some way, and at least it would be memorable and spruce up their humble home.

She stood and looked around, deciding what was next now that she had Charlie occupied.

Dishes.

She went to the sink and squeezed in a dollop of soap, then started the water. She frowned at the hardened syrup on the breakfast plate and the nonsensical number of cups that one little boy had used in a day.

She had to do better. Leaving dishes undone for hours just wasn't her. She needed more organization.

What stopped her? Fatigue. Frustration. And if she was honest, maybe a little bit of laziness.

Sometimes she felt like a failure. But then, she had successfully kept her fear from showing in front of her son. Shouldn't she get brownie points for that?

Fear came new to her as an adult. It definitely wasn't something she'd ever experienced growing up. With three protective brothers, there was never a chance for anything too scary to penetrate her world, and if it had, they'd somehow managed to make her forget it. Even now, all she had to do was make one phone call or send one email, and they'd rally around her to make her problem go away.

But one of her brothers was battling his own demons, having basically sunk into a deep depression after his girlfriend left him. He needed to work on getting his own life together.

Between the other two, one was busy with his many start-up ideas, his competitive spirit sending him in a million directions to find the one concept that would catapult him to success, and the other one was still a newlywed and enjoying his life with his young wife.

Calling in the troops was tempting, she'd admit that. But it had taken her years after leaving home to finally feel independent and not like the protected kid sister. So her mother was the only family member who knew of the nightmare Maggie had gone through with her stalker, and she'd been sworn to secrecy. Maggie had opened the door to the madman, and it was her job to close it.

Her mom had begged her to reconsider, but Maggie stood firm. All her life, she'd been sheltered and protected. That's not who she wanted to be. She wanted to be strong. Competent. Self-sufficient.

Colby couldn't know either. Being who he was, he'd think he needed to move in with her just to protect their son. Who knew? He might even petition the court for custody. It made Maggie feel a little guilty, but no one could protect Charlie like she could. And if someone took her son, she'd have no reason to live. So far, Colby knew nothing about why they'd been on the run. He—and her brothers—just thought she was having trouble figuring out what she wanted to do in life, so she followed her best friend as a guiding light. Colby knew her better than anyone and could attest to her spirit that wandered at the same time it sought stability. The island would seem to him like the perfect place to satisfy those dueling sides of her personality. In reality, it was.

Despite always having a shadow behind her, Maggie was careful not to let him know the truth, and she made sure that Charlie lived the life of a carefree little boy. She'd learned something through this motherhood gig of hers: having a child meant being an expert at compartmentalizing.

She'd done a damn good job tonight too.

After they'd picked up the stuff for flowers, she'd stopped at a hardware store and purchased a drill and dead bolt, which she installed herself. At least it gave her a tiny bit of security, though she'd heard stories of doors being kicked down despite multiple locks. She couldn't afford a full-blown home security system, so the dead bolt would have to do—the dead bolt and her watermelon-carving-fort-making knife.

She felt the anger come rushing back.

It just wasn't fair. She'd thought their move to Maui was a new beginning—one that was free of always looking over her shoulder for the relentless Martin Andrews, aka the Ghost. How and why had he found her email account? Or was the culprit a random scammer and the rose emoji a coincidence? She didn't know for sure, but she was really pissed off that the sense of safety she'd had since moving to Maui was now in jeopardy.

Just the whiff of something awry was enough to reinstate many of the precautions she'd left on the mainland. And now she wasn't going to be able to put Charlie in a public day care as she'd planned. Having to juggle a job and childcare was more complicated when you added a stalker to the mix. Maybe she wouldn't be able to slip some yoga into her schedule after all.

Suddenly she realized she was clutching her coffee mug so hard her fingers ached. She let go, allowing it to drop into the water as she braced herself against the sink and closed her eyes.

She counted to ten, taking deep, cleansing breaths before finishing the last of the dishes and hanging up the towel.

The clock on the wall said half past eight. Half an hour to get everything in order, give Charlie his bath, and tuck him into bed.

She took the broom from the small pantry and began sweeping the wide span of crumbs, dog hair, and other tidbits from the floor. She moved from the kitchen to the ratty carpet, wishing she could afford a vacuum cleaner.

A few years ago, she could buy anything she wanted. Her job was great and her bank account thriving. Now she lived like a pauper.

Sometimes she wondered what she'd done to deserve having her life upended by some lunatic. She was a model citizen—okay, so maybe not *model*, but she'd never been arrested. She paid her taxes and didn't litter. She tried to be a good person, and she never hurt anyone.

Colby didn't count.

They'd hurt each other.

But she'd been kind to the rest of the world. And for that, she was a target?

It truly sucked, and the more she thought about it, the angrier she got.

She paused once she'd swept the last of the debris onto her makeshift dustpan—a sturdy piece of junk mail—then dumped it in the can.

She listened, looking at the door.

When she heard nothing, she put the broom away and took a look around the small room. It wasn't much. The apartment held the tiniest kitchen she'd ever had, a not-much-bigger living room, one bedroom, and a humble bathroom. She would've loved to have a two-bedroom, but first of all, she couldn't afford the extra rent, and secondly, it wouldn't make much sense since she and Charlie slept in the same bed. But there would be time to move up. She was just glad to have reconnected with Quinn and found a fresh place for her and Charlie to start over. And a short walk or drive anywhere filled her eyes with such magnificence that she immediately forgot their modest living conditions and focused on the inspiring natural beauty of the island.

But she was tired. Bone-tired, actually.

Quickly she made the rest of the rounds, picking up toys and returning the couch cushions to their place. She tackled the laundry basket next. It could've waited another day, but to be honest, she was weary of it watching her accusingly from the corner of the room, its sullen silence reminding her of being a horrible housekeeper each time it caught her attention.

She held up a pair of Charlie's jeans. Both knees had grass stains, and she didn't have any stain remover. Despite the stains, she smiled, knowing that they represented the fact that she'd kept her son safe while still allowing him to be a little boy. All kids' jeans should have grass stains, she told herself, then folded them and added them to his pile.

When she was done, she felt proud that she had two stacks of clean clothes and an empty basket. She kicked it as she went by on her way to put the clothes up.

"Take that, you ungrateful piece of plastic. Don't you know you should be thankful to even have a job?"

"What, Mommy?" Charlie called out.

"Nothing. I was talking to the laundry basket."

Her son knew her well enough to not ask why. Talking to things was normal in her household. It had been a lonely year with just herself and a tiny human most of the time, her social life cut short so she could have eyes on her boy as much as possible.

However, tonight she was feeling a little more than her normal crazy. Finally she was settled and wanted to put down roots for Charlie, and now everything was going to start up again?

She paced the floor, feeling angrier by the minute.

A knock on the door stopped her in her tracks.

Her pulse raced, and she could feel the pounding of her heart through her shirt. Quickly she tiptoed into the kitchen and to the box. She knelt down.

"Charlie," she said, curbing her annoyance.

He looked up at her, shining the flashlight into her eyes, blinding her.

"Stop it," she hissed.

He moved the beam and she could see his face.

"Listen, I want you to be quiet. Someone's at the door."

"Why don't you open it?" he said.

"Because! We don't open the door to strangers! We went over this."

"Sorry, I forgot."

Maggie took a deep breath. "Okay, Charlie, I'm going to see who it is. But promise me you won't come out of the box until I tell you to. If someone comes through our door, you be the invisible man. You can listen, but you can't talk, and I don't want anyone to see you. Okay?"

"Okay," he said, easily persuaded as long as it had to do with magical powers.

Woodrow crept out of the box, taking his place at her side.

They tiptoed to the door, Maggie wishing it had a peephole. Even the window at the porch didn't afford a view of the front step.

More knocking. Harder this time. Whoever it was wasn't giving up.

Woodrow growled. Maggie put her hand on his head, shushing him.

"Who is it?" Maggie called out, despising the fear her voice conveyed.

"Your neighbor," a girl replied.

"I don't know my neighbors yet." Maggie didn't trust anyone in the dark. Not even a female.

"You know me. It's Juniper. From the clinic. I have your key and the scrubs," she called out impatiently. "But if you want to wait . . ."

Maggie gave Woodrow a stay command and opened the door. Juniper stood there with a pile of scrubs in one hand and a bottle of wine in the other.

"Welcome to the neighborhood," she said sarcastically as she held the wine up. She looked completely different in real clothes versus the scrubs from the clinic. Her short tie-dyed T-shirt matched her hair, and the leggings showed off her curves. Maggie couldn't pull off leggings herself. Some things were meant to be left to the imagination, and the exact shape of her butt cheeks was one of those things. Or maybe it was that she didn't have the confidence to pull them off. Either way, Juniper proved that leggings could look flawless and pack some serious attitude.

With her colorful appearance and spirit, combined with her petite body, she reminded Maggie of some sort of woodland fairy.

"What the hell took you so long to open the door?" Juniper said.

A fairy with a potty mouth.

Just what everyone needed.

"I was busy," Maggie said, still blocking the doorway. "How did you know where I live?" She only had a post office box listed on her résumé, so the girl hadn't gotten it from work.

"Um . . . on my way out, I saw you and that little booger-eater getting out of your car, with that shaggy dog trailing behind you like a ghost. I live a few doors down. Come on, let me in. This bottle cost me ten bucks, you know. For that, I could've gotten two drinks down at Casanova's ladies' night."

Maggie couldn't help but laugh. What near stranger had the nerve to call a little boy they'd never met a booger-eater? She must have brothers too.

"Come in. Thanks. I'm sorry. I just—well," Maggie stammered.

Juniper held a hand up. "Stop. It's fine. You're new here, and really, you can't be too careful. Maui might look like paradise, but between the millionaires and common folk like us, we have our share of meth heads and thieves. You're smart to be careful."

Maggie was relieved she didn't have to say more. Then embarrassment followed. Despite the quick cleanup, her apartment wasn't really presentable. Even for Juniper. But something told her the girl wouldn't mind a little mess.

Juniper headed straight for the kitchen. As she turned her head to tell Maggie something else, she tripped over the laundry basket and was sliding toward a fall.

"Shit!" Juniper called as she reached out for something to steady herself and hit the wine bottle smack on the edge of the kitchen counter.

It shattered, red wine exploding everywhere. At least Juniper was wearing tie-dye . . . Maggie would have to remember that fashion trick since living with a preschooler left her looking like a walking painter's palette half the time.

All that was left of the bottle was the neck, which Juniper grasped in her hands. She looked down at it as though it were a precious family heirloom that had just shattered to pieces.

"What was that?" Charlie exclaimed, his little blond head popping out of the cardboard window like a jack-in-the-box. He spotted Juniper. "Mommy, why did you let a clown into our house?"

Gosh, Charlie must be referring to Juniper's blue hair. Maggie was totally mortified, but she had to admit, the red wine dripping off Juniper definitely added to the sad-clown effect.

"Well, there goes my ten bucks," Juniper said, ignoring Charlie. Then she looked at the scrubs she'd somehow managed to hang on to. "But by some miracle, you still have a clean uniform. You're welcome."

If a dog could look amused, Woodrow did as he stared, obedient in his stay command.

"Oh no," Maggie said. "I'm so sorry. I shouldn't have left that basket there."

Juniper shrugged. "It's your floor. I'm okay, but I was hoping to have a glass of wine with you. Do you have any? Please tell me you do. It'll help make it easier for us to clean this mess if you can hook us up."

Maggie sighed but appreciated her attitude. Juniper was a little quirky. And a lot comfortable in her own skin. Maggie could use some of that in her own life. Suddenly she was glad that fate had put her and Juniper in the same apartment complex.

She headed over to the drawer that held her one and only clean dish towel. "Yes, I have wine, thanks to the supermarket genius who put a display of Chardonnay near the cereal aisle. In the hour it took for Charlie to pick out what box of cereal he wanted, one bottle in my shopping cart turned into two."

Juniper raised her eyebrows at Maggie. "Mommy juice?"

"I'm a single mom," Maggie said. "Don't judge me."

Juniper laughed. "I knew we'd be friends."

At least a half hour later, Maggie shut out the bedroom light and backed out the door, leaving it open just a crack.

She tiptoed into the living room, relieved Charlie was tired enough not to beg for another story. Woodrow was sound asleep, his nose resting on Juniper's feet. Juniper sat there like some high-society dame, holding a wineglass with one hand and flipping through a children's book on counting in the other.

"Sorry it took me so long," she said. "Charlie won't let me leave him unless he's falling into twilight land."

"That must've been rough when he was still in a crib," Juniper said.

"Yeah, I wasn't too good at sleep-standing."

"Well, of course not. Only Coneheads can successfully sleep standing up."

Maggie laughed.

In addition to putting a spell on her dog, Juniper was proving to be resourceful. By the time Maggie had Charlie dried, dressed in pajamas, and tucked in for the night, the kitchen was clean again.

"Thank you so much for dealing with the mess," Maggie said, pouring herself a glass of the white wine. She took a seat at the end of the sofa. Woodrow moved over to her side and curled up next to her feet, his warmth deliciously comforting.

"You're welcome. That was only fair since I made it," Juniper said, then held the book up at Maggie. "Do you really think this is a good book for your son, considering his age?"

"What's wrong with it?" Maggie said, feeling a lecture coming on.

"Isn't he too old for flap books?"

"He's had it a few years," said Maggie. Book buying wasn't in the budget these days, not that it was anyone else's business. "I wanted Charlie to know how to count. And now he does. Now, can we have some grown-up conversation? What's it like working for Dr. Starr?"

Juniper rolled her eyes.

"Uh-oh," Maggie said. "Did I make a mistake accepting the job?"

"No, but Joe's a clown. So you'll need to get used to that. And sometimes he's a scatterbrain. Like most of the male species, he's got a few character flaws. I have to constantly remind him to stay on time with his appointments. He can't understand that if he gives Rover and his overdramatic mom an extra fifteen minutes, then Mittens the cat more time than allotted, the day just keeps getting behind, and we all end up locking up late."

"Sounds like he really cares about his patients," Maggie said. "That's a good character flaw, if you ask me."

Juniper shook her head. "Okay, Mother Teresa. I can see you'll be no help in the let's-keep-it-moving department."

Maggie loved how easy it was to banter back and forth with Juniper. She needed that. Easy relationships were hard to come by. Quinn would always be her best friend, and Maggie would do anything for her, but sometimes she was just too serious, always trying to please everyone at every turn. Knowing someone who didn't seem to care what others thought was a rare and welcome relief.

"So what's your story?" Juniper asked.

Maggie took a sip of her wine, then leaned her head back against the worn couch that had come with the apartment. It smelled like cats.

"I don't have much of a story," she finally said, breaking eye contact to hide the truth. "But I'll fill you in on the basics if you don't think that'll put you to sleep."

"If it does, I'll just blame it on the wine." Juniper chuckled while leaning in closer to listen. "Refill my glass and lay it on me, why don't ya?"

Chapter Four

It was late and Maggie was tired, but it had been a long time since she'd enjoyed having company so much, and she didn't want Juniper to leave. So she started talking. However, she was careful as to what bits she shared about her life. It was a fine line to straddle, being friendly yet being careful about revealing too much. Over the past year she'd learned to be guarded about the details. One never knew when someone posing as a new friend could be storing facts to use against you later.

To stay safe, she told Juniper about growing up with brothers and how they made sure she learned how to do things for herself. At school she was all girl, but at home she'd pull her hair back and fall in right alongside her brothers mowing grass, trimming trees, or learning what each car part does under the hood and how to fix the easy stuff.

"You're lucky. I only have one sister, and she's six years younger. I spent every summer babysitting her, and I had to hear constantly how I needed to set a good example for her. It would've been cool to have a brother. I don't even know where to find my dipstick."

Maggie laughed. "It's not always easy to have a pack of boys around you. I didn't have my first kiss until I was seventeen, and then he was so worried my brothers would find out that I had to initiate it. But yeah, they did teach me a lot of good things. Made me independent. And competitive. Which is why I can change a tire faster than any of them."

"So what you're saying is that if I'd have met you a month ago, I could've saved a couple hundred bucks by letting you install my new brake pads?" Juniper said.

Maggie laughed. "Yep. I can be quite the grease monkey when the need arises."

Juniper eyed her suspiciously, her eyes taking in Maggie's long hair and slim legs, as well as the last remains of her makeup from earlier that day. "I can't see it," she said. "But what about Charlie's dad? You haven't mentioned him."

Maggie adjusted herself on the couch, suddenly uncomfortable.

"Ohhh . . . ," said Juniper, noticing the overabundance of fidgeting. "Sore subject?"

"No, not really," said Maggie. "He still lives on the mainland. We aren't together anymore." *Don't give city and state of hometowns until you are sure you can trust,* Maggie remembered.

Juniper looked disappointed. "No chance of reconciliation? You don't think he'll fly over and try to make amends?"

Maggie had to give it to her, Juniper said whatever popped into her head. No reservations about boundaries.

"No, he won't. There's nothing to reconcile and no amends to be made. I realized early in that he really didn't want to be saddled with a family, so I decided to make it easy for him. I agreed to let him co-parent as much as he can, but not have to be too involved."

"You made the decision for him?" Juniper asked, her eyebrows climbing.

"Yes, I did," Maggie defended herself. "If I hadn't, he would've grown to resent Charlie, and I didn't want that. This isn't the Dark Ages where a woman must have a man to take care of her. I can take care of myself and my son."

"Point taken," Juniper said.

"But he wouldn't come here anyway. He's afraid of flying, and there are no charter boats going from the East Coast to Maui that I know of." She cringed, realizing she'd just narrowed down which side of the mainland her family lived on. She was getting lazy. Must be the wine.

"He can't be that afraid," Juniper said. "Afraid enough that he won't even visit his son?"

"Yes, he's that afraid," Maggie said. "He was in a small aircraft crash on his way to a fishing trip as a gift for his graduation. His best friend and the pilot were killed. Colby walked away, at least physically, but he still has a hard time with survivor guilt. He swore he'd never fly again."

"Jeez, that's jacked up," Juniper said. "How will Charlie get to see him? Or is he the kind of dad a boy shouldn't see?"

"No, it's not that. He's a good dad. He just needs to grow up some. But we'll go back a few times a year so Charlie can see his dad, and I can check on my mom. It's not the best scenario, but we'll make it work."

"That's going to be expensive."

"Not so much if I plan far enough ahead and get the cheap seats. I'll also have my tax refund to use, and anyway, I'll figure it out. I always do."

Juniper looked bothered about the situation with Colby. Some people didn't understand that a single mom could fill in for a father just fine. She'd just have to show her.

"What about you?" Maggie asked, eager to get the limelight off her own details.

"Not much to tell," Juniper said. "Clean record, I don't do drugs, and I haven't made any babies yet. Despite how I look, I'm basically your boring next-door neighbor who likes a few glasses of wine every once in a while."

Somehow, Maggie doubted she was boring. Maybe anything but that. "Boyfriend?" she asked.

"I date. No one serious. I like to keep my options open. I'm not yet the person I plan to be, so how would I know what kind of man I should saddle myself with?"

"So you haven't found your soul mate yet then?"

Juniper looked playfully offended. "Hell no. I'd be happy to find someone I don't want to beat the hell out of every day, then go from there."

"Good point," Maggie said, laughing at the ridiculous thought of the tiny woman beating anyone. "Do you have family here?"

"Nope. I left home when I was eighteen. My parents called it a temper tantrum and accused me of refusing to conform to society's expectations. They were right on the second part, but I also like to think of it as my pursuit of freedom. I'd saved enough for a one-way trip to Maui and just knew that something amazing awaited me. What I found was that if you don't have money or contacts here, you might as well be just another beach bum."

"You lived on the beach?" Maggie asked.

Juniper nodded. "I lived out of a tent and a backpack for about a year. Then I got tired of feeling unwashed and hungry, and I decided to set some goals. I got a job, saved some money, then lucked out and got a better job. After six months, I finally had enough for an apartment, making me a reputable citizen like my mother so wanted."

"Do you stay in contact with them?"

"No. They weren't willing to get to know the real me when I was under their roof, so I block them from knowing me now. The last thing my mom told me was that I'd amount to nothing. My dad stood there, silent, afraid to go against her when she was raging."

"Wow—that's tough," Maggie said, thinking of her own mother who was loving and supportive.

Juniper shrugged. "I actually appreciate that those were our last words. If she hadn't said them, I probably would've amounted to nothing. But now I'm driven to prove her wrong. After I got my apartment, I started going to the library. One day there was a woman recruiting for college."

"She got you to sign up."

"Not exactly," Juniper said. "I was too embarrassed in my cheap clothes and messy hair to approach her. But seeing her there got me thinking, and I did some research into how someone like me could get an education. Eventually I applied for scholarships, and wouldn't you know it, I qualified for a few. The rest you can probably figure out. I got the job with Dr. Starr, and I'm doing school on the side. I take care of myself without asking for handouts from anyone."

Maggie smiled at her. "You sound like a warrior. Nothing can stop you."

"I don't know about that. But one day when I get my degree, I'll fly home. I'll walk through my mom's door and hand that piece of paper to her. And I'll still probably have blue hair and this nose ring that set her off before I left."

They both laughed. Maggie would love to be a fly on the wall of that reunion.

"So what are you majoring in? Animal science?"

"Actually, no. My goal is to earn a degree in information technology. I used to spend so much time at the library that when a computer started acting wonky, the staff would ask me to get it back on track. Turns out I'm a natural computer geek. One that loves animals too."

Maggie instantly thought about her email issue. Quinn had texted that her computer guy was on a hiatus for the rest of the week. She hesitated, though. How much would she need to tell Juniper to get to the bottom of her hacker scare?

"What?" Juniper said. "You look like you want to ask me something."

"Oh, it's nothing. Just a problem with my email. I don't want to bother you. I'm sure everyone you know asks you to look at their computer."

"I really don't mind, though I can't promise I can help. Some issues need equipment to fix. Bad hard drives and such. What's going on?"

"Nothing like that," Maggie said. "Someone hacked into my email account and changed the password so I can't get back in. They sent out messages to my contacts too."

"Well, that's Hacking 101. Kiddie stuff. Any idiot can figure out how to do that."

Maggie shot her an exasperated look.

"Oh, sorry. Not just any idiot," Juniper said. "What kind of messages?"

"One of those *I'm stranded overseas, please send money* kinds."

"Did anyone bite?" Juniper asked, looking suddenly much more interested.

"Yeah, my uncle fell for it immediately. His wallet took a hit."

"Yikes. That sucks. Want me to take a look to see if I can get you in?"

Maggie hesitated. She didn't actually have to tell Juniper more of the story or her suspicions about who her hacker was. And if Juniper could get her back into her email, it would save her having to bother Quinn's guy. The less people she let into her online world, the better.

"Okay." She went to the bedroom, tiptoeing so she didn't wake up Charlie. She grabbed her laptop from the bottom of the nightstand and returned to the living room.

"Oh, you reminded me," Juniper said. "I need a photo of you to add to the website for the clinic. There's a "Meet the Team" page. Obviously, I'm keeper of the website. Dr. Starr can't even figure out how to open his phone some days."

Maggie stood there for a second, trying to think fast.

"I'd rather not be on the website, if you don't mind," she said finally.

Juniper stared at her, then nodded slowly. "Um . . . okay. I won't ask."

That relieved Maggie because she was so tired she couldn't think up a single reason that sounded plausible. She handed Juniper her computer.

"My password to get into the laptop is CharlieWoodrow1980."

"You're shitting me."

"I know, I know. I should have a more complicated password. I've been meaning to do that."

"You think?" Juniper said. "I could take one look at your social network and figure that one out." She typed in the password, and all of Maggie's icons popped up on the screen.

"I'm not on social networks."

That earned her another deadpan look.

"That's odd," Juniper said. "I thought all young, hot moms were on every platform posting pictures of the one moment their kids were smiling sweetly during the day, which off-screen then led to the fifteenth major meltdown of the week. What's your email provider?"

Maggie laughed. "Yahoo. And nope. I'm not on Facebook recommending recipes I've never cooked up either. Or crafts I'll never try." No wonder, considering the deranged felt fox she'd made earlier that night. "I'm about as far from a Pinterest mom as you can get. But hand me a slow cooker and a can of cream of mushroom soup, and I'll make you wish I gave all my secrets away online." She didn't state the real reason she avoided social networks, other than the fact that one positive about her exit from social media was that it was nice to not have to compete with the photographs of strangers.

"Email address?"

Maggie told her, then poured the last bit of wine into her own glass. She couldn't believe they'd drunk the entire bottle. She usually limited herself to one glass a night.

Juniper tapped some more and then looked up briefly. "And never give someone your login to get on the computer unless you know 100 percent they aren't going to try to use it in the future. You just met me. I could be some blue-haired, nose-ring-wearing hippie who will sell off all your information for twenty bucks." She went back to work.

"Well, you are two out of the three," Maggie said, hiding her smile. She was willing to bet that Juniper was safe. Some things you could just feel.

"Have you tried the lost password option?" Juniper asked.

For the next fifteen minutes, Maggie watched as Juniper took on a serious persona, barely looking up as she asked the occasional question, until finally she turned the laptop around.

"You're in. Change your password immediately. Use twelve digits and make it something hard to guess this time. Then we'll check and make sure someone didn't change your alternate email or the phone number attached to the account."

Maggie sighed. "I hate computer stuff."

"That has to change. Computers rule our lives, and you need to become aware of how someone can use it against you. Once we've done these steps, you then need to send a message out to your contacts that you were hacked, and tell them not to send money. Unless . . ." She looked up at Maggie. "We can change the flow to us and split it? I need to buy books next week."

For a second Maggie couldn't tell if she was kidding, but then Juniper gave her a naughty grin.

Maggie laughed nervously. "You don't know my mother. She's probably already called and warned everyone who I've known since the first grade. But yeah, I'll need to email the rest. Can I do that tomorrow?"

Juniper shook her head.

"I'd advise you to get it done tonight before your hacker discovers you in here and locks you out again."

Maggie let out a long sigh of exhaustion but took the laptop that Juniper was holding out to her.

"Tell you what," Juniper said, standing and stretching. "Didn't you say you bought *two* bottles of wine? That gives me just the ammunition I need to stay and keep you company."

She headed to the refrigerator without waiting for an answer.

Maggie was tired, but she didn't regret the long evening. She had a neighbor she could trust now. And best of all, she had a new friend. Seeing how she'd had to disconnect from most everyone in her life recently, she'd call that a win.

Chapter Five

Quinn listened to Liam quietly strum the ukulele and tried to allow the soothing tunes and the gorgeous view of the ocean to calm her mind. Saturday nights usually ended with her feeling nervous about the next day's scheduled events. Since she'd discovered her biological parents and siblings, Sundays were reserved for her family to get together, and Quinn was expected—and so far hadn't let them down—to be present for lunch.

Liam finished the soft song. "You look lost. What are you thinking about?"

It was after dark. They'd met on the terrace to enjoy the sunset and a few moments of peace. Liam was a little disappointed earlier that day when she turned down his offer of a dinner date at Mama's Ribs in Napili. He'd taken her before, and she'd loved the restaurant's spin on southern food—the chicken and ribs were to die for—but it was located near Lahaina, which was on the west side of Maui and would've taken far too long to go there and back. She had so much to do these days that dinners out were few and far between. Hana was just too remote from the happening spots on Maui.

She was just glad to finally sit back and take a deep breath. The evening check-ins were done, and she'd also completed her lengthy daily checklist. She'd calmed down the hysterical woman in room two and single-handedly caught the offender, a three-inch gecko, and relocated him to a place far from their room.

She was getting to be quite the wrangler as well as part-time therapist as she explained that Maui was a tropical place, and with that came tropical insects and other slimy creatures.

To finish off her day, she'd done the dreaded firing of the afternoon housekeeper who had only lasted two days.

It wasn't easy. Rosa was a sweet young woman. She just wasn't cut out for housekeeping. People tended to think that cleaning the rooms was a stress-free position, but that was far from the truth. The housekeepers had to be organized and efficient, turning the rooms over in the small pocket of time between checkout and the new guests checking in. Rosa couldn't keep up, despite the multiple chances Quinn had given her.

Not having rooms ready as scheduled caused angry guests and the ripple effect of stress on everyone on staff. Quinn hated to do it, but that was the hard part of being in charge. She had to send a message to all employees that they were responsible for getting the job done.

It was Management 101.

Still, the memory of Rosa's fallen face lingered.

Being a boss was not everything Quinn thought it would be. But the week was over, and now it was almost time for her one day with family.

"Earth to Quinn," Liam said, his voice teasing. "Anyone in there?"

"I'm sorry. Just thinking about tomorrow. Are you coming with me?"

"Sorry, I can't. I have a job that's behind schedule. The investor is flying in from China next week and is expecting to see everything finished in his new property so he can get it back on the market. I sanded the floors today, and Jaime is going to help me stain them tomorrow. We'll probably work until dark."

Quinn felt disappointment surge through her. Liam was her security blanket. With him beside her, she didn't feel so exposed to her family. Since she'd first met them nearly a year ago, it was easy to feel as though she were under a microscope. And with her mother, that was even harder. While Quinn was happy the woman had finally found her long-lost daughter, it was hard to make her understand that Quinn was no longer the toddler they'd once known.

She'd grown up as someone else—a new identity with a different mother, the only one she'd ever known. A good one too. It was hard to suddenly change allegiance. Even though the woman who raised her was dead, Quinn still felt a loyalty to her that couldn't be broken. But on the other hand, there was an attachment growing with Jules, or being rediscovered, that she couldn't deny.

Jules—Quinn's biological mother—had asked Quinn to share about her childhood. Friends, favorite memories, accomplishments, and so on, but thus far Quinn just couldn't do it. The death of her mom—or the woman she'd known as her mom—was still too fresh. Sharing their lives together would feel like a betrayal.

So as happy as Quinn was to meet Jules, there was still some distance between them, and that would take a while to overcome.

Her new sisters were another story. Eight and ten years younger than she was, they were immediately nosy and in awe, all at the same time. Having never lived on the mainland, their questions were less intrusive and more about what it was like to grow up on the East Coast, when she had started dating, what her college years were like. The topics that most interested sisters.

At first it was a lot of fun suddenly having siblings. But once the novelty wore off and they were no longer on their best behavior around her, she realized that being a part of a big family wasn't always the rosy picture she thought it would be.

For starters, she was beginning to understand sister rivalry. She felt in the middle of the two most of the time, always being asked to take sides. She'd had no idea that grown sisters still fought as though they were children.

Sometimes it was ridiculous.

Quinn refused to take sides, of course, but if she had the guts to say what she really thought, she'd tell them that they spent too much time together, that maybe branching out in different directions would be good for their relationship.

She still didn't feel as though she had that kind of say in the family pecking order, though. Someday, maybe. But it would take time.

"What about Maggie?" Liam asked. "Could she go in my place?"

"I asked her, but she needs to stay home and mentally prepare herself and Charlie for her first day of work. Which, by the way, have I said thank you enough for pulling the strings to get her the job?"

He reached over and took her hand, and she felt warmth climb up her fingers and fill her body.

"It wasn't just me. She still had to pass the interview. Joe said he thought she was great, so obviously she knows how to present herself well."

Quinn laughed. "She told me about the cat."

Liam held his hands up. "I told him not to do it. I thought I had him talked out of it. Luckily she didn't run screaming from the room."

"I knew she'd be good," Quinn said. "She really needs this. I've offered to help her out financially but she's too proud."

"I can see that. I hear redheads are stubborn."

Quinn laughed. "That's a stereotype but actually true when it comes to Maggie." Then she fell into silence again.

"What else? Spit it out," Liam said. "Something's bothering you."

He knew her so well.

"I'm just worried about her. You didn't know her before, but she's changed. She used to be a lot tougher. Her brothers made her that way so that she could take care of herself. I mean, the old Maggie would've given Dr. Starr a piece of her mind for pulling a prank on her. It seems like now she's cautious all the time and afraid of dishing it back. It's just not her."

"She's been through a lot."

"Yeah, she has," Quinn said. "I just wish I could make it all go away for her. I feel like her life is still in limbo. And Charlie, he's as sweet as they come, but I think he's a little confused. He misses his nana. And his dad."

"Any news on that front?"

Quinn shook her head. "She won't really talk about Colby too much. I think despite her trying to pull it off like she doesn't care, she knows it's not the best situation for Charlie. Or her. Being a single mom has to be rough. Especially when you think you have a stalker on your trail. When she first visited me here, I told her she should've gotten her brothers involved. They would've taken care of that creep in no time. But she said it wouldn't be right to bring that kind of crazy into their lives on top of everything else. She wouldn't even tell Colby what happened. Only her mom and the authorities were there for her to lean on, and as you know, the authorities take forever to do anything."

"It's crazy they can't do more. A woman shouldn't have to go through life looking over her shoulder constantly. If he really hacked into her account, then that should be grounds for more charges." He sounded angry.

"I agree. The thing is, he isn't supposed to have access to the internet where he's at. And they're supposed to let her know if he comes up for parole, and she hasn't heard a thing."

Liam sat up. "How are they supposed to contact her?"

"I don't know. Why?"

"Because if he hacked into her email, he could've deleted any correspondence giving her notice."

"She could always call and find out," a voice from behind them said.

Both Quinn and Liam sat up quickly and turned around to find David, their guest. His wife wasn't with him, but he sat on a lounge chair only feet away, balancing his laptop on his knees.

"I'm sorry. I didn't mean to eavesdrop, but I was here first. Julianne is sleeping, and I slipped out. I should've made myself known."

"Oh, that's fine," Quinn said, though it really wasn't. Talking about family issues and stalkers wasn't the professional front she wanted to present to her guests. They were there to enjoy a drama- and stress-free vacation, not feel like they were on the sidelines of a soap opera.

"How are you enjoying Hana?" Liam asked him, picking up on Quinn's awkwardness.

"I love it. The untamed beauty of Hana compared to the rest of the island is magnificent. It's like a wild sanctuary. Makes me feel isolated from a lot of the worries I've been dragging along lately."

"Hana has that quality, we've been told," Quinn said.

"We should've moved here years ago. Julianne wanted to. She says in Maui she can always hear music. In the wind. On the waves. She said it was everywhere. But I wanted to keep working. I thought I needed to keep pumping up that retirement fund. I spent the last twenty years planning for life instead of living it. And now it's too late."

He sounded so resigned. Quinn couldn't imagine the emotional load the man was carrying, knowing he would have to say goodbye to his wife soon. Forever.

"Oh, thank you so much for all the effort you put into making the room nice for Julianne. She enjoyed looking at the scenery today from the chair. And she absolutely loved the shawl. So thoughtful," David said.

"You're welcome," Quinn answered. "Just let us know if you or your wife decide you want to do something touristy. I can arrange private transportation or whatever you need." She didn't think his wife would feel up to it, but she had to at least offer.

"I doubt we'll be taking you up on that offer, but thank you. I'll keep it in mind." He paused for a moment. "Listen, I don't mean to bring this up again, but I couldn't help overhearing you talking about your friend's dilemma. I'm a retired detective and closed many cases that involved some sort of stalking. If I can help, let me know. But she can at least call and find out if the offender is still incarcerated. That much is easy and will give her peace of mind."

"Thank you," Quinn said. She was glad that the lights in the patio were dim so David couldn't see her face flushing with embarrassment.

"And if he has been released and she's worried, I'd be glad to talk to her about some safety precautions she can take," he said. "There are some real crazies out there."

"That's for sure," Liam said. "Some people just can't accept that someone doesn't want them back, or at all."

"I think she'll be okay," Quinn said. "She's been dealing with this guy a long time, and she's learned to be quite effective at outrunning him."

"That's just it," David said. "She shouldn't have to outrun him." He closed his laptop and walked over. "Here's my card. I still do private work, but I don't charge a thing just to talk to her. If she needs me, let her know I'm here."

Quinn took the card. "Thank you. I'll tell her, but I'd rather you enjoy your time with your wife and not worry about a thing."

He smiled. "It's my job to worry about people. Always has been. But, of course, Julianne is my priority. She just sleeps a lot right now, so I have time for a chat here and there, and honestly, a distraction might be welcome to keep me from focusing on . . . the inevitable."

No one said anything. Quinn nodded.

"Good night," David said. "Enjoy the moonlight."

When he walked away, she and Liam didn't speak. Quinn was still thinking of the look on David's face when he talked about his wife. She could only hope someone would love her like that one day. After she'd broken up with her fiancé, she'd decided it would be easier to be alone. But Liam was patient, never bitter, as he waited for her to think differently. Quinn just couldn't shake off all the years of being in an unhealthy relationship and who she'd become at the end of it. She'd realized she wasn't herself but rather someone who'd morphed into what her ex had expected her to be. Finally, she was finding herself again. It was like she was being reborn, back into her family and with a new sense of self and purpose.

No, she wasn't ready to commit to long term, but she hoped what she was able to give was enough to keep Liam in the picture.

"Quinn," he said, prodding her out of her serious thought.

"Hmm?"

"You're giving off those intense vibes again."

"I know. I'm sorry."

"Didn't we agree to live in the moment and not worry so much about the future?" he said, making her wonder how he always seemed to know along what line she was thinking.

"We did."

"Then take my hand. Stop all the worrying. My *kahuna* says that only the blind grope in the darkness. Tomorrow will come soon enough, so don't waste tonight."

She took the hand he held, intertwining her fingers with his. She really did care for him. He made her feel good about herself. He made her feel loved. But her ex was probably that way in the beginning too. How could she know this time that it was for real? That he was for real?

She no longer trusted herself when it came to relationships.

Then the other side of her, the soft one that longed for the happily ever after, reminded her that life was short. And right now, in this instant, she had a good man beside her.

She ran her nails softly up his arm, and he laid his head back against the lounge chair and sighed.

Quinn chuckled at how fast the action made him quiet. "You're right. But since you can't come with me tomorrow, how about you stay tonight to make up for it?"

He let out a low, sexy growl. The kind that started the familiar warmth deep in her belly. He leaned over and whispered, his breath tickling her ear in a seductive dance that brought on a delicious shiver.

"I think I should start making it up to you right this moment," he said, and picked her up, laughing, to carry her inside.

Chapter Six

Quinn's stomach felt so full it could pop, but she shoveled in the last bite of Jules's creamy macaroni salad, then headed back to the table to make a take-home plate. It was astounding how fast she'd taken to the comforting Hawaiian recipes, as though somewhere deep inside, her appetite knew this was the food of her heart—and her culture—and was just waiting for her to figure it out.

Her grandmother, Helen, had left a half hour or so before, but on her way out had encouraged Quinn to start arriving earlier so she could learn how to make some of the recipes herself. Helen was trying hard to be a part of the family without being overbearing, as everyone told Quinn she'd been in the past. Considering she was a big part of why Quinn didn't grow up knowing her family, the old woman carried a lot of guilt and seemed thankful to be allowed to join them at all.

As she passed Quinn, Helen had given her a thankful smile, then slid quietly out the door without any further goodbyes.

Quinn wished she could know the Helen of thirty years ago—the grandmother who was so broken by the bad deeds of her family and her fear that a curse was on their name. A woman who, in one tragic decision, thought it better to send a little girl away for her safety than to reunite her with her parents.

Though Quinn still didn't connect with Nama, the child she once was, she grieved for her, as well as for Jules and Noah, who felt not only devastated for the loss of their daughter but responsible for leaving her on the boat with only her brother to look out for her safety. If they had only known she'd washed safely ashore, the entire trajectory of their family history would've been changed, and so much heartache would've been avoided.

Yes, Quinn felt sorry for Helen and agreed that perhaps the next weekend she'd come an hour or so early so that Helen could teach her how to make something special. Sometimes when she felt the family's coldness toward her grandmother, she wanted to remind them that Helen had tried to get her back just months after sending her away. She never thought that Elizabeth would disappear with Nama, using new identities that couldn't be tracked. The irony couldn't be denied and the deed couldn't be undone, thus giving Helen the burden of silently carrying her remorse for the last thirty years.

Quinn considered the other dishes. Her other mom, the one who'd raised her and had also been born on Maui, had cooked Hawaiian cuisine often before her death, but it was usually recipes that could be made on a budget—nothing as extravagant as the recipes she'd been sampling at Sunday lunches lately.

Besides more macaroni salad, she added a serving of *kalua* pork with cabbage. The delicacy was usually the main event at a *luau*, but presented on a much bigger scale, with the entire pig prepared for the crowd. Her mother's version was cooked in a slow cooker but tasted just as succulent, as though it were freshly carved and shredded from the *kalua* pig.

From the living room she could hear her dad begin a light snore from his place in the worn leather chair no one else ever tried to snag. It still amazed Quinn that after growing up without one, she finally had a father. Not just a name but a living, breathing man who made a point to make her feel special whenever he could. He cared about her. Worried for her. Lectured her, even.

All the things a dad should do.

Sometimes it still didn't feel real. Today he'd quizzed her about Liam and what stage of seriousness they were at. He genuinely seemed to want her to be happy, and in his world that meant finding one's soul mate and locking it in.

Luckily her mom was busy in the kitchen during the conversation, or Quinn would've never been able to break away.

Sunday lunches were important to her mom, a way for them to honor their gift of *ohana*—the Hawaiian word symbolizing family— and the food was always delicious and plentiful. Quinn made her way around the table, adding a few more things of this and that, creating a mound of food she couldn't possibly finish but would have fun sampling.

At the dessert end of the table, her sister Lani stood, her arms around the platter that held Quinn's favorite of all, the malasadas—soft and delicious fried doughnuts sprinkled with sugar.

She grinned at Quinn, looking like the cat who swallowed the canary.

"I'm taking all of these home," she said, picking up the platter and holding it to her body teasingly. "You can have the leftover butter mochi."

"Don't make me fight you," Quinn said. "I'm not leaving without my doughnuts, and you know I have the advantage. You take the mochi."

Lani, definitely a more petite version of Quinn, looked her up and down, then set the platter back on the table. "Mom is going to have to start making a batch just for you at the rate you eat them."

"Fine by me," Quinn said, smiling as she added a few to her plate. A year ago she wouldn't have touched them with a ten-foot pole. Just looking at them made her waistband whine. But now that she'd accepted the curves that were such a part of who she was, she would never turn one down. Surprisingly, though, her weight hadn't gone up in the past year.

She attributed her newfound ease of maintaining her target number to the fact that she'd finally stopped worrying about it so much. It also helped that Maui was a much healthier place to live. With all that it had to offer in the ways of staying active without it feeling like torture, Quinn would never have to climb on another dreaded stationary bike or force herself to live on salads again.

Anyway, Liam said he liked his women to have something he could hold on to, and that Hawaiian women were meant to be women of substance.

"How's it going up there in the wilds of Hana?" Lani asked. "Have any celebrities checked in yet?"

"Nope, just normal people like us." As soon as the words were out, she looked at Lani, and they both burst out laughing.

Their family being brought together by a swab of saliva could definitely be considered anything but normal. And the fact that Quinn was lost at sea when she was a young girl, then found and raised with another identity, sounded like something out of a movie. But Quinn had to admit, it felt good finally knowing her biological family and having a sister to banter with. Two, actually, though Kira was currently not in the bantering mood and sat outside in a rocking chair, staring at her children playing.

Quinn wondered what all the seriousness was about. But Kira wasn't as open to talking to her as Lani was. It was going to take more time to solidify that sisterly bond. Quinn had a feeling that Kira was having trouble with her husband, as the two had barely spoken at dinner or afterward. Kira was such a young wife and mother, working full-time, that it wasn't hard to imagine that she might be burned out and exhausted, her marriage strained.

But it wasn't Quinn's business until her sister decided it was. She would never dig unless invited.

When she'd filled her plate, she took it to the kitchen to look for the plastic wrap. Lani followed her.

"You couldn't get Jonah to come today?" Lani asked, her expression serious now. She opened a drawer and plucked out the wrap, handing it to Quinn.

"I haven't seen him all weekend. He got his list of tasks and somehow completed every one of them when I was elsewhere. Before I left to come here, I went by his cottage, and he wasn't there."

Lani sighed. "Mom and Dad would really like to see him more. Now that he's not staying on the beach, they don't have as much contact, and they're afraid he's going to backslide. I miss him too."

Of all of them, Quinn had noticed that Lani was the closest to Jonah. He was protective of her in the way that he probably was of Quinn long ago, before the accident and her disappearance. Lani also seemed to have a way with Jonah, putting him at ease when she was near. Of course, she would be the most concerned about their brother.

Quinn finished with her plate and leaned against the counter. "I'm trying to help him. He does his job, but he's quiet. Too quiet. I don't think he's using, though. I really don't."

"I hope not. If he relapses again, it'll crush them. All of us."

She didn't have to tell Quinn that. The minute she'd driven up, she could see her mom looking out the window, searching for Jonah. It was sad, but it seemed that no one could reach him. It felt as though he were adrift, and no one could pull him in. Quinn knew he'd suffered a lot of trauma—first as being the big brother who was supposed to be watching out for his little sister who was swept away at sea. This guilt had followed him into adulthood, driving him to enlist and head off to Iraq for a few tours of duty that left him scarred even more.

Her mother said that Jonah's post-traumatic stress triggered night terrors and worse. Deep down, though, he was still that lost little boy who felt like he had to carry the years of grief his parents went through after losing their daughter.

In a perfect world, with the reunion of Quinn and her parents and the knowledge that she'd lived a satisfying childhood, her brother would find healing. But thus far that hadn't happened. What he didn't understand was that Quinn now also carried a heavy burden of guilt over what he'd lived through because of her and how he continued to let it drive his actions. She didn't have any memories of that fateful day, but her own questions nagged at her, like what if she hadn't wandered so close to the edge of the boat? Was she the one responsible for bringing so much pain to her own family?

Her parents were another story, but they'd somehow turned their early hard times into a story of resilience. Her mother, Jules, had been a wild child, choosing her boyfriend—Quinn's father—over her family and rejecting the wealthy lifestyle she'd grown up with.

Instead, they'd gone it alone, overcoming every obstacle as they fought hard to make a living, turning their pennies into dollars and their stubbornness into a thriving business of their own. The years of hardship they went through together before becoming successful had not pulled them apart as it did some couples. Instead, their relationship grew stronger until it was more like a fairy-tale romance than a story of rags to riches.

But that didn't erase all the hardships. Those memories were always there, threatening to pop up and upset a stable and happy family if they weren't careful. And Jonah's troubles were a constant reminder to them all that it wasn't always rainbows and sunshine in paradise.

Life was complicated, and it astounded Quinn how humans ever endured the constant sorrow and traumas to their souls to continue to strive for peace and happiness.

As though her thoughts were the magic needed to produce her brother, Quinn heard her mother call out happily, "Jonah's here!"

Quinn and Lani went outside to join Kira and their mom in welcoming Jonah, their dad suddenly awake and alert right behind them. None of them cared that Jonah was late; they were just overjoyed that he'd come at all. Kira's husband, Michael, stayed behind, his attention on the midday news.

Her brother climbed out of his old Ford truck slowly, his reluctance visible in every move of his body and the expression on his face as he made his way to the porch, to the family so glad to see him.

Jonah turned to Quinn, giving a pained smile as he readied himself for the onslaught of affection coming his way.

It amazed her how much he looked like a younger version of their father. Tall and lithe, his hair still blond even in his thirties. Even the sun lines around his eyes and mouth mimicked those of their dad's, adding character and maturity to an already too-handsome face.

But unlike their father, Jonah lacked the natural confidence and seemed not to know how he stood out from other men. It was clear he wasn't comfortable in his own skin.

Kira's boys reached him first, wrapping their arms around his legs.

"Come play with us, Uncle Jonah," five-year-old Micah said.

"Yeah." Lukas added his much younger voice to that of his brother's.

It still amazed Quinn that Kira was such a young mom, but any doubts of her mothering skills disappeared when she watched her sister with the boys. She was protective, loving, and everything a mom should be, without even looking like she was trying.

"In a little while," Jonah answered as he untangled himself from their grasp, just to find someone else vying for his attention.

Quinn watched as their mom enfolded him into her arms, whispering her thanks to him for coming as she held him a few seconds too long. He obviously had a soft spot for her, as he let her linger, her affection a direct opposite reaction to the way he avoided physical contact with everyone else. Their dad patted him on the shoulder and encouraged him to come in and fix a plate.

"Come on, Jules," her father said. "Let the man come in and eat."

Quinn decided to sit outside and be one less person on his trail. He saw her enough at the inn, anyway. Much more than he saw the other members of his family.

Kira had returned to the rocking chair, and Quinn joined her. They watched as the boys dejectedly left their uncle, then went to the end of the yard to work together to try to make a boomerang out of a small piece of rope and a stick.

"He looked good, didn't he?" Kira said quietly. "His eyes were focused. Bright, even."

"Yes, I think so. But I don't think I've ever seen him when he's not sober," Quinn answered, feeling guilty talking behind his back. Out of all of them, she felt the closest to Jonah and would never want him to think she was questioning his sobriety.

"You'd know it," Kira said. "He's much happier and quite the chatterbox when he's high. He's been called the life of the party, believe it or not."

"Well, that would be a drastic change."

Kira rocked back and forth, her eyes on her boys. "Micah is his mini-me. It infuriates Michael, but it worries me."

"Why does it infuriate Michael? Because of Jonah's past?"

"No, it's not that. Michael wanted his firstborn son to be exactly like him. Instead Micah looks like Jonah and acts just like him. He even slips into the same kind of quiet, contemplative moods."

That was an interesting tidbit.

"So are you saying that Jonah was quiet and contemplative even before the accident?" They always referred to her being lost at sea as "the accident." It sounded much less terrible that way.

Kira nodded. "Well, I wasn't around yet, obviously, but Mom said he was. She agrees that Micah acts just like Jonah. She even calls him Jonah half the time. By mistake, of course. I would say she's getting old, but even I see my brother in my child's face and his mannerisms. It's a bit uncanny."

"But Michael and Jonah get along, right?" Quinn asked.

"They do, but between me and you, Michael feels a little resentful that Jonah doesn't work on the boat anymore. He says if Jonah would step up, it would make it easier for us to do our own thing."

"What would you do?"

"Oh, I don't know. We just dream a little here and there," Kira said.

"Well, I hope you don't pin any of those dreams on Jonah, because I think he's just happier on land," Quinn said. "And he's doing a good job at the inn. Being the caretaker keeps him outside and busy but also allows him to avoid most people."

"But is that really good to let him continue to do that?" Kira said. "Don't you think he should stop being such a hermit?"

"Well, he's made an effort to be here, right? Your mom said he didn't always come to the Sunday lunches."

"Yeah, a lot has changed since you came into the picture," Kira said.

Quinn thought she heard a tinge of resentment in her statement, but before she could answer, their dad called everyone in for a family meeting.

"This can't be good," Kira said. "Dad is not a fan of formal family meetings. Come on, let's go find out what this is all about."

She led the way into the back door and Quinn followed, feeling unsure if she should even be a part of it.

Chapter Seven

Quinn took the seat closest to the back door. She wasn't sure what the family meeting was about, but if it got too serious, she would make a quiet exit.

Most likely, her brother was going to be the subject. All of them had been whispering about him at some point during and after the meal, so what else could there be to talk about? She felt a flush of pity for him and hoped whatever the discussion, it wouldn't be too intrusive. In her opinion, he was making strides to be more involved with family than he had before, at least according to everything she'd heard about his past tendency to disappear for months on end.

Kira and her husband, Michael, took up half the couch, and Lani sat at the other end. Their mom pulled a chair up to be beside their dad, and Jonah stood against the front door, an even faster escape route than Quinn had in place. The only evidence that he'd eaten was the toothpick he twirled in his mouth, his expression nonchalant but also guarded.

Quinn wondered how long it had taken him to perfect the I-don't-really-care look, or if it was genuine.

"Jonah, please take a seat. I'd like you to weigh in on this too," Noah said.

Surprisingly, her brother didn't argue. Along with everyone else in the family, the unspoken respect for their father was evident in the way he followed the request. He grabbed a chair from the table and placed it where he'd been standing, perhaps a last effort at finding his way to freedom as soon as humanly possible.

Jules looked at Noah, nodding for him to take the lead.

He looked sad, but he took a deep breath and began. "Let's go back to the weeks after Quinn was returned to us, and we discovered the family betrayal that took her."

Quinn stopped breathing when he said her name. Being the topic of a family discussion was on her list of Never Want to Do Again.

She hung her head, acknowledging the painful memory. When Quinn discovered her family, her one condition of having a relationship with them was that they'd forgive Helen for her involvement. She'd suffered enough by her own hand.

"Well, once the dust settled and we began to work on forgiveness, we all pledged there'd be no more secrets in this family."

Now all of them looked nervous. Just because you say no secrets doesn't mean that's going to happen, and Quinn could just bet that every member of her family had something they hoped would remain buried.

Her dad turned to Kira and Michael.

"Your grandmother told me that you asked her for a substantial loan," he said to them.

Quinn saw relief flash across Jonah's face before disappearing. She was glad that he wasn't the one on the hot seat this time.

Kira's face fell, but she didn't answer. She looked at her husband, Michael.

"We sure did," he said, raising up in his chair to sit taller.

Noah nodded. "Well, Michael. You and Kira are adults and normally I wouldn't interfere on something you obviously wanted to keep private. However, as you know, you both are a huge part of our operation, and if you plan on leaving it, don't you think that's something we need to discuss beforehand?"

Quinn could see a line of perspiration forming on Michael's upper lip. Kira also looked painfully uncomfortable.

After many years of struggling when her parents were young, the family business was now successful. Quinn wasn't involved in it, but the others operated twin vessels called *Holoholo I* and *Holoholo II*. They set out to sea six days a week off Front Street in Lahaina where most of the tourists flocked. The boats offered multiple scuba and snorkeling trips, carrying up to forty-nine passengers each time, with three trips per day. One of the reasons they always had a full load was because their ticket prices were affordable. They were honest and never tried to gouge the green tourists. Besides, they catered to the average couple or family, not the rich crowd. Her father said that the size of your bank account shouldn't be the deciding factor on whether you got to enjoy the magical world under the water or not—that it should be open to everyone. He always made sure of it and rarely raised their prices.

Michael and Kira managed the original *Holoholo*, with him the captain and her overseeing the operations. They had a small crew of six, mostly transplants from the mainland eager to live a beach lifestyle and ready to work cheap. Their dad used to captain the other boat, and Jules ran it, but when they decided to step back from operations, they employed a captain and taught Lani to take over the management of that one. It was a lucrative business, built from the ground up by both Noah and Jules, with the profits now shared equally among their girls.

"Easy for you to say, Noah," Michael said. "You married into money, but somehow none of it has yet trickled down to Kira."

Quinn saw a shadow of anger cross her dad's face and then just as quickly disappear. Jules looked disappointed, and Quinn was glad she wasn't Kira. The hot seat was looking mighty toasty at the moment.

"Hmm. That's an interesting take on my beginnings on Maui," Noah replied. "I like how you tried to rewrite the script, but you know damn well—or at least Kira does—that Jules walked away from her family and their money after we met. So if you call living in a tent on a beach and pulling ourselves out of poverty one inch at a time easy, then I'm happy to 'trickle' that challenge over to you."

"So this house sits on property you bought yourself? The craftsmanship's not much but the land could bring in a pretty penny," Michael said.

Quinn cringed. Michael knew good and well that the land was given to her parents by her grandmother Helen, Jules's mother. He was trying to rub it in that they hadn't paid for it.

"You'd better check yourself, man," Jonah said, his voice quiet and steeled. "This is our family home. And Kira gets plenty of the family money, but she has to work for it just like everyone else. If you thought you were stealing away a trust-fund baby, you thought wrong."

"Jonah, stay out of it," Kira said.

"He doesn't have to," Lani said, glaring at her sister. "This is a family business and a family meeting. And I suppose you don't care that if you back out now, I'm the one who's going to be left figuring out how to run both boats?"

"I didn't say that," Kira said.

"Then what's the loan for?" Lani demanded.

Quinn began to feel very uncomfortable, and Noah held up a hand. "Calm down. We can discuss this like adults. And Lani, you won't be left hanging no matter what happens. Don't jump to conclusions."

Jules put her hands up. "Everyone, take a breath. This doesn't have to turn ugly. We're here to talk through it. As a family."

Quiet settled uneasily around the room, but the vibes of frustration bounced off the walls. Quinn was glad the boys were still outside and not able to hear what was probably going to be even more heated words. A battle had been brewing between Lani and Kira for a while, and now Quinn thought it just might come to a head.

"Yes," Michael said. "We want the loan so we can buy our own business and be sole owners. Kira wanted to come to you first, but I talked her into waiting until we knew for sure we could swing it. We were going to tell you. Eventually."

Lani shook her head, visibly disgusted at her brother-in-law. "And after all we've done for you, Michael. Dad taught you everything there is to know about boating."

"Shut up, Lani," Kira said.

"You can't tell me to shut up!" Lani's face reddened.

"Both of you, stop it," Jules said, as though talking to bickering young sisters instead of the adult women before her.

Noah sighed, his anger gone and his eyes sad. "Okay, so you don't like working in the family business anymore?" he asked Michael. "Is that what you are trying to tell us?"

Michael's expression was hard to read, but Quinn thought he looked like he was planning for an argument, getting his thoughts lined up before he spoke.

"Of course I like it," he finally answered, his tone softening. "I worked behind four walls most of my life, and then you showed me a way to leave that behind and work on the water, in the sunlight and beauty of the ocean's shadow. And I appreciate everything you've taught me, Noah. You have to believe that. But I want to be my own man."

"You're a captain of a successful venture. You aren't paid hourly or by charter. Instead you get a split of the profits. How is that not being your own man, Michael?" Noah asked, his voice gentle. "Can you explain this to me? To us?"

"Damn it, Noah. Can't you understand? I want to go further. Make more money. Why don't you get your own son to take my place? It's about time he started pitching in anyway."

"Michael," Kira said, putting her hand on his thigh and scolding him with the tone of her voice.

Jonah was silent, but Quinn could see the rage well up in his face. His struggles were known in the family, but yet too personal to speak aloud. Quinn didn't even know her father that well yet, but she could tell those words hurt him. Of course, he probably had always wanted his own son on the water with him.

"This isn't going well. Let's try it from another angle. Kira, why don't you tell us what it is you and Michael want to do?" Jules said, her voice soft and inviting, a balm to the hurt and resentment floating around the room.

"There's a man who wants to sell his luxury private yacht charter business. It's a newer boat, looks amazing, and he gets a thousand dollars for two hours and two thousand for four. He already has repeat clientele and can prove he's made a profit for five years plus. You both know how hard it is to get recreation permits on Maui. This way we just take over a lucrative business without fighting the city to start from scratch," Kira said.

"Sounds suspicious to me. Might be a scam," Lani said.

"It's not a scam," Kira shot back at her sister. "The boat owner is ill and needs to retire. He's spent a long time building his clientele."

"Oh, I get it. You want to cater to the snob society that flies in and out," Lani said. "The snowbirds and celebrities. The common people aren't good enough now."

"No, Lani," Michael returned just as heatedly. "We want to build a legacy for our boys. Our own legacy. Not one they have to split across fifteen cousins."

"Anyway, the celebrities have their own boats, idiot," Kira said, glaring at Lani.

"Wait—what do you mean, fifteen cousins?" Jules asked. "You two are the only ones with children so far."

"You know what I mean, Jules. You've got another daughter in the picture. Who's to say she doesn't get married and start popping out kids?" Michael said. "And Lani over there is just burning to find a husband. This family is getting bigger by the minute, and that means my family will get smaller pieces of the pie as the years go on."

Lani looked flabbergasted at his comment. And rightfully so. Quinn could relate. She felt heat rise up her neck and fill her face. She wanted to leave but was mortified someone might see her. Her childless life was a sensitive subject to her. Not to mention that she wasn't getting a penny from the charter business and never planned to. She wanted to earn her fortune, not be given it. But the inn—that was probably going to be pulled into the discussion soon, and she wished she could disappear before that happened.

Noah stood. He pointed his finger at Michael. When he spoke, it was calmly but with authority. "You listen to me very carefully. I don't know what's gotten into you, Michael. I've never heard you disrespect anyone in this family like that before, and I'd better not ever hear it again."

Jonah stood too. He was deathly quiet and still. Like a panther.

Kira burst into tears, though Quinn wasn't sure if it was because she'd disappointed their father, or if she was upset for her husband. Or maybe both.

"Take a seat," Jules said, pulling on Noah until he sat back down. She beckoned for Jonah to do the same. "We aren't going to draw battle lines in this family. I won't have it."

"So I guess you're going to tell Helen not to loan us the money?" Michael said. "Going to ruin our one and only chance at finally catching a break because you want to keep all the money tied up in the family business."

"My mother is in charge of her own accounts," Jules answered, her voice soft. "But before you do this, I'd like for us to decide the future together, as a family. Like we've always done."

Michael stood and beckoned for Kira. He ignored Jules altogether. "Kira, get the boys. We're leaving. No one is going to tell me how to make decisions for *my* family. You aren't a child in this house anymore, and we don't owe them anything."

Jonah stood and launched at Michael then, but just as fast, their dad stepped between them, stopping Jonah without Michael ever knowing what just about befell him.

"Let it go, son," he said, putting his hands on Jonah's chest. "Let them go on home and we'll discuss this later, when everyone has had time to cool down."

"He disrespects Mom like that again and there won't be a later for him," Jonah said, so quietly that Quinn had to strain to hear. As she did, she realized she was trembling.

Jules came to her and pulled her into a hug, then let her go. "I'm sorry, Quinn. This wasn't what we'd hoped to accomplish with a discussion, and I'm sure you aren't used to all this family drama."

"No, not really." She didn't think the few years of teenage angst and gray hairs she gave her other mother could quite compare.

"That's just because you didn't have your siblings around then. But I promise, it's worth the growing pains to have family. Just bear with us," Jules said, her eyes pleading for Quinn to understand.

"It's okay, Mom. Really. But I have to get back to the inn," Quinn said, collecting her bag. "I'll talk to you later this week."

She didn't say goodbye to anyone else. There was too much chatter going on behind her, and her nerves were frayed from being a witness to her first family feud. She went out the back door, waited under the cover of the porch for Kira's family to get in their van and leave, then went to her Jeep and climbed in.

Once on the road, she picked up her phone to call Liam. Even if he couldn't come to the hotel, she needed to hear his voice.

Chapter Eight

Maggie shifted in her seat, leaning in to give her total attention. Quinn had asked her over for a late Sunday afternoon chat. Maggie was tired but despite that, Quinn needed to vent, and that's what best friends were for. Liam had Charlie, and they'd gone off on a short hike. Maggie didn't want him too far from her, and Liam had promised to stay within earshot of the back of the inn.

"And then Michael just stormed out of there with Kira and the boys," Quinn said. "Jonah looked like he wanted to chase Michael and beat the piss out of him."

Maggie smiled gently. "I'm so sorry. But this kind of stuff happens in big families. We've had get-togethers where my brothers drew blood from one another, then the next day went out hunting together. It's just the way it is. You'll get used to it, I promise."

They heard footsteps behind them, and Maggie turned. A tall, older man came into view. Quinn greeted him.

"Maggie, this is Mr. Westbrooks. He and his wife are guests here at the inn."

He held his hand out and Maggie shook it. He had an official look about him, even in his casual polo shirt and shorts.

Quinn cleared her throat. "Maggie, Mr. Westbrooks—David—is a retired detective and has offered to talk to you about some precautions you can take. Just to be safe."

Maggie felt cornered and a little peeved at Quinn. This was an obvious setup. Woodrow sat at her feet, the only thing keeping her from jumping out of her chair to go look for the wine bottle to fill her nearly empty glass. She had a feeling she was going to need a round two.

She smiled politely. "I really appreciate it, but I've kind of been through the whole gamut of precautions, considering what's happened in the past. I'm sure Quinn filled you in."

Quinn looked guilty, as she should.

"Good for you," David said amicably. He gestured toward Woodrow. "And kudos for getting the dog. I've told many clients that a dog can be their first and best defense, especially if he is trained."

"He's only trained as a service dog, but he's very protective too," Maggie said, winding her fingers through the hair on Woodrow's neck.

"Great," David said. "He'll be a huge help to you if someone comes back around. And just so you know, stalkers are a strange breed. They're lonely and lack self-esteem, yet they think they are extremely important."

"That sounds about right," Maggie said, taking a sip of water.

"I just don't understand what they get out of it," Quinn said. "Why spend your time going after someone who doesn't want to be with you?"

"That's a tricky answer," David said. "There are different variations of stalkers, but the two most common that I've dealt with are the predatory stalker and the rejected stalker. The predatory stalker is obviously the most dangerous, as he—or she, in some cases—seeks sexual gratification by using dominance and control. They get off on planning the process and fantasizing about the victim. The rejected stalker is someone most likely looking for vindication."

"Mine is the rejected stalker," Maggie said. "We met on a dating site. I felt something was off about him, so after the first date I told him I wasn't interested. He didn't want to take no for an answer."

David nodded. "Very common. What mode of harassment did he choose?"

"At first it was just irritating things. Flowers. Letters professing his love. I nicely tried to dissuade him for a while. Then when I finally told him outright to leave me alone, he got weird. He befriended people on my social network, then sent them messages with lies about me. He called my boss and told him he had a nude video of me. Which he didn't, but at the time I worked as a publicist, and that's the last kind of rumor we want making the rounds to our clients. He started showing up randomly at places I was at, like the grocery store or at a gas pump. One day I came out of a doctor's appointment, and he was sitting in the lobby as if he were a patient too."

"Would it have been possible?" David asked.

Maggie scowled. "It was at the gynecologist. I got a restraining order then."

"So what finally sent him to jail?" David asked. "He broke the order?"

Maggie nodded. She felt sick. The memories never got easier to reprocess.

"For weeks I thought someone was coming into my house, but I couldn't prove it. I'd find little things out of place. Things I knew weren't the way I left them. The police wouldn't—or couldn't—do anything without proof. So I set up a hidden camera, tucked into a teddy bear I had sitting on my dresser. It caught him doing, well . . . let's say, *unsavory* things, with items from my lingerie drawer. Of course, he knew my schedule, so he made sure I wasn't at home. I guess he didn't think I was smart enough to set up surveillance. Still, they couldn't catch him right away because somehow, he got wind of the warrant for his arrest."

She felt Quinn's stare on her, but she didn't look up. It would be full of pity.

David sounded even more serious when he spoke again. "You're right. He meets the criteria. But what I want you to understand, if you don't already, is that a rejected stalker might seem harmless, but in some circumstances they can become predatory. Out of the many types of stalkers, the predatory and the rejected stalkers are the two most likely to assault their victims. If you had surprised him, there is no telling what he'd have done. Or what he had planned for another time."

Maggie felt ice water creeping into her veins. It was a balmy afternoon in Maui, and suddenly she was chilled.

"Yes, I know that. I did my own research when this all started, and what I found was the catalyst to my year on the run. I quit my job, packed up my house, and went from town to town, jumping states to stay ahead of him, to keep my son safe, until they finally caught him."

David's expression changed. "Oh, I wasn't aware you have a son."

"You met him when you checked in," Quinn said. "That was Charlie."

He nodded. "Oh, the curious little boy. That makes things a little more complicated."

"Were you able to find out if he's still incarcerated?" Quinn asked.

"I can't call until tomorrow." Maggie bit her lip, then realized Quinn would catch that and know how worried she was, so she let go.

David leaned forward. "I get the impression you are fairly buttoned up and probably doing all the right things. But if it will make you feel any better, I'll make a few calls and see if I can dig up any intel."

Maggie hesitated. She hated to involve a stranger, and she also didn't like that this was all becoming real again. That old fear was settling into her bones, and it made her mind skip ahead to the next possibility. Where would she go next? And would she ever be able to settle Charlie somewhere?

"Maggie, I can see what's going on in that head of yours," Quinn said. She reached over and grabbed Maggie's hand. "Don't feel like you have to be alone in this. Let David check it out. Just as a precaution. You're safe here, though."

Maggie nodded, but she didn't believe that. She didn't believe she could ever feel safe again. She gave him the name and brought up the phone number and address of the correctional facility.

David jotted it down, then turned back to Maggie. "Let's talk about further defenses. Do you have a firearm?"

"No, and I won't have one. Guns and children in a small apartment are not a safe combination." She was firm on that one, and her tone let him know it.

"Even if she wanted to, she probably couldn't get a license to carry here anyway," Quinn said. "Hawaii gun laws are strict and especially in Maui."

"Then she should be taking some self-defense courses," David said. "I'm sure there's someone on the island."

"Listen," Maggie said, "I grew up in a family of brothers. I can take care of myself."

"It never hurts to refresh what you know, Maggie. There's a woman on the island who does formal classes," Quinn said. "I can get you her number. I'll even go with you."

Maggie almost laughed at that, imagining Quinn in a martial arts stance with her hands up in defense just wasn't easy. She smiled at her. "We'll see."

David stayed serious. "Next up is simple things. Put dead bolts on all outside doors. If you have a sliding glass door, get a wooden dowel cut to fit. Install an interior and exterior alarm bell. Something loud enough to wake the neighbors. Make sure you have lighting outside your windows, preferably at a height no one can reach. Be alert for any unexpected packages or mail, and don't open anything that looks suspicious."

"Yes, I know all that," Maggie said, mentally noting to work on getting alarm bells. She couldn't afford a real system, but he was right, bells could help.

"Are you working?" David asked.

"I'm supposed to start tomorrow," Maggie said.

"Make sure your son knows how to dial emergency on any phone. Will he be in school? If so, you walk him straight to the door, and pick him up there too. No bus stops."

"He was supposed to start day care, but now I'm not sure what to do," Maggie said. She had been trying to figure out something all day. If it came to it, she'd have to tell Dr. Starr she couldn't take the job. She needed the income, there was no doubt of that, but her first priority was Charlie.

Quinn cleared her throat. "I was thinking about that last night, Maggie. And I might have an idea."

Maggie looked up.

"You said your hours are noon to six. I just fired a housekeeper who was working the afternoon shift. I could possibly rehire her as a nanny. She could keep Charlie here, and that way, I can keep an eye on him too."

"Why did you fire her? How do I know she's trustworthy?"

Quinn held a hand up and smiled. "Slow down, tiger. Her name is Rosa, and she's a local. She's a super nice girl. She's just not house-keeping material. It's harder than people think. She could be okay at it someday—with some extensive training—but I don't have time for that. However, I could totally see her as a good caretaker for Charlie. I think he'd be smitten with her."

"I don't know, Quinn. How do I know she's even good with kids? Charlie is a handful."

"She met Charlie one afternoon in the café. I remembered that last night and how she seemed to be fond of him right away. She was a natural with him, but I'd be here to make sure I'm right. And I always work until at least seven or eight, so they could use my rooms when they aren't exploring the grounds. Oh, and her background check was clean too. I check all my employees before hiring."

"That sounds like a much safer alternative to day care," David said. "At times, if a stalker can't get to you, he'll try to scare your friends or family."

"I would kill him if he came anywhere near my son," Maggie said, all traces of her earlier smile gone.

"Let's hope it doesn't come to that," David said. "Just to be safe, though, it sounds like if you are going to take the job, he would be better here under Quinn's supervision."

Maggie hesitated. Technically Quinn wouldn't be around every minute. Could she leave Charlie knowing it would be a stranger who was keeping him safe?

"You know how he loves it here," Quinn added.

"You're right," Maggie said, trying to keep the defeat out of her voice. She wasn't fond of imposing on Quinn. But it was for Charlie's best interest.

Maggie sighed, thinking of her sparse finances. "What do you think she'll charge?"

"I'm sure you were going to pay the day care more than she was making as a housekeeper, but I'll negotiate a fair price with her. I have a feeling she'll be so pleased to have a job again that she'll be easy to work with. I can have her come over early in the morning," Quinn said. "You can meet her, and then if you like her, we can offer her the job. If you don't, I'll keep up with Charlie for the day and until you figure out something. But I think it's going to work out."

"Okay," Maggie said.

That was one worry down.

A million more to go.

Chapter Nine

On Monday, Maggie was sitting in the parking lot at half past eleven, dressed in scrubs that were half an inch too short, her feet already sweating in her new Crocs. Her hands left moist prints on the steering wheel as she breathed in and out, closing her eyes to focus on calming her spirit.

It's just a job, she told herself. *You've done this sort of thing before. You can do it again. You won't make an idiot of yourself. You are competent and professional.*

She released a long breath. Positive thoughts weren't working this time. Beside her on the seat was the poke plate for Dr. Starr, and it didn't smell all that delectable to her. Her stomach gurgled, way down low, and Maggie hoped it wouldn't revolt. It would be just her luck to get inside, begin to assist Dr. Starr, and then have to run and lock herself in the restroom.

"Woodrow," she said softly.

He leaned over the console, setting his head on her arm. Maggie buried her face in his fur, inhaling the sweet scent of grass. She felt her pulse slow. Her breath came easier.

She hated the toll that anxiety took on her, making her feel like someone other than herself. It wasn't just the new job. That was enough to make her sweat, but now she had the added stress of worrying about

Charlie's safety. Her calls to the Victims' Services Department had gone straight to voice mail.

The detective, David, had promised to call her as soon as he had some answers.

Waiting wasn't an easy thing for Maggie to do. She thought of Charlie, excited when she'd dropped him off. She'd explained to him that he couldn't bother Quinn or the guests during the day and that all his needs were going to be met by Rosa. The girl was at the hotel bright and early, and Quinn was right: Charlie had taken to her immediately, and Rosa was thrilled with her new position. Maggie prayed it would work out.

Life had gotten so complicated.

Again.

"Woodrow, what do you think?" She looked at him. "Maui was supposed to be our safe haven. What happened?"

He sat in the passenger's seat, his expression serious as usual, though she thought she detected one eyebrow raise just a fraction as though to say, *You talking to me?* He didn't care what she did as long as he was there with her. She hadn't broken it to him yet that once she felt comfortable at the clinic, his hours were going to go part-time, leaving him plenty of time for squirrel gazing off the balcony of their apartment. Unless, of course, her uneasiness panned out to be more than paranoia, and in that case she'd have to keep him by her side.

What if she really was being tracked again?

Her spiral into worry was diverted when a rusty red truck pulled up beside her and an old man climbed out, then went around to the back and opened the tailgate. He adjusted the strap of his overalls, then bent over with his head out of sight.

Maggie watched through her side mirror, and when she saw him struggling to lift something, she opened her door and stepped out.

"Would you like some help?" she asked.

He let go of the bundle of blankets and stood, holding his hand up over his eyes to block the sun.

"You work here?" he asked, his voice shaky.

Maggie hesitated. She looked at the bundle but didn't see anything except a lump under it. "It's my first day, actually. But why don't you tell me what's going on?"

At the sound of his voice, Maggie saw the tip of a brown nose rise from one of the folds.

"It's my hunting dog, Cooter. I think a snake got to him."

Maggie moved closer, feeling her pulse quicken.

"How long ago? What kind of snake?"

The old man shook his head. "I let him out at sunrise, and he was gone for hours. He always comes when I whistle, but when he didn't this time, I went looking for him and found him lying halfway in the creek. Don't know how long he'd been down. He was shivering and couldn't get up out of the water. I had to climb down there and carry him up. Didn't see no gunshot wounds, so either he fell and broke a leg or it was a snake. My gut tells me it's the latter."

"I thought Hawaii didn't have snakes?" Maggie said, opening the dog's eyelids to check his pupils.

"Yeah, tell that to the scumbags who smuggle them in then let 'em loose when they get too big to handle at home."

Judging by the old man's feebleness, she couldn't see how he had climbed down anything, much less come back up with a fifty-plus-pound dog and carried it back to his vehicle. But she knew this—the bond between human and dog was strong, and loyalty could work miracles. Still, the man looked exhausted enough to drop, and Maggie wasn't certified to work on humans.

"Let me get him," she said. She didn't know if it was a snakebite or not, but they needed to move fast. A dog out on his own could get into all sorts of trouble, and snakes were not just one of the hazards of letting dogs roam free, but they were also one of the deadliest.

"Oh, no, I can't do that, ma'am. He stinks bad enough to knock a buzzard off a shit wagon. And you're just a slight little thing anyway."

"I'm stronger than I look." She moved around him, putting her arms under the bundle and then lifting it. The dog was heavy, but she was used to carrying Charlie. Using the strength in her legs, she straightened and turned around. "Get the door. We need to get him to Dr. Starr stat."

Woodrow was right behind her as she followed the old man, who hurriedly hobbled to the door. Suddenly all her nerves were gone, and in their place she felt the adrenaline crank up. She remembered now the passion she had for her job as a tech so long ago—the rush of being needed and allowing her skills and love for animals to make a difference in their lives.

Juniper had the door open before they even got there with the dog. The old man stood aside, letting her pass, and Maggie turned so she could walk through without bumping Cooter any more than necessary. Francine was behind the desk, her face pinched with concern.

"We need a table," Maggie said. She directed Woodrow into a lobby chair and commanded him to stay. He jumped to her bidding immediately.

"This way," Juniper said. Maggie was glad to see she was all business and didn't waste time with questions.

In the back, Juniper led her to a clean table and called out, letting everyone know they needed all available hands on board. Maggie laid the dog—bundle and all—on the stainless-steel table. His head had come uncovered and his eyes were dilated, fixed and staring off somewhere.

"He's in shock," she said.

"What do we have here?" Dr. Starr asked, appearing from nowhere as he began to unfold the blanket.

"Met him in the parking lot. Brought in by his owner who found him in the creek bed, shivering and unable to get up. I didn't get a look, but he suspects a snakebite," Maggie said.

"I doubt that," Dr. Starr said. "He'd have to be one unlucky dog to find one of the few snakes on the island. There hasn't been a sighting in years. Let me see him."

Francine appeared, wringing her hands. Dr. Starr waved her out of there, and then he began a physical examination. It was clear as soon as the blanket was pulled back that one of the dog's front legs was swollen to at least twice its normal size. He searched, sorting through the hair, trying to find a wound.

He found a spot that made Cooter wince when touched, but he didn't see any sort of visible source of pain.

"Josh," Dr. Starr called out. "X-rays, stat."

Maggie stepped back, allowing a young man, obviously another vet tech, to pick the dog up and carry him to a small room, kicking the door closed behind him.

It wasn't five minutes and he was back, setting the dog on the table again.

"Start a line," Dr. Starr said, then left to go read the X-rays.

A girl Maggie hadn't met yet elbowed her way in and prepared to give intravenous fluids.

Dr. Starr was back quickly. "It wasn't a snakebite. I'm going to talk to the owner. Maggie, you come with me since you brought him in."

She followed him out to the lobby where the man was standing at the door, looking out at his truck, his expression stoic as he stroked the gray scruff on his chin. By that time, there were a few other clients out there with dogs and one with a cat in a crate, and they all watched silently.

"Excuse me, you own the hunting dog?" Dr. Starr said.

The man turned, and Maggie saw him try to blink away the moisture in his eyes. He set his jaw and lifted his head higher.

"That's right," he said, nodding solemnly. "Is the old boy going to make it?"

"That's depending on what you want to do. His leg is broken. But unlike most bone fractures in dogs that can be treated with a simple bone realignment and a cast, this is a dirty break. It's not clean enough to fit back together with traction. He's going to need surgery if you want him to return to a normal quality of life."

The old man shook his head slowly from side to side. "I just don't know what happened. He's down in that creek bed a dozen times a week. I thought for sure a snake had got him. But breaking a leg? How's that possible?"

"He could've been after a wild hog or something and slipped on some rocks, fallen down the bank," Dr. Starr said. "I don't know, but he definitely did a number on himself. We could amputate that leg, but there won't be any more creek runs. You'd have to keep him closer to home."

"What would you do if it were your dog?" the old man asked.

"He can do without a leg. I just wish it wasn't his front one. That's a different story when it comes to mobility. If he loves to roam and you don't think he'd adjust to being yard bound, I'd save the leg, but it's going to be expensive. I'm assuming I'll have to insert a rod to keep it stable."

The man wrinkled his brow. Maggie could tell he didn't have much.

"How expensive?" he said.

"With the amount of time, equipment, anesthesia, and aftercare that'll be required, it may cost upwards of a couple thousand," Dr. Starr said softly. "And there's always a chance it won't heal properly and we'll have to take it anyway." He paused for a moment. "Or we could give him a few shots to put him to sleep and take him out of his misery, if you can't afford surgery and don't want to take the leg."

Maggie didn't know how the doctor could even say that without emotion. She was glad it was him doing the talking and not her.

The old man looked out at the parking lot again, taking a full minute before responding. "See that truck out there? I bought it brand new more than twenty years ago. It's been a good one. Me and that truck have been through some messes. But I know I can get at least three grand for it from some high school kid who wants to look like a man behind the wheel of something tough."

"So . . . are you saying . . . ," Dr. Starr said, trailing off to wait for official permission.

The old man nodded. "Hell yeah, I'm saying to save my dog *and* his leg. Ol' Cooter is all I got left in this world that really matters. I ain't taking away his freedom, and I sure ain't putting him down."

Maggie swallowed past the lump in her throat and followed Dr. Starr back to the emergency area. She wished she had a few grand sitting unused in her pocket that could keep an old man and his beloved truck together.

Maggie didn't assist in Cooter's surgery, but she got to watch and found it just as fascinating as she remembered: the magic of skill and medicine combined to heal a living thing.

After nearly three hours of surgery, Dr. Starr sent her out to tell Cooter's owner—William Hill, but everyone called him Red—that his dog had made it through the surgery fine and that he could come back and visit tomorrow. Red nodded, obviously choked up from relief, then made a beeline for the door and the trusty truck that would probably not be his much longer.

Once Cooter was moved to a large kennel, Maggie squatted in front of him and whispered that it would be fine, his pop would be by to see him soon. With that, she moved on to the next task. Then the next, and the next.

When the last patient was seen, she pitched in to help the assistants clean up the day's mess. Maggie settled the overnight patients in with fresh food and water, then washed her hands. She checked in once more with Cooter, saw that he was stable, and finally let her shoulders relax.

She felt completely spent, but she realized something interesting.

In the six hours that she'd been there, she had helped treat Cooter, then cleaned and dressed the wound of another dog that was brought in with a piece of barbed wire wrapped around its ankle, as well as held down a squealing pig that needed to be neutered. She suddenly realized that she had not thought about her own troubles at all.

The diversion felt good.

"You did all right today," Dr. Starr said as he locked the door then turned to her. Other than the vet assistant who had volunteered for the overtime and would sit through the night with Cooter, they were the last ones out. Francine had left only minutes earlier, but not before she'd hugged Maggie and told her how grateful she was to have her at the clinic. It was a little awkward, but it made Maggie miss her mother. She made a mental note to call later and let her talk to Charlie.

"Thank you. But Liam said you needed a vet tech, and I noticed you already have a few. So why did you hire me?" A suspicion was gnawing at her and had been throughout the day.

He gave her a sheepish grin.

Realization flooded over her, and Maggie felt her face flush. "You've got to be kidding me. Liam came to you and asked you to give me a job as a favor to him, didn't he?"

Dr. Starr held his hands up. "Wait—simmer down. I did, I mean I *do* need a tech. I'm going to be taking on a partner next year, and there's so much business to be had here on the island that we need to ramp up the staff."

She shook her head. "I'm so embarrassed. I mean, seriously, what was he thinking? I'm thankful for the job, but I didn't think I was a charity case." She rummaged in her purse for her keys, unable to find them through the humiliation that burned her vision. "Woodrow, heel."

Woodrow came to attention beside her.

"Maggie, please. Stop," Dr. Starr said. "Liam and Quinn care about you. And I legitimately need your help. What I saw from you today in there is that you put your heart and soul into your work. That you really care. That's the kind of vet tech I need beside me. And to be honest, the others haven't really accepted me. I thought it was a great idea to hire someone myself. I need someone who I can depend on and know is not comparing me to the amazing Dr. Kent."

She stopped. He sounded desperate. And he did have a lot to live up to; that was no joke.

"What makes you think *I* won't be comparing?" she asked, turning around even as she realized her anger at Liam was coming out at him.

He laughed. "For one, you don't know him. But I'll be honest, Dr. Kent is a legend around here that I'll never measure up to. All I can do is try to make my own name. I swear—this isn't a pity offer. Stay and work with me."

She hesitated. She was still mad that he and Liam had conspired together. It made her feel . . . well, she didn't know how it made her feel but she didn't like it. Then she couldn't help but smile at Dr. Starr, who stood there looking like a little boy caught with his hand in the cookie jar, waiting for his punishment.

"Hasn't anyone ever made a call to help you get another job?" he asked.

Maggie thought of her very first job when she turned sixteen. Their local grocery store had a Starbucks inside, and their pastor knew the manager. He'd put in a good word, and Maggie found herself working there every Saturday through high school. It wasn't easy at first because the college kid who was supposed to be training her would stay out all night on Fridays and come in on Saturdays hungover. He'd try to sleep it off in the supply closet while Maggie struggled to learn on demand to make a skinny latte or whatever it was the next frazzled mom across the counter ordered.

Now she was that mom.

And this mom needed to pay the bills.

She breathed slowly, letting her temper simmer down. Her mom always said it liked to jump the gun and make a mountain out of a molehill. "Fine. I'll stay through the ninety-day evaluation period. At the end of that, if it isn't working out for me, I walk."

He straightened, putting his chin in the air and taking on an arrogant stance.

"And what if it's not working out for me?" he said, a sparkle in his eyes.

So he wanted banter. She sighed. So much for the professional doctor-employee relationship that he should be striving for. She needed to set that straight right away. Her motto these days was not to let anyone get too close, or even merely confused.

"Then you can give me my walking papers and I'll be out of your way," she said, keeping her tone professional and curt. "But I'll have you know, that's not likely to happen. I'm good at my job, as you saw today, and I'll prove that to you over and over again so that you'll forget that Liam ever got me in the door in the first place."

With that, she left. She didn't have to turn around to know that the good doctor was still standing there, a bemused grin spreading across his face.

Chapter Ten

Fifteen minutes later, Maggie was getting out of her car at the inn when she spotted an older man with a camera hanging around his neck. He stood back and snapped a photo of the hotel, then the license plates of several cars in the lot.

He turned and saw her watching, nodded, and then continued inside.

She let Woodrow out, and they followed him inside. The man was decent looking—though a little weathered—but for his age he carried himself well, his gait smooth and energetic. He stopped at the bellman and waited for him to look up from the phone he was scrolling on.

The bellman startled, then slid his phone into his pocket.

Maggie heard the man ask for Quinn.

"Last I saw her, she was outside by the pool," the bellman said, beckoning to the other side of the lobby where the doors led out to the poolside.

Maggie frowned. She was going to have to talk to Quinn about educating her staff in giving out too much information. The bellman should've gotten the man's name and purpose and then called to ask Quinn if she was expecting anyone or wanted to come out. Why would they send a stranger off the street to find her?

With Woodrow behind her, Maggie trailed the stranger outside and watched as he surveyed the guests, then walked toward the pathway that led to a lower level of chairs arranged in the sun.

He'd missed Quinn. She squatted at the edge of the small pool next to where Rosa sat, her legs dangling in the water, with Charlie hanging on to them like a little spider monkey. Maggie approached, glad to see he was wearing the sun hat she'd brought and still had a streak of white cream across his nose.

Woodrow saw his boy and beat her over there. He knelt beside the pool, his face as close to Charlie as he could get, his tail bobbing excitedly.

"No, Woodrow," Maggie said. She didn't want to deal with a wet dog on the way home.

Charlie looked up and saw her, a huge smile spreading across his ruddy face.

"Hey, buddy," she said.

"Mama!" Charlie exclaimed. "Rosa is afraid of the water! Tell her it's fine."

Rosa's cheeks flushed with embarrassment. She looked up at Maggie. "I'm not afraid. I just don't particularly like getting wet."

Maggie laughed. Woodrow whined, his plea to get in getting more insistent.

"Charlie, not everyone is a little fish like you," Quinn said. "Be glad she's okay to get that close."

Rosa smiled her relief.

"It's okay. I love Rosa," Charlie said. "Can she come home with us?"

They all laughed, and Maggie's spirits lifted seeing that putting Rosa in the nanny role seemed to be going well. Charlie looked happier than she'd seen him in a while.

"Rosa has to go home to her own family. As a matter of fact, you need to get out now, Charlie, so she can get going."

The expected groans and whining ensued, but he obeyed, climbing out and straight into a fluffy towel that Rosa held out for him.

"I'll go get him into dry clothes before I go," she said, leading Charlie away.

"Thanks, Rosa. Take Woodrow with you. He's burning up out here."

"Come on, Woodrow," Charlie called.

The dog looked at Maggie and she nodded, giving him permission to fall in behind Charlie and follow him to the room.

Maggie sat on the edge of the closest lounge chair and patted the one next to her. "Want to sit for a minute before your visitor finds you?"

Quinn sat. "What visitor?"

"Some man asked for you in the lobby. He went that way," she pointed at the path. "But he'll be back. He seemed pretty determined."

"Probably another vendor trying to get on board with us," Quinn said. "Once you announce all your goods and foods will be handled locally, they start swarming. I'm going to have to pass some of the orders around more to give everyone a chance."

Maggie loved that Quinn wanted to focus on sustainability for the small farmers and vendors on the island instead of ordering in from the mainland. That meant more to the people of Maui and might even earn her more points with those in Hana who weren't happy about another business opening up in their small town they tried to keep off the radar.

"First," Quinn said, "tell me if I'm overstepping my boundaries."

"Okay," Maggie said, feeling wary.

"Did I tell you about Julianne, Mr. Westbrooks's wife?"

"No, but Charlie mentioned something about her and the chair," Maggie said. "I hope he didn't embarrass you too bad."

Quinn waved her hand. "No. That was nothing. They thought he was cute. Anyway, she was a dancer before she got sick. She even taught dance."

"And?"

"And," Quinn said, drawing the word out, "I found out that Maui has an academy of performing arts. I want to have one of their teams come do a special show for Julianne and David's anniversary."

Maggie smiled. "Didn't I say that you were born to own an inn? That's a great idea and will really set you off from other inns that just push the regular excursions."

"I didn't even think of that," Quinn said. "I just want to find something to take her mind off her illness."

"Of course. I know that," Maggie said. "But you know what would be even better? If she's up to it, what about letting her help them train for the show? Or rehearse—whatever you call it. Might make her feel useful and give her something to look forward to."

"I love it," said Quinn. "I'll call them tomorrow and see if it's even a possibility. Then I'll talk to her husband. He might think it's too much for Julianne to help but would welcome a show to lift her spirits."

"Yeah, he'd know best," Maggie said.

"How did it go for you today?" Quinn asked.

"Good. It started on a low note when an old man was going to have to sell his truck to pay for his dog's surgery, but then Juniper set up an online campaign to raise the funds. In four hours, it surpassed the goal, and now he can have his dog back *and* keep his truck."

"That's really sweet of—"

"Nama Monroe?"

They both turned and got caught off guard when the man from the lobby snapped a photo. Then he snapped another. Maggie was shaken. How did the man know Quinn's real name from when she was a child?

"Are you Nama Monroe?" the man asked, lowering his camera.

Maggie saw Quinn hesitate, then recover.

"No, I'm Quinn Maguire. Who are you?" she demanded, standing to face him.

Maggie stood too.

He appeared completely unruffled.

"My name is Simon Lang, and I'm a journalist. Can you confirm you are, or were, Nama Monroe?" He squinted at the sun behind them, bringing more attention to the lines around his eyes and the leathery, baked look of his skin.

"I already told you I'm Quinn Maguire. Now you answer me. Who do you work for?" Quinn said, her face flushing so red it was nearly purple.

Maggie put a hand on her arm.

"Calm down," she whispered.

"I work for myself. Freelancing," he said, pulling a card from his shirt pocket and holding it out. He was fit, the muscles in his arm bulging with the weight of the camera. "I retired a few years ago but still put in some stories here and there."

Quinn didn't take the card.

Maggie did. It might come in handy later to check him out.

"Look, I know who you are whether you confirm it or not. I was a fresh-faced reporter for the *Maui Times* way back when you disappeared. I've waited three decades to see this case solved. I can't just walk away, so you might as well talk to me."

Quinn looked crestfallen. Since she'd found her family, they'd done everything they could to keep it out of the news. And they'd been successful. Until now, it seemed.

"You aren't planning on writing a story, are you?" Maggie asked him.

"I am. It's only fair that everyone who took part in the investigation knows how it turned out," he said.

"Please, I don't want this public," Quinn said. "I'm a private person and—"

"Freedom of the press," he said, cutting her off. "I can write what I want. The entire island was trying to find you. Don't you want to let them know you're alive?"

"I'm not that girl," Quinn said. "And you cannot use that photo. I want you off this property. Right now."

He nodded. "That's fine, but you are in fact the missing girl, Nama, who fell off her family boat and was thought to be lost at sea. That's been confirmed by a very credible source. And if you won't give me the story, I'll piece it together on my own and run it. Right now I'm giving you the opportunity to work with me."

Everyone around the pool was looking at them now, and Maggie could see that Quinn was visibly shaken.

"There isn't any story," Quinn said. "Get out."

He nodded, then headed for the lobby doors. "If that's how you want to play it."

"Wait," Maggie called out.

He turned.

"Who sent you here?"

He smiled gently. "I don't give up my sources. But I'll give you forty-eight hours to contact me for a meeting. Or I run with what I've got."

Then he was through the doors and gone.

"Quinn, maybe you should rethink sending him away," Maggie said. "There's no telling what he'll run with if he only has bits and rumors."

"You're right," Quinn said. She sat on a lounge chair and put her head in her hands. "I'm too shaken up to talk to him right now, though. What if he knows that my grandmother was involved in keeping me away from my family? That she arranged for a stranger to raise me? What if he publishes that?"

"Well, it is the truth," Maggie said gently. "But you could guide the narrative, to make it sound less ugly."

Quinn had dropped her face into her hands as she spoke, her voice sounding anguished as it filtered through her fingers.

"Oh my God. This could ruin my family, Maggie. Their businesses. The tarnished Rocha reputation that my grandmother has tried so hard to salvage all these years. It would all come back, and even though she made her own way, she'd get dragged into the feud. Not to mention the inn. I just opened the doors, and this could end my business before it has a chance to take off."

Maggie sat beside her and put her arm around her shoulders.

"Breathe, Quinn. We can call him. Invite him back and see what he knows. It could be that he doesn't have all the information and is just hoping you'll give it to him. Trust me, this is PR 101. I figured this out in my first month of my public relations job: You fake it until you make it. Anyway, I bet he knows next to nothing."

"But he knew something, and someone had to have told him I was here. Who? Only my family knows. And you."

"And Liam," said Maggie.

Quinn looked at her, narrowing her eyes. "What are you trying to say?"

Maggie held her hands up. "Nothing. Just helping you remember who all knows. And don't forget Maria and her family. Do they know the details?"

"No," Quinn said, shaking her head quickly. "They don't know everything. And they for sure have no idea about my grandmother's secrets."

Suddenly the lobby doors opened and Charlie burst out, Rosa and Woodrow right behind him.

"Mama! I'm hungry," he said, breaking the tension.

Maggie held her arms out and he fell into them. He smelled like chlorine. And little boy. She kissed his forehead.

"What's for dinner?" he asked.

"Chicken, potatoes, and apples," she said, giving him a wink.

Charlie pumped his arm in celebration. "Yay! A Happy Meal!"

"No, buddy. Maui doesn't have a McDonald's on every corner. This time it's for-real food," Maggie said.

He looked crushed.

She locked eyes with Quinn. "You going to be okay?"

"Yes. Go, Maggie. Take care of Charlie. It's been a long day away for him, and you both need to be home."

"I really don't want to leave you right now," Maggie said.

Charlie laid his head on her shoulder and wove his fingers into her hair, a sign that he was getting sleepy. She had to admit, she was exhausted too. All she wanted was to get Charlie fed, bathed, and into his pajamas. Hopefully his day with Rosa was just as tiring as hers at the clinic, and they could get to sleep early.

"Please, it's fine. I need to call my parents. And Liam should be here any minute. He'll help me figure this out. Just leave me that cockroach's card. This is my dirt to sift through, not yours."

"Your dirt is my dirt," Maggie reassured her. "I'm here for you, Quinn. Just call me."

Chapter Eleven

Maggie awoke to the sound of her phone ringing a full hour before her alarm was set to go off. She fumbled for it, knocking it from the nightstand. Thankfully when it hit the floor, John Lennon instantly stopped crooning the key verse to "Imagine."

"Damn it," she muttered, glancing over to make sure Charlie still slept. She'd rather be showered and dressed before His Highness took over her morning, demanding nutrition and cartoons.

His tiny eyelashes fluttered, but otherwise nothing. Beside him Woodrow thumped his tail on the bed.

"Shh . . ." She put her finger to her lips and he froze.

She picked up the phone and glared at the screen. It showed *Quinn SoulSister* as one missed call.

They'd talked late the night before after Quinn had met with her parents about the reporter. Quinn said they'd decided to sit on the threats for a day or two while their family attorney investigated. Quinn had calmed down, and Maggie promised to come by a little earlier than usual to drop Charlie off, with doughnuts.

The phone rang again and she almost dropped it.

"Hey, what's up?" she whispered.

"Maggie," Quinn said. "That reporter is a liar."

"About what?" Maggie asked, stumbling to the bathroom and shutting the door behind her so she could talk louder.

"He said he'd give us forty-eight hours, but my dad just called to tell me to check the internet. He's livid."

"What does it say?"

"Get on your computer," Quinn said. "You need to read it yourself."

Maggie sighed, then rubbed her eyes. "What site?"

"Maui Now. Only the most popular online news site for the island. I'm about to have a nervous breakdown. Dad already talked to our lawyer before he called me, and there's nothing we can do."

"Okay, let me look at the damage." *Crap.* Quinn sounded crushed. How had Mr. Creeper gotten anyone to accept a story without facts to back it up? Maggie pictured him looking smug and wished he was close enough for her to wipe the smirk off his face.

Instead she went back to the bedroom and sat down on the bed next to her makeshift desk—which doubled as the nightstand. Charlie stirred, so she carefully and quietly opened her laptop and typed in "Maui Now." The first thing at the top was a photo of her and Quinn, taken poolside at the inn. The caption under it read Quinn Maguire AKA Nama Monroe and Maggie Dalton at Hana Hamoa Inn. Photo credit: Simon Lang.

Maggie felt the blood drain from her face. Her photo and location, plastered on the internet for any wacko to take note of.

The headline was in bold:

Rocha heir lost at sea thirty years ago reemerges as the new proprietor of the Hana Hamoa Inn

"Well, that piece of—"

"Exactly," said Quinn. "And the front desk phone has been ringing off the hook already this morning."

"Well, that would be good, right? Filling up reservations?"

"No. It's people asking for confirmation on the story. More reporters, police, and just locals, all wanting to know if it's true. This is going to be a circus. And who knows what else he has up his sleeve?"

"I'm so sorry, Quinn." Maggie could hear the anguish in her friend's voice. Beside her, Charlie mumbled, and she pulled the covers higher up on his shoulders.

"Yeah, me too. I bet my family is going to wish I'd never found them. Especially my grandmother. Despite what she tries to present to the world, she's actually quite sensitive. This will kill her."

"Hold on, let me scan the rest of it," Maggie said.

She read the article.

> Information from a reliable source has confirmed that Quinn Maguire, the new proprietor of the Hana Hamoa Inn, is none other than the daughter of Jules and Noah Monroe, granddaughter of heiress Helen Rocha. Maguire is reported to be Nama Monroe, who disappeared at sea more than thirty years before.

"He doesn't know any more than he did yesterday," Maggie said.

"But now he's set all the vultures on me. Every reporter in this county will be trying to dig up the facts."

"He must've thought someone else was going to scoop him, so he went with what he had," Maggie said. "He's vermin."

"Yep. Bottom-of-the-barrel kind too. Read the comments."

Maggie scrolled down, and after a few comments, felt sick to her stomach. Some people were saying that Quinn might be a fake—a con artist here to claim the lost girl's place in the family. Take her share of the Rocha inheritance when the grandmother dies. Others claimed it was a miracle, orchestrated by God. Most of them wanted more details. Where had she been? How did they find her?

She felt livid for Quinn and the breach of her privacy. "So now what?"

"Now I have to try to do damage control," Quinn said. "The thing is, I don't have any idea what kind of story to give them without throwing my own grandmother under the bus. Or the mom who raised me. I know I shouldn't worry about her reputation since she's dead, but I still don't want her name dragged through the mud and have her branded as a kidnapper. You know how much she loved me, even if I wasn't supposed to be hers."

Maggie closed her eyes, trying to think. Yes, growing up, Quinn had the best mom ever. Technically, Elizabeth had kidnapped Quinn, but there was no doubt she'd loved Quinn and had given her a good life. It was just that Quinn's story was so absolutely incredible—albeit tragically so—that of course it made for good news. The truth of it was that when she fell overboard and somehow miraculously made it to the beach and was found, her own grandmother arranged for her to disappear again.

All to avoid some supposed curse on their family.

"I've got it!" Maggie opened her eyes wide.

"What?"

"You can say that when you were found, no one claimed you, and child services arranged for you to be adopted."

"Maggie," Quinn said, "the entire town was looking for me for weeks. There's no way child services wouldn't know who that little girl was."

Maggie felt defeated. She was right.

"Amnesia?"

"It wouldn't have mattered. Anyone would've known a child washed up was the Monroes' daughter."

Maggie noticed Quinn still acted like the child lost at sea was a different person than she was. It was going to take much longer for her to come to terms with her identity, it seemed. But that was talk for another time.

"I just don't know then. Maybe the truth is the best option?"

"And let everyone know my own grandmother sent me away with a stranger? Never to see my family again? Crushing the hope of her own daughter who grieved her lost child? They will crucify her, Maggie."

"I know, but she might have to be the sacrificial lamb to keep the entire family and your parents' businesses safe. And the inn. If you're painted as a fraud, it's going to affect your vision for the future here. You don't want to lose everything you've worked so hard for already."

Maggie hated that Quinn had been through so much in the last year and now was having to face it all again. It just wasn't fair how some of the nicest people had the heaviest burdens to bear.

"Liam said the same thing," Quinn finally said after a long pause. "But what she did is a crime. A felony even. I can't let them know. I have to protect her."

"At the cost of your own integrity? Quinn, you're innocent in all this. And you damn sure never asked for any of their money. You're earning your own way here. Stop trying to shield everyone before yourself."

"I don't know what I'm going to do," Quinn said.

Maggie saw a notification for two new emails at the bottom of her screen, and she clicked her in-box open.

She zoned out on what Quinn was saying when she saw the first one in the queue was from the email address iSeeyouInmaui@Lmail.com.

When she clicked it open, the same photo from the Maui Now site popped up, but this time it was edited. A crude-looking heart was drawn around her face. The email contained nothing else, but the point was made. She knew who it was from, and he knew where she was.

She felt the bile rise up in her throat and a loud ringing began in her ears.

"Quinn," she said. "He's found me."

She couldn't keep the hysteria from her voice, and Charlie heard her.

"Mommy? Is that Daddy on the phone?" he asked.

"Maggie? What are you talking about?"

"Just a minute," Maggie said, then held her hand over the phone. She took a deep breath and softened the fright on her face before she turned to Charlie. "No, this is Auntie Quinn."

Charlie's lip quivered and a tear slid out. "I was dreaming about Daddy."

"I gotta go, Quinn. I'll see you in a little while." Maggie hung up and tossed the phone onto the bed, then gathered Charlie up into her arms, pushing aside her own terror. "I'm sorry, buddy. I didn't know you were missing Daddy so much. You want to call him?"

Charlie nodded. In his sleepy and sad state, he looked younger than usual, and Maggie wished she could go back to those days when he was happy just rocking in her arms and staring up at her face. But now that he was older, he loved another person as much as he did her. Well, maybe not *as much*, but somewhere close.

She sighed a long and lengthy breath to try to expel the sudden onslaught of anxiety rushing through her. Not only was she being hit this morning with the mess about Quinn, then knowledge that her stalker knew where she was now, but like a cherry on top, she felt guilty that she hadn't noticed how much Charlie was missing his dad. It was all just too much.

Things with his dad were complicated. She and Colby had issues. He didn't understand her need to be independent. And she wanted him to be with her because he was madly in love with her, not because it was the responsible thing to do.

Would she always have these complicated feelings about Colby? As the father of her child, she knew there would always be a connection, but she hoped one day they could simply be friends. Or at least pretend to be as they co-parented their son.

Charlie was her world, and to know that she was the cause of any of his disappointment just broke her heart. It was probably going to be an ice-cream-sandwich-for-breakfast kind of day, just to keep him happy on the way to the inn. But at least she'd bought the good kind made with whole milk. Calcium and protein. Naysayers could bite it. She had bigger things to worry about.

She hoped that the detective was up and about when she dropped Charlie off. Maybe he could direct her to the next steps. She also needed to talk to Rosa about being extra careful not to let Charlie out of her sight.

But right now there was only one thing that would make Charlie's frown turn upside down.

She reached for the phone and hit the last number called, then realized it was Dr. Starr's and not Colby's number. She hung up before the first ring ended. Carefully this time, she brought Colby's name up and flinched when his photo filled the screen. He was wearing the hat they'd bought together before their first rodeo date. It was startling how much the photo made her miss him. Or at least miss the years they'd had together before things went wrong. She didn't even want to hear him talk about her moving back.

She handed the phone to Charlie. It would be midafternoon on East Coast time, and Colby was probably still working, but he always said there was never a bad time to take a call from his boy.

"You talk while I take a shower. Tell him you love it here."

He gave her a confused look before concentrating on the phone.

Maggie left him to it and headed to the bathroom. She planned on standing under the hot, streaming water and thinking only about what new safeguards she needed to work on. She'd also imagine cats, dogs, fleas, and hair balls—anything to get the vision of Colby's twinkling green eyes out of her head and the sneaky feelings they'd brought back up. She reminded herself again that she had bigger things to worry about.

Chapter Twelve

"How many of these are legitimate guests and how many are people looking for a story?" Quinn asked Emily. While she'd love to celebrate the fact that they were booked solid for the next two months, she wasn't naive enough to believe that suddenly the Hana Hamoa Inn was the best stay on the island.

"I haven't had time to research them. I've been too busy doing checkouts and taking calls. Mr. Westbrooks asked to extend their stay, by the way. He also said he needs to talk to you, and it's important."

"David? Oh. For how long does he want to extend?"

"He said to go ahead and put it in for two more weeks if it was okay, and then he'll let us know if it'll be longer."

"Interesting," Quinn said. She wondered if that meant Julianne was too sick to travel. She also hoped he had some news about Maggie's stalker. "I'll call him when I can get five minutes to step away."

Emily slid over the spreadsheet they kept printed out for daily maintenance issues—a piece of paper that Quinn would rather see empty. Unfortunately it already had a pile of to-dos going.

"I had to call Jonah in, and that took some tracking. He was helping mow the side yard and didn't hear his phone. The coffee maker in room four isn't working, and the bathroom sink in six is stopped up. Four is cranky, and six has threatened to leave a bad review if the sink isn't repaired immediately."

As soon as the words were out of her mouth, the phone rang again. Emily raised her brows but picked it up. "Hana Hamoa Inn, how may I help you?"

Quinn turned away. Everything was in an uproar at the inn. She needed to get a guest list and google each of them. She needed to hire another morning shift front desk person, and she'd already promised David she was going to do something about getting the dance team there to talk to Julianne. She was overwhelmed, and the perfect life she'd carved out for herself went from being within her reach to spiraling out of control overnight. It felt like a storm was brewing, and she didn't like it. Not one little bit.

"Good morning, Mr. and Mrs. Monroe," the bellman at the doors said.

Quinn looked up to see her parents on their way in, making a beeline straight to her. That was all she needed. She was just as helpless as they were to hide from prying eyes, yet here they were, coming out to check on her. She couldn't deny they genuinely cared about her well-being, even if they didn't really know her yet.

"I'll be back up in a few," she mouthed to Emily, who nodded with a look of panic in her eyes.

"Let's go to my rooms," she said, beckoning for her mom and dad to follow.

Jules had already seen her suite, but Noah hadn't. When they walked into the sitting area, he whistled.

"Nice," he said. "I could live here."

"Thanks. It works out great for me to be here on-site. At least most of the time. Though right now I wish I lived on the other side of the island."

Noah went to the bookshelf in the corner and appeared to be reading each book title, as though he could get a glimpse inside her head by knowing what she liked to read. They were always trying to dig a little, but usually in unassuming ways.

Jules sat down on the small settee but was looking toward the bedroom. Quinn was glad she'd made her bed and put away her laundry from the day before.

"I'll bet you do," Jules said.

"Would you like some fresh-squeezed juice?" Quinn asked.

They both nodded. Quinn went to the corner of the suite where her mini kitchen was and opened her fridge, pulling out the juice she'd squeezed at five o'clock that morning when she couldn't sleep any longer. She was glad for a moment to busy her hands while they looked around. She didn't blame them for being curious about how she lived. They'd fallen in love with their own sweet, tiny brown-eyed girl and then lost her for thirty years. Quinn figured they were always going to try to see some of that child they once knew inside the woman they'd recently met.

When she had three glasses full, she brought them over on a tray, handed her parents theirs, and settled stiffly into the armchair facing them.

"Before we get on to the drama that my presence has caused, have you heard anything from Kira or Michael?" she asked.

"No. And she's blocked me from her phone and all social media," Jules said. She looked stricken as the words left her mouth. Noah put an arm around her, giving her a comforting squeeze.

Quinn never tired of seeing the two of them together, so connected and still obviously in love after so many years. These days, it was a miracle to have a relationship stand the test of time. She could only dream of a love like that someday. She supposed she had some of her father's hopeless romantic quality inside her after all.

"I'm sorry. She'll come around." Quinn really didn't know what to say.

She wanted to call Kira and make her see what was happening with Michael trying to drive a wedge between her and the family. But they weren't close like that yet. Quinn also didn't want to ask if her grandmother had loaned them the money or not. All she knew was that if Kira and Michael went ahead and started their own charter business without the blessing of Noah and Jules, it was going to be trouble. She hated to see a solid family suddenly fracture over money. Especially when her parents had been so generous with the profits from what they'd built.

"I don't know about that," Jules said. "Kira has always taken things too personally. She's had a history of feeling attacked, when that's the furthest thing from what is really happening. Her teenage years were not easy. For her or us."

Noah raised his eyebrows and nodded, his face giving away that Jules had made an understatement.

Quinn was surprised. This was the first she was hearing of Kira being less than perfect.

"The girls joined Jonah in therapy when they were old enough to understand that we'd lost a child. Kira more than Lani had a problem with feeling like she was only wanted in order to replace you," Jules said.

"Which is ridiculous," her father added. "Children have a hard time getting that we love them each the same but differently. Just because we lost you didn't make us love Kira any less for who she was as an individual, and she sure wasn't meant to be a replacement for you. That would've been impossible. Still, she always questioned her place within the family, craving reassurance. I thought she'd gotten past it, but maybe I was wrong. I don't know."

"I'm sorry," Quinn said. He looked so sad. And that made her sad.

"Don't be," Jules replied, her voice soft. "You have nothing to be sorry for, Quinn. None of this was your fault. You were the victim."

Quinn knew that, but it didn't make it any easier to accept that her disappearance was the cause of so much anguish in one family. For thirty years she'd wished for relatives, but she'd made the most of her circumstances and appreciated the mother and the life she had. It was still surreal that all along she'd had a family in Maui, longing to know what had happened to her. Her parents and brother grieving over her, and her sisters trying to compete with a ghost they'd never met.

"The girls were always with us on charters when they were growing up, but when Kira turned eighteen, she didn't want to be a part of it anymore," Noah said.

That really surprised Quinn. She thought Kira had always been a part of the family business.

"She met a boy—just like I did," Jules said, smiling. "Who talked her into rejecting the family and the work we do. She quit, telling us it was too painful to be near the water that took her sister. She knew that was the one thing we wouldn't argue with. Their emotional well-being is always our top priority. We thought she needed some space. Some distance from everything to be able to finally heal."

Quinn winced. Her fault.

Again.

Noah chuckled. "She went to work in a boutique, catering to the rich tourists. It was a nightmare for a girl used to being out in the beautiful seascapes of Maui to be cooped up with an onslaught of demanding shoppers. She was miserable, although she tried to hide it."

Jules smiled at the memory, but the smile slowly disappeared. "Then she met Michael, and he talked her into coming back. Told her she was crazy to walk away from such a dream job. Turns out that it was his dream all along, and she was the ticket."

"And now he's the one who talked her into walking away," Quinn said. "This has to hurt both of you."

Noah shrugged. "Your kids grow up, and in their quest for independence, they sometimes hurt you. You can't do anything about it but let them go and hope they eventually figure out that their parents aren't the villains they think we are."

"She'll see that starting a business isn't as easy as she thinks," Jules said. "And when she does, we'll be waiting. She'll always have a place with us."

Quinn suspected her parents were afraid to lose another daughter and wanted to keep Kira in their sights. She also noticed that Jules didn't mention saving a place for Michael. It was time to change the subject.

"So, I guess we should talk about the reporter and how we want to handle this. He's made my job here much harder, to say the least." Quinn had already decided she was going to have to stay in the background and try to work from the small office behind the front desk. She didn't want any other cheap shots from someone aiming to cash in on a possible juicy story or candid picture. To them, it was like a reality show.

To her, it was her life.

"I had a feeling this would come up one day," Noah said. "We should've addressed it when we found you. Now a year has gone by, and it makes everything look suspicious."

Jules shook her head. "I disagree, Noah. How could we have addressed it then any better than we can today? No matter how we spin it, my mother—from the infamous Rochas that so many on Maui already hate—orchestrated a kidnapping. All the good she's done over the years to try to make up for it will be forgotten if this comes out."

Quinn could feel the walls closing in on her. Her grandmother had committed an unforgivable act, but that was the thing—she'd been forgiven. Now it would all be dredged back up. All the old woman wanted was to go to her grave with a clean conscience, which her family had granted her and which she'd finally accepted.

This wasn't going to help that goal.

Quinn wished she could turn back time. Every bad thing that was happening was her fault. Why did she have to even try to find her biological father? Her search had netted results but at her family's expense.

It made her feel horrible. And how could she ever make the inn a success on her own terms now? Sure, the calendar was filling up, but it wasn't because she'd made it a valuable destination. It was because people were curious. Everyone wanted to see the woman who was once the little lost girl—the island's own prodigal daughter.

Profits or not, it made her sick to her stomach. Privacy was priceless, and hers was now being offered for the fee of one night's stay at the Hamoa Inn.

Really, there was only one way to make it all go away. It was going to be the hardest thing she'd ever done, but it was best for everyone.

She took a deep breath, then let it out slowly.

"I have a solution."

Her parents waited, letting her have the floor.

Her phone beeped, alerting her to a text message.

"Just a minute," Quinn said. "Let me make sure the front desk is okay." She reached for her phone and read the message.

Maui county detective at the desk, asking for you.

"What's the matter?" Jules asked. "Something's wrong. Spit it out."

Great. Her mother could already read her like a book.

"Quinn?" Noah added.

"There's a detective at the front desk asking for me," Quinn said, looking up at them. "What do I do?"

"There's nothing else to do but bring him back here and talk to him," Noah said. His brow furrowed even more than it had talking about Kira.

"But what will we say?" Quinn asked. Her hands had turned to useless limp noodles, and she nearly dropped her phone.

Jules stood and began pacing. She wrung her hands in front of her, then turned around. "I know. We'll say she's our niece. Not our daughter."

"That's a thought. Only our family and closest friends know the truth, and they surely aren't going to say anything," Noah said. "Not taking your birth name back has kept everyone else from being suspicious."

"But the authorities can prove I'm your daughter with a DNA test," Quinn said. "We all saw how easy that was. Then you could be charged with interfering with an investigation if they figure it out."

"We're not lying to the authorities," Noah said. "I don't know what I'll say, but just let me do the talking. We'll meet in the lobby. This is your home, Quinn. Let's keep the negative energy out of it."

She agreed. This needed to remain her safe place without the taint of accusations being made within it. She led her parents out of her suite and to the main area. They chose the most private seating area; then Quinn approached the uniformed man who leaned on the front desk.

"Excuse me," she said.

From the back she could see he was a stocky man, his dark hair peppered with gray. He was at least her father's age, if not older. He could've been past the age of retirement, but here on the island she'd heard that many people worked well past their sixties.

He turned. "Are you Quinn Maguire?"

She nodded. Now she could tell he appeared to be of Hawaiian and Japanese descent.

He showed her his badge. "I'm Detective Kamaka of the Maui Police Department. Is there somewhere we can talk?"

"This way," she said, leading him to where her parents sat.

Noah stood up and held his hand out. The detective took it, and they shook. "Noah Monroe. And this is my wife, Jules."

The detective pulled a notepad from his pocket and flipped it open. "I suspected as much."

They all took a seat.

"I'm glad you are all here, as the questions will pertain to all parties," Detective Kamaka said. He took a pen out of his pocket and clicked the tip out, ready to write.

Noah cleared his throat. "We would like to respectfully decline questions without an attorney present."

Quinn blinked. She hadn't seen that one coming.

The detective looked up from his pad. "Why would you lawyer up on me? This isn't a criminal case. As far as I know. Is it?"

Jules looked from the detective to Noah. Quinn could see the alarm on her mother's face at just the word *criminal* mentioned.

The detective switched his attention to Quinn. "Ms. Maguire, would you like to make a statement in regards to the article that was published in the Maui Now news that claims you are Nama Monroe, the child who was lost at sea?"

He tapped his pen onto the pad, making bold marks along the edge. Marks of frustration, no doubt. His stare felt like it was burning holes through her forehead.

"I—" she stammered, but stopped when her dad put his hand on her arm.

"Again, my wife and I, as well as Ms. Maguire, will be glad to talk to you with our attorney present. I'll need to give him some notice and see if we can match up an afternoon to your schedule," Noah said.

Quinn had to give it to him. He was firm without being the least bit rude. He also didn't mention that her mother came from a family of attorneys, and having one by his side in a matter of minutes was possible. If the detective already knew it, he didn't let on.

"Look, people. This case has been open for far too long. If you have answers, I'd appreciate you giving them."

"We'll be glad to talk to you with our attorney present," Noah said, repeating his mantra, but this time with more compassion.

The detective didn't care for his compassion. He flipped his notebook shut, then pushed it and his pen into his pocket. He gave her father the death stare and stood.

"We'd like to thank you for wanting to get to the bottom of any unfounded rumors," Noah said. "And we look forward to speaking to you again."

The detective seemed unnerved at the over-the-top cordiality of the man in front of him. He looked like he didn't know whether to spit or smile.

Noah was impressive, and Quinn had to wonder if she'd inherited some of his peacemaking abilities, as the way he spoke felt similar to how she'd mediated with people in the past.

"You'll be hearing from me," the detective said to Quinn. "I'll show myself out and begin my investigation from another angle. I'll expect to see the three of you at the precinct by this Friday at five p.m."

He walked away, and Quinn breathed a sigh of relief.

It was short-lived, though. She knew this was only a reprieve.

There was sure to be more to come. This was one story that was too good for the town to let go. She just hoped she could figure out a way to keep the mobs and sticks of fire off her family's doorstep.

Chapter Thirteen

"This is the narrowest place on the Maliko Stream. We'll cross here," Liam said, holding his arm out to help Quinn find each stone strategically put in place to get across the span of rippling water. She almost wished they'd fall in, as it looked cool and inviting, and the hike up was testing her newfound physical endurance abilities.

Liam, however, wasn't the least bit winded. So Quinn quietly suffered.

He'd shown up shortly after the detective left, then her parents, and found Quinn alone in her suite. To her humiliation, he'd caught her huddled on the couch, looking like a total wreck.

"Tell me what's going on," he'd said, pulling her into his arms.

She'd melted against him. He smelled of freshly cut wood and hard work. And he felt so solid. So safe. It would be easy to let him help make sense of things or sort everything out, but that was the old Quinn, the one who allowed everyone around her to guide her life.

The new Quinn—the one who'd been found and reborn in Maui—had to suck it up and be a big girl. She also had to sort out some details and get plans in motion. Before Friday. That meant they had three days. But first, he deserved to know.

"Liam, I'm leaving," she'd whispered in his ear as he held her.

They broke apart and settled on the couch, where she told him she'd made up her mind that the best thing for her to do was leave the island.

Permanently.

She'd figured it out. A second disappearance from the island was the only way to save her family from public shaming, as well as protect the reputation of the mother who raised her. Even if she was gone from this earth, Quinn could feel her around, guiding her to make good decisions. For that mother to be painted as a criminal was something Quinn wasn't about to let happen, even if technically, it was true. The simple truth was that Elizabeth had been deprived of love until Nama came into her life. She'd grown up in a dysfunctional family without siblings, or the affection of her parents, and when Nama gravitated toward her so easily, Elizabeth couldn't give her up. Against the law, yes. Malicious, no. At least not in Quinn's opinion.

"The mainland isn't that far, Quinn. They'll find you."

She shrugged. "Maybe not. I unknowingly lived under an alias for decades. It can be done."

Leaving the inn and all the sweat and tears she'd put into it would crush her, but she planned to start pulling résumés for hotel managers that very afternoon. She couldn't be too picky, considering the immediate need. She'd talk to her grandmother as soon as she found a replacement. It was possible she might only go to Oahu, or the Big Island. But somewhere that no one cared who Nama Monroe or Quinn Maguire was or wasn't.

Liam listened quietly. That was his way. Take things in and let them simmer. He didn't try to talk her out of anything.

Finally she ran out of things to say. Then he spoke.

"Take the rest of the morning off and come with me," he'd said. "There's someone I want you to meet."

"I can't. Emily is swamped up there, and Maggie will be bringing in Charlie."

"I'll have you back by one o'clock, and you can send Emily on a long lunch to recover. Rosa can handle Charlie alone for a few hours. Please."

Since he rarely asked her for anything, she'd agreed. They'd dropped by Colleen's for breakfast, a local restaurant in Haiku, and though the food looked and smelled delicious, she'd barely eaten a bite.

She didn't know she would be jungle-jogging afterward or she might've made herself eat more.

Now here they were, climbing steep terrain and crossing streams that were fairly full because of the previous night's small squall. It was a far cry from fielding phone calls and maintenance emergencies, and she felt like a fugitive on the run. Emily was probably losing her mind by now, handling the midmorning rush alone.

However, she had to admit the fresh air and serenity of Haiku calmed her. The area was similar to Hana in that it was a beautiful, remote part of Maui. Unlike Hana, though, Haiku was still yet undiscovered to most visiting the island. She was pleased that they hadn't passed a single person on the way up. What they had passed was a quiet rainbow of colors and scents in the many tropical flowers she spotted. Heliconia, angel's-trumpet, several types of orchids, and even a few birds-of-paradise.

Leaving Maui was going to hurt. It truly was a tropical utopia to those who knew how to appreciate the gift of nature. Quinn couldn't get enough of it, and she counted her blessings often that on her deathbed, her mother had sent her to the island of her birth.

The island she now needed to leave.

"We're almost there," he said.

"Are you sure?" Quinn said. She saw no sign of any sort of landmark or place to rest. They'd hiked for at least an hour, first through thick grass, then a bamboo forest, and now simply thick vegetation that was crisscrossed with a few streams of water.

She was beginning to worry that they were lost.

He chuckled. "I'm sure."

"I don't know how you could be sure of anything up here. I can't even tell north from south."

"Look at the sun. And I should know this by now, but are you a Jimi Hendrix fan?"

"Uh, I don't think so," Quinn said. To be honest, she knew he was a legend, but she couldn't name a single tune he once sang. "Why?"

"We're not too far from a property where he stayed when he was here for his 1970 Rainbow Bridge concert. He stayed in a 1930s-era cottage, and they've left it that way."

"Up here? In the wild?" Quinn couldn't even imagine a rock star wanting to be so far from everything. Though she could relate to a person needing to hide from prying media and fanatical strangers.

"It feels remote and it is, to a point, but actually we aren't too far from a lot of places. Haiku Town Center is only a few minutes to the east. And Paia Town, the so-called hub of the North Shore, is about ten minutes west. Even the airport is less than fifteen minutes from here. It's not as isolated as it looks."

Maybe not, but Quinn couldn't imagine who they were meeting way up in what *felt like* the middle of nowhere. Over the last year she'd met Liam's mother, brothers, and many more relatives of his than she could count. She'd also met lifelong friends that had all sang his praises, showing that he was exactly what she'd thought: a good and loyal person.

He came to a stop so fast that Quinn nearly ran into him.

"Whoa, what's that?"

In front of them she could see a small path through the trees. Nothing official, just a trail that appeared to be trodden down from frequent use. At the start of it was a fierce-looking wooden statue with a tall headdress.

Liam nodded at it solemnly. "It represents Lono, the spirit of peace and healing. Also agriculture."

The eyes on the tiki-looking piece were carved on the side of its head. They were round and huge, and quite frightening.

"Is it an idol?" she asked.

Liam shook his head. "No. That's what people who don't under-stand like to think. But we Hawaiians know the truth. Since you're a true Hawaiian, you also know the truth deep down, but I'll help you remember," he said with a smile. "It's just something we use to focus on, like the Catholics pray to Mother Mary on the altar. Lono is a spirit, and if we acknowledge him, he will help guide us."

"Who put this here?"

"The man who carved it. My father," Liam said, his voice low and quiet. Almost reverent.

"It's . . . Well, it's really a magnificent piece. Your father must've been a very talented artist." She was a little taken aback. This was only the second time she'd heard Liam mention his father. When she'd asked, he'd said they lost him years ago. It felt like a subject that was off-limits, so she'd never brought it up again.

Liam nodded. "Yes, he was, and still is. Come on."

He continued on and Quinn followed. His father was still alive?

They followed the path and came to a wooden fence erected in front of them. It was ragged, obviously built from scraps and weather-worn, but hanging on the front of it was a sign.

ABSOLUTELY NO TRESPASSERS! DO NOT ENTER! BEWARE OF DOG!

Quinn felt a ripple of alarm, but she trusted Liam—with her life if need be. He opened the gate and held it for her, and she slipped in.

"My father doesn't like visitors," Liam said. "He hasn't left this property in many years and rarely allows anyone in. But I think it's time you meet him."

"I'd be honored." Quinn held in the rest of her questions. If Liam wanted her to believe his father wasn't in the picture, there must be a reason. She'd have to wait and see if he wanted to share it with her.

Contrary to the jungle they'd just traversed through, when the gate closed behind her, Quinn was astonished at the beauty that lay before her.

It was still wild and somewhat untamed, but the Maui flora and all the tropical trees formed a protective circle around what she thought of as some sort of homestead. There was also order in the chaos. And so much beautiful woodwork. The first thing she saw in the distance was a rustic cabin. It was small, and a porch ran the length of the house with a solitary chair set out. Quinn could imagine the porch lined with rocking chairs, soft cushions, and colorful flower pots.

It could be so much more inviting.

But she wasn't here to judge. Or redecorate.

"That cabin is only three hundred square feet. There's nothing fancy about it. A bed and tiny kitchen area. A wood-burning fireplace for when it gets cool at night. No electricity and not even indoor plumbing. There's an outhouse for that, and he bathes in the creek."

"No comforts?" Quinn asked, noticing a cast-iron water pump about thirty feet from the cabin. Beside it were a half dozen or so empty buckets. She thought of her brother, Jonah, noting the similarities between the way he lived compared to Liam's father.

"Nope. You won't find items that are for looks, comfort, or even memorabilia. Other than one framed photo that hangs on his wall."

"So he's a minimalist."

Liam gave a strange little snort. "I guess you could say that. He became one before it was a thing."

He pointed toward another structure, built much bigger than the cabin but with the same exquisite craftsmanship. "Over this way is his workshop. That's where he spends most of his time. I'm sure he'll be in there."

As they walked, Quinn marveled at the many different fruit trees that flanked the property fencing. "It's like Eden."

Liam laughed. "Not sure he'd agree. Much of this was here when he came, but my father also grows tangerines, bananas, oranges, grapefruit, and guava. He's got a greenhouse in the back of the property, higher in elevation, where he has organic vegetables growing. He passes the majority of it to my mother, who distributes it throughout our family."

Quinn also saw a coconut tree nearly bursting with ready coconuts. No wonder the man rarely left the property. It appeared he had everything he needed to sustain himself, right outside his front door.

Just before they arrived at the shop, a huge black dog stepped out from behind a tree and lumbered toward them. He wasn't the most graceful of dogs; his eighty pounds or so swayed back and forth with each stride.

"Is he nice?" Quinn asked, remembering the sign.

Liam laughed. "Nice is an understatement. Bodhi is the best dog on the island. He doesn't bite, bark, or pester. But he will lay at your feet and relish any attention you decide to give."

Quinn bent down and held her hands out.

Bodhi took his time, but when he got to her, he sat down in front of her and looked up, straining through the curly black bangs that adorned his face.

"Good boy," Quinn said, rubbing him behind his ears. He cocked his head, pushing into her hands, and gave a little moan of pleasure. "I like him. And I'd count Bodhi as a comfort item, wouldn't you?"

"I would but my father, probably not. Bodhi is security, and that's needed out here. He might not attack on command, but he'll sure sound the alarm if anyone tries to come in uninvited."

"He didn't make a sound for us."

"Oh, he's got the nose of a bloodhound. He can recognize my scent a mile away. He knows I'm welcome."

Quinn thought of Woodrow then, and that made her remember that Maggie was also dealing with too much stress. Quinn felt a rush of guilt that she hadn't been more help to her best friend and that she'd be even less so when she was gone.

Everything was falling apart.

She sighed loudly, then rose and followed Liam to the door of the shop.

He gave three successive knocks, a pause, then two more. With that, he opened the door and stood aside, letting Quinn cross the threshold first.

Chapter Fourteen

Maggie pulled up to the pump at the Ohana Fuels station and put down all the windows before shutting her car off. All morning as she'd gotten herself and Charlie ready, she'd felt jittery. Nervous. It was just her luck that a summer storm had hit on her way home last night, and though she knew she should stop, she'd skipped the gas station.

Now the tank was on empty without even enough gas to get Charlie to the inn, let alone get her back down Hana Highway to the clinic.

"Can we stop at Komoda Store for a doughnut on a stick?"

"No, Charlie, we can't. That was in Makawao, and it's a long way from here. Mommy's in a hurry this morning. They probably already sold out anyway."

Maggie could feel pools of sweat beginning to form in her shoes. To top it off, her eye began the nice little dance it did when the nervous tic came to play.

She turned to look at Charlie. "Sit tight while I get gas."

He barely acknowledged her. He was concentrating on chewing the skin from the side of his thumb, a habit he must've inherited from his dad because Maggie had seen Colby doing it a million times.

"Charlie, stop that."

He immediately stopped and looked at her with his most innocent grin, his green eyes big and round.

The doughnut Charlie was craving was one they'd picked up at a famous bakery when they'd gone to Makawao one evening. The family business was over a hundred years old and so popular that it was said they usually sold everything out by midmorning, then closed shop. It was good stuff but way too far out of their way.

But now she felt guilty.

Little heartbreaker. Damn, she loved her kid.

She climbed out and ran her debit card through the pump scanner. It beeped, and she picked up the pump, ready to use it. She peered at the screen, putting her hand up to shade it. The words were hard to make out through the bright rays of an extraordinarily warm Maui day.

PLEASE SEE CASHIER

Exasperated, she scanned the card again.

Same message.

The morning was not being kind to her. She had hoped to be able to talk to Quinn, and maybe David, before heading on to work. She needed every spare second she could get.

She went around and opened Charlie's door. He was back to chewing his fingers. "Come on, bud. We need to go in the store."

That got his attention. Usually the only time they went inside a gas station was for treats. He hopped out, Woodrow right behind him. Maggie was glad she'd had a strange feeling that morning and put on the dog's official vest.

"Give me your hand," she said a little too brusquely to Charlie.

He complied, and they hurried across the parking lot.

Inside, Maggie approached the counter, with Woodrow obediently at her side. A young man stood behind the counter.

"Mommy, can I have candy?" Charlie said, tugging on her pants.

"No," Maggie said. "Hush while I get this straightened out."

She turned her attention back to the cashier.

"Your card was declined. Can you try another? Or do you want to pay cash? Oh, and we don't allow dogs in here."

"He's a service dog. And there must be something wrong with your system." Maggie was beyond using her polite voice.

"Nope."

That's it? Just a nope?

Charlie tugged again, then gave another plea for sweets.

"Do you have another card?" the cashier asked. "Or cash?"

"Nope," Maggie said, using the same deadpan voice as he did.

"There's an ATM at the back."

"Come on, Charlie." She had just deposited a check from Colby the day before, and now she could kick herself for not getting some cash out of it. She tugged Charlie by the neck of his shirt, then grabbed his hand and headed for the back.

Before she could reach the machine, her phone rang.

It was a Hawaii area code. Was it one of the clinic numbers? She wasn't late yet, was she? She continued the beeline to grab some cash and answered the phone midstride.

"Yes? I mean, hello?"

"This is the fraud department of Bank of Maui calling. Is this Margaret Ann Dalton?"

Maggie froze in place, right between the aisles of automobile oil and cheap souvenirs. Woodrow stopped, too, but she had to let go of Charlie so she wouldn't lose a limb.

When he turned around, she waved him back.

"Yes, it is." She looked down at the debit card in her hand.

"Please verify your phone number, Ms. Dalton," the faceless female voice said.

"It's the one you just called." She rolled her eyes at the phone.

"Mommy, are you mad?" Charlie asked, tugging on her hand again.

Maggie put her finger to her lips and shushed him.

The woman wasn't a bit ruffled with Maggie's attitude. She asked again. "Please verify your phone number. It's bank protocol, and we have an important message for you in regard to the safety of your account."

Maggie gave in and rattled off her phone number, date of birth, and her mailing address. Last, they asked the name of her favorite dog.

"Toby." Then she covered the phone and glanced down. Woodrow's tail thumped the ceramic floor, and he looked up at her with sad eyes. "Sorry, it was my first dog," she whispered to him.

She could hear the rep tapping on computer keys. "Have you recently changed your basic information such as your email address, password, and pin number?"

"No," Maggie said. She felt her heart rate soar.

Woodrow nudged her leg and whined.

"Ms. Dalton, did you request a new account and debit card?"

"No, I sure didn't."

As she shuffled Woodrow and Charlie toward the sign that indicated the restroom, she listened to the rest of the call, which was nothing less than terrifying. The rep told her that someone had opened a new account in her name, using her address and social security number, then attempted to withdraw funds from her existing account. The bank fraud team caught it, but her account—and all access to her money—was frozen until the investigation could be completed.

She hung up the phone after being instructed to call back in a few days. The nausea took hold, and she felt the Pop-Tart she'd eaten for breakfast trying to rise up in her throat. It wasn't as though she had a gold mine in her account, but what she did have, they needed to live on.

Goose bumps started to creep from her fingertips, up her wrists.

"Charlie," she gasped.

Woodrow got more insistent, nudging her knees to try to make her sit.

"No, Woodrow!" She couldn't sit down in the middle of the store.

Kay Bratt

"What's wrong, Mommy?" Charlie said, his face scrunching up with worry.

Maggie began to see stars swirling in front of her eyes as she stood there. No money. No gas. No groceries for their empty pantry. No dog food for Woodrow. Payday two weeks away. The emailed photo that morning. Now this.

He'd found her.

No security.

No protection.

She felt like she couldn't breathe.

And Charlie looked terrified.

"Bathroom," she croaked out, letting go of his hand and pointing to where a restroom sign hung on the back wall.

Charlie headed there, and Maggie staggered behind him.

She could feel her chest tightening, and she was breathing too hard. Woodrow nipped at her heels and gave a sharp bark. He knew it was coming, and she couldn't stop it.

She had to get Charlie to safety.

"Ma'am?" the guy at the front counter called out. "Is everything okay back there? You've got to move your car if you don't want gas. We've only got two pumps!"

"Get in the bathroom," she said to Charlie as the tears began to stream down her face and she struggled for breath against the sudden intense chest pain.

They got there, and she pushed him in, then followed with Woodrow on her tail. Charlie immediately wrinkled his nose at the sour smell of the toilet and the dirty paper towels strewn everywhere. Under normal circumstances, Maggie wouldn't let him into a bathroom in this condition, much less let him touch the sink like he'd immediately done.

Her head pounded, and her chills gave way to intense sweating.

She sank to the floor and pulled her knees to her face, then struggled against Woodrow as he tried to squeeze under her trembling arms

140

and flatten her legs. He succeeded and laid his body across her knees, his training to keep her from hurting herself kicking in admirably.

"Stay right here," she hissed between sobs, not even looking up until she heard Charlie moving. Before she could react, he'd grabbed her phone from her purse and slipped out.

She tried to push Woodrow off, but she was on the top level of an anxiety attack, and he wasn't letting her go anywhere. Even through the trauma, Maggie could see he was trying to apply deep pressure to her torso to comfort her.

It wasn't enough. Things were escalating.

Everything around her blurred and blended with the sound of an oncoming freight train in her ears. And then the world faded to black.

Chapter Fifteen

An hour later, Maggie sat on a stretcher outside the gas station, Woodrow at her side as a paramedic checked her blood pressure once again. She was horrified that leaning on the emergency van in front of her was Dr. Starr, aka Joe—aka her boss!

He was helping Charlie open his second bag of potato chips. They looked comfortable together, as though this wasn't their first time meeting.

She saw Charlie fidget with a new shark tooth hanging around his neck, the leather of the necklace resting low on his tiny chest. She'd noticed Charlie glance at them on the souvenir aisle when they'd gone to the back of the store for the ATM.

Obviously Joe was doing whatever he could to make Charlie feel comfortable in the midst of what to him must've felt like the end of the world.

"Are you sure this is real?" Charlie asked, holding up the tooth for Joe to inspect.

Maggie recognized the hopeful expression that went with his question.

Joe nodded. "It sure is. Probably from a great white right off the waters of the North Shore."

"Wow. Thank you," Charlie murmured.

She was reminded of her current situation—no access to funds and a lunatic still tracking her—and she pushed the thoughts away, the fingers of her free hand running through Woodrow's soft hair.

He looked up at her, worry still in his eyes.

"Good boy," Maggie whispered. "Such a good boy."

The machine made a racket as it filled up and then deflated. The paramedic quickly pulled the cuff from her arm, the rip of the Velcro like a gunshot in her ears.

"Can I please go?" Maggie pleaded with the man who hovered over her, whose thumb now pushed down on her wrist, taking her pulse. "I'm fine. This is embarrassing."

Joe handed the bag of chips over to Charlie and looked up. "No, you can't go until you are cleared."

"The numbers are better but not stable yet. She needs to drink some juice," the paramedic said, then headed to the van.

"Mommy, can I have a Coke?" Charlie asked innocently. He'd finally come down from his fear over her safety. Kind of quickly, too, considering how fast he'd accepted the invitation to climb into the fire truck and blow the horn.

He'd looked proud of himself as he'd climbed down wearing an oversize fireman hat, having earned a new nickname.

Little *Makoa*, they called him. Brave man. He'd saved his mother and had earned their respect. Something she could've done herself—with Woodrow's help—if he'd just have waited a few more minutes before bursting out of the restroom with her phone. But she had to give it to him, for being so young, he'd also been responsible.

"No. You can have milk. I'm sure it goes great with all that salt you're ingesting." She gave Joe a look that was meant to chastise, but he only smiled.

"Aww, he's a kid. A Coke once in a while won't hurt him."

"Tell that to your local dentist and see what his response is. Anyway, I really appreciate you coming, but don't you need to head back to the clinic?" Maggie asked. "You had a full morning of appointments set up, I'm pretty sure."

He shrugged. "They can wait. My employees and the animals under my care are my first priorities. Our current in-house patients are fine for the moment, and Mom rescheduled the morning appointments for later today. Everything is under control. Except you."

"I'm under control." She left off the key word *now*.

Maggie could just die. There was no doubt going to have to be some explaining later. He wasn't just going to let someone who collapsed in a soggy mess in a public bathroom continue to be employed without knowing his clients were safe.

"We can talk about it later," Joe said, nodding his head toward Charlie.

Was he reading her mind now? Maggie flushed.

It was just her luck that when Charlie had grabbed her phone and run out of the bathroom during her meltdown, the door had locked behind him. He'd charged the young man at the register, telling him to call his daddy as he pushed the phone up onto the counter.

First, the cashier tried to get into the bathroom as Maggie sobbed between heaves.

Since he could hear her through the door and knew she was conscious, the young man tried to reach a family member. He'd tried Colby's number, as it was last on the call log, but he got his voice mail. Then he dialed the person called before that, which happened to be Joe from her accidental dial earlier that morning.

With Charlie at his side, the cashier had told Joe he wasn't sure what to do, but a little boy named Charlie was freaking out because his mother was sick and locked behind the bathroom door in the gas station.

Joe had instructed him to call the paramedics, then jumped in his car and made the usual half-hour trip in record time. He was already there when the paramedics called the fire department to come break the door down.

Joe had spoken to her through the crack, his voice loud but soothing, just as he had used it during the surgery yesterday.

"Maggie, it's Joe. Open this door so we can help you."

Thankfully, though shocked to hear her own boss, Maggie was finally able to pull herself together enough for Woodrow to let her stand and unlock the door. Just in time, too, because two of Hana's volunteer firemen were about to use a massive crowbar to break it off the hinges.

Most likely the cost for that repair would've landed on her plate. One more expense she couldn't pay for. Because why? Her bank account was frozen.

Deep breaths.

Her phone rang just as the paramedic came back, slipped the cuff back on, and began pumping it full of air.

Maggie looked down and saw Colby's face pop up.

She hit "Ignore."

A text came through ten seconds later.

WHAT THE HELL IS GOING ON?? CALL ME!

A jolt of alarm went through her.

"Charlie?"

Her son looked up, his mouth full of potato chips.

"When you and the nice man from inside tried to call your dad, you didn't leave a message, did you?"

Charlie shook his head.

Relief flooded through Maggie.

"The nice man did, though," he said, crumbs shooting out of his mouth and onto the front of his shirt.

Maggie hung her head. She could only imagine what the store clerk had said on the message he'd left.

There's a worried kid in front of me because his hysterical mother has locked herself in the bathroom and no one can get her out. Please help.

Colby would not be easy to settle down. Unfortunately he knew about her anxiety attacks. Before he'd agreed to let her move to Maui with Charlie, she had assured him repeatedly that they were now nearly nonexistent. That with Woodrow's presence, she was cured.

She typed out a quick message and hit "Send."

We are fine. A complete misunderstanding. Will call you later.

She prayed it would be enough. Having Colby breathing down her back was the last thing she needed when her life was already crumbling around her. Only one thing had changed. She *would* talk to Colby about everything that was going on. As Charlie's father, he deserved that much. But first she needed to get it sorted out.

On her own.

Chapter Sixteen

The first thing that hit Quinn when she stepped into the shop was the intoxicating and bewitching scent of wood. Liam followed her, and the door shut behind them.

"Can't Bodhi come in?" she asked, already missing the sweet boy.

"He's on duty," Liam said.

Quinn peered around. The building was immaculate, every inch swept clean and kept orderly, a collection of tools hung in precise rows on the wall nearest to her. Below them against the wall was a pristine line of carved wooden statues, similar to the one outside the gate.

It felt warm and inviting, though besides a few wooden stools, there was no place to sit. And it was quiet, other than a methodical swoosh that sounded every few seconds. Visually, there was a lot going on that made sense in a workshop, but after a quick scan, her eyes were drawn to a canoe mounted on the opposite wall. It was set tipping out to them, arranged like a trophy.

"That's an outrigger canoe," Liam said, following her gaze. "It's my father's pride and joy. Carved from a one-hundred-year-old koa tree, just like in the old days."

The swooshing noise stopped, and Quinn followed Liam to the mounted canoe. It was definitely a masterpiece, and she felt honored that she would meet the master wood-carver who'd created it.

"It's beautiful," she murmured, reaching up to run a hand along the bottom.

"He spent years carving and chipping away at it, taking his time to get it absolutely perfect. Years that I barely saw him."

Quinn turned to Liam. "I'm sorry. I know sometimes an obsession can tear a family apart."

"It wasn't his obsession," Liam said. "It was his penance."

Before Quinn could ask what he meant, an elderly man walked forward from the shadows. He was tall, and though not a heavy man, his upper body rippled with muscles. His hair was thick, only a few stripes of black streaking through the faded gray like tributaries into a river.

She could see Liam in the lines of his face, Quinn decided, though his countenance was far different from his son's. Liam usually came across as welcoming and at peace. But this man—his very own father—looked sad.

Deeply, deeply sad.

He pulled a rag from his pocket and mopped his forehead with it, then stuffed it back into his jeans.

Finally, he looked up at them and made eye contact. "Son. Good to see you."

"And you," Liam said. He squeezed her hand. "This is Quinn."

The man nodded shyly at her.

Liam turned to Quinn. "And this is my father, Ano."

"It's a pleasure," she said. "Your property is gorgeous. I feel like I'm on a deserted island."

He didn't smile. Only nodded again. It wasn't unfriendly. He just seemed distant. His energy reminded Quinn of her brother, Jonah. Protective of himself and sparing with conversation.

Quinn's thoughts swam with curiosity. Why had Liam let on that his father was gone? What was really going on between them?

"I wanted Quinn to see your workmanship," Liam said.

"She must be important for you to bring her here."

Liam nodded. "She is."

Quinn felt her cheeks flush. There was something going on. Something she didn't quite grasp. It felt like a secret was being passed from father to son and back again.

"I heard you back there," Liam said. "You must have been sanding."

Ano nodded. "I have a canoe going out on Saturday. I'm doing the final prep."

"Another for the club?"

"Yes."

There was an awkward silence for a few seconds; then Liam directed his next words at her.

"My father plays an important role in keeping Hawaiian customs alive."

"That's wonderful," Quinn said. She looked at Ano, but he kept his eyes down. He was humble.

Liam touched the canoe—reverently, as though it were alive. "He's one of the few who does craftsman work while keeping with the oldest techniques. The shape, length, and weight requirements are all very strict. His canoes are highly sought after, but only a few will ever own one."

"The only value to me is what they feel in their heart as they use the vessel to be one with the sea," Ano said, his voice softly echoing in the big room.

"Believe me—the value is much more than just sentimental," Liam said. "If only he could finish them faster."

Ano looked up. "It takes time to get it right."

"Interesting," Quinn said. "How do you know how to do this?"

"It's complicated," Ano said.

"I'd love to hear."

Liam glanced at his father, an invitation for him to speak. When Ano remained silent, Liam began, "Polynesians from long ago were natural experts with navigation, and they discovered the Hawaiian Islands, which brought about the influx of migration. My father believes the spirits of these same discoverers come to him with details, dimensions, and their wishes for what he must work on next. All of it is shown to him either in meditation or when he sleeps."

Over the last year that she'd lived in Maui, Quinn had become much more spiritual. She now believed in visions and spirits.

"You've memorized my words well, son." Ano looked pleased for the first time.

"We've shared so few that, of course, I remember them all," Liam said.

He didn't sound unkind, but knowing him like she did, Quinn could hear just the tiniest bit of resentment hidden within the smile. She didn't judge—she knew well how complicated a parent-child relationship could be. She was still trying to figure out how to be the daughter her newly discovered mother wished her to be.

"I hope that your brothers were as good of students," his father said gently. "But somehow I doubt it. You were always the thoughtful one. As well as the one most interested in the canoes."

Quinn had met Liam's brothers at a weekend cookout. Big, strapping goofballs who were much more talkative and demonstrative than their brother. To her they seemed more interested in their own pursuits— mostly catching the biggest fish and drinking on Friday nights—than they were in anything creative. She could see how they would be considered less likely to take on their father's craft or listen to his words.

Liam was different. He was a listener, a trait that made people confide and trust in him. Though he was young, he felt more like a Hawaiian elder, his entire being reverent and protective about their culture.

"Anyway," Liam continued, "the knowledge of ocean navigation began to fade with modern times until some decided to bring it back. Now cultural classes include lessons on navigation as well as racing. There are dozens of canoe clubs across the islands and more forming all the time. My father's gift is very valuable as the new generations try to embrace their Hawaiian culture."

It made Quinn happy to hear that Maui wasn't letting its traditions be forgotten.

"I've never been in an outrigger. I can imagine how close to the sea you feel in one," Quinn said.

Liam raised his eyebrows in a challenge. "If you'd like, I could set us up for an outrigger tour. There're a few companies that do them on Maui. Of course, it's not like the old days, but you can see what it's like to be on a canoe with no land views in sight. They'll even take you to snorkel with the old sea turtles."

Quinn thought of the sea turtle that she believed had saved her from drowning, guiding her up toward the light and the surface. With that experience, she'd finally overcome her fear of water. Now she loved to swim in the comforting sea, but she stayed close to shore. She still had unresolved trauma from falling overboard when she was a child, and she wasn't sure she was ready to go out on such a small boat. Thus far her family had not been able to persuade her to even go out on their much larger vessel.

"Make sure you use someone reputable," Ano said. "Last April a group went out, and the whole thing was flipped over by a wave. All eight tourists went overboard."

"Lest you're thinking they were eaten by sharks, don't worry, they were rescued," Liam said, winking at Quinn. "The instructors are usually really good, but sometimes you can get someone green. I wouldn't book us with anyone but the best. We could even do an outrigger whale-watching excursion."

Quinn remembered all the trouble she'd left behind at the hotel. She doubted she'd have time to do anything other than get all her responsibilities covered before jumping ship—metaphorically speaking, this time. The flood of reality made her feel like her energy was suddenly being sucked out of her.

"Is there someplace I can sit for a minute?" she asked.

Liam put an arm around her. "Of course. I'm sorry. It was a long hike."

"No worries. I just need a minute. And some fresh water if possible. My Hydro Flask is on empty."

"Take her into the cabin and let her rest where it's cool before your hike back down," Ano said. "I have more work to do." He turned and headed toward the back from where he'd first come.

Without so much as a *goodbye* or *nice meeting you*, he was gone. Liam looked after him, then shook his head.

"I'd hoped to have a little more conversation, but he's done," he said. "Come on."

They left the shed and found Bodhi waiting right outside the door, his tail thumping out a beat on the dirt at the sight of them.

"Bodhi," Quinn said, kneeling down to rub him behind both ears.

"Don't spoil him," Liam said. "As you can see, my father isn't very affectionate, and Bodhi will just feel abandoned when you leave."

"Aww, poor baby," Quinn crooned to him. She decided that wherever she ended up settling next, she wanted a dog. One just like Bodhi if possible.

Liam helped her stand, and they walked up to the cabin with Bodhi right behind them.

"You go on in and rest while I fill your flask," he said, taking it from her and heading to the pump in the yard. "There's no air con, but it feels better in there than on the porch. Bodhi can go in with you if you like. We'll take him off duty for the moment."

Quinn hesitated, her hand on the door. She felt like an intruder, but he'd insisted. Since Quinn had already seen the condition of the workshop, she felt sure the interior of the cabin would be similar.

But she was wrong.

She stepped through and stopped suddenly. Sparse wasn't even the word to describe what she saw. It barely looked like anyone lived there.

Bodhi moved around her and went to the hearth, dropping down on the cool tile laid around it. He released a long, tired sigh.

"He working you too hard, Bodhi?" Quinn teased. She noticed that the dog was quite plump, and his hair shone. Ano might not be affectionate, but he took good care of his companion.

The cabin was only one room. It held a cot against one wall, a wooden stool near the large kitchen sink, and another wooden stool by the hearth.

She saw one framed photo on the wall. As she approached it, she could see it was a family shot of parents with three boys. She tried to pick Liam out from them, but the brothers looked so much alike she couldn't tell.

Liam came through the door and handed the flask back to her.

"Sorry there's nowhere comfortable to sit." He took a seat on one of the stools, close enough that he could use his foot to rub Bodhi's belly, which was now shamelessly splayed out for attention.

"Which one are you?" she asked, gazing back at the photo.

"None of them. That's not our family."

Quinn turned to him. "But—I don't understand."

"Come sit down."

She took the other stool and carried it to the hearth, easing down gently and glad to be off her feet.

She took a sip of the water from her flask.

"This water is delicious."

"Straight from a spring. Listen, Quinn. There's a reason I brought you up here, and it wasn't just to get you away from the hotel."

"I'm listening."

"My father left us when I was six years old. I only saw him a few times a year."

Sudden sadness overwhelmed Quinn. So much so that she didn't even know what to say. She grew up without a father, too, and knew it was probably the hardest part of her childhood.

Liam took a deep breath. "All three brothers in that photo were killed one night when my father left a bar on Front Street, thinking he was okay to drive. Turns out he wasn't, and he crossed the center line of Piilani Highway, pushing the car in the oncoming lane over the embankment."

Quinn realized she was covering her mouth, frozen in horror. She dropped her hand in her lap, not sure what to do with it. Thoughts swirled faster in her head than she could keep up with, her brain trying to sort it all out and put it back together again.

"But—but—why the photo?" Liam looked so sad that it was nearly unbearable for Quinn not to go to him.

"Miraculously the parents lived, though they didn't want to without their children. The mother was severely and permanently disabled. The father was in traction for months before the trial. We lost everything in the restitution order. Our home. The family land that has been ours for generations. I was too young to understand it all, other than the fact that I no longer had my favorite playing spots to wreak havoc on."

"I'm so sorry."

He took a deep breath. "The restitution, of course, wasn't enough to make up for their loss. In their victim impact statement, they asked that my father be required to hang a photo of the boys in his prison cell to remind him every day what he'd taken from them. He gave his word he would do it."

Nausea and pity rolled in Quinn's stomach. She could understand the parents' request because she knew she'd never understand their loss.

"So he kept the photo even after he was released," she said. "To punish himself."

Liam nodded. "He was paroled after seven years for exemplary behavior. But he wouldn't come home. He said he didn't deserve to have the blessing of his three sons after taking three sons from someone else."

"But that was punishing you. And your brothers. How cruel." Quinn didn't care how it came out. She couldn't imagine Liam's mother trying to explain to them why they couldn't see their father. "Where did he go?"

"First he walked around Maui, living without a home. Denying himself sanctuary from family and friends. The more that people pitied him, the more enraged with himself he became."

"Did he drink in his anger?"

"No. He's never touched alcohol again since that night. He was a law-abiding citizen. He checked in with his parole officer when he was supposed to, and that was really the only way we knew he was still alive."

"Your poor mother," Quinn said.

"Yeah, watching her suffer was the worst part of all of it for me."

"So how did he get here?"

Liam crossed his feet at his ankles, his eyes on Bodhi. "It was a blessing, really. One day a few months after he'd been living on the beach, he decided to go farther up into a remote area of Maui. He found a cave to make camp in where he could be away from people. My father lived in that cave for nearly a year, meditating to try to find peace. He didn't even go to town for food. He lived on plants, berries, and whatever else he could from the land around him."

"It's a miracle he survived."

"Yes, he knows that now," Liam said. "Inside his cave were a few rotting old canoes left there from many years ago. As the months went on, he studied the ancient canoes, trying to understand why each part was carved the way it was. That was when the dreams first came and the deeper knowledge—we call it *huna* from the ancestors—spoke to him and awarded him his gift, which would become his life's work."

"A wood-carver."

"A wood-carver and a canoe maker," Liam agreed. "He began to see in his dreams how the canoes were made, but he needed more guidance. He found and worked with one of Maui's few remaining canoe masters for another year, and when the man died, he left this land to my father with the agreement that he would continue his studies and help keep the old ways alive."

"And he has."

Liam looked at her, raising his eyebrows. "Yes, he has. My father never goes back on his word. This has been his home ever since. The only time he leaves it is to go see another uncovered ancient canoe or to the museums to study those on display, and even then it's been only a few times all these years."

"But not to your home? Or family events?"

He shook his head. "Never. He didn't watch my brothers play football. Wasn't there to teach us to drive. He even missed seeing me surf in the Maui championships back in the day. Anything and everything a father would do, he avoided."

"But why couldn't he move your family up here to be with him?"

"Because that would defeat his purpose of isolating himself. It wouldn't be a punishment if he had the support of his family around him."

"So you and your brothers took his place as the man of the house. You got to share in his punishment after all," Quinn said.

Liam shrugged. "My mother worked two jobs for many years until my brothers and I were old enough to work and help. She needed us to grow up fast. She still needs us. Or at least, she needs me. My brothers have a lot going on in their lives."

"I can't imagine how much it hurt you to not have a father around." She knew what it was like to grow up without a father, and it brought about a stirring of anger toward the old man. But she also felt pity, for he had to have led a lonely life. A life of isolation and quiet.

"He did what he had to do. Is still doing what he has to do to serve penance. My brothers and I at least got to visit once he moved here. He tried to teach us what a father should during those quick visits. Lots of life lessons and lectures. His greatest fear is that we will not be men of our word or noble enough to own up to our mistakes."

"So he has to continue showing you forever?"

"Yes. He feels that the death of those boys is forever, so his penance is forever. But I don't agree. I think mistakes can be forgiven, and one made shouldn't lead to many more. Quinn, what I'm trying to say is that you can never outrun your troubles. My father could've suffered the same, staying in his home as he does here. Without the distance leaving us fatherless. He could've made penance in another way."

"You think leaving my family and running away won't solve my problems."

"You tell me. People here love you, Quinn. Why make them suffer more with your absence? Why punish them all over again?"

He didn't name himself among those who would be punished by her absence, but she could see in his eyes that he was hurt for her to even consider leaving him behind for another life. If she did, she would be doing to him exactly what his father had done.

It would shatter her, especially knowing she'd hurt him, but he had to think of her family. She had to make him understand that staying would hurt so many people. It would be all on her. Once again she would be the reason they suffered. Maybe they'd miss her, but at least their lives wouldn't be upended. It wasn't enough that she'd disappeared for thirty years. Now that they'd been reunited, fate wanted to use her to bring them all down.

It wasn't fair. Not to them. And not to her.

He watched her, his eyes sad as he waited for her to answer. He was the last person she would ever want to hurt. But as a native Hawaiian, he knew that *ohana* was everything.

"Liam, I get what you are trying to make me see here, but what about my grandmother? She could go to jail, and that would surely speed up her death. She'd die of humiliation. And my family's business and reputation? What if—"

He held a hand up. "Quinn, mistakes can be forgiven and reputations repaired. I'm not telling you what to do. Just think about it."

"You could come with me." The words slipped out, and Quinn wanted to pull them back in. She didn't want to sound needy. Or ask him to make such a sacrifice.

"Then both of us would have to leave our family. My mother depends on me. Even more so than my brothers. You are very important to me, and I'm sorry, but I can't leave Maui. My heart is tethered to the 'aina of this island. My responsibility to my family is still heavy."

Quinn had a vision of herself alone on a property far away, too far for anyone she loved to visit. Too complicated if she didn't want her story to harm them. Could she start over again? Should she have to?

Liam stared at her, his eyes beseeching her to think deeply about her choices. Reminding her that he was the first person to care for her completely, without expectations, despite her many flaws.

Her thoughts spun through her head like a tilt-a-whirl.

It couldn't be decided right here. Not right now. "Are you ready to go? I need to get back to the hotel."

There was a lot to think about, and all she wanted to do was get through the business day and hide in her room for the rest of the evening. Bedtime would mean plenty of hours for her to be wide awake, and she hoped to figure everything out so she could get the ball rolling by morning.

Chapter Seventeen

Maggie pulled her car into the alley behind the Shakti Yoga studio, put it in park, and stepped out. Dr. Starr had insisted that she take the day off. Do some yoga, he'd said, as though that would solve all her problems. If it wasn't enough that her brand-new boss had seen her at one of her weakest moments, now he was ordering her to stay away from the clinic. It was all so humiliating that the prospect of *not* facing him over the examination table at work was what made her accept his offer of the impromptu afternoon off.

Then she'd realized her gas gauge was hovering on the full mark. He must have taken it upon himself to fill it, and she'd owe him for that too. Another chink in her armor of pride.

She'd considered keeping Charlie with her for the day, but one look at her reflection in the mirror changed her mind. It wasn't often she put herself first, but she needed some time alone. He would be happier at the inn too.

By the time she'd dropped Charlie off at the inn and was told that Quinn was out somewhere with Liam, yoga followed by a walk on the beach sounded inviting.

She swung by her apartment, leaving Woodrow for a celebratory nap that he'd well earned. She changed, grabbed a bottle of water, and was back on the road in less than five minutes.

She barely remembered the drive from the apartment to the studio. Her mind was on Quinn. Where had she and Liam gone that was more important than talking to her about the photo uploaded online? And Maggie needed to tell her about the latest catastrophe with her bank account. And the ensuing panic attack.

But obviously, it could all wait.

She entered through the door to the small front room that smelled of sweet, flowery incense.

Quietly, she unfurled her mat and set her blanket and strap to the side, then crossed her feet and lowered herself gracefully until she was in lotus pose. She closed her eyes. A few minutes of meditation before class always settled the chaos in her mind.

Only here in her yoga class could she be completely anonymous.

She only had to do one thing.

Just *be*.

She kept her eyes shut while others filtered in, shuffling around barefoot as they set up their places.

Long breath through the nose, out through the mouth.

Suddenly she felt a new presence moving close to her. A heavy footstep, then a drop as someone squeezed a mat between her and the wall, where there was obviously not sufficient room for it. She felt a rush of irritation that her space was being trodden upon. Aside from work, which didn't count, this was the only time she had strictly for herself, and it was precious to her.

She cracked one eye open and was shocked at who she found there.

"What are you doing here?" she hissed at Dr. Starr.

He raised his eyebrows at her. "Yoga?"

"You don't do yoga. You said it was for New Age millennials."

Their exchange caught the instructor's attention, and she gave them an admonishing look.

Dr. Starr turned his face away and fought with his legs, bending them as he tried to work himself into a cross-legged pose. He wore shorts, and he was hairier than Maggie had imagined. His calves were muscular, too, as though he did some sort of physical recreation in his spare time.

But judging by his struggles, it definitely wasn't yoga.

He held out his hands, touching his pointing fingers to his thumbs. "I'm trying something new," he whispered. "Listen to this. *Ommm.*"

"Don't you have patients to be seeing to?" she whispered back.

He shook his head. "I have a two-hour gap."

Maggie had to fight the urge to get up and leave. His uninvited presence just put a dent in the gratitude she felt for him caring for Charlie during her crisis.

Before she could tell him what she thought, Shaila, the instructor, stood at the front of the room. She closed her eyes and lowered her head, doing what she'd explained to them before as taking their collective pulse so she'd know how to start the class.

Maggie really enjoyed the classes taught by Shaila. She was a truly talented (and serene) yogi from India and focused on healing mind, body, and spirit in many series of restorative poses. And she did everything quietly, with only gentle and subtle corrections.

Shaila looked up and smiled. "I see everyone is seated comfortably, and there are a few new faces. We like to begin each class by silently declaring a positive, simple intention. Close your eyes for a moment and think about yours. It could be your intention to breathe with awareness or to leave class with your spirit recovered. Or you can even be ready to offer up your practice to a higher god. It's up to you and totally personal. While you set your intention, keep your eyes closed and breathe deeply."

To get through this class without strangling Dr. Starr is my intention, Maggie thought. So much for an hour of relaxation and restoration. She could barely wait to get out of there so she could really give him a piece of her mind. He might be her boss, but damned if he was going to insert himself into her personal life.

Dr. Starr sighed long and loud, and though she refused to look at him again, she could only imagine how hilarious he looked sitting there on the yoga mat, his lanky frame hanging over the narrow strip of padding as he tried to figure out what his intention was. What *was* his intention here, come to think of it?

"We can now move into the sun salutation," the instructor said. "Remember, Buddha says that the mind is a restless monkey. We must work to tame that restlessness."

Speaking of monkeys, Maggie rose, and through her peripheral view, she could see Dr. Starr do the same.

"Arms spread wide, backs arched, then support your spine with your hands while you bend back." The instructor began to walk around, adjusting each student when needed. "Now fold into *uttanasana*."

As soon as Maggie folded forward and clasped her ankles, she chanced a peek at Dr. Starr.

He was bending as much as he could, fumbling for his own unreachable ankles. He was teetering, close to falling on that thick skull of his.

She bit her lip to keep from grinning at his ineptitude as she stretched farther, feeling the delicious burn behind her knees.

"Now go into downward-facing dog."

Maggie gracefully sent her legs back, settling into downward dog.

"I should know all the dog poses," Dr. Starr whispered. "'Cause I'm a vet. Get it?"

Okay, so chilling out today isn't going to happen.

Beside her, Dr. Starr struggled to get positioned correctly, and the instructor came to him.

"First this leg. Gently, now. Guide it back."

Maggie heard some ungentle movement.

"Now the other leg," the instructor said. "Feel your core energy firing up."

When Maggie peeked, she saw the worst-looking downward dog she'd ever seen in her life. She closed her eyes again, trying to shut out his heavy breathing. She focused on the light sounds of nature coming from the speaker high on the wall.

The instructor led them through the next series of poses, and she had to give it to Dr. Starr—he gave each one a valiant attempt.

Maggie kept up her silent litany, trying to concentrate on anything but him. *Stretch. Breathe. Move. Stretch. Breathe. Move.*

The instructor definitely earned her pay for the night. After a few minutes, she simply stayed beside Dr. Starr, adjusting his body or adding blocks and blankets to help him achieve at least a semblance of what everyone else in the class was easily doing.

At last, they were brought back to the original cross-legged pose to rest. This was usually her favorite part of the session, when each part of her body tingled from the energy expended, knots and tightness of the days before finally worked out, her mental state calm and restored.

Today that wasn't going to happen. Thanks to the good doctor.

"We want to be sitting in *asana*—and that means to be seated in a firm but relaxed position," Shaila said.

Usually after a few minutes of peaceful reflection, the class ended the session with one long *om* together, and with it, Maggie always felt a sense of gladness. Today, when they reached that point and then the instructor dismissed them from the mats with her quiet *namaste*, Maggie only felt relief.

Relief that it was over.

She stood, grabbing her mat, blanket, and strap, then quickly took them to the closet. She wanted to get out of there before Dr. Starr had a chance to initiate a conversation. He demanded that she take a day off, fine. She would show him what that really meant.

Chapter Eighteen

Maggie saw Quinn was at the front desk with Charlie when she finally made it back to the hotel. He sat in a rolling chair, pushed up to the low side of the counter, his focus on a stack of crackers and cheese. Rosa was nowhere in sight.

"I'm so sorry, Quinn," Maggie said, rushing across the lobby. "After yoga I took a walk on the beach and laid down on my towel. Next thing I know, I woke up to sand kicked in my face and freaked out when I saw I'd been sleeping for over an hour. I rushed here—"

Quinn held her hand up. "Stop. It's fine. Sounds like you've had quite a day. Your body was telling you to recharge. Charlie filled me in on some of this morning's events."

Maggie hadn't counted on Charlie giving away all the juicy details. She wondered how he'd described her incident.

"Don't worry," Quinn said. "I only picked up the highlights because he was most concerned with talking about the fire truck."

"Did he tell you who else was there?"

"No, who?"

"You're not going to believe this. And he showed up to my yoga class—"

"Mom, look. It's a tower," Charlie said.

Maggie let out a sigh of impatience before he could catch it in her voice. She would really love to have a few minutes alone with Quinn, but Charlie missed and needed her too.

"That looks good, Charlie. I can tell exactly what it is." A stack of cheese and crackers, with a splash of imagination. But that's not what he wanted to hear.

"Me too," said Quinn. "What's the name of your tower? Is it the Empire State Building?"

Charlie looked around her.

"Where's Woodrow?"

"He's at home. He needed a break today. But Auntie Quinn was talking to you," Maggie said.

Her son shrugged and went back to his crackers. It was one of those embarrassing parent moments when you can't believe how stinking rude your kid can be. Unknowingly too.

Quinn shrugged. "Oops. I guess I lost him."

"Probably good we diverted his train of thought before he started asking you one question after another about what the Empire State Building is," Maggie said.

Quinn laughed.

Maggie was glad to finally see a smile on her friend's face. She'd have to reward Charlie for that later. And though he had his moments when he made her want to have invisibility as a superpower, she was proud of him too. He was a smart and imaginative child, and she wasn't just saying that because she was his mom.

"Want to have a chat?" Maggie said, then lowered her voice to a whisper. "We've got a lot to catch up on. And I have to tell you why my new friend, Juniper, is on my shit list."

It was far too coincidental that Dr. Starr had just happened to show up at the same yoga studio that Juniper had recommended to her. Maggie smelled a tiny blue-haired rat.

"Okay, but the evening clerk is running late too," Quinn said. "Why don't you take Charlie out by the pool and I'll join you in just a few minutes. Jonah is supposed to call me back to talk about the frogs keeping some of my guests up all night. Not sure what to do about that. And Rosa will be back any minute. She's gone to get Charlie's clothes out of the dryer. He decided he didn't need swim shorts to jump in the pool today."

Maggie noticed now that her son was wearing his swim trunks and sun shirt instead of what she'd sent him in. "Charlie, what in the world? And where are your floaties?"

Quinn waved a hand. "No worries. He had supervision every second, and he's promised to never do that again. Speaking of Rosa, she can entertain him for a little while longer while we have a conversation. I'll have the chef make her up some dinner to take home for the family."

Maggie nodded. She had a lot to tell her. Quinn might know something happened, but probably not all the details. Like how now she didn't have five cents to her name because a lunatic had gotten into her account.

"Oh, there's Josh now," Quinn said. "He can take over up here."

The young man that Quinn nodded at moved slightly to the left, and Maggie saw an elderly woman behind him, then heard Quinn let out a long, frustrated breath.

"Just what I need," she said.

"Were you expecting your grandmother?" Maggie asked. She'd only met the woman once, actually at the same time that Quinn had met her, but no one could forget someone like that. All regal and fragile looking at the same time. Her hair was in a different style, pulled back in a classy ponytail instead of the sleek and tight chignon she'd worn before. She appeared to be dressed for tennis, though Maggie had never seen that style of long tennis shorts. Especially not with long white socks. The knobby knees that barely peeked out were a bit scary, so she could see why the woman wanted to cover most of her legs.

Helen approached, her stride strong and without hesitation, her expression solemn. She ignored Maggie, dropped her purse on the counter, and leaned in, fairly close to Quinn's face.

"We need to talk."

Maggie could see the woman had that look that she wasn't taking no for an answer. From everything she knew about Helen, she could be a stubborn force of nature.

"You go, Quinn," Maggie said. "We can talk later. Do me a favor: when you see Rosa, tell her to just keep Charlie's clothes here for an extra set. In case he pulls that stunt again."

"Okay. Bye, Charlie." Quinn shot Maggie a look that begged for rescue, and Maggie grimaced, trying to convey sympathy.

As Maggie led Charlie toward the door, she heard Quinn give in.

"We can talk in my room, Helen."

The old woman said something that Maggie couldn't catch.

"Come on, Charlie. Woodrow's probably wondering where we are."

At the car, she locked Charlie into his car seat and climbed in.

"It's hot, Mama," Charlie said, already starting to squirm.

"Yeah, I know. It's Maui, son. Give it a minute for the air to get cool." She cranked the air conditioner up as far as it would go.

They rode another mile and Charlie fussed a little more, his rarely cranky side rearing its head.

"I can't breathe," he said.

She looked in the mirror at him. His face was red, a sheen of sweat making him glitter in the reflection. She looked at the air-conditioner knob. It was set right. All the way on cool. She put her hand in front of it.

It was blowing nothing but hot tropical air.

"Crap, Charlie. The air-conditioning isn't working. I'm sorry, buddy." She hit the electric window buttons and put them down on all sides. It didn't feel great, but it was better than the stagnant warm air from the vents. While her hair whipped into her face, stinging her eyes, she tried to remain calm.

What else could happen to her in one week?

Charlie didn't try to talk over the sound of air rushing through their windows, so it gave Maggie a little time to think. She was going to call the bank as soon as she got home and demand they open her account. But even that wouldn't pay for maintenance on her air-conditioning if the coil was bad. Hopefully it just needed a few cans of Freon, and she could do that herself. She hoped it was that simple. According to Liam, used cars on Maui had a bad reputation for being junkers, but Maggie had gotten the best that she could find with what little funds she had to work with. If it was a lemon, she was sunk. There'd be no way to get Charlie to the inn or her to work.

Her pulse began to race, and she felt her eye twitch.

She took a deep breath, trying to calm herself before Charlie could feel the stress. He'd already dealt with enough because of her gas station fiasco.

"Did you like jumping in the pool with all your clothes on, Charlie?" She looked in the mirror and watched him perk up at his name.

"I thought it would be fun, but my clothes made me heavy," he said. "I couldn't float as good."

Maggie laughed. His shoes alone probably weighed a few pounds. He had big feet, just like his dad, and they were growing every day. Soon she'd have to buy him new shoes.

"Can we try not to do that again, Charlie? You need to ask Rosa's permission before jumping in the pool. Even if you are wearing your swim clothes. Okay?"

He nodded, but she wondered how much he heard with the wind blowing in his ears. Her tone was evident, though, and he was smart enough to agree.

No Place Too Far

They pulled up to the apartment, and Maggie shut off the car. She was eager to get out of the hotbox. She also wanted to stop by and see Juniper as soon as she got Charlie settled. Maggie had a bone to pick with her. And it was called Dr. Starr. She would at least make Juniper run out and get the Freon to make it up to her.

She helped Charlie out and slammed the door. "Hurry up, I'm sure Woodrow is dying to go outside. He needs a walk."

They climbed the stairs to their level, Maggie holding Charlie's hand to make sure he didn't stumble. For the hundredth time, she wished they could find something on ground level. It would make her life so much easier.

"Can I have some cereal, Mama?"

"I think we need to eat something more than cereal for dinner, Charlie. Some real food." However, if cereal was what it took to get him to bed early, Maggie wasn't above handing it over. She'd at least make a valiant attempt to give him something a bit more substantial.

"Cereal is real food, though. Cap'n Crunch has berries. That's fruit."

She barely heard what he said because of what lay before her. Five feet from their door, Maggie stopped in her tracks.

"What's wrong?" Charlie asked, coming to a halt beside her.

The flowers that she and Charlie had planted together and placed beside their door to make their shabby apartment look more inviting had been sabotaged. Every flower head appeared to have been snipped off at the same height and lay neatly, like a carpet of color, around the boxes.

"Nothing. Let's get inside to Woodrow." She looked around, scanning the landing and the parking lot below. She saw no one, but she nearly dropped her keys in her rush to get to the door and lock her and Charlie behind it. With her heart in her throat, she tugged him faster than he could walk and ended up dragging him the last foot or so.

"Mama, stop," he chided her, getting his feet under him again.

169

"I'm sorry, Charlie. Stand here." She put him in front of her legs, between her and the safety of the door. First she tried the knob, making sure it was still locked. It was, and she fumbled through the keys until she found the one for the dead bolt.

"I hear Woodrow whining," Charlie said.

"I know. We're coming, Woodrow!"

She hoped Charlie wouldn't notice the flowers from his limited view. How would she explain it? How could she tell him the chilling thought that filled her up inside? This had been done to her before. And it indicated something real and concrete. And terrifying.

The Ghost was on Maui. And he knew where she lived.

Chapter Nineteen

Quinn led her grandmother down the hall, feeling upset that once again, she and Maggie couldn't find the time to discuss everything going on. She felt pulled in every direction, physically and emotionally. How her life had gotten to that place again so fast she wasn't quite sure.

However, she no longer had someone to fix everything for her. She had to put on her big-girl panties and figure it out herself.

She opened the door to her suite, and her grandmother just about ran her over going in. With all the traffic her room had gotten lately, it was starting to feel less like her sanctuary. The only positive was that it wouldn't be so hard to leave.

Helen looked around. Quinn watched her take everything in, her eyes settling on the soft, cozy blanket thrown over the couch, then the tattered secondhand ottoman that Quinn had found in the Rainbow Attic in Kihei. Quinn had added several gently loved—used—items to soften the hard lines of all the new things in the room. It made it feel more like a home, though she doubted her grandmother felt the same. She was so rich that she even smelled like money, and Quinn couldn't imagine her sifting through a bin of used blankets to bring home.

Finally Helen turned to her.

"It's nice." She looked surprised.

"I'm overwhelmed with your abundance of compliments," Quinn said, not cracking a smile.

Helen did, though. Just a tiny lift at the corner of her mouth that let Quinn know she liked it that her granddaughter had a little sass. And if Quinn was honest with herself, she also liked that Helen was a firecracker. The fact that she'd arranged for Quinn to be kidnapped as a child and taken off the mainland, well, that was another matter altogether. But one she'd already forgiven her grandmother for.

"Have a seat," Quinn said. "I'll make you some tea."

Fixing her grandmother's favorite steaming pineapple tea would give her a chance to figure out how she was going to say what needed to be said. She wasn't exactly afraid of Helen, but she'd admit her grandmother was intimidating, to say the least. She set the kettle on to boil and took a peek at her phone, then turned it on silent. Her grandmother wouldn't appreciate any interruptions. She expected full attention when she was around.

Quinn restrained herself from peeking to see what Helen was doing, knowing without confirmation that she was probably looking at the same book titles that her father had. Her grandmother would have no qualms about judging Quinn's literary choices, and she doubted that the entire collection of Denise Grover Swank's Rose Gardner series lined up would make the cut, even if they were situated on a shelf just above at least a dozen Maui history books. Those books had kept her from being too lonely on many long nights.

She didn't have to sleep alone. Liam would probably come over and stay anytime she'd let him, but Quinn was still wary about letting another man have too much of her life. After years with her ex-fiancé and the way he'd molded her into being who he wanted her to be, Quinn was determined that it would never happen again.

"It's ready." She put the hot cup on a saucer and brought it to her sitting area, then set it on the side table next to her grandmother.

"Your parents were here earlier," Helen said. She didn't touch the cup, only watched the steam rise and twirl from it.

"Yes, they were."

"They came to talk about the article."

"Yes, they did."

Quinn crossed her legs and then recrossed them. She wasn't going to make this easy. If Helen wanted all the details, she was going to have to work for them. Jules claimed to have forgiven Helen for everything that had happened when Quinn was a child, but Quinn wasn't so sure. You could feel something between the two of them when they were in the same room, and it didn't feel like forgiveness.

Reluctant truce, maybe. But there were definitely no olive branches slapping them in the face. Their lack of communication was a testament to that.

"I talked to Jules for a few minutes. She filled me in," Helen said. "But just the highlights."

That took Quinn by surprise. From the beginning when they'd all been reunited, Quinn had laid down the rules that either all was forgiven so the family could pursue healing, or she wouldn't stick around. She knew that Jules would bite back anything too harsh she really wanted to say to her mother, but it was hard to imagine them having tea and discussing Quinn's current issues.

It was a work in progress.

"So what's the plan?"

Quinn hesitated—because really, Helen wasn't going to like her plan at all—but then there was a knock on the door.

Thank God.

She rose and crossed the room, opened the door, and found Jonah there. And he wasn't alone. He gestured toward his guest.

"Quinn, this is Kim. She's the field crew leader on the Maui Invasive Species Committee. I asked her to come for a consult about the frogs."

Quinn looked from her brother to the pretty young woman. She wore camouflage pants tucked into black work boots, a long-sleeve red T-shirt, and a headlamp. Her long dark hair cascaded down her back. But back to her head—yes, Quinn was shocked to see she wore a headlamp.

Was Jonah serious, or was he really stupid enough to be trying to prank her during this stressful time? But her brother wasn't the joking type. And this was definitely a reprieve from the current uncomfortable conversation.

"Come in." She stood aside.

Kim sat down beside Helen on the other edge of the small couch. Jonah stood next to her, crossing his arms across his chest in his usual protective stance.

"You needed a committee for the frogs?" Yes, the guests had been complaining about the loud sound of the critters at night, but a committee?

"He absolutely did the right thing," Helen spoke up. "If you've got a few of those little monsters now, soon they'll be everywhere, and your guests will never get any rest. You'll find yourself handing out refunds or at least comping additional stays."

That didn't sound good.

She took a seat and looked at the young woman. She was pretty, and that made Quinn wonder if Jonah had known that before he'd reached out to her. Thus far in the time that Quinn had been on Maui, she hadn't seen her brother date anyone. It was one of those things she was dying to ask him but didn't think they were close enough to do it. He was a very handsome man, and he was a good person. It seemed such a waste for him to live his life alone.

Quinn would entertain the frog-buster, if only for Jonah's sake.

"Is this really that serious?" she asked.

Kim nodded. "It will be if you don't nip it in the bud. The Big Island didn't take it seriously, and now they have a major problem. In the tourism industry, the last thing your guests want to hear as they settle in for the night is a coqui frog shrieking at eighty to ninety decibels all the way until morning."

"They can sound as loud as a blender or garbage disposal in your ear if they get close enough to the building," Helen said. "When I was young, my daddy used to send us out onto the ranch and whomever brought one back would get five dollars to spend in town. Obviously, he had his own committee of six kids and a few hound dogs."

"I lead a five-person task team," Kim said. "We hunt the frogs; then when we find where they're bedding, we bring in high-pressure hoses and douse the area."

"With what?" Quinn asked.

"Citric acid," Jonah said. "And before you go getting all upset about the poor little frogs, you know how you love the birds and want them here for the guests. You spent quite a chunk of change to save the native trees, plants, and flowers, too, when you were renovating. Well, these frogs are threatening Maui's fragile ecosystem. They're already trying to take over Maliko Gulch. There's an ongoing fight against them there."

"They gorge on insects that are food for the birds," Kim said. "If the insects are gone, the birds will disappear too."

"And so will the guests," Helen said. "I loved hearing the frogs when I was a kid, but guests want to sleep. And they aren't going to be doing it if you don't take action. I approve the eradication."

"Hold up," Quinn said, being gentle. "Remember, I have a stake in this place too. I need to know more. I'll do some of my own research before we send a team traipsing through our property and killing off anything green that jumps."

Kim laughed. "It doesn't quite work like that."

Jonah didn't laugh. "Her team is careful where they go. Remember, the ecosystem is important to them, too, or you wouldn't see Kim here crawling around the jungle in the dead of night with a machete in hand and a headlamp on, hunting a frog the size of a quarter."

Well, thought Quinn. *My brother is defending the pretty woman. That is interesting.* "I see what you're all saying, but just give me until tomorrow. I have a lot going on, and I just need to wrap my head around a few things before I make any decisions. On anything."

"If it makes you feel any better, if we only find a few, we can come in with backpack sprayers and do a more targeted eradication. Sometimes what sounds like dozens is in reality only a couple. But that can change fast, so we recommend acting on it as quickly as possible. There are no natural predators on the island that keep them under control, so it comes down to us," Kim said.

"I agree," Helen said.

"Same," Jonah added.

"Fine. I'll let you know," Quinn replied, already planning on calling Liam to get his perspective on the subject.

"*Mahalo*, Kim. I can show you out," Jonah said.

She stood. "No need. I know the way. Remember, we really need to act on this. Not just for your business but for the good of the island. Give me a call."

"Will do." Jonah opened the door for her, then closed it softly and turned to them.

"So what's this cozy little meeting all about?"

"Helen wants to know what we plan to do about the reporter."

Jonah looked from her to her grandmother. "It doesn't appear that we can do anything. If it all comes out, it comes out."

Quinn noticed he said *we*. It touched her that he considered it his problem too. Every day she felt a little closer to this brother she'd only known for a year.

"I know that," Helen said sharply. "And I also know that this is all my fault. We aren't going to be able to stop this horse, because it's already left the stable. But what I can do is save you from the brunt of it, Quinn. I at least owe you that. Thank goodness there was a need for six bulletproof vests in the department. My donation bought you two more weeks before you have to show up and talk to the detective."

Quinn couldn't imagine how she'd already managed that, considering the deadline was all set just hours before. It wasn't too surprising, though, because Helen worked quickly and efficiently when she wanted something. Her own disappearance was a prime example of that.

"But I can't head them off forever. That's why I've got a plan."

Jonah sighed hard. "That sounds noble, Grandmother, but remember that you taking it upon yourself to do what's best for Quinn is what got her into this mess. Maybe before you start handing out bribes, you need to step back and talk to the rest of us about it."

"We're family, Jonah. And as long as I'm alive, I will do what I can to protect Quinn from further damage. I know I'm responsible for the past. You don't have to remind me."

Quinn felt sorry for Helen. What she'd done in sending her granddaughter away to be raised by a stranger was something she'd have to live with for the rest of her life. The old woman worried about how it had impacted Quinn, but she ignored the trauma she'd caused Jonah, who was supposed to be watching Quinn on the boat when she disappeared into the deep ocean.

"Speaking of family, did you loan Michael and Kira the money to start their own business?" Jonah asked.

"I did not. I told your mother about it, and I am waiting for her to tell me what to do."

Quinn could see her brother was getting worked up. Jonah wasn't known for having any sort of temper, but his resentment about what their grandmother had done to Quinn appeared to still fester.

"Can we get back to the issue at hand?" Quinn said, trying to get them back to a civil tone. The room crackled with tension, and she didn't like it.

Helen's chin went a tad higher before she began talking, making it the proudest chin Quinn had ever seen. Her grandmother was something else.

"It's not an idea. It's a confession. Or at least it will be. It's time I took full responsibility for my actions. I plan to organize a press conference and tell them who you are, Quinn, and then lay out the facts."

"That's ridiculous," Jonah said, sighing loudly. "It solves nothing."

"Grandmother, I would never let you do that," Quinn said, tears springing to her eyes at the gesture. "You would go to prison. Accessory to kidnapping—or something like that."

Helen nodded solemnly. "I know. I'm prepared for that possibility."

"Oh really? How have you prepared? Have you isolated yourself to a room for a week? Sworn off real food? Sunshine? You have no idea what going to prison would be like," Jonah said.

"Jonah, please," Quinn said.

He shook his head with disbelief but he quieted.

Quinn stood and went to her grandmother. She knelt beside her and took her hand. It was cold, and so very thin. "Even if you did this, it wouldn't set things right. It would only cause more chaos and put the family business in jeopardy. And Grandmother, I pledged to the Makenas that I would protect their daughter's name. You know she was still a wonderful mom to me, despite what she did to get me."

"They should've been protecting *their daughter* while she was under their roof. Then this wouldn't have gone as far as it did," Helen said. "She couldn't wait to get away from their bickering, not to mention the substance abuse. From what I've heard, they barely knew their daughter was there, until she wasn't."

"They've admitted they were terrible parents, and both have been clean for many years. Believe me, they are in enough pain knowing they drove their only child away." Quinn kept her voice even, though it unnerved her for anyone to talk about Elizabeth.

Helen looked deep into Quinn's eyes. "Please—I need to do this."

"No, you don't," Quinn said. "You have to stop punishing yourself. I have my own plan. I came across something last night. I found a listing for a floundering guest ranch in Montana that needs an inn manager. I've thrived here because I'm passionate about making this inn profitable. That tells me I can do that same thing there. I was up until after midnight doing research, and the place needs a lot of work, but it's got good bones. It comes with horses and other animals. They have a ranch manager that supervises the outdoor staff who has agreed to stay on. I'll have full authority to hire my own indoor staff as well as a renovation team."

Jonah looked stricken. "And you think no one will know who you are? Sorry to tell you both, but Montana has internet these days."

"Of course they do," Quinn said. "But if I up and leave, and there's no confirmation that I am Nama, it's just one more lost lead. I won't be here for the questions to continue. On the mainland, I'm just another single woman with no family to speak of and no connection to Maui. Especially in Montana. To most of them cowboys up there, Hawaii is just a postcard dream."

Helen looked thoughtful. "I still think the truth would be better for this family."

"No, it wouldn't," Quinn said. "And I don't want to be under the microscope if it comes out that my own family instrumented my estrangement. I want this inn to be successful, but not because people want to come see the girl who disappeared for thirty years. And think about it, if they can't verify that I'm Nama, they can't get the rest of the story and come after anyone. That would save you, Helen, and also keep the Rocha name from taking any more hits. Then Mom and Dad would be spared and not have to worry about losing their business, which would impact everyone's livelihood."

"And you're going to just up and leave and never see any of us again?" Jonah asked, his eyes clouding over as though thunder was coming.

"I'm not saying it's a bad idea," Helen said. "But let's slow down a minute and consider the pros and cons."

"Con number one: Mom would be devastated," Jonah said softly. "It would kill her to lose you again."

That cut Quinn to the heart. "Yes, she'll be sad, but after some time passes and the Maui media moves on to the next big story, she and Dad can visit. She'll need to understand that I want to spare her any more pain from something she had no control over."

"She would also want you to be free to live a life of privacy," Helen said. "A true mother will sacrifice her own needs for those of her children. Every time. She will see that other than me coming forward, it's the only way."

Quinn's head was spinning. Now that she'd spoken her idea out loud, it sounded so much harder. She would need to find a better way to explain it to Liam. "I need some time," she said. "If you two could excuse me, I think I'll spend the evening in here and just slow down and think this through."

Helen rose and Jonah made it to the door first, holding it open.

They both paused, turning to Quinn.

"I hope you'll do the right thing," Jonah said.

Of course, she wanted to do the right thing. That's what she'd been doing all her life, to the detriment of her own wants and needs. But Quinn knew she was slipping back into her old ways of trying to please everyone around her—a trait that had almost made her forget who she truly was. Did she really want to go back to being that person?

"She will," Helen said. "She's got the Rocha blood raging through those veins. She's smart, and she's a survivor."

Jonah took her on one more time. His tone was respectful, as always, but firm. "She's also a Monroe, and there's not a one of us who would want to be landlocked away from the crashing waves of the sea. It'll call out to her. It's a part of us."

"Um, hello . . . ? I'm still right here," Quinn said, waving a hand in the air. "It's my decision to make."

"Sorry," Jonah said, breaking his competitive gaze from his grandmother. "Come on, Grandmother. Quinn needs some time alone."

"Fine," Helen said. "We've got two plans laid out, and now we just decide which way to go."

"I'll think about it," Quinn said. However, she knew she'd never pick a lane that would land an old woman in jail.

"Yes, think hard on this, Quinn," her brother said. "This is *your* life."

With that they were gone, and the door closed with a sharp click, leaving Quinn feeling like she'd just survived a tsunami of stress. So many decisions and barely any time to make them. The deadline was looming down on them quickly. She had to figure it all out.

It was going to be a long evening.

Chapter Twenty

Maggie eased the bedroom door closed, leaving just an inch or two cracked in case Charlie woke up so she'd hear him. Thank you, Jesus, for melatonin gummies because this was one night that her son needed to hit the sack early. Woodrow was a huge help too. He'd curled up next to Charlie, somehow knowing that Maggie needed him there, watching over the most important thing in her life.

She dialed the phone, whispered a request, then hung up and waited. Normally she was always moving in the evenings. Having a small child meant that until her head hit the pillow, there were a million things to get done. But tonight, all she could do was sit in the middle of her couch and clutch her phone.

Panic. Fear. Anger.

She didn't have to wait long before she heard a gentle knock. Woodrow immediately came from the bedroom and put himself at the door, his stance a protective one.

"Stay," Maggie said. "No bark."

She went to the kitchen drawer first, grabbed the sharpest knife she had, then went to the door.

"Who is it?" she leaned against the cool surface.

"It's me, Juniper."

Maggie hurried over and put the knife back in the drawer before opening the door. Juniper rushed in, and Maggie locked the dead bolt behind her.

"Where's Charlie?" Juniper said, looking around the small room.

"In bed."

"You feeling better?"

Maggie nodded, though to be honest, now she was feeling quite sick.

"You said you needed to talk. What's up?" Juniper asked, moving into the living room and plopping down on the sofa.

"Quinn should be here any minute, and then I'll tell you both together." Maggie had called Quinn before she'd started Charlie's bath. It was time that her closest people knew the full details of what was happening. She needed them more than ever now.

When all this had started for her, one of the first things she'd learned was to alert your most trusted people as to what was going on in case you needed them. Build an army around you, the first detective had told her. Back then, Maggie had chosen to run instead, not wanting to drag her family and friends into a mess of her making. But she was tired of running. She now knew running wasn't the answer. Obviously there was no place too far to be found.

"Fine, but tell me you have wine," Juniper said. "You're making me nervous."

"Yes, you're going to need a glass. Or two." Maggie went to the fridge and pulled out a cheap white wine. Just as she was pulling out glasses, another knock sounded.

"That's probably Quinn," she said. Woodrow was still relaxed, reassuring Maggie that she was right. After confirming, she opened the door. Quinn rushed in and held her arms out. First Maggie locked the dead bolt behind her friend; then she accepted, falling into Quinn's embrace.

It felt safe there. But Maggie knew it wasn't. She wasn't safe anywhere anymore. A pain ripped through her gut, and she remembered she hadn't eaten all day. That was okay. It would just make the wine work faster.

They broke apart and Quinn looked at her, a stricken expression on her face.

"Oh, Maggie," she said.

"What the hell is going on?" Juniper said from her place on the couch. "Did someone die?"

"Quinn, this is Juniper. She's my neighbor, and I work with her at the clinic," Maggie said. "We're friends, and I trust her."

"Sorry," Quinn said, directing her gaze toward Juniper. "I didn't notice you there."

"You mean the blue streaks and nose piercings didn't make me stand out against this gorgeous brown couch?" Juniper said, lightening the awkwardness of a new introduction.

Maggie let out a long, ragged breath. "Okay, ladies. Wine first, then talk. Quinn, go get to know my little hippie-fairy friend while I fill your glass."

~

"You have to call the police. Not tomorrow. Not next week. Now," Quinn said. "It's gone too far, and you need more protection. The MPD here are serious about keeping people safe."

Maggie watched as Juniper nodded emphatically, in total agreement with Quinn.

"Yes, I know," Maggie said. She sat on the floor with Woodrow's head resting in her lap. Quinn and Juniper shared the couch, sitting on opposite ends and creating quite the contradictory picture. Two people who couldn't be more different except for the fact that they were the two on Maui that Maggie trusted the most.

"And I'm going to give you a loan," Quinn said when Maggie got to the part about her account being frozen.

"No. I'll get that straightened out first thing tomorrow," she answered.

"If they don't open your account tomorrow, ask for your request to be escalated to another level of management," Juniper said. "They can't hold your money hostage because of something someone else did. And you know Starr will give you an advance if you need it."

"I won't need it," Maggie said. Getting anything extra from Dr. Starr wasn't going to happen. He'd been dragged into her personal life enough.

"Well, you and Charlie are definitely coming to the inn to stay with me," Quinn said. "You're going to have to stop being so stubborn."

Maggie paused. That was complicated. While she knew they'd be safer at the inn, the Ghost had obviously seen the photo of her there, and a quick google would tell him where it was. He'd probably even followed her from the inn to her apartment one day, falling back behind other traffic so she couldn't see him. Most likely he knew all her routine stops.

"I know that I might be safer there with more people around, Quinn, but honestly, I don't want to leave yet another place. Charlie is comfortable here. It's not a palace, but we've made it into our home. I don't want to uproot him and start bouncing around again."

"Maggie, your stalker was *here*. It's not safe," Quinn said, her voice rising with emotion. "You can't possibly be serious."

"Shh. I don't want him to wake up. He'll never go back to sleep if he sees you here," Maggie said. "And don't worry. I have Woodrow."

Woodrow flicked his ears, letting her know he was still awake beneath the ecstasy of her rubbing the velvet lining of his ears.

"I'm sorry. But you really need to think this through a little better," Quinn said.

"It is her decision," Juniper said, her voice gentle. "And if she stays here, I'm taking the couch. Maggie, don't even try to dissuade me."

"Well, I guess you'll have the couch then because tonight we aren't going anywhere. I'm too overwhelmed to make any big decisions. I have Woodrow, a dead bolt, and tomorrow I'll go to the police department. I need to talk to your guest, David, too."

Quinn sat forward abruptly. "Oh crap. I forgot that Emily told me this morning that David was looking for me. Is it too late to call him? He might have some intel."

"Who's David?" Juniper asked.

"He's a retired detective staying at Quinn's inn, and he's been doing some checking around for me," Maggie said. "Trying to find out the status of this psychopath on my tail."

"Call him," Juniper said. "He might have some advice you need to hear before you put in the police report."

Quinn went to her purse and pulled out the card David had given her, retrieved her phone, and dialed the number. She put it on speaker.

"Hello?"

"David, it's Quinn. Sorry to call so late, but Emily said you wanted me to reach out. I've got you on speakerphone, and I'm here with Maggie and a friend named Juniper. You can talk freely. Were you able to find some news?"

"Yes, I'm glad you called. They took forever to get back to me because they were trying to cover up an administrative disaster that's still unraveling. After the lecture that I gave them, you should be hearing from a victim's advocate soon, but the spoiler is, he's out."

Maggie felt her stomach drop. She'd already known the Ghost was the one stalking her again. She could feel it. Hearing it confirmed made it that much more terrifying.

"Ironically enough, it turns out there were two Martin Andrews in the facility. One was due for release, but they screwed up and let your guy go. There's a search going on for him now."

Maggie cringed at David calling the Ghost *her guy*.

"The prison systems are a disaster," Juniper said. When Quinn shot her a curious look, she nodded. "Don't ask me how I know."

"Ms. Dalton," David said, "you need to take necessary security measures to keep yourself safe in case he tries to find you."

"He's already found her," Quinn said.

There was silence on the phone for a second.

"How do you know?" David asked, his tone now much more serious.

Maggie quickly told him what had transpired since they'd last talked.

"Damn," he said. "This is really bad. They need to get him back into custody."

"Can't they just run his name with all the airlines and start tracking him?" Quinn said.

"No doubt he's traveling under an alias. He's gotten good at this by now," David said. "Okay, listen. First thing you need to do is go to the police and file a report for harassment and stalking. I can tell you right now they'll ask for proof before naming him as a suspect. You don't have proof, but at least your report will put something on file. You can request that they keep an eye out around your neighborhood on patrol. Next, you should probably go to another location for a few weeks and not tell anyone where it is."

"I want her to come to the inn," Quinn broke in.

"Nope, if he is here, he's been following her and knows about the inn. Can you take a few days off of work and perhaps go to another island? Think of it as a small vacation," David said. "Pay for all travel and lodging in cash."

"No. I can't do that. I just started my job, and that wouldn't be fair to already ask for time off. Not to mention that I'm broke," Maggie said, no longer caring how humiliating the confession was.

"I'll talk to Starr," Juniper said. "He'll understand."

"And I'll pay your way," Quinn added. "You can give it back when you're on your feet. Take Charlie to see the Big Island. He'll love seeing the most active volcano in the world and can even walk through a lava tube."

"Nope," said Juniper. "They've been closed since the eruption."

Maggie held her hands up. "Wait. Just wait one second before you all go a little crazy. I ran from him for more than a year. Do you know how exhausting it is? Not only physically but emotionally too. I'm not going anywhere, and I'm sure not going to jeopardize my job. If you've noticed, jobs don't just grow on trees around here."

"Starr won't fire you," Juniper said. "I'd kill him."

"Please, don't joke about killing right now," Quinn said.

"Who said I was joking?" Juniper said, her expression deadpan.

Maggie gave Juniper a scowl and put her fingers to her lips to tell her to be quiet. The detective was going to think they were all a bunch of crazies.

On the phone, David cleared his throat. "I'm going to pretend that I didn't hear that. I've got to go, ladies. Julianne isn't having the best night."

"Oh, I'm so sorry, David. Is there anything we can do at the inn? I can call the night clerk," Quinn said. "Any special foods they can go out for?"

"No, we're set. She just wants me close. I'm going to read to her," he said.

They said their goodbyes, and Quinn put up her phone. When she did, she pulled a bottle of wine from her bag.

"Who is ready for round two?" she asked, holding it high.

Maggie saw it was a good wine—not one from the discount shelf at the local gas station. She expected Juniper to jump for joy, but when she looked over, the girl had taken the liberty of opening Maggie's laptop and was working away.

"What are you doing?"

Juniper looked up and gave a sly smile. "You don't need a detective to track someone when you've got my kind of skills. What's his birth date?"

Maggie wasn't sure but remembered his age from when he'd first contacted her on the dating site. She told Juniper and watched as the girl tapped at the keys furiously.

"How is that going to help if he's here under a fake name?" Quinn asked.

"He might have gotten here under a false identity, but I doubt in the little time he's been out that he's had time to set up credit cards under an alias, transfer money, and all those details," said Juniper. "He's probably got someone's license but is financing the trip under his own name. I can also find out who his connections are. Relatives. Friends. Find him that way."

"You're relentless," Maggie said. A flash of hope ran through her. If Juniper could track him down, that would get him away from her and Charlie that much faster.

"Okay, find him," she said. "In the meantime, I'll go first thing tomorrow and put in a report. At least they'll be on notice."

"I think you should do it right now, Maggie," Quinn said. "They'll send someone here to talk to you and take down the details. They can at least put together a description and send it out to the staff by morning. And they'll know to patrol here to keep an eye out for anyone strange."

Juniper looked up. "Just don't tell them what I'm doing. They won't want me playing cops and robbers."

Quinn raised the bottle of wine. "I'll just put this in the fridge. After we make the report, I'll open her up. This pretty pink superstar is bound to make us all feel a little better."

The three of them laughed, then were instantly silent when a sudden noise startled Woodrow and he jumped to his feet to look around for a culprit.

Maggie checked the window and saw one of her neighbors carrying a basket of clothes up the stairs.

"Down, Woodrow, it's okay," Maggie said. "Now where's my phone?"

She turned and found Quinn and Juniper directly behind her. And for just a second, Maggie forgot her life was in shambles. It was just three friends, all as different as could be, but forging new bonds over trauma. Those were the best kinds of friendships, too—the ones built during hard times—because they were built to last.

Chapter Twenty-One

Quinn felt a stirring of affection as Charlie burrowed deeper under her arm on the couch. She'd turned on cartoons and draped her softest throw across his lap. He had a cup of hot chocolate with marshmallows and a stack of cookies waiting on the side table, but so far he wasn't interested in moving enough to test either.

Even Liam hadn't been able to distract him with an invitation to wrestle or ride on his shoulders. He wanted to be close to her, she supposed, because she was the next best thing to having his mom.

Quinn had missed seeing Maggie when she'd dropped Charlie off. She probably wouldn't have seen him for a few more hours, but Rosa had knocked on her door, with a pouting little boy clinging to her hand and a desperate look in her eyes.

"He's asked for his mom a dozen times. I'm so sorry," Rosa said. "I can't get him interested in anything else."

Despite the fact that Liam had only just arrived and they were looking forward to a light lunch alone together to talk over her situation, Quinn had invited Charlie in immediately. She told Rosa to go take what looked like a much-needed break while she got to the bottom of why Charlie wasn't being his usual good-humored self.

After making him comfortable, it was time to get down to it. "Charlie, can you tell me what's wrong?" she asked, her voice soft and inviting as she traced little circles on the outside of his hand.

Liam looked a little jealous from where he sat at the end of the couch, but she gave him a grateful look. He had such a soft heart for all kids, but especially Charlie because the boy lacked a father figure in his immediate life. Liam liked the rare times they were alone together, but he'd never turn the boy away either. They were both way too fond of him not to be concerned over the dark look he wore.

"I wanted to stay home with Mommy."

"Are you feeling okay?" Quinn felt his forehead but didn't detect any unusual warmth.

"Mommy isn't."

"Oh? Why do you think that?" She raised her eyebrows at Liam over Charlie's head.

"She's scared."

That sent an alarm surging through Quinn. Had he heard them the night before? They all thought he was sleeping soundly. Even when the officer came and stayed for nearly an hour taking down all the information, Charlie hadn't made a peep from the bedroom. When Quinn left, Juniper was already decked out in Maggie's pajamas while Maggie promised to dead bolt the door and get straight into the bed.

"And you thought you should be with her today to make her feel better?"

He nodded.

His admission broke Quinn's heart.

"Charlie, I've known your mommy for a really long time, and I know she isn't afraid of anything. But why do you think she's worried?"

He shrugged. "I don't know."

"Well, Mommy is doing important things today. She's helping make all the dogs and cats feel better. But is there anything else bothering you, Charlie?"

He looked up at her with the saddest expression ever.

"I need a soccer ball."

"Oh, that's right. You're going to play on a team next year, aren't you, buddy?" Liam said.

"I'm s'posed to practice."

He sounded so distraught that Quinn squeezed him before getting up and going to her small desk. She came back to the couch with a pencil and a stack of sticky notes.

"Charlie, sometimes we have worries that want to stick around in our head. Life is full of worries. But also full of happy times. We don't want to give more of our headspace to the worries than the happy times, do we?"

"No," he said.

She wasn't sure that he got everything she was saying, but she had to try to do something.

"Okay, this is what we're going to do. I want you to tell me every worry that you have right now so I can write them down on these little papers. Once we get them all done, we can store them in a jar and ask the universe to take care of them."

"Or God?" he asked, finally looking hopeful.

She shot another look at Liam, this time a plea for help.

"Whichever one you'd like," he said.

Good answer, thought Quinn. She wasn't sure yet how much religion Maggie had introduced to her son, and she wasn't about to create even more worries. Or questions.

While she wrote out Charlie's worries, Liam retrieved an empty jar from her cupboard. He set it down in front of them.

When the notes were done—at least eight or nine, with one being that Charlie was worried about whether Santa would find Maui when Christmas came around—they tossed them in the jar and Quinn let Charlie twist the lid tightly.

"Okay, the worries are safe. Now we can stop thinking about these things and focus on having a good day, right?" she asked him.

He nodded, smiling now.

Quinn would tell Maggie how well it went, and at bedtime maybe he could write positive thoughts from the day to highlight the good stuff before he fell asleep.

"Good. So are you ready to go get in the pool? Want me to call Rosa?"

"Yes!" he said, jumping up from his spot on the couch. He grabbed his small bag and headed for the bathroom to put on his swimming trunks.

When Quinn heard the door shut, she looked up at Liam and found him still staring, a strange look on his face.

"What?"

"Nothing," he said.

"It must be something, because you're looking at me weird. Did you have a better way of bringing him out of his mood?"

He smiled gently, sparking that little fire inside her that only he could summon. "No, not at all. That was amazing. I was just thinking about what a wonderful mother you're going to make someday."

The warm little fire low in her belly went out instantly, and her stomach dropped. She'd made up her mind years ago—with the persuasion of her ex—that she wouldn't have children. Now she didn't even know what she wanted. She only knew she'd never want to raise an only child and make them go through the loneliness she'd felt growing up. She wasn't so young anymore, and the thought of planning for more than one child overwhelmed her.

"Liam," she said, her voice pleading. But before she could continue the conversation—one that definitely needed elaborating on if only to keep him from being disappointed later—Charlie busted out of the bathroom.

With his shorts on backward.

Liam laughed. "Those pants don't look quite right. Let me help you. And before you go home today, I'm going to make sure you have a soccer ball."

Charlie beamed as he backed up to Liam to fix his swim trunks.

"You guys need to eat a proper lunch before I call Rosa. I'll make sandwiches," Quinn said. She stood and with one more look at the two of them laughing together, she smiled. She had to admit, Liam would make a heck of a father too.

After a quick lunch, Quinn sent Charlie out to the pool with Liam, then called Rosa to meet them out there. The time for a private talk with Liam would have to wait. She took care of some calls from the front desk, then called back the frog-buster. Emily said they'd had three more noise complaints from guests the night before, and although Quinn hated to sign the death note for anything, it was going to have to be done. There was a lot of money invested in getting the inn up and running, and she couldn't let a few frogs be the cause of customer complaints. These days, with Yelp and TripAdvisor and all the other popular review sites, a few cranky tourists could put a wrench in future bookings.

She texted Jonah and let him know the frog quest was scheduled, then looked at the clock. The day was flying by already, and she had more to do than even three people could handle.

She started with answering emails from guests and sending confirmation emails, then moved on to collecting deposits. When she'd caught up with that, she put aside her list, opened a new window on her laptop, and signed in to an employee/career social site that she'd made an anonymous profile for. Looking for someone to take her job felt like swallowing knives, but things were quickly progressing out of her control and the truth was, she had to seriously consider the Montana offer. Her leaving might not totally shut down the noise about her past, but it would help. Not to mention that at least Quinn wouldn't have to be in the middle of it. Starting and running an inn wasn't a walk in the park, but she had no illusions about her inability to withstand public criticism and attacks on her privacy.

Maggie was different. She had always been tough, and she'd be okay on Maui without Quinn. Just thinking about the hell some deranged lunatic had put her best friend through over the last year made Quinn seethe, but Maggie had handled it like a boss. Quinn would've crumbled. She'd come a long way since leaving Ethan and breaking out of the person he'd molded her to be, but privacy was important to her. Whether running from a stranger or having her childhood and the actions of her adoptive mother scrutinized, both would break her down.

Quinn knew this. She'd grown stronger—but not that strong.

Finding a proper replacement wouldn't be easy, and the faster she got started reviewing résumés, the better. So she began the search, narrowing down those experienced in hospitality. She found only two candidates that she'd even consider, but she had to admit, her concentration was lagging.

Liam was outside with Charlie. Probably laughing and having fun. It wouldn't be long before she wouldn't be able to see either one of them. Time was running out.

She snapped her laptop shut, grabbed her phone, and went to find them. In the hall she passed one of the housekeepers who informed her they were low on toilet paper again, and their order wasn't coming in for a few more days. Quinn made a mental note to check the cameras in the employee locker room. Too much toilet paper was passing through the inn, and she was sure some of it wasn't through the sewage system. The new innkeeper might have to start keeping supplies under lock and key at this rate.

As soon as she pushed open the door to the poolside patio, she could see Charlie's little head bobbing up and down in the water. Rosa was on the edge, her thin brown feet dangling as she stretched her toes toward him.

Quinn scanned the area and found Liam.

He was in deep conversation with the woman next to him, his face solemn as he listened to her. At first Quinn felt a tinge of jealousy, but it turned to embarrassment when she realized it was Julianne, their ailing guest. She was stretched out on a chaise lounge, tucked protectively under one of their umbrellas. Another look at the pool told her where David was. She watched as he came up underneath Charlie and grabbed his feet, then popped out of the water.

Charlie squealed in delight.

She approached and crouched, beckoning for Charlie to come closer.

"Mr. David is playing shark with me," he said, grinning as he whipped his head around to see where the Shark was.

David came up and waved.

"Just the lady I needed to see," he said, approaching the side. "Charlie, you tread water like I showed you. I'll come back and play in a minute."

Rosa heard him and called Charlie over to her, and he immediately dog-paddled right between her outstretched legs and used them to support himself while he practiced treading water.

"Okay," David said, grabbing the sides of the pool so he could look up at her. "We can talk now."

"About Maggie?" Quinn asked.

"No, this is about Julianne. She would really love watching a dance team, but I don't think she's up to helping coordinate their routine. And actually, if you're on board with it, I have something better in mind."

"Oh," Quinn said, glancing at Julianne and Liam. They were still in deep conversation.

"Do you think you could help me set up a vow renewal ceremony? Of course, you can add all charges to my room," David said, his voice coming out in a whisper.

"Oh, I'd love to help," Quinn said. "Do you have anything special you want to do? A specific theme?"

He shook his head. "Nope. Just flowers, candles, and music. And someone to officiate. Julianne doesn't like anything too showy. Simple but special has always been our style."

"Easy," Quinn said. "That's manageable. Is this a surprise?"

David looked over at Julianne and smiled sadly before turning his attention back to Quinn. "No, I jumped the gun and told her it was in the planning stage. I wanted to give her something to look forward to. She's not doing well, Quinn."

Quinn didn't know what to say. Was *sorry* too morbid?

"I understand," she finally choked out. "When do you want to do this?"

He paused. "I know this is short notice, but do you think we could pull it off Friday night?"

Quinn's mind raced, already trying to put things in place. It would take a miracle, but she was determined to make it happen.

"Sure. Friday evening. Shouldn't be any trouble at all. And please, if you need anything at all between now and then, call me on my cell phone."

"I will," David said. "I've begged her to let me fly her to Oahu to see a special doctor there. She refuses, says she's tired of modern medicine. She wants to let her body decide what's next, even if it's not what we both want."

Quinn swallowed hard. She could see the fear and worry in the man's eyes. She didn't know what he would do without his wife. Julianne seemed to be his everything. It was endearing and tragic, all at once.

"Well, let me drag Liam away from her so she can get a nice nap," Quinn said, sending David back to shark duty.

Julianne saw her coming and broke off midsentence in whatever had Liam so transfixed.

"Hi," Liam said. He looked so happy to see her.

"Hi." She nodded at Julianne. "Hello to you too. Enjoying the afternoon?"

Julianne's lips were pasty white, and the dark circles around her eyes were much worse than when Quinn had last seen her. She'd gone downhill so fast that it seemed unbelievable.

"Well, yes, I am," Julianne said. She smiled gently. "Liam and I have been talking, and I have to tell you, he's a great storyteller. He's been telling me all about Maui's long history of love stories." She winked at Quinn.

Liam looked guilty, as though he'd been caught telling secrets. "I told her about naupaka, the beach plant that grows half flowers, and the legend of how it came to be."

"Oh?" Quinn teased. "You've never told me about it, and you know I love to hear the legends."

"It's not a long one. We believe that the naupaka is the incarnation of a beautiful Hawaiian princess who was separated from her lover."

"Tell her why they were separated," Julianne encouraged. Quinn noticed she looked very pleased with herself.

Liam smiled apologetically, then began again. "Because she was forbidden to marry her lover, a mere commoner. The last time that they were together, she took the flower from behind her ear and tore it in half, giving him a piece. She went up to finish her life in the mountains, and he lived down by the water. The naupaka plants witnessed their goodbye, and to show their sorrow, they bloomed in half flowers ever since."

Quinn was struck silent for a minute. Liam looked at her like she was the princess and he was the commoner. Or was she reading too much into it?

"Your Liam is one of a kind," Julianne said. "And quite a catch."

"Yes," Quinn said. "I guess you could say that."

He'd be a catch to some lucky lady on Maui, but it wouldn't be her because she wouldn't be there to enjoy him.

"What are you doing out here?" Liam asked, suddenly concerned. "I thought you had a to-do list a mile long?"

"I do. But I just wanted to see you for a little while before you head out."

Liam looked pleased. He stood and took her hand. "Julianne, if you'll excuse me, I'm going to take this pretty lady for a walk."

Quinn called out to Rosa to let her know they were going and that she had Charlie-watch on her own again.

Rosa waved her off.

Julianne smiled up at them. "Enjoy your stroll. I think I'm about to convince my better half to get out of the pool and rub my feet. So he's going to need your chair anyway, Liam."

As they walked away, Quinn leaned her head toward Liam. "It won't take any convincing. That man is mad about her."

Liam looked off in the distance, not answering.

Before he did, Quinn could've sworn she saw a sheen of moisture in his eyes. It was so convincing that she also looked away. Theirs wasn't a love story for the ages. This was real life, and if she'd learned anything in the last thirty years or so, it was that real life was hard. If she kept a jar of handwritten worries, it'd be overflowing. But in this moment, she chose to squeeze Liam's hand and simply enjoy their walk.

Focus on the moment.

The future was bearing down on them, and for Quinn, it was coming much too fast.

Chapter Twenty-Two

Maggie got to work still feeling sluggish at a quarter to twelve. The officer had assured her that he would conduct routine checks on the parking lot in front of her apartment until morning, but between listening for every tiny noise, then worrying herself over the predicament Quinn was in, she'd barely slept. It felt surreal that both she and her best friend were dealing with something that could be written straight into the script of a Lifetime movie. Except they wouldn't, because at this moment, she couldn't see a happy ending for either of them.

Her morning had been a total shit show. It took more than two hours on the phone with her bank and half a dozen threats before finally convincing them to release the hold on her account. Then a race to the auto parts store for refrigerant to put in her car, then dealing with Charlie who woke up on the wrong side of the bed and surprisingly didn't even want to go to the inn. He was extra clingy and wanted to stay with her for the day, forcing her to bring out her mean-mommy voice even though all she wanted to do was grab him and go back home to spend the rest of the day snuggling.

Maggie wished she could live by Charlie's rules and say, "Okay, we aren't adulting today so let's stay home." Instead she had to be responsible, and leaving him with his lip dragging the ground and teary eyes filled her with guilt.

She walked through the small lobby and noted a young barefoot man with a bearded dragon on his shoulder. On the other side of the room sat a couple with a pit bull puppy between them, oohing and aahing over it as though it was their first child. Those kinds of people usually cheered Maggie up, but she couldn't shake the exhaustion that permeated every fiber of her being.

She was going to have to reconsider Quinn's offer to stay at the inn. She couldn't go through many more sleepless nights, and it would be easier if she didn't have the logistics of getting Charlie from the apartment to Rosa. At least until everything blew over.

But wow, she hated to be that woman. Needy and afraid. The thought of giving up her freedom incensed her.

Even her double dose of green tea didn't help her mood. Dr. Starr's mother sat at the desk, wiping the countertop with a Clorox wipe. She took one look at Maggie and smiled sympathetically. In her lap, her little dog lay sleeping comfortably.

"Juniper's late coming back from lunch," she said. "I'm filling in."

"Thanks. How's the calendar look?" She hoped for an easy morning.

"Joe's finishing up a dental, but next he needs you to help prep for a neuter," Francine said. "He's in a pretty good mood because there was a woman concerned that her duck wasn't swimming, and he got to give her the news that there was nothing wrong with it because it was a chicken. He did it without cracking a smile too. Until she left, that is. Took him ten minutes to get himself under control, and that was only after I nearly pinched his ear off."

Maggie could just imagine her scolding Dr. Starr for being inconsiderate to the poor pet owner. The door opened and Juniper glided in, a vision of color in her long tie-dyed skirt and crazy hair. She wore bangles on both wrists, and every step seemed in tune. Far from looking exhausted, the girl oozed confidence and energy.

"Good afternoon," she said.

"Hi, girlie. I'm out of here," Francine said, picking up her dog and heading for the front door. "I have a pedicure scheduled, so I'll see you ladies later. Maggie, you hurry on to the back now."

"I'm on my way," Maggie said, wishing just this once she would've caved and had a cup—or a pint—of coffee instead of her usual herbal tea.

She went around the desk and tucked her bag into a cubby, then sat down. "Wait a second, before you go back there," Juniper said when Francine had cleared the door and was headed for her car.

"What's up?"

"I found him." She smiled like the cat that ate a canary.

Maggie leaned in, her chest lying over the counter. She whispered. "You found *him*? Are you sure? Where is he?"

"I don't know where he's staying yet, but I worked backwards through the email he sent you and found out he's been using the Wi-Fi of a little café in Lahaina. It's on Front Street, across the way from the famous banyan tree and the old courthouse."

The confirmation that he was so close made Maggie swallow hard with anxiety. "Let's let the police know where to find him."

"We need to wait until I can get an address on him," Juniper said. "If they go to the café looking, he might go into hiding. Then who knows how long it will take to find him again. Maui's small, but there's a lot of places where a person can disappear."

"He's really good at hiding too," Maggie said. "Once I finally secured a warrant for his arrest the last time, it took them a month to find him. But this is so frustrating. Maui isn't very big, so that means he's close and yet we can't do anything."

"I wouldn't say that," Juniper said. "I was able to get into his computer remotely."

"What did you do?"

"I fixed the icons on his desktop to jump around every time he tries to click on one. That will cut down on him troubling your internet life."

"You're a genius, Juniper." Maggie felt her mood lifting.

"But back to next steps. He must be staying close to that café unless he's got money to pay for a ride. I doubt he's been able to get a car."

"We know he has access to money or he wouldn't have been able to get a flight here," Maggie said.

"Oh, right. I guess he could've bought a junker off someone on the island. But would he? That's just one more way for the authorities to find him once they start hitting the Maui news with his photo. If I was a criminal, I'd lay low with making substantial purchases, even if I had fake identification."

"You're right. I guarantee the police will be investigating the small car lots to ask if any foreigners have bought something recently," Maggie said.

"Yeah, probably. But listen," she lowered her voice a little more. "If you can get a sitter for tonight, I'll pick you up at dark, and we will ride to Lahaina for a quick investigation. I might have one tip."

Maggie hesitated. She didn't like to leave Charlie after dark. But if he was with Quinn, and she was only gone for an hour or two . . .

The door swung open, and a small woman walked in carrying a cat who looked a little worse for wear. They approached the desk and Maggie stepped aside.

"Can I help you?" Juniper said.

"Yes, I need an appointment for Hazel."

"Oh, hi, Mrs. Kaufman. What's going on with Hazel now? Didn't we just see her last week?"

"Yes, but she's still peeing all over my condo. I can't take it anymore. I've spent a fortune on carpet cleaners."

"Did you put the litter box inside the house like we told you?" Juniper asked.

Mrs. Kaufman shook her head and looked guilty.

"Ma'am, listen carefully. Hazel is old now. She doesn't want to do her business outside anymore. Get her a litter box. Stat. I promise you'll see a difference. You don't need to pay Dr. Starr for him to tell you that, but if you want to, I'll work you in."

The woman looked unsure of what to do.

Maggie decided to intervene. "Mrs. Kaufman, I'm a vet tech. Would you like me to check Hazel's vitals to make sure everything is all right? And I can listen to her heart too. Complimentary, of course. Just have a seat, and I'll get you back as soon as I can."

The woman beamed, then headed for a chair. On the way over, Maggie heard her shift to baby talk as she held the cat against her chest. "You'll like that, won't you, Hazel? They can listen to that old heart of yours to make sure it's still ticking. I don't want my girl checking out on me now. Later I'll give you a bath and trim your claws."

Maggie shared a knowing smile with Juniper. Some customers just needed attention.

"Yikes," she said, glancing at the clock. "I've got to get back there before Starr comes looking for me. Thank you so much, Juniper, for doing all that investigation. And yes, we're on for tonight. I'm sure Quinn won't mind looking after Charlie."

She went through the swinging doors and scrubbed, then headed to the surgery room.

Inside, Dr. Starr's back was to her, and she noticed he wasn't in his normal light-blue scrubs. He wore the pants, but his shirt was white.

He heard her and turned, and she saw the big black bold words across it that said, "Move Your Asana." The shirt was at least two sizes too small and stretched across his chest.

She stopped in her tracks, her smile disappearing.

"I felt bad for your yoga instructor having to give me so much attention, so I bought a T-shirt. They're made for women only, I suspect. This was supposed to be a large."

"I see that. Real funny."

He held his hands out, his expression earnest. "Not trying to be funny. Just supportive."

Maggie paused. He really did look earnest. And the shirt—well, it was kind of hilarious, if she admitted the truth. Maybe not so much to the next crazy dog mom he'd have to address. The thought of that exchange was too much.

She laughed.

Dr. Starr raised his eyebrows. "Oh, so she does have happy emotions bottled up behind that tough facade. I'm thrilled."

Maggie shook her head and forced a serious expression forward. He was growing on her. "Dr. Starr, you're one of a kind. Come on, we have work to do."

"Wait, Maggie. I'm sorry for crashing your yoga class. But what it looks like to me is you need more friends. I could use a few, too, to be honest."

"You're my boss."

He shrugged. "So what? This is Maui. Mainland rules and etiquette don't apply. I'm not going to be slipping you hundred-dollar bills for being friendly, so no worries."

He had no idea how welcome that sounded. If only she didn't have so much pride.

"I have friends." She thought of Quinn. And Juniper, who between her work and studies was rarely around. Liam? Could she count him as a friend without Quinn? If yes, that made three.

Yeah, her friends list was terribly short these days.

"Can't you handle one more?" he asked.

There it was, that earnest look again. Like a puppy with big eyebrows and a wet nose, just waiting for her to pat him on the head. That made her think of Charlie and how happy he'd looked at the gas station when Dr. Starr was giving him so much attention.

Having one more person in their court wouldn't hurt anything. He was harmless, after all.

"Sure," she relented. "We can be friends. Now, can we get to work?"

He grinned, a huge one that spread across his face like the sun coming out from behind a cloud. "Only when one: you call me Joe. And two: you promise to go surfing with me this afternoon. If we get everyone out of here at a decent time."

Maggie hesitated, then nodded. "Charlie will love that."

"And you'll call me Joe?"

"Yes, I'll call you Joe outside the clinic, but not while I'm on the clock."

"One more thing, Maggie. I don't want there to be any awkwardness between us, so I just wanted to say that you don't have to feel weird about what happened at the gas station. When I was a kid, my mother used to suffer from anxiety, so I know a lot about the subject."

Surprisingly, Maggie felt relief that he'd brought it up and now she wouldn't have to. But she didn't want to extend the conversation. "Thanks, Joe. Now, are we good here?"

"Yep, and before I forget, we need to preserve the testicles of our next patient. His owner wants to put them in a jar and show them to his daughter's boyfriend as a warning to what happened to the last guy that did her wrong."

Maggie couldn't hold it in this time. She laughed big guffaws all the way from her belly, and it felt good. Dr. Starr—or, um, Joe—might just be a salve to her suffering soul. She needed more laughter in her life.

～

The water was perfect for her first surfing lesson, and Maggie tried hard to totally enjoy it. So far she was putting on a good show, but it wasn't proving easy for her to stop thinking about who was out there watching her and just relax. It had been an exhausting day, despite the change of atmosphere between her and Dr. Starr, and she wished she could have canceled all promises and just collapsed.

Joe had brought two surfboards and Maggie straddled one, resting from the exertion she'd just put her body through as she practiced standing and dropping back to the board. They'd been out for nearly an hour, and now he lay over the second board, most of his body in the water as he grinned at her.

"I need to get out here more often," Joe said, his breaths coming fast. "I'm showing my age."

He really wasn't, though. At first she'd thought he was in his midthirties or so, but Juniper had let on that he was closer to forty. His body was toned and he was strong. The only thing that remotely gave away his age was the gray that was mixed in with the dark hairs on his chest.

She'd met Dr. Starr at the beach near Quinn's inn after going home to grab her swimwear. Since that's where Charlie was, it made it easier for her than retrieving him and going to a different beach altogether.

At least now that it was getting near dinnertime, the Maui sun was less intimidating, and most everyone was somewhere else, leaving the water and beach wide open and nearly private.

Never in a million years when she took the job at the clinic did she imagine herself out in the water with her boss, both of them showing too much skin to even pretend to be professional.

She hoped the streaks of white under her eyes and down her nose didn't look too ridiculous, but it was true about redheads and the sun. Maggie knew from experience that a day at the beach without protection could result in medical care for her. She burned much quicker than the average human, and it was frustrating.

She scanned the sand in the distance, wishing she'd opted for contacts instead of just glasses. It was blurry, but she found Charlie by the brightness of the new soccer ball, the black-and-white colors a contrast against the sand.

He and Liam kicked it back and forth. Quinn lay in a chair, her arm over her face, either sleeping or thinking. She stood out, too, the turquoise of her swimsuit a spot of color easy to find.

If she wasn't sleeping, then she was stressing. Her book lay flat on her stomach, untouched. Maggie envied the sun-kissed, mellow color of her skin that her Hawaiian genes afforded her. She looked like a beautiful cover model out there, and the crazy thing was she didn't even know it.

Something tickled past the toes on her left foot, and Maggie silently pulled her legs up as far as she could. She didn't want to look like a wimp, even as she imagined a jellyfish or some other unnamed but toxic creature trying to get close.

"Ready to give it a go?" Joe asked. "I see one coming, and you'll have to paddle hard."

"Nope, I need a minute." They waited and the wave came, lifted them both in a gentle, fluid motion and let them back down. It felt like heaven.

"You're a fast learner," he said. "I think you can probably take a small wave now."

That was an overcompliment if she'd ever heard one. She hadn't yet been able to stand up for more than few seconds, and the scrapes on the insides of her thighs were burning like fire. She had to admit, though, she should be spending more time in the water or at least on the beach, breathing in the fresh air and letting nature soothe her mind. In the warm caress of the sea, she'd nearly forgotten her troubles.

"I've never surfed, but I do have a competitive spirit," Maggie replied. "Growing up with brothers will do that to you. I never wanted them to baby me, so I was always trying to prove myself."

"I can see that," Joe said. "Even in the clinic, the more I give you to do, the less likely you are to ask for help. Is everything a challenge to you?"

She nodded. "I guess you could put it that way."

"Don't you ever just want to let your guard down?" He bobbed up and down on another wave as he squinted at her. "Or let someone help you?"

"Nope. I let my guard down once, and it brought me nothing but trouble." She looked for Charlie again.

She saw Liam first. He'd gone to sit by Quinn, and they appeared to be deep in conversation. Then she saw Charlie, kicking his ball down the beach. Woodrow was near, frolicking each time the ball dropped out of Charlie's reach.

Charlie was too far for her to tell his expression, but she guessed he was lost in his daydreams of becoming a soccer star.

A man coming down the path that led from the hotel caught Maggie's eye. He didn't look like a beachgoer. From her perspective, it appeared he was wearing jeans and closed shoes.

He shielded his eyes to look over the water, then scan the beach.

"I wonder who that is," Maggie said. "He's looking for someone."

Joe turned and looked. "I don't know, but he's headed in Charlie's direction."

Maggie watched as the man turned toward her son and began a determined stride. Her pulse accelerated, but she tried to tell herself to calm down, that not every stranger was danger. Probably just a tourist with an interest in soccer.

Or little boys. Hers in particular.

That thought spurred her into action. She lay on her belly and headed to shore, paddling as fast as she could. "Charlie," she called out, but her voice was drowned out by the wind and waves, and he didn't turn.

She called again, desperate this time.

Even Liam and Quinn didn't hear her.

"Now that's what I mean about putting your all into it," Joe yelled from behind her. "But you're going the wrong way."

Damn it! The man was bridging the distance between him and her son. She wanted to scream at Woodrow, command him to be on guard.

"Maggie, wait. What's wrong?" Joe yelled.

He was right behind her now, probably thinking she was a maniac, but Maggie didn't care. What if the man snatched Charlie and ran? She was moving so recklessly that the saltwater continued a direct hit to her eyes, burning them with every splash.

Only a few yards from the sand now, she saw Charlie turn as though the man had called out. Then he stood there, staring at him.

Maggie reached, paddling harder, digging deeper.

The man covered the distance between him and Charlie, and to her horror, he picked up her son. Woodrow jumped up on his legs but didn't appear aggressive. Why wasn't he intervening?

A new strength she'd never known she had filled her, and she seemed to float over the water, her board barely skimming the waves as she paddled in.

Luckily when she got close enough to get her feet under her, she recognized the stranger who held her son in a bear hug. It was no less shocking, though, as it had to have taken a miracle for Charlie's dad to conquer his fear of flying in order for him to get there. She felt instant sympathy for his seatmate for the more than five thousand miles.

"Colby," Maggie barely got out between the panting and coughing up water. She struggled to get to the shore and made it down the beach the last few feet to them. She wanted to collapse from the sudden exertion, but she held herself together with just her hands on her knees, doing her best to control her ragged breaths.

Obviously she needed more exercise.

Yoga was letting her down.

Woodrow came to her and tried to help, but licking the salt from her legs was less than helpful to her heart, which was pumping out of her chest from exertion. If anything, the dog was sucking up more of her energy.

"No, Woodrow," she gasped. Anyway, he was a traitor. She'd expected him to at least show some ferocity toward a man he hadn't seen in months.

"Mama, look! It's Daddy! He's here!"

Charlie had a look on his face that Maggie had rarely seen in the last year. It was pure and unadulterated joy. Disbelief too. But mostly the kind of happiness that can only come from a child who thinks his world is complete because he now has his two favorite people at his side.

In her peripheral view, she saw Joe change direction behind her. He'd obviously heard the word *daddy* and didn't want to intrude on the welcome.

Liam and Quinn were turned their way, watching but not interfering.

"Yes, I see that, Charlie. What a surprise," she finally croaked out.

Colby turned and set Charlie down.

"Daddy, I'm practicing soccer! Liam got me a ball."

"That's great, buddy. Go kick a few while I talk to Mommy." He rubbed Charlie's head and then their son was off, intent on showing off for his dad.

"What are you doing here?" Maggie asked as soon as Charlie was out of earshot. They stood together, watching him go after his ball. It felt surreal that one moment, he was thousands of miles away across the ocean, and then he was here.

Maggie couldn't remember the last time Charlie had seen his parents in one place, side by side, as though it was meant to be that way.

"Do I get a hello? Or a hug?" Colby said. He looked over her head. "People are watching. Can you at least act like you're glad to see me?"

The truth was, Maggie wasn't glad to see him. She'd kept her secret from him for a long time, never letting him know the problem she was running from. Having him here now just wasn't what she needed.

He held his arms out, and she suddenly felt next to naked in her bikini, even though by Maui standards, it was quite conservative.

"I'm wet," she said, backing up a step. "And you're wearing jeans. And boots. On a Maui beach. Do you have any idea how silly you look?"

He grinned, and her stomach flipped. She despised that he could still do that to her. It also puzzled her how most men would look like idiots dressed that way on a beach, but somehow, despite what she said, Colby pulled it off. All he needed was his sweat-stained old cowboy hat and he'd have a line of beach babes at his beck and call, if it was just a bit earlier in the day.

"I'm serious, Colby."

He lost his grin and tipped his invisible hat, reminding her just how southern he really was. No act, just genuine country-boy etiquette. "Sorry, little miss. I didn't have time to shop. I was kind of in a hurry after your last call. Or should I say, the last call I received from this island by someone I didn't know who had possession of your phone."

Maggie thought of the poor fellow who manned the gas station. He would probably lock the door the next time he saw her coming.

"That was . . . Well, that was unfortunate. But I handled it. You know I have issues with anxiety, but nothing happened to Charlie, and we were both fine. You didn't have to come all the way here."

He turned and put his arms around her, pulling her close to his side. And the embrace felt good. She had to admit it.

Colby's arms were familiar. Her body knew him and reacted immediately. Even with the slight chill of the evening breeze on her damp skin, she instantly felt warm all over.

That wasn't a good thing, and she broke away.

He sat down on the sand and put his arms around his legs, staring out at the water. "Mags, don't be mad. I could hear Charlie crying in the background of that message. It was a cry I've never heard. You didn't call me back, so I was worried about you too. How could I not come?"

Woodrow sensed his distress and lay down next to him.

"I sent you a text message."

He gave her a disappointed look. "Yeah, that one is what drove me to the internet to book my ticket. Kind of cold, don't you think? I could've called you back, but I needed to see what was going on for myself."

Maggie sat down beside him. "I'm sorry. I should've talked to you after everything settled down, but I just didn't want a lot of questions. You know how I am about that problem. It's humiliating. Not to mention that I'm going through a lot here right now."

"Obviously. And I came to see if I can help. And to make sure Charlie's getting on all right. He's thousands of miles away from me, his father, and when I hear him cry like that, it kills me not to be there to comfort him." He looked hopeful.

"But I don't need any help, and Charlie doesn't need you confusing him."

He looked at her, taken aback. "How am I going to confuse him?"

Maggie sighed. "Oh, Colby. Now he's going to think you're here to stay."

Colby shrugged and looked at his boots. The same worn-in shitkickers he'd been wearing for probably ten years. He hadn't changed. "I don't have to leave right away. I gave my job notice I wasn't coming back. I'm ready for something else. Building fences gets old, if you know what I mean. Thought I'd try mending a fence this time instead, which is why I'm here . . ."

So many thoughts were going through Maggie's head that she didn't even know what to ask next. His arrival had definitely put a wrench in things. And now that he didn't have a date to be home by, this was going to get complicated. She had to find a way to send him home without breaking Charlie's heart.

"So the airplane thing, how did you do that?" she asked, softening her tone.

No Place Too Far

He looked at her then. "It was hard, I'm not gonna lie. But I kept telling myself that what I loved the most was on the other side of that ocean, and there was only one way to get there."

She smiled. "He really missed you too, Colby. Maybe this visit will do him good and help you see that we're both thriving here. So that you know I've got everything under control when you go back."

Colby started to say something else but was interrupted by Quinn and Liam walking up.

"Hi, I'm guessing you're Charlie's dad," Quinn said, holding her hand out. "You look exactly like your photo."

Colby smiled broadly. "So you must be the infamous Quinn that she's told me so many stories about. I can't believe it's taken this long to meet you." He shook her hand, then took the one that Liam offered.

"I'm Liam. You've got a good kid there," he said, nodding toward Charlie who was now trying to kick the ball up to the top of his head to bunt it. He bent too far over as he tried again, and the ball smacked him right in the face.

He recovered fast, and the next time, he nailed it.

"Did y'all see that?" he called out to them before getting back to training.

"He's committed," Colby said. "Good job, Charlie!" he yelled out.

He and Liam laughed like they were old friends. Something about the way that Colby fell into her friends group so easily irritated Maggie.

"I'm guessing the desk clerk told you where to find us," Quinn said. Colby nodded.

Maggie shot a look of concern to Quinn. This was the second time one of her staff had led a stranger straight to them: first the bellhop and now the desk clerk. No one should be giving out their whereabouts. It was already a miracle that some reporter wasn't skulking around while they were out there. Or worse, a deranged stalker.

215

Colby noticed the exchange. "Ah, don't blame him. I told him I was Charlie's dad here to surprise him. He thought that was awesome."

But what if it hadn't been Charlie's dad? Maggie couldn't very well bring that up to Colby, so she seethed in silence.

"Josh has a soft spot for Charlie, but he needs to be a little more discerning," Quinn said. "I'll have to talk to him."

"I'll do it," Liam said. "He's my third cousin, and he'll listen to me without thinking he's about to lose his job."

"Well, maybe he needs to have a little fear," Maggie said. She stood and brushed the sand off her wet bottom, or at least tried to.

"I need to start guiding Charlie toward a bedtime. Where are you staying? Did you book a room here at the inn?" she asked Colby.

"I—um—no. I checked the rates, but well, you know, it's a little pricey for my budget. I didn't even rent a car. Thank goodness for the waiting taxi."

He looked embarrassed, and it dawned on Maggie.

Colby expected to stay with *her*.

She felt her independence closing in on her a little bit more. He was right, though. You could buy a small car for what lodging in Maui would cost you for a week. And she couldn't expect Quinn to lose a room just to comp him for her.

As for Colby, she stared at him and could read his mind. All he had to do was summon his little mini-me minion, and Charlie would insist that his dad come home with him.

Maggie wouldn't win this one. And just like with a child, you also had to learn to pick your battles with your ex. This was small compared to what it would take for him to agree she was fine and leave the island. She needed to save her mental strength.

"Fine. You can take the couch," she said, unable to wipe the grimace from her face before speaking. "Wait, where did Starr—I mean Joe—take off to?" She hadn't even noticed that while they were talking, he'd disappeared.

"He said he had a patient to call about," Quinn said, raising her eyebrows at Maggie.

He didn't have any patients. Maggie knew that. Yeah, it was a little awkward, she had to admit. She'd call him later and apologize. Joe had really been good with Charlie, and surprisingly, she'd enjoyed the surfing lessons too. Away from the clinic, her boss was a lot of fun.

Actually, even in the clinic, Joe was a lot of fun.

Colby reined Charlie in, and they all headed back up to the hotel.

"Our sleepover is off, right?" Quinn asked.

"Yep," Maggie replied.

Charlie stopped. "I want Daddy to stay with me."

They were almost up to the hotel. Everyone was silent, and it got awkward.

"Yes, Daddy is coming home with us for tonight," Maggie said, heading off a whining campaign. "Because I decided, not because you ordered it."

Charlie jumped up and down, his excitement of seeing his dad now surpassed by his joy of taking him home and probably showing him every Tonka truck and book he owned. He was going to talk until his dad was ready to wave the white flag.

She smiled slyly. Colby at least had that coming.

Maggie was already planning a long, hot, and uninterrupted bath. While Colby was here, he was going to be taking more than his share of parent duty. She'd make him beg for an airport drop-off.

"Colby, grab your bags, and I'll meet you in the parking lot. Look for the biggest piece of junk out there, and you'll find me and Charlie." She sounded as disgruntled as she felt, but her good manners wouldn't do anything less than let Colby stay with them.

Hell, she couldn't afford Maui lodging either. Not unless it was a pup tent on the beach with the moon as her night-light. She pushed the thought away before it could slip out of her mouth. She knew her son and he'd jump all over that idea, probably with his dad backing him up.

And while the Ghost was on the loose, Maggie meant to keep Charlie behind lock and key.

The ride to her place was filled with Charlie asking questions, a blessing because that meant she didn't have to find something to say. Her son was never at a loss for words, and he was also good for entertainment in awkward moments.

"We can go to the park but not at dark because Mama says the boys smoke marinara there at night," Charlie said.

"Good call. We sure don't want to be around any saucy smoke," Colby said, laughing as he grinned over at Maggie.

They pulled up at the apartments and she bit her tongue, worried what he would think of her sparse living. He didn't judge, other than to tease her about having a black thumb when he saw the boxes of flowers on either side of her door.

The lines of stems with no heads did look a bit creepy.

Maggie had told Charlie that the dragonflies ate them, but something told her Colby knew enough about nature to know that would be a bunch of bull.

While she fumbled to unlock the door, she felt Colby staring a hole through her.

"That's some serious hardware," he said.

She declined to comment and showed him in, feeling her cheeks burn as he walked into their tiny home. If he noticed how shabby it was, he didn't say a word, and for that she was grateful.

Two hours later, she was ready to strangle Colby. He'd used two pots, three wooden spoons, two cups, four bowls, and a colander to make Charlie a simple box of macaroni and cheese, all the while narrating each step loudly and obnoxiously as though he were some sort of television chef.

Charlie loved the show.

Every. Single. Second.

He thought his dad was some sort of celebrity.

As for her, she should get more for giving him birth and keeping him alive each day. But then she smiled as she heard Colby's voice from the bedroom, reading their son his sixth bedtime story. As predicted, Charlie had not stopped talking to his dad.

And talking.

Then talking some more.

She'd almost rescued Colby a few times, but then she figured he needed to know the feeling of thinking your ears would bleed if you had to listen to one more question or read yet another story.

Even Woodrow had enough by book three and came out to join her in the kitchen, lying between her legs and the cabinet, just to make her last chores that much more unbearable as she strained to reach the dishes.

But his loyalty was admirable.

"You're such a good boy," she mumbled to him. "Aren't you glad it's not us tonight?" He looked at her, and she swore she saw a barely perceptible nod of his head.

When she finished the last dish, Colby stumbled out, looking quite shell-shocked and red-eyed from reading in the dim light. He was wearing just basketball shorts and no shirt—his farmer's tan shining from day after day of planting poles and hanging wire. Which the muscles confirmed.

She tried not to stare.

"God, Maggie," he said, falling into the couch right on top of the clean sheets she'd just set out for him. "I couldn't find an off button."

She laughed. There were many evenings she'd thought the exact same thing. She didn't know why there was such a thing as waterboarding when the government could just send in a four-year-old, and the suspect would soon beg to spill his guts if the kid shut up.

"I finally had to promise to teach him how to do a judo kick as soon as he wakes up," Colby said.

"Well, that was a mistake. You'd better be ready as soon as his tiny toes hit the floor. You promise a preschooler something before they go to sleep, and the second they open their eyes they're demanding you pay up."

"Crap," Colby said. "I thought he'd forget. That'll be fun first thing in the morning. He'll be pulling moves, and I'll be standing there trying to remember who I am and how I got here."

Maggie laughed. "Welcome to Charlie's world."

She opened the fridge and pulled out two cans of beer. She took one to Colby, then popped the top on hers and sat down beside him.

"Thanks." He scooted a little closer, and she felt her guard creeping up. "I have no idea what time it really is, but my brain is telling me that I missed a night's sleep somewhere."

"We're six hours ahead. You should've slept on the plane."

"I couldn't. I was too worried about what you'd do when you saw me. I expected a hard right to my center or something like that. I know how much you hate surprises, so the mellow way you took it kind of surprised me."

"That's because I couldn't catch my breath from paddling in to the beach. If you'd have come out to me, I'd have drowned you," Maggie said.

She leaned her head back on the couch, and he followed suit. They sat there side by side, heads back and beer in hands. It felt comfortable.

"Come on, now," he said. "You know I've changed a lot in the last few years. Don't I get any credit?"

She didn't say anything, though she'd noticed he had changed, actually. He was never late sending a check for Charlie's support and sometimes even added a little extra. Despite the time difference, he was always available by phone—no matter what time it was, he would pick up. He'd also never missed a visitation or was late for anything he'd agreed to do with Charlie.

But Maggie most appreciated that when they exchanged their son back and forth, Colby was always the perfect gentleman. They'd never let Charlie think there was anything but fondness between them.

Co-parenting at its best.

Though, honestly, Colby had always had impeccable manners. From their first date when he'd opened the truck door and helped her in, then paid for dinner. Afterward he took her for a simple ice cream cone before delivering her back home without even one attempt to talk her into his bed. It wouldn't have taken much. Maggie had fallen hard for his southern charm during dinner that night; then the deal was sealed even more when she witnessed how well he treated his mama.

He was just a good man.

That simple.

She'd never denied that fact.

"You shouldn't have moved so far away, Mags. I wasn't ready for that."

"I know. But you have to admit it's beautiful here," Maggie said.

"And expensive," Colby said. "Someone left behind a real estate magazine on the plane. The prices for even modest living are insane. You can't really ever have a life here, can you? I can't imagine how much you'd have to make to even qualify to buy a house."

"I do okay," Maggie said. "And you know I wanted to be close to Quinn again."

"And far from me," he said softly.

She wasn't touching that one.

"Have you made any new friends?" Colby asked.

"I have a friend named Juniper. She lives a few doors down and works with me. But I'm not looking for more. I get enough mom-shaming when I look in the mirror each night and rewind my day. I don't need a group of overzealous young moms comparing their children's accomplishments against Charlie's."

"Sounds fair. But I was talking about the male sort."

"Oh. Well, not really," Maggie said, embarrassed now at her tirade against other young moms. They weren't all that competitive, were they? "I've been busy with work. And Charlie." *And a relentless stalker.*

"What about the guy you were surfing with? He didn't stick around long enough to meet me, did he?"

Maggie hadn't even been sure that Colby had seen Joe, since he hadn't said anything about it. But she should've known. That was his way. He liked to take things in, think about them, and let them simmer, then bring them out for discussion when he was ready.

"That's my boss, the veterinarian."

"So you're sleeping with your boss? Those are some great fringe benefits."

She picked up a throw pillow and threw it at him. "No! And if I was, why do you care?"

He didn't answer, and she didn't press it.

"Joe is just a friend, Colby. He's safe, and you don't have to worry about me having random boyfriends around Charlie. I'm very careful who he is exposed to. A little overprotective, probably."

"Does Joe know he's just a friend?"

"Yes, Joe knows. And that was actually the first time he's met Charlie. I made sure Quinn and Liam were there too. Just in case. It's also the first time I've been around him outside of work."

Colby was silent for a moment. Maggie could tell he had more to say.

"Mags," he said, "I don't know if I've ever said it, but you're a great mom. Don't doubt yourself."

"Oh, you might not think that if you'd been around more in the first two years. I went weeks without a shower, and more often than not, I felt depressed and inadequate. It's a miracle Charlie is the awesome kid that he is."

"I wanted to be around more. If you remember right, you wouldn't let me," Colby said. "You basically kicked me out, Maggie."

She didn't quite remember it that way. Her recollection was that he had a hard time going from bachelor to daddy. It wasn't that he'd ever said anything, it was just what she suspected. She'd just made it easy for him and showed him the door, narrowing his responsibility down to child support payments and scheduled visits.

But if that was all true, why did she feel so guilty about it?

"You need to get some rest," she said, diverting the conversation. "And I'm exhausted too. That was my first surf lesson you saw out there, and it kicked my butt. My shoulders are fighting for the title of worst pain ever, but my thighs are winning. Gripping that surfboard makes marks that are felt deep."

Colby gave a little growl.

"Don't talk about your thighs, please," he said.

She gave him a stern look. "Stop. Get your mind out of the gutter."

He set his beer down on the side table and patted his lap.

"Lay here and I'll rub your shoulders," he said.

Maggie was tempted. Even before the surf lessons, she'd spent hours bending over the surgery table, assisting Joe in one procedure after another. Then wrestling the surfboard, followed by the hard paddling, and topping it off with standing over a sink full of dishes left by two mischievous boys. And that didn't even count the time spent on her hands and knees scooping up Legos and toy trucks.

Her upper body was screaming.

"No. Thanks anyway," she said.

"You really don't want a massage?" Colby asked, his voice unbelieving.

"Not if it involves a penis."

Colby threw his head back and laughed loudly until he was wiping tears. "Now whose mind is in the gutter?"

Maggie just smiled. She was serious. She knew what his *massages* always led to, and her mama didn't raise no fool.

"Oh, Mags," Colby said, finally catching his breath. "God, I missed you and that sassy mouth. You have no idea how much."

They both got quiet for a minute; then Maggie jumped up, hoping he wasn't waiting for her to return the sentiment. She didn't believe in pursuing lost causes. She also didn't trust herself to make the right decision if she started going down that path.

"I'm going to bed," she said, deciding a massage wasn't worth the risk of falling under his spell again. "I work at noon tomorrow, and I won't be home until after dinner. You can drop me off and use my car if you'd like."

"Can I keep Charlie with me?" He looked so earnest.

"If you promise not to sneak off the island with him." Maggie was only half kidding.

Colby held his hands up defensively. "Are you crazy? I've seen that red-haired temper of yours, and I ain't looking for some enraged mama bear to come after me."

"Good. There's a Walmart in Kahului if you want to go pick up some more appropriate clothes for Maui weather. Just look it up on your phone. It's an easy drive. And while you're there, can you get some sunscreen? Rosa, his babysitter, said the one I sent is almost gone."

He gave her a thumbs-up.

"I'm serious, Colby. If you take Charlie in the sun, be sure to coat him down good. Get his ears too. He'll go from milk to lobster in five minutes if you forget. He's got my dysfunctional skin."

Unlike Colby's skin, which was a delicious-looking bronze on the parts that got to see the sun. She looked away again, peeling her eyes from his chest.

"Sure. Face. Ears. Got it. Any specific kind?"

"Something that doesn't kill the environment and poison our son at the same time would be great."

"Cool," Colby said. "I'll ask Google."

"Good night, Colby," she said softly, then went into the bedroom and eased the door shut. What she couldn't say aloud was that whether she wanted to admit it or not, this might be the first full night of sleep for her in far too long. She still resented him for showing up uninvited, but she knew she could rest easy with Colby between her and anything on the other side of the front door.

Chapter Twenty-Three

Maggie felt an ache in her fingers as she gripped the door handle. If she had known that Juniper was such a crazy driver, she probably wouldn't have agreed to this little field trip. She hoped that they could get done quickly, as Charlie was home waiting for her.

Well, maybe not exactly *waiting* for her. She'd called before they left the clinic, and Colby said he hadn't asked for her all day. He and Charlie had spent the afternoon on one of Quinn's family boats—a complimentary excursion, no less. They'd lucked upon a pod of dolphins that decided to be playful around them. Charlie was now on a quest to learn all he could about the cute little mammals and was begging Colby to take him to the library.

Imagining Colby in a library brought a smile to her face. He wouldn't know the first thing about finding the right book. She could just see the glisten of perspiration on his forehead.

She glanced at Woodrow in the back seat, and they exchanged knowing looks when Juniper tapped her brakes too fast. She shot him a silent apology.

This morning he had quickly made friends with Colby again, sitting pretty for him and for cheese, of course. Maggie had been a little grumpy, admittedly, because what she'd thought would be a night of good rest had turned out to be mostly tossing and turning. Somehow 'nowing Colby was outside her door, sleeping half naked on her couch, made falling asleep a goal she didn't reach until what felt like minutes before a loud noise woke her.

She'd stumbled out of the bedroom to find Colby midair in a judo kick, with Charlie wide-eyed and ready for his turn.

"I told you," she said, then went back to bed and tried to block out the noise with a pillow. It hadn't worked, and she finally got up and made eggs and bacon, then took Woodrow for a walk before it was time for Colby to drop her off at work.

Now she was dragging.

"Ooh, no you don't," Juniper mumbled under her breath, slipping into the other lane to pass the car in front of them, then quickly back into the right.

"Juniper, please," Maggie said, nearly hitting her head on the window as she was forced to lean each way. "Don't forget Woodrow isn't harnessed in."

Juniper laughed. "Sorry, I know I drive too aggressive. It's an emotional release for me."

Aggressive was an understatement. Maggie hoped they made it back to the clinic in one piece. For such a free-spirited hippie type, Juniper sure needed to let out a lot of steam.

They were on a rescue mission.

It was near the end of her shift when a call had come in that someone had heard what sounded like a dog whining coming from under a dumpster behind a store near Front Street. Juniper had told them to call the Maui Humane Society, but the lady said she kept getting a recording.

Juniper informed Joe, and he suggested they team up and go take a look.

"I'm glad Joe let us go early," Maggie said. "It's nearly a hundred degrees today, and there's no telling how long the dog has been out there."

Juniper nodded. "I know. It might even be too late when we get there."

The irony of the situation hadn't been lost on either of them. Juniper said that the café she thought the Ghost had worked from was near that same store that the dumpster was behind. They would have to be careful because Maggie sure didn't want him spotting her or sneaking up behind them.

"I heard about your ex dropping in," Juniper said. "Starr wasn't too thrilled."

"Why? Did he say he wasn't?"

"Nope, but I could tell by his tone. You do know that he's crushing on you, right?" Juniper glanced at her, smiling.

"He is not," Maggie said. "We're friends and that's it."

"Okay," Juniper said. "Think what you want, Miss Gullible. But I'm telling you, he was bummed that Charlie's dad is back in the picture."

Maggie let that sink in for a moment. She wasn't oblivious. There was something weird brewing between her and Joe. She could feel it when they worked together, the vibes bouncing off the stainless-steel table between them. But it wasn't something she'd planned on pursuing. Friendship was enough. Her life was too complicated to add a love interest right now, especially if that interest was her boss and especially with Colby breathing down her neck.

"He's actually not back in the picture. He's just visiting."

"Oh. Well, in that case, Joe wouldn't be too bad of a catch for you," Juniper said. "You wouldn't have to scrape by anymore, just barely making it, and Charlie could have a father figure in the picture all the time."

"Not funny," Maggie said.

"I'm not joking. All you need to do is give him one ounce of encouragement, and I swear you'll have a ring on that finger so fast your head will spin."

"I barely know him, Juniper."

Juniper laughed. "Just wait until you've been on the island a while. It's slim pickings finding a good partner, and a few weeks is considered a long-term relationship here."

"Please stop talking about this," Maggie said, rubbing her temples. The truth was, she felt guilty because the thought had crossed her mind. Life could be easier if she just let her guard down and learned to trust someone else.

But she wanted to be head over heels in love. Not be with someone for convenience. She wanted her person to feel like he couldn't take another breath in a world that didn't have her in it. And she wanted to feel the same.

On the other hand, she didn't know too many married couples who were head over heels anymore, so maybe that was just a fantasy.

They turned behind the row of shops.

"Okay, look for the one that has an orange bicycle locked up beside it. She said we should see it easily," Juniper said.

"I'm looking. But just so you know, Colby will be leaving Maui soon."

"Willingly?" Juniper asked. "Without you?"

Maggie shot her an exasperated look. "Yes. Willingly. He knows that part of our relationship is long gone and over."

"I thought you said he doesn't fly? If he overcame that fear to get here, I'd think that was pretty significant. Have you always been this blind when it comes to men?"

Maggie sighed loudly. Juniper had a great memory.

She was saved from answering when she saw the orange bike.

"There it is." She pointed.

Juniper pulled up next to it and put the car in park mode. "We'll leave it running so Woodrow doesn't get too hot."

She popped open the glove compartment and took out a pair of rubber gloves.

"Should I ask why you keep rubber gloves in your dash?" Maggie asked. "Please tell me you don't have a gallon of bleach and a shovel in the back."

"True-crime addict?" Juniper asked, raising her eyebrows.

"A little," Maggie said, then opened the door. True-crime television used to be her guilty pleasure but lately much less so with her own story still going on. The occasional episodes she watched now hit a little too close to home.

She looked back at Woodrow and told him to stay put. Maggie was rewarded with a look of disappointment, but she and Juniper didn't know what they were up against, and she sure didn't want to scare off the pup if it was still out there.

"This isn't my first dumpster rescue. I come prepared." She opened the back door, grabbed a leash that was lying on the floor, and tossed it to Maggie. "Hold this until I need it."

"I don't hear anything," Maggie said.

They stood perfectly still next to the dumpster for a moment, straining to listen. Maggie fought not to gag from the putrid smell of rotting leftovers.

Juniper kneeled down and peered under the dumpster.

"Nothing under here. It must have moved on. That's disappointing," she said.

"Maybe someone else got it?" Maggie hoped so.

"I doubt it," Juniper said, standing and brushing the debris from her gloves.

Suddenly they heard something. But it didn't sound like a whine. It was more of a low growl.

"It must be in the dumpster," Maggie said. She flipped the lid open, giving it a big push to make it fall to the other side. "Whew!"

Juniper made a face. "Well, we know what kind of shop it is now."

"I'll never eat fish again," Maggie said, holding her nose. "I really ope a pup hasn't been unfortunate enough to be dumped in here."

They both peered over the side. At first Maggie didn't see anything amid the trash and scraps, but then she saw an empty box seem to move by itself way back in the corner.

"Over there," she pointed. "That box moved."

Much to Maggie's relief, Juniper climbed over the side and carefully settled onto her hands and knees. "The trick is to crawl across the trash and not get stuck in it."

"I'm thinking I won't need your tutorials," Maggie said. "You can have the dumpster privileges infinitely."

"Oh, thanks. Nice teamwork," Juniper said. She approached the corner, and they heard the growl again. "Oh, he's in here."

"Be careful, Juniper."

Juniper reached out and flipped the box over. A small black face peered up at her, baring its teeth, or what was left of them.

"It's okay, buddy," she crooned, trying to stabilize herself as she got a little closer. "Maggie, go around behind him. When his attention is on me, loop the leash around his neck loosely. Don't tighten it unless he lunges."

Though they couldn't see his lower half, Maggie could tell it wasn't a big dog at all. Maybe just twelve or so pounds. But even a five-pound dog could do a lot of damage if he wanted to. She pulled the leash through the handle to make a noose and crept over behind the dog.

He turned his head up and growled, then turned back to Juniper, who was closer to his protective space.

"Come on, now. Don't be afraid. We just want to get you out of here," Juniper said, reaching a hand out closer. "He needs to smell me so he knows I'm not dangerous."

Like a snake, the dog lunged forward, and before Juniper could pull her hand back, he made contact.

"Damn it," she said, examining the fingers of the right glove. "I felt that, but it doesn't look like it broke through. I thought you were my safety?"

"Sorry. I wasn't expecting that." Maggie saw an opening and leaned over the side, then quickly dropped the loop of the leash over the dog's head. He instantly began writhing around but still couldn't dislodge himself from the trash.

"He's really not in that deep," Juniper said. "I think something else is wrong. Just let him fight it out for a minute."

His eyes were wild, and after a few moments of struggle, the dog stopped. He panted and looked around at Maggie, his eyes bulging.

"Shh, shh . . . ," Maggie soothed. "Calm down, baby. Let us help you."

"There's a small bowl and a bottle of water in the back of my car," Juniper said softly. "Go grab it."

Maggie dropped the leash and went to the car, opening the back door. A rush of cool air hit her in the face. Bob Marley was playing on the radio.

"You chilling in here, buddy?" She leaned in around Woodrow and grabbed the water and bowl, and also an old towel wadded in the floor. "Good boy," she said, patting him on the head before shutting the door again.

When she returned to the dumpster, she was shocked to see Juniper sitting upright, leaning against the inside wall and holding the dog. Even more shocking was that, though he was still panting heavily, he wasn't fighting her.

Now that he was out of the mounds of trash, Maggie could see it was a little Chinese pug. A black one, with a lot of gray around the muzzle.

"Everything calmed down when you walked away," she said, smiling up at Maggie.

"Oh, thanks. What am I? Cruella de Vil?" She handed over the water and bowl.

"You brought out the leash. They hate the sight of it. I had to make move because it's getting dark. I'm not wrangling dogs I can't see."

Juniper poured the dog some water and let him lap at it for just a moment. "Not too much at once, pup."

"Do you want me to get him so you can climb out?" Maggie asked.

"Yes, hold on. But it's a she, and she's a senior." She gently got back on her knees and handed the small dog up to Maggie, who scooped her up in the towel, keeping her teeth far from her skin.

Juniper climbed over the side and took her gloves off, then went to the car and came back with a packet of moist ground dog food. She sprinkled a little of it on the ground. The dog caught the smell and instantly became alert.

"Set her down and let's see if she's strong enough to walk."

Maggie gently set the dog down on the pavement, balancing her on the legs. As soon as she let go, the dog collapsed.

"Something is wrong with her back legs," Juniper said, crouching down in front of the dog.

When they looked closer, it was obvious that whatever was wrong with her legs was an old injury. They were too thin and looked useless, but the dog tried to crawl to the food using her front legs.

"Poor old girl," Maggie said. She picked her up and set her at the food. The dog began gobbling it up. "I guess she wasn't too keen on eating rotted fish remnants. She's starving."

"She's probably incontinent too," Juniper said. "Barely any teeth and back legs paralyzed. Someone got tired of being her caretaker."

"They should be arrested for dumping her," Maggie said.

"Yep, but it happens all the time. The dog gives them a lifetime of loyalty, then gets old and the favor isn't returned. Some people are just evil."

Maggie turned around, checking out the alley around them. She hadn't forgotten they could be close to another evil too. She breathed a sigh of relief when she saw the only other human was an old woman sweeping the back stoop of a floral shop a few yards away.

"Let's get her back to the clinic and get her settled," Juniper said. "Starr can do a full exam tomorrow and see what all we've got on our hands."

Maggie used the towel to pick the dog up again, thankful that she'd gotten over her fear-based aggression. They returned to the car and Woodrow jumped around the back seat, relieved for them to get back in.

Woodrow stuck his nose between the seats, sniffing at their guest. Then he turned his snout toward Juniper and after one whiff, shrank back.

They laughed.

"I don't think you'll ever get this smell out of your car," Maggie said. She looked down at the little dog. Her face was so dark and night was coming fast, so she could barely make out her expression. "I think we'll call you Cinder."

"Oooh . . . I like it," Juniper said.

Maggie sighed, her sadness audible. "Do you think anyone will adopt her? She's old as the hills and possibly paralyzed."

"I definitely do," Juniper said. She put the car in drive and started down the alley. "For all the jackasses in the world who would throw their old dog out just when she needs them the most, there are two more compassionate humans willing to give this dog a loving retirement. Don't worry, we'll find just the right one."

Maggie hoped she was right.

"Haven't you read the book, Maggie?" Juniper said. "Evil doesn't win."

They laughed but inside, Maggie knew a little more on the subject than Juniper did. In many cases, evil did win. It was a constant battle, and she herself had seen enough of it to know.

She looked down at the flattened nose of the pug. Even with the gray peppered all over her face, she was cute.

"You thought you were in the last chapter, didn't you? That you'd take your final breaths in that gas chamber? Well, guess what, Cinder?"

"Plot twist," called out Juniper.

They both laughed.

"Speaking of plot twists," Maggie said, "I got my bank account back."

"I'm glad you brought that up. Have you heard anything from Maui's finest?" Juniper asked.

She pulled out into traffic, and the dog flinched. Maggie held her closer and soothed her with a whisper.

"Not a thing. I'm hoping the silence means they're busy tracking leads."

"Well, I have a few more things up my sleeve to find your weirdo. A friend of mine has developed an app that might help us out. He's coming over tomorrow."

Maggie cringed. "I really don't want to involve anyone else, Juniper. The police won't take kindly to us doing their work for them. We could just get in the way."

"You said yourself it was hard to catch him. Do you really want to send him back into hiding even deeper?"

"It's an island. How far can he go? They'll also be watching the airports," Maggie said. She rubbed circles around Cinder's ears, making her sleepier than she already was after eating and filling up with fresh water. "I just feel like this cat-and-mouse game could end badly for me. I have Charlie to think about."

Juniper sighed. "You're right. I really wanted to be the one to pinpoint exactly where he is, but that's just my hero complex."

Maggie was glad that was settled. The thought of Juniper toying with Andrews had plagued her all night, interspersed with the thoughts of Colby outside her door, and she felt relief that they could stop playing detective and let the police do their job.

They pulled up to the clinic, and Juniper cut the engine. The parking lot was empty, and the windows to the lobby were dark.

"I've only got my front door key," she said.

"Oh, I've got the one to the back door," Maggie said.

"Then let's pull around there. Easy in and easy out. I know you need to get home. You've got two rambunctious boys to rein in for bed."

Juniper was right about that. She'd seen several text messages pop up from Colby that she hadn't been able to answer. Her hands were full with the pug, and since the dog wasn't fighting her, she was afraid to move.

Juniper drove around to the back and parked.

"I'll come around and open the door," she said.

She did and Maggie climbed out, cradling Cinder close to her. She no longer cared that the dog smelled like death—she was a living creature who needed to feel safe.

"Can you lock the door? I'm leaving my purse and my phone," Maggie said. She wanted to keep as still as possible for the dog, without reaching and juggling for things.

Woodrow hopped out first. Maggie jumped when Juniper slammed the door shut behind them and sounded the horn with the lock function.

"What the hell?" Juniper stopped walking midstride.

Maggie did too.

The back door to the clinic appeared to have been taken off the hinges. It sat neatly leaned up against the building, as though someone had set it aside and planned to come back to it.

"Do you think Starr did that?" Maggie said, bewildered.

"No way. He wouldn't leave it like that. Someone else must have done it. But why wouldn't they have just kicked the door in? Why take it off in such a precise manner?"

Maggie thought of the rows of stems in her flower box, their heads neatly removed instead of haphazardly torn off.

Woodrow growled, deep in his throat.

A warning.

They were less than ten feet from the open door, but with only one small light usually left on in the back, they couldn't see inside.

Maggie felt invisible cold fingers trailing down her spine. She backed up, cradling Cinder closer. "Woodrow senses something, Juniper. Let's get back in the car. Woodrow, heel."

He growled louder, and in the beam of the lone parking lot light, she could see the hair standing up on his back. "Woodrow, heel! Now."

For the first time since she'd adopted him, he didn't obey. Instead he charged into the door opening at a full bark.

"Someone's in there," Juniper said. "Come on, Maggie. This is unsafe. I'm calling the police."

Maggie looked from Juniper to the door of the clinic. She called for Woodrow again, but he didn't come out. He'd gone silent, and that terrified her.

Quickly, before Juniper could react, Maggie shoved Cinder into her arms, then turned and ran for the door.

"Wait!" Juniper yelled.

"I'm not leaving Woodrow in there alone," Maggie shouted back. She hesitated for just a second when she reached the door, knowing that what she was doing was careless, but he was more than a dog to her.

Woodrow was family.

She took a deep breath and barreled through.

Chapter Twenty-Four

As soon as Maggie was through the door, she could see why Woodrow had gone silent. He was lying on his side, and a man stood over him, his booted foot holding him down by his throat. Other than his feet twitching, Woodrow seemed paralyzed there, his eyes bulging and pouring tears as he waited for release—and oxygen.

The man turned when he heard Maggie but didn't release his hold on her dog.

Woodrow whined, his eyes rolling up until he found hers.

Maggie saw red. "Let him go, you son of a bitch," she said, stopping just inside the door. It was Andrews, and he looked ragged. And just as dangerous as he had the last day she'd seen him before they'd dragged him off to prison.

"Margaret Ann Dalton," he said, smiling eerily. "I thought I was just going to cause a little ruckus in here. Didn't know I was going to be rewarded with the honor of your company."

"Fuck you," she seethed. "Give me my dog."

"Your mangy mutt bit me," he said.

Maggie saw now that his hand was bloody, and she wondered how the idiot had turned the tables and gotten Woodrow down. Then she saw he held a spray bottle in his other hand.

It was the bleach mixture they used to clean out the parvo cages. Another look told her that the scumbag had sprayed it in Woodrow's eyes.

She looked around, trying to see what she could use as a weapon. Their back room looked like a tornado had run through it. Contradictory to the way Andrews had neatly removed the back door, he'd obviously lost control inside. Cabinets were pried open and contents strewn about, once-sanitized surgical tools littered the tiled floors, and a few cats wandered around. One still had the remnants of an IV in his leg and wasn't even supposed to be walking yet.

Old Man Carlson's Congo African gray parrot they were boarding was loose too. It perched on the highest cabinet and looked distressed. Carlson would be devastated if anything happened to his bird. He'd told Maggie that it'd been his best friend for more than fifteen years.

She couldn't take all that in right now. Her first goal was to get Woodrow free. She prayed that Juniper already had the police on the way before it was too late for her dog. She needed to keep Andrews talking.

"How did you know I work here?"

He scowled, his face darkening. "Do you think I didn't notice how you were down there on the beach flaunting your body to the good doc? I saw how he looked at you. How you *wanted* him to look at you. You two were a little obvious, don't you think? And he's a bit forward for my liking, thinking he can just swoop in and take my place."

"You've been following me," she said.

He shrugged, shifting his weight, and Woodrow yelped. At least Andrews dropped the spray bottle then, but Maggie could still see the madness glittering in his eyes.

"I mean it, you'd better not hurt him," Maggie bellowed.

"Where's your chivalrous doctor now?" he asked, pushing his foot a little deeper.

She changed her tone. "Listen, Andrews. You don't need to hurt my dog. If you let him go, I'll leave here with you."

He was considering her words. She could see the emotions play over his face, and she prayed he fell for it.

"Bullshit. You're a liar," he said. "But I see he's your soft spot. What if I just choke the life out of him and make you watch? Do you know how much hell I've gone through in that prison cell? The inmates are disgusting pigs."

"I'll bet they are. You shouldn't go back there, Martin. You're much too sophisticated a man to rot with the likes of criminals," she said, taking one step closer. "Martin, let him go and I'll send him out the door. But I'll stay. You don't have to chase me anymore. We can finally be together."

"Why would you even say that?" he said, suddenly uncertain at the sound of her using his first name.

"Because your commitment shows that you're serious about me. No one has ever put this much effort into pursuing me."

"But you sent me to jail."

"Technically, I didn't. The state put you in jail."

He looked angry again. "Because of you!"

She spoke calmly. Her voice soft and cajoling. "I know, and I'm sorry about that. I didn't know how much you really liked me. I had to put you to the test. God, Martin, you broke out of prison to be with me. That's a big deal."

When he didn't respond, she slowly bridged the distance between them and dropped to the floor at Woodrow's side. Now that she was so close, she could see the panic in his big brown eyes, and she began sobbing, pulling at Andrews's foot to take the pressure off his throat.

"Please," she begged. "Just let him go."

"Don't cry, Maggie," Andrews said, lifting his foot and stepping back.

Woodrow popped up as though he had a string attached to his head. He took ragged breaths and struggled to get to his feet. He looked confused but immediately started to growl, the hair on his neck standing at attention as he tried to lunge at Andrews.

"No, Woodrow," Maggie said, holding him around his neck. She was afraid the sudden rush of air might make him faint. "Stay, boy. Please, stay."

"My hand is bleeding," Andrews said. "This is a clinic. Where're the damn bandages? Get me something for pain too."

Maggie stood, keeping her hand firmly on Woodrow's collar. "Listen. My friend is outside. I'm going to send Woodrow out there and tell her to take him home. Then I'll clean up your hand and find you something for the pain."

"What friend?" he demanded, his eyes darting to the door.

"It's the front desk receptionist. She's harmless. I swear, I'll just send Woodrow out there and I'll come right back. I'm not doing anything for you if you don't let her take him."

He came closer, and she shrank into herself. Woodrow growled and tried to lunge again, but Maggie held on. He panted hard and fast.

"And you won't run?" Andrews asked, kicking at Woodrow but missing.

She shook her head. But she had every intention of trying. "Of course not."

"Fine," he said, pushing her toward the open door. Just before she got there, Andrews looped his hand in the back of her waistband. "I'm making sure you don't go anywhere."

Frustration poured over Maggie. He wasn't going to let her go that easily. But at least she could make sure Woodrow was safe. Straining against the hold he had on her clothes, she looked out but couldn't see Juniper. The car was still there, and she hoped her friend was too. She practically had to drag Woodrow, but when she was just about to push him out the opening, she heard someone.

"Maggie, is that you? Are you okay?"

It was Juniper, and she sounded like she was crying. The sound was coming from behind the car.

Andrews tightened his grasp on her waistband, and her skin crawled at his touch. She wanted to run, but there was no way now.

"I'm good. Juniper, I want you to take Woodrow on home for me. And take care of Cinder until tomorrow. I'm going to stay here and visit with an old friend." She tried to keep her voice from cracking, but at the last minute, it broke off.

There was silence and she could just imagine Juniper thinking, trying to figure out what Maggie's plan was. She would know immediately who the *old friend* was.

"Are you coming?" Maggie called out. "Please, Juniper. Come get him."

She saw a shadow emerge from behind the car and heard Juniper's shoes slapping the pavement slowly. Finally they were a foot apart and she felt a hand cover hers, then slip under Woodrow's collar.

Maggie nudged him over to her.

"Please wash out his eyes," she said. "He was sprayed with bleach water."

Juniper put her hand over Maggie's and clutched it tightly. They both held Woodrow between them. Andrews kept hidden around the inside of the doorframe but kept up his secure hold.

"Just run, Maggie," Juniper whispered.

Andrews heard and jerked Maggie backward so hard that she instantly let go of Woodrow and fell on the floor, an excruciating pain hitting her tailbone and traveling up her spine.

"Take Woodrow, Juniper!"

"Stupid cunt. Who does she think she is?" Andrews spat out above her.

Maggie could hear Woodrow whining and straining to get back to her, but thankfully she also heard shoes slapping on the pavement again. Then a car door open, pause, and slam.

They were safe. At least Andrews couldn't kill her dog.

Now Maggie just had to figure out how to get herself out alive. Andrews grabbed her shirt and dragged her backward; then she heard the first siren.

Chapter Twenty-Five

Quinn set her pen down and leaned her head back. Her neck hurt. It was late and she was tired, but somehow the stars were shining down on her, and she'd finally finished confirming every task to make David and Julianne's vow renewal happen without a hitch.

She considered for the millionth time that day how surreal it was that if things hadn't changed drastically for her when she'd come to Maui a year before, it might be her own wedding she was planning, instead of the vow renewal for her favorite guests.

One thing she'd always done well was compartmentalize, but in this case it was proving to be more difficult than usual. It wasn't that she had any second thoughts about leaving her fiancé to pursue a different life, but she had been planning her own wedding since she was a small girl, and letting go of that dream had been harder than letting go of the relationship.

Still, she had a job to do and she wanted it to be perfect.

The flowers would be delivered in the morning, and the housekeepers were going to weave them into delicate garland leis. She'd secured a white carpet to lead up to a flower-covered arbor, and the rep said it would be wheelchair friendly, just in case. Liam had arranged a local Hawaiian band to play soft music off in the corner, and best of all she'd gotten a promise that one of the local *kahunas* would be there to officiate.

Just like she'd promised, the ceremony would be simple but elegant. And afterward there would be an intimate reception. David had asked her to invite some family members and friends so that it felt celebratory. He said Julianne loved people and would be pleased.

Quinn and the chef had worked out a proper menu, and it included *kalua* pig, the traditional roasted pork with Hawaiian sauces. There'd be plenty of fruit, too, in case Julianne didn't feel like eating anything heavy.

For dessert, she'd called the first friend she'd made in Maui. Maria made the best cookies and had branched out into other things now. She was going to put together a special cake.

Quinn put Jules on the task of rounding everyone up, though whether she could manage getting Kira on board was still in question. Secretly, Quinn was glad for a reason to bring everyone together, as it might be the last special event she would attend with her family before she headed off to Montana. She'd called Helen that morning and insisted she was going forward with her relocation plans and taking the opportunity in Montana. It would be the best way to settle things down and at least try to give her family some semblance of peace.

Liam would know tonight, after everyone left. He'd already told her he was staying over, but Quinn had a feeling that after their talk, he might change his mind.

That thought brought a whole new wave of fatigue over her. While David and Julianne held a private second honeymoon, more than likely Quinn would be sleeping alone.

As for the inn, it pained her to leave her baby, but she'd made two appointments with possible candidates to take her place. First interviews would be video chats; then if they passed that, she'd meet them in person. Both candidates knew this was on a fast track and had agreed to drop everything for the opportunity.

Then she'd be headed to Montana. She wondered how rough the winters would be. Maybe she could finally learn how to ride a horse. She forced herself to think about this as an opportunity and not a tragedy.

A soft knock on the door brought her out of her thoughts about cowboy country, and Quinn rose and crossed the room.

"Who is it?" She leaned against the door, glad she hadn't yet taken a shower and climbed into pajamas. She might look like an exhausted mess, but at least she was dressed.

When no one answered, she called out again. "Jonah?" Her brother was usually the only one who bothered her in the evening. He hated phones and, more times than not, just showed up if he needed to talk to her.

"It's Ano," a voice said.

"Who?"

"Liam's father."

Quinn opened the door slowly, unable to keep the look of shock from her face when she saw the man standing there. Liam had said he rarely ever left his land, so what was he doing coming all the way to Hana to talk to her?

"Is Liam all right?"

He nodded. "Everything is fine. I would just like to talk to you, if you don't mind."

She was still trying to figure out how he knew which room to find her in when she heard a familiar voice.

"Would you rather talk to him in the lobby? Or on the patio?" Jonah stepped out from the shadow. "Or I can stay."

"What are you doing here?" Quinn said. At least now she knew how the man had found her room. She was going to have a talk with Jonah.

"I found him walking around the hotel grounds," Jonah said.

"I was trying to get up the nerve to come ask for you," Ano said.

"Please, come in." Quinn held the door open. She didn't ask Jonah what *he* was doing walking around the grounds after dark, but she sure would later.

Ano came in and took a seat at the small dining table, but Jonah hesitated.

"He and I had a long talk, and if I didn't think this was important, I wouldn't have brought him to you," Jonah said, keeping his voice low. "He's a good man, Quinn."

"You don't know everything about him, but I'll let him talk," Quinn said. His story wasn't hers to share, even with her own brother.

"He's told me a lot. I don't need to stay unless you just want me to."

Quinn hesitated. "No, I'll be fine."

Jonah nodded, then disappeared down the hall, as quiet as he'd come.

"Does Liam know you're here?" she asked, taking a seat across from Ano.

"No, he doesn't."

"This sounds serious," Quinn said. "Can I get you something to drink?"

"A glass of water would be appreciated."

Quinn remembered that he didn't drink alcohol and was glad she hadn't mentioned it. She rose and made them both a tall glass of ice water.

She took them to the table and set them down, then sat.

"Okay, I'm ready."

Ano laughed softly. "You act like I'm here to give you bad news."

Her face flushed red.

"I'm not really sure why you're here."

"Can I tell you a story?" he asked.

She nodded and he took a sip of water, then began.

"Many years ago when my sons were younger, I made a decision that turned out to be tragic. It affected many lives—the hardest ones hit were strangers. However, my own family suffered as well."

Quinn kept her face expressionless. She'd never tell him that she already knew his deepest shame.

"Everything in me was sorry for what I had done, but remorse isn't enough. I felt I should be punished further. So it took me some time, but I finally decided to stay in the place that you visited and not allow myself to partake in the joys of fatherhood. It hurt my sons. And it hurt me. What father doesn't want to teach his sons how to be a man?"

His eyes glistened and his voice took on a new thickness, yet he continued.

"Liam took it the hardest. He visited me, begged me to come down and join the family again. I told him maybe one day. That's how our exchange went for many years until he stopped asking. During those years, he stepped into a role that was far too mature for him. I wanted to stop it, but I just couldn't come back. Liam slowly took on every responsibility that a man of the house would."

Quinn's heart felt sad for the boy that Liam lost too fast in his decision to fill the empty hole his father left.

"He took care of maintenance on the house, the car, and even keeping the yard clean and manicured. He was gifted with his hands but was also smart. With his grades, he could've gone on to college. But instead he worked a job after school, helping a local carpenter on projects, learning skills that even I could not teach him. When he graduated high school, he worked full-time and still took care of the home, never considering leaving his mother alone to pursue his own life."

"Why are you telling me this?" Quinn finally asked. It wasn't her story, but it brought her pain as though it were. She didn't want to hear any more about how much Liam had given up to help his father find his penance.

"I'm telling you because he has never brought a woman up to see me. And I've never seen the look in his eyes that he had when he looked at you."

Quinn blushed.

"He's a very caring man," she said, struggling for the right thing to say to a man she barely knew. "He's special."

"Yes, he is. More than you can imagine. I've been a horrible father and husband. I was blinded by shame and didn't see that my penance was also theirs, for a crime they didn't commit."

"I'm sorry, but I agree," Quinn said softly. It wasn't fair, and she wouldn't pretend like she understood. Liam deserved more than that from her.

"My wife has also seen how Liam looks at you," he said. "And she came to see me yesterday. She told me how my absence has hurt her over the years and how lonely she has been in her bed at night. She doesn't want that for Liam."

"I can't imagine any mother would want that for a son," Quinn said.

He nodded. "You know, marriage isn't really about the physical things. It's about having a friend for life. Someone you can turn to when you feel everyone else has let you down. Someone who will back you up even when you are wrong. My wife, she's done that for me. Even when she has turned to her empty bed year after year, cold and lonely, she has never spoken to me in anger."

"She talks about you fondly," Quinn said. That much was true. She'd been there many times when the woman had reminisced about the old days, before one fateful night had taken her husband from her side. She only spoke about him in affectionate terms.

"Yesterday was the first time that she told me everything she has felt. She bared her soul to me, and I thought that I would die right there in front of her, the pain in my heart was so bad. I'm telling you now, this is the truth, I knelt before her and I cried like I've not cried in all these decades of feeling alone and guilty. She let me cry, and she patted my head. But she said she couldn't forgive me."

Quinn was taken aback. Liam's mother was not the type to hold a grudge.

"She said that there's still time for us to share our golden years. To be together to welcome grandchildren and watch sunsets over the ocean. To enjoy the bounty that Maui has given us."

"And you rejected her," Quinn said, feeling hollow as she traced the rim of her now-empty water glass.

"I did not."

She looked up in time to see one tear slide down his face.

"She convinced me that continuing to dwell on what I did in the past is defining who I am now. But I know I'm not that same man. So I've decided to forgive myself."

"I'm glad to hear that."

He smiled. "My wife is going to join me at my property. She's going to make that empty house a home. Not only for us, but for all the generations to come. It will be a place to build new memories. Happy ones that hopefully will help heal the sad ones."

"That's wonderful, Ano," Quinn said.

He smiled slowly. "It is. But I came here to tell you because I know how Liam feels about you."

"I don't understand."

"Liam wasn't totally yours before. But you need to know, he is free now. It is time for him to stop feeling responsible for his mother's well-being. I'm strong and healthy, with many good years ahead of me. I'll spend the rest of our lives making sure she knows she is the most important thing to me in this world. Not the canoes and not the penance I've been seeking, but her. My punishment is over, and I'm just glad she made me realize it before it was too late."

Quinn was crying now.

Not only for Liam's mother, but for him. What a burden would be released from his shoulders. Not that he didn't want to take care of his mother, but he knew there were the lonely parts of her that he just couldn't fill. And that knowledge grieved him.

She also cried because it was too late for her.

Montana was the best option for her in order to keep her family's privacy intact.

Her phone rang before she could form a response to Ano's declaration.

"Excuse me," she said, reaching to rub away a wayward tear as she picked up her phone.

It was from a number she didn't recognize. She sent it to voice mail, and immediately they called back. She knew it could be a reporter, but something felt weird and she answered. "Hello?"

"Quinn?"

"Who is this?"

"It's Colby. Have you heard from Maggie? She was supposed to be home an hour ago, and she's not answering her phone."

"No, I haven't," she said, then heard a pounding at the door. "Hold on, Colby. Someone's at the door. Maybe it's her."

She went to the door and opened it to find Jonah there again. This time he looked alarmed. He looked around and saw that Ano was still there.

"I'm really sorry to interrupt, but Quinn, have you heard the news at all this evening?"

"No, what's going on?"

"I'm not sure, but there's some kind of standoff going on down at the vet's office that Maggie works at. Maui PD has it surrounded."

Quinn looked at the phone she still held in her hand. She could hear Colby, his voice frantic as he demanded to know what it was that Jonah had said about Maggie.

She handed the phone over to Jonah because her hands were shaking badly. She didn't trust her voice either. Something told her that Maggie was in that building.

And she wasn't alone.

Chapter Twenty-Six

Maggie scooted back against the wall and watched Andrews pace back and forth, ranting about the sirens that were getting louder. Above him the parrot squawked, stuck on his favorite phrase.

"Here we go. Here we go," it repeated, a mantra that felt too ironic at the moment.

Andrews picked up a stainless-steel tool tray and threw it at him but missed the bird. It jumped, squawking louder as it flapped its wings, then settled a little higher.

Maggie could see the lights flickering around the open door, and it sounded like dozens of cars screeching to a stop, one after another. Was the entire Maui police force coming to her aid?

That was good and bad. She hoped their arrival didn't push Andrews over the edge before she could figure out what to do. She considered trying to make a run for it, but she knew he'd probably overtake her before she could even get to the door. He'd already proved he was strong and had fast reflexes. She needed to be strategic and plan an escape that would work.

"She called them, didn't she? Didn't she?" he screamed. He was holding his bloody hand to his chest, obviously in pain.

"I—I don't think so. I think a silent alarm was activated when you took the door off." Maggie knew there wasn't an alarm system, but she was terrified that Andrews might go after Juniper, who no doubt was probably sitting in her car with Cinder and Woodrow, too stubborn to leave.

He stopped and stared at the door. Maggie saw the sweat dripping from his face. He was losing it. And fast.

She thought about Charlie. He'd hugged her legs that morning, so happy that his dad was there. He looked like he was just bursting with joy. It was bedtime now, and she wondered if Colby had gotten him to sleep. She forgot to tell him that Charlie likes his night water in his turtle cup with two ice cubes.

Her throat choked up. Would she ever get to see that smile again? Feel those warm, chubby arms around her and listen to him call her mama? And Colby. How would he be as a single dad? Would he find a good woman right away to step in and be a mother, to replace her?

"What do you want to do?" she asked, trying to divert herself from thinking about Charlie, Colby, and all the possible outcomes of her current living nightmare. That was a road to despair.

"We have to get another room," he said finally, coming at her and holding his good hand out. "Come with me."

Woodrow was safe, but Maggie knew to save herself, she'd have to keep up the game. She didn't like to think that Andrews was crazy enough to really hurt her, but who ever knew what was going on in someone's head? Especially someone like him.

"Yes, and I've got to clean up that nasty bite."

She took his hand, and he pulled her to her feet. His fingers were cold and clammy, and Maggie felt like she would be sick. She let go as soon as she could, but when she looked at him, he had that strange grin on his face again.

He liked her touch.

His made her shudder.

"Let's go in the surgical room. That's where the bandages are," Maggie said. She led him there and he closed the door behind them, then locked it.

When Maggie heard the click, she flinched. It would make her escape that much harder, but it wasn't hopeless yet. She was slowly forming a plan. She led him over to one of the surgery tables where a crash cart was parked nearby.

"Sit up here," she gestured.

He looked around suspiciously but followed her direction.

"You better know what you're doing," he mumbled.

"Yeah, I agree." She hoped she knew what she was doing—more than he knew.

While sirens screamed outside the building, Maggie worked on cleaning and bandaging Andrews's hand.

"We can't have a vicious dog," he said, staring down at the bloody cotton balls.

Maggie felt like screaming at him that there was no *we*, but she remained calm. "What kind of dog would you like to have?"

"A Lab. I had one when I was a kid, and he was my best friend."

She dabbed some antibiotic on his wound. "What was his name?"

"*Diablo.*"

"Oh, why call him a devil if he wasn't vicious?"

He shrugged. "My dad gave him the name. I don't know why. He never liked him."

"How can someone not like a Lab?" Maggie asked as she started rolling the bandage around his hand. "They're eighty pounds of pure affection."

"I don't know. That's what I asked him after he put a bullet in his head for pissing on his truck tires."

Maggie jumped at his words and put too much pressure on the wrap. He cursed, and from behind him he pulled out a scalpel that must've been tucked in his back pocket.

"What the hell are you trying to do, Maggie?" he demanded, waving the blade in front of her face.

"I'm sorry. I didn't mean to hurt you. The story about your father startled me."

She backed up a step.

He studied her face, then lowered the blade to hold it beside his leg.

"Just hurry. It fucking burns like fire," Andrews said, rolling his eyes up to the ceiling as he strained to remain in place.

"I've got access to morphine," she said, still shaken up at the sight of him wielding a scalpel. One swipe and he could've slit her throat. "Just let me finish this up. And it's going to need a shot of antibiotics or you might risk infection. I can do that here."

Maggie fumbled through the crash cart, looking for what she needed. Her eyes fell on the bottle of antibiotics, then behind it, another bottle. She picked up a clean syringe and the antibiotic.

"Let me see it," Andrews demanded. "I don't trust you."

She handed over the bottle and he read it, then handed it back.

"Doxycycline. Isn't that what they give humans?"

She nodded, then shook the bottle, uncapped the needle, and stuck it through. She held the bottle upside down, letting it fill the syringe to the halfway mark. "Many human medications are dog friendly. Just have to do it in smaller doses."

She stopped and sighed impatiently. "That bottle didn't have enough. I'm going to have to uncap another."

She turned, blocking his view of the crash cart. Quickly, before he could ask questions, she picked up another small bottle and clean syringe, working faster than she thought possible as she filled it, then set them aside and grabbed the original syringe.

She turned back to Andrews and he was cradling his hand against his chest.

"Let me see," she said.

He put it out for her and she took it, feeling revulsion again as she touched him.

She'd done a good job cleaning it up, but Maggie was a little surprised at the damage Woodrow had inflicted. The puncture wounds were deep even if they wouldn't require stitches.

She mentally gave Woodrow an *attaboy*. She knew her dog and she could bet that right now, he was having a fit because he couldn't get in there to protect her. But he was where he needed to be, safe from the possibility of more abuse. That was the downside of falling in love with your pets. You'd risk your life for theirs without even blinking an eye because you knew they'd do the same.

Woodrow had, in fact.

"The antibiotics aren't pleasant going in, but my son's pediatrician taught him a trick."

"I'm not a toddler," Andrews said. He looked doubtful, but Maggie was banking on the average man's big fear of pain.

"If you look away, it doesn't hurt nearly as much. I swear, it works."

He hesitated, then turned his head.

As soon as his gaze was averted, Maggie reached around for the second syringe.

"What are you doing?" Andrews demanded.

"Nothing," she said innocently. "Don't look."

He scared her so badly that her hands shook.

Suddenly the clinic phone rang, and Andrews turned to look.

Quickly, she put the syringe in her back pocket and said a prayer she wouldn't break it, then picked up the original one.

The second ring sounded even shriller than the first.

She looked at the phone on the wall and saw the light blinking.

"Don't get it," Andrews warned. "It's them. I know it."

"But they might want to negotiate," she said.

"There's nothing I want from them other than to get out of here with you."

He stared her down until she lowered her eyes.

"And you know they aren't going to allow that," he finished. "Give me something for this pain so I can think clearly."

The phone stopped ringing. Then began again.

"Damn it," Andrews yelled, slamming his good fist on the examining table. "They need to stop! My head is killing me!"

"What about transportation?" Maggie said. She needed to hear a voice. Any voice other than Andrews's. "We need a way out of here. I can tell them that."

He hesitated, then nodded. "Tell them to bring a helicopter. With a full tank."

Maggie picked up the phone.

"Hello?"

"Miss Dalton, this is Detective Kamaka. I've talked to your friends. Say yes if you are in there with Andrews."

"Yes," Maggie said. She looked up at Andrews, and he gestured for her to hurry up. "We need transportation. He wants a helicopter with a full tank."

She hated using the word *we*, as it sounded like they were together, but she had to keep him convinced she was on his side.

"Tell him that's going to take some time. The precinct doesn't have one, and we'll have to find someone to lend theirs willingly."

"Just do it," she said, suddenly remembering where she'd heard his name. He was the detective who'd talked to Quinn and wanted to close her case.

"Say yes if he is armed," the detective said.

"Yes," Maggie replied, still seeing the glint of the scalpel Andrews held in his free hand. After so many years of complaining about her freckles, she decided right then and there that if she walked out with all of them intact, she'd praise every single one.

"Say yes if he is alone."

"Yes!" Maggie could see Andrews getting suspicious.

"Ask him if there's anything we can get to make you both more comfortable while you wait for the helicopter," the detective said.

Maggie held the phone to her shoulder and looked at Andrews. "He wants to know if we want anything else. It's going to take some time for the helicopter."

Andrews shook his head.

"I haven't had dinner," Maggie said softly. She hoped that would help humanize her in his eyes even more.

He waved the scalpel again. "Then get something. I don't care. Wait—a bottle of fine wine. And two glasses."

Maggie repeated his request into the phone and added a small pizza. She doubted she'd be able to eat anything, but in every hostage scene she had ever seen, they called in pizza. Maybe that was how someone from the outside slipped in a vital tool she'd need to get herself out of this hell.

"Hang up," Andrews said.

She really, really didn't want to hang up the phone. The detective that she'd once wanted to punch in the throat for dogging her best friend was now her lifeline.

Maggie finally placed the phone back on the wall receiver and turned back around. Andrews was using his good hand to cradle his bad one around the wrist. His face was contorted into a grimace. For a man who thought he was big and tough enough to stalk someone, he sure didn't take pain well.

The scalpel was on his lap.

"Get me something for pain," he said.

"I may not be able to get you anything strong enough," she said. "The controlled substances are in the locked closet, behind another locked door, and then in a locked box. Only the doctor and his mother have the key."

"You said you had morphine."

"We do, but I forgot it's locked up. The DEA requires it."

He looked like he might put his fist through the wall. Through gritted teeth, he told her to show him to the closet.

Maggie took him to it, and immediately, Andrews eyed the dead bolt, then tried to pull the door. It didn't budge. He blasted every curse word in the book as he pummeled it with punches and kicks, only to stop when he was out of breath and his hair was plastered down with sweat.

She could see the scalpel was tucked in his back pocket again, but she didn't trust herself to grab it and back away fast enough for him not to take it from her. Having her skin sliced open didn't sound like a fun way to end the evening, so she waited, keeping her back pocket out of view.

He turned to her and glared. "You know where the key is, don't you?"

"No, I don't!"

He punched the wall with his good hand. "I'm in a *fucking* clinic, and I can't get drugs? This can't be happening."

The phone rang again.

"Don't answer it!" Andrews shouted.

"It might be important." Maggie really wanted to talk to the detective again. Andrews was looking crazier by the minute. She had a thought. "Were you on medication in jail, Martin?"

He sank down to sit on the floor in front of the closet, his hands over his ears. When the phone stopped ringing, he put them down and looked up.

"Yeah, on some mental health bullshit. It was supposed to calm me down, but all it did was make me sleep. And then came the nightmares."

"You haven't had any medication since you got out?"

He shook his head. "Nope. Why? You think I'm hearing voices telling me to kill you?"

She stared at him. He didn't sound like he was kidding.

"I hope not. I was asking because I'm sure that whatever you were taking, you probably aren't feeling well going off of it cold turkey." She could only imagine what they were treating him for. Bipolar disorder? Schizophrenia? The possibilities were endless.

His confession upped the ante for her. Quite a bit, actually. Maybe he was in as much mental pain as physical, and that was making him more unhinged. She had to be careful.

"Can I call my son?" she asked, feeling very afraid now.

"For what? You changing your mind? What happened to us getting out of this together?" He looked at her with such venom, it amazed her that he had an infatuation with her at all. If looks could kill, she'd already be dead.

"No, not at all. I'd just like to tell him goodbye." She didn't add that in a way, that was the truth. If she didn't make it out of there alive, she wanted to hear his voice and tell him she loved him one more time.

"You'll have more kids," he said, then leered at her, his eyebrows raised. "*We* can have our own son. Daughter, too, if you want one. So don't go getting all morbid with wanting to say your goodbyes."

Maggie cringed at the thought of making a baby with Andrews, but she didn't let him see her revulsion. She needed him to believe she wanted to be with him, in every way possible.

Then she thought of Colby. There were a few things she'd like to say to him, too, but nothing that could be said in front of Andrews that wouldn't make him react in a jealous rage.

The phone rang again.

"I know they don't have the damn helicopter yet," Andrews mumbled. "And I'm not up for chitchat."

"I can tell them we need the keys to the drug cabinet," Maggie said quickly, before he could scream at her not to answer.

He nodded. "Now you're thinking."

She picked up the phone. "We need the keys to the controlled substance closet. Get Starr here stat."

261

"Miss Dalton, we can't very well hand over keys that would enable an already-deranged man to further complicate things with heavy drugs. Surely you understand?"

Maggie repeated it to Andrews and he stood, slowly coming at her.

She backed away, but he caught her and slipped behind her, bringing the scalpel to her neck. He took the phone with the other hand.

"Understand this," he shouted into the receiver. "Send those fucking keys in with the pizza, or I'll send her out in a bag. And you've got an hour to find a helicopter."

"He's got a knife to my throat!" Maggie yelled.

Andrews slammed the phone down, then dropped the scalpel to his side. He grinned at Maggie.

She was afraid and that pissed her off, because she hated to show fear.

"They bought it, didn't they? Good job, Maggie."

Now she dropped down to the floor, her back to the closet. It wasn't really planned, but her legs would no longer hold her up. Then the tears came again.

Chapter Twenty-Seven

Quinn wiped at the tears that ran down her face. Liam pulled her in closer. They leaned against her Jeep, and Colby paced the six feet in front of it. The police wouldn't let them any nearer, and he was about to give himself a stroke.

He let out a litany of profanity and kicked his boot across the ground, sending up a trail of gravel. He still hadn't calmed down from being restrained at the yellow line when he'd tried to get to the back of the clinic. No one cared that he was Maggie's child's father. They'd told him to either get off the property or go to jail.

Liam had talked him into the former, pushing him back until they returned to the Jeep, but it wasn't easy and took a lot of manhandling.

"Colby, please," Quinn said. "Maggie is getting out of there, and when she does, she'll need you. What good will you be if you're sitting in a jail cell right beside Andrews?"

He stopped and bent over, his hands on his knees. "I'm losing it. I swear to God if I could just get in there . . ." He trailed off. Then he looked at the Jeep where Woodrow sat alert on the seat.

Quinn could see Charlie in Colby's face as he fought through his emotions.

Thankfully their curious boy was still sound asleep and didn't know that his mother was in danger. She'd picked up Rosa and brought her to stay with him, and Liam had called and arranged for a police officer to stand guard outside the apartment door. She had to give it to the young woman, Rosa was obviously frightened, but she'd still agreed to stay with Charlie as long as it took. Quinn prayed the ordeal would get under control and be over fast.

On their way to the clinic, Liam and Quinn had taken turns filling Colby in on Martin Andrews and how he'd made Maggie's life hell. Understandably, Colby had at first been furious at Maggie for keeping it from him, but now his anger was aimed directly at the faceless man who held Maggie against her will just yards away.

"This is killing me," Colby said, throwing his arms up and then letting them drop to his sides again. "I need to do something!"

"Let the professionals do their job," Liam said. "They'll get her out."

"Hell, they probably don't even have a hostage negotiator on this little piece of shit island," Colby said.

Quinn shushed him up. It wouldn't do for any of the native Hawaiians to hear him talk about their town that way.

Colby shook his head again, then restarted his pacing. Even Quinn could feel the pent-up anger and energy about to explode from his body.

She felt the same inside, but acting it out wouldn't make things any better. It was frustrating not to know what was happening. They'd had to park across the street and didn't even have a good line of sight to the back of the clinic. Gawkers were lined up as close as they could get, most of them not even knowing what was going on, other than that it was a hostage situation.

Even that was leaked from a detective's wife on Facebook and had spread through social media and now the crowd. Quinn hoped he lost his job for that slip. Anything could set Andrews off. A loud crowd. Noise. Who knew what he would do if the wrong thing traveled back to him?

She wished they'd all go home.

Juniper had found Quinn and crossed the line to bring her Woodrow and fill her in with what information she knew, but then she'd gone back to the clinic in case they needed to ask her more questions.

"Quinn," someone called out.

Speaking of the little devil, Juniper was making her way across the street again.

"What's going on?" She, Liam, and Colby faced Juniper, leaning in to hear what she had to say.

"He asked for a helicopter, but he'll never get it. Maggie asked for pizza and wine," Juniper said.

"Pizza and wine?" Colby said. "What the fuck is this? Some kind of psycho date? The police need to go in and get her, right now. No more games!"

"Stop, Colby," Quinn said, putting her hand on his arm. "Maggie must have a plan. Let Juniper talk."

Juniper was out of breath. She gave Colby a nasty look but continued.

"They're trying to make him think they're open to his requests. It's called negotiation. He also wanted the keys to the closet with the controlled substances."

"Damn drug addict," Colby muttered.

"Maybe not," Liam said. "Didn't you say that Woodrow came out with blood on his muzzle? Maybe the guy is hurt and in pain."

"That's what they think," Juniper said. "They called in Starr, and he gave his permission if it's going to help keep Maggie safe."

"Wait," Colby interrupted. "Starr? Isn't that the vet? Why is he allowed to be over there when I'm standing out here with nosy neighbors?"

"I own the clinic," said a voice coming around the Jeep. "I'm Joe Starr. You must be Colby."

Quinn stood back and let Joe into their circle.

He and Colby faced off.

"I was just telling them that he wants a helicopter, and Maggie asked for food and wine," Juniper said.

"That's right. And it's buying us time to let his anger fizzle out a little. I was able to bring the floor plans, and they know the layout in there now. I overheard them talking about having the SWAT team in place in case they need it."

Quinn cringed. "A team could end up getting her hurt, couldn't it?"

Joe didn't answer.

"What the hell was she doing out after work looking for strays anyway?" Colby asked, looking at Joe. "If she hadn't come back here, she wouldn't be in this mess."

"Technically, she wasn't supposed to be with me," Juniper said, shrugging. "Not his fault."

"Colby," Quinn said. "Stop it."

Joe held his hand up. "No, he's right. I take full responsibility. I can't say how sorry I am that all this has happened. Maggie is a good woman. She doesn't deserve this."

Quinn couldn't agree more.

"Look," Joe continued, keeping his voice calm, "I know we're all tense here, and Colby, you have more reason to be than anyone. Why don't you come over there with me?"

"We tried. They won't let us anywhere near the building," Liam said.

"They will if you're with me," Joe said. He looked at Colby. "I'm thinking that Maggie needs your face to be the first one she sees when she comes out of there."

Quinn could see Colby falter, unsure how to respond to Joe's kindness.

"And she *is* coming out of there," Joe said, reaching out, putting a hand on Colby's shoulder, and squeezing it.

Colby's Adam's apple bobbed up and down, and Quinn could tell he was swallowing back a lot of emotion. To get past the moment, she turned to Juniper. "What did they decide? About the keys?"

"They said they're working on it," she replied.

Colby pulled away from Joe and clutched his head again, running his fingers through his hair until he looked like a mad scientist. "Holy shit. I can't believe this is happening. Why in the hell did she have to come here to this place?"

"Andrews would've tracked her down on the mainland too," Quinn said. "This guy was relentless. Letting the wrong man out of prison was just his lucky break."

"If she had just told me this has been happening," Colby said. "I would've made it stop before it got this far. The bastard wouldn't have been so lucky to even make it to prison."

"And I would've made sure we had more safety precautions in place," Joe said.

"Don't feel too bad, guys. She didn't even confide in her brothers," Quinn said. "The only one who knew was her mom, and she was sworn to secrecy."

Colby shook his head, his frustration all over his face. "That's Maggie's biggest problem. She thinks she can do everything by herself—that needing someone makes her weak, so she pushes away anyone who wants to help. It's ridiculous, and it's made our relationship harder than it needs to be."

Quinn put a hand on Colby's arm. "I agree. When this is over, both you and I are going to have to talk to her about it. But let's just get through this first."

"If you're ready, we can walk back over there," Joe said. "All of you."

Colby's phone rang, and he wrestled it from his pocket. Quinn didn't even see him look to see who it was. He hit the button and shouted into the phone. Thankfully, it was on speaker and she could hear too.

"Hello?"

"Colby? It's Maggie."

All the energy seemed to drain out of Colby at once. He hit his knees, one hand covering his eyes as he began to talk, his voice broken by tears.

"Maggie? Oh my God, Maggie. Are you okay?"

Chapter Twenty-Eight

Just hearing Colby's voice was like a salve to Maggie's soul, but she had to be careful. Andrews was listening, just waiting for her to screw up. She struggled to clear her throat so she could make good use of what would probably be her only call to them.

"Maggie, can you hear me? Please tell me you're okay!"

Her hands were shaking so violently that she could barely keep the phone to her ear. After she'd gone into hysterics, Andrews had calmed her by negotiating with her. Two minutes to talk to her son and she wouldn't cry on him again. For a man drowning in his own madness, it seemed that seeing a woman cry was his kryptonite.

"Yes, but I'm only supposed to talk to Charlie," she said carefully. "I have to hurry. Pass the phone."

"Baby, please. Charlie's asleep and safe, but he's not here. He doesn't know what's going on. Has that creep hurt you? Talk to me, Mags. Talk to me."

Maggie wanted to climb into the phone and out the other side, straight into Colby's arms. His voice nearly made her melt with need.

She looked up and saw Andrews staring a hole through her. He was smart, and tricking him wouldn't be easy. And if he thought she was even trying . . .

It was worth the risk. "Hi Charlie, it's Mama," she said, hoping that Colby would take the hint that for now, he was going to have to be Charlie.

"Maggie. Okay, I got you. Tell me what to do. I'm listening, baby."

The desperation in his voice slayed Maggie. She couldn't say anything that she really wanted to, and it was killing her.

"Charlie, I don't want you to do anything. Listen, I'm going away for a while with a friend. And I might not be able to talk for a few weeks. But I—I . . ."

She looked at Andrews again.

"I love you. Okay? I really, really love you, and I'm sorry I haven't said it enough. I've been so stupid."

On the other end, Colby broke down into sobs. "Maggie, I love you too. I hear you, baby. You're coming out of there. Don't even think he's taking you anywhere. I'll kill him first, I swear to—"

Maggie hung the phone up. Colby was getting too loud, and she was afraid Andrews might hear him and know it wasn't Charlie.

"Now, you feel better?" he asked. "And suck it up. You said you wouldn't cry."

She nodded through the rain of tears. She didn't want to talk to him. She wanted Colby's voice to stay in her head for as long as possible.

"They should be coming with that wine and the keys any minute," Andrews said. "Once they scoot it in the door, I'm going to hold on to you again as you reach out and grab it."

She didn't reply.

"Maggie? You listening to me?" He sounded angry again.

"Yes, I'm listening, Martin."

His voice calmed. "Pizza in this mess of a place wasn't what I'd dreamed of for our reunion," he said, "but at least we'll have wine. Are there candles anywhere here? Doesn't the island get storms?"

"No," she lied. "We have a backup generator."

She didn't know if they had candles at the clinic or not, but there was no way she was going to sit down to candlelight and wine with him. Her acting skills only went so far, and if he tried to touch her again—

"When we get out of here, we'll go off grid. I've been studying about it, and I know all the natural edibles out there just ripe for picking. We'll camp near a natural spring and . . ."

He continued to talk and Maggie nodded occasionally, but she was thinking about Colby. She was glad now that he was on the island. Charlie was going to need him. Especially if—if . . .

She pushed that thought aside and went back to remembering Colby's voice. She'd always teased him that he sounded so much more country than she did. The fact was, he never cared what people thought of his accent. That was something that she really liked about him. He was who he was and no apologies—just like walking onto the beach in jeans and boots.

And looking damn good doing it too.

"Why are you smiling?" Andrews said, sounding suspicious.

She wiped the small smile from her face, irritated because she'd forgotten for a moment where she was.

"I was just thinking of a place in Haiku that Quinn told me about. It's wild there, even more so than Hana. It's a great place to walk into the jungle and hide from everyone."

"That sounds good," Andrews agreed. "But what about the shuttle to Lanai? Don't you think we should get off the island?"

"Lanai is too small. Nowhere to hide for us to finally be together."

He seemed to like her input and nodded, then lowered his head like he was thinking again.

"We're going to need transportation," he said, looking up.

The phone rang, and they both jumped. Andrews instructed her to answer it. The detective quickly told her that there was a delay finding a pizza joint still open, but they were working on it, and they had calls out about the helicopter too.

The detective wanted to talk more, but Andrews jumped up and took the phone. "What the hell is taking so long?"

Maggie watched as the rage crossed his face. He shouted again. "I don't give a shit about the pizza. Don't call back until you have the keys to the closet or the helicopter!" he yelled, then slammed the phone back on its hook.

He took his seat on the floor again, and Maggie stayed silent. She wanted to give him time to calm down.

She went back to thinking about Colby. It made her feel better, remembering him in happier days. She recalled years before when he would take her in his truck, all the way out to the country after a big rain. They'd hit every mud spot there was and laugh and shriek as they went around winding curves, barely able to see because of the filth that covered the windshield. Sometimes on summer nights they took a blanket and a cooler of beer and lay in the bed of his truck, counting stars and planning their future.

They stopped doing that when Charlie was born.

Actually, they'd stopped doing a lot of things. Maggie now knew that she'd kind of lost herself for a while there. As much as she loved having her newborn son against her breast, feeling his heart beat against hers, somewhere deep inside she had wondered if she'd made the right decision to become a mother.

She hadn't considered that maybe Colby felt the same, that fatherhood scared him. The pregnancy was a surprise to both of them, and neither of them brought up the possibility of not going through with it. But Colby worried about everything they would need to raise a child, constantly doing the math against their combined financial responsibilities to see where they could squeeze out a few more dollars.

Maggie quietly watched him give up spending money on his hobbies. He never complained, but she thought he should have been more upset about it. His whole life had changed, and she resented it *for* him.

Now it grieved her to think that she'd turned that resentment against him.

She recalled now that Colby never once said he didn't want to be a father. Before she'd told him to leave, he'd gotten up with her every time she fed Charlie in the night. He said he'd bottle-feed but, though Maggie's breasts were swollen and painful, she wanted her son to have the healthiest start possible.

Colby didn't let her be sleepy alone. He was always there.

She felt like such a stupid fool.

"What are you thinking about?" Andrews said, breaking her out of her memories and self-contempt.

"My son," Maggie answered, wary of giving too much detail.

"What's it like?"

"Having a son?"

He nodded.

"It's the scariest but most wonderful thing in the world," she said softly. "It's so incredibly hard, but then there are these most amazingly rewarding moments of pure love that slip through just often enough to keep you going through the difficult times. I wouldn't have it any other way."

"I made it harder, didn't I?" he asked.

It was quiet between them. No sirens. No phone ringing. Just a man and a woman having a moment of truth.

She turned and looked him in the eye. "Yes, Martin. You did. He was really upset about what you did to those flowers. That was one thing I couldn't hide from him."

He took it in, hesitating before he spoke again. "I bet you think I had a horrible childhood and it messed me up. Like you hear of those serial killers who were abused and later took their frustration out by murdering people."

"Well, your dad sounds like a real piece of work," Maggie said, forgetting that she was supposed to be minding her words.

Surprisingly, Andrews laughed. "You could say that. He wasn't one for animals, and I guess I inherited that from him. I just can't understand these people who are obsessed with dogs, putting clothes on them and carrying them around in purses. I think they're the mentally ill ones."

Maggie smiled. "They just want something to love."

"So did I," he said softly.

She wasn't sure how to answer that one. She couldn't very well sympathize with his obsession for her. She wasn't a stray dog that he could just claim as his. Why did some men think that once they chose you, they possessed you?

"But just for the record, I had a great childhood," he said. "I have a brother, and we were best friends. He was the good-looking one, though I was a year older. He was my wingman in high school. If it wasn't for him, I'd never have had a date."

"I've got a few brothers myself," Maggie said. Remembering them made her think of her mother, and she felt a lump rise in her throat. She hoped her mom knew how much she loved her.

"I know. I checked out each of them, making sure you weren't there before I figured out you were in Maui."

"Was it the picture online? At the inn with Quinn?" she asked, curious to at least know that.

"No. It was your banking. You shouldn't use your debit card. It was easy to hack in and follow you with each transaction."

"I thought you didn't have access to computers in prison?"

"I didn't, until I offered to do the warden's tax returns and I saved him a bundle over what he paid last year. Wardens are people too. We all like to save a buck."

He said it like it was funny, but Maggie didn't see the humor. If she made it out alive, she was going to let that warden know what a piece he was. So much for victims' rights.

"I'm not the average dumb criminal, Maggie. I graduated magna cum laude, you know."

"Good for you," Maggie said. Too bad he had done nothing with that distinction of honor, except managing taxes for a prison warden. It always amazed her how many idiots in the world held college degrees.

"I had an accounting business once too. It was even profitable. But my brother, he was my partner, and I found out later that he was doctoring the numbers. We had one good year, and then we were in debt up to our eyeballs. He screwed over a lot of our investors too. Family. Friends. Our name was mud."

"Great wingman," Maggie said. She couldn't even imagine one of her brothers doing something like that to her.

"He's dead now. Couldn't take the humiliation of being bankrupt. He had a pretty little wife and 2.5 kids. Nice house in the suburbs and two new cars. He didn't want to just keep up with the Joneses, he wanted to be the Joneses. Instead of facing his downfall like I did, he ate a bullet."

Maggie stared at him.

"I'm sorry," she said. She meant it too. No one deserved to lose someone they loved that way. Not Andrews, but especially not the man's wife and two children, who were innocent and now had to live with that shadow of loss over them.

He shrugged. "Turns out he might have been better looking, but I was the stronger of us both. He was a coward in the end."

"To some people, pride is everything," Maggie said, nearly choking on the words because she was having an epiphany about herself and the mess she'd made of her life. She'd thought she could outsmart Andrews without bringing anyone else into it. Poor Charlie lived day to day without a father because of her damn pride too.

"But I miss him," Andrews said, still talking about his brother. He dropped his head down to stare at the floor between his knees, choosing not to look at her to finish the story. "My parents were devastated.

They thought I could've stopped it from happening. We never spoke again after the funeral. As a matter of fact, I feel like I was ostracized from every relative I know."

"I'm sorry, Martin." Maggie couldn't imagine how alone that would feel. Her big family was her safety net—or at least they were until she decided to shut them out of her problems, therefore her life.

She'd been such a fool.

He looked up. "You're really not at all like I thought you were."

"What do you mean?" Maggie asked.

"I thought you were going to give me much more of a fight. You're not really living up to that fiery hair."

"I'm not much for fighting these days, Martin. After all the running I've done lately, I guess I'm just tired. Sorry to disappoint."

"Look, I'm not an idiot. I know I'm not getting out of here with you. But it was fun pretending for a little while."

He looked sad. And weary.

It was time for the truth.

"You're right, Martin. They'll never let us go."

"I'm not delusional either. There is no *us*. And they'll shoot me if I walk out there." He pulled the scalpel from his pocket and ran his finger along it. A line of blood popped up.

"Maybe not," Maggie said.

He made another stripe down another finger, as though testing to see if the blade would work twice.

"Don't do it, Martin."

"Do what?" he asked, smiling at her.

"Don't be your brother. You're better than that. Be a man and face the music. What you've done is a crime, and you're going to have to pay for it. You said it yourself—only cowards take the easy way out."

He struggled to stand, and when he was up, he smiled down at Maggie.

She looked at him from her place on the floor, still sitting against the wall. "What are you doing?"

He took a step toward her.

Then another until he was hovering over her. "Not what you expect," he growled.

Chapter Twenty-Nine

Maggie stared up at the hand that Andrews offered her. It was pasty white and, for a man's hand, not that big. It looked pathetic. But what really stood out was that it was steady.

So damn steady.

She recalled how hers had shaken when she'd worked with the syringes. But not his. His was solid. If he were giving up, going back to jail, truly thought this was the end, wouldn't he seem more . . . afraid? Angry? Something?

"Here, let me help you up," he said, stretching his hand farther. Eagerly.

Something didn't feel right.

He'd seemed coherent in these past few moments, but just a short time ago he'd been completely deranged and suffering withdrawal symptoms.

Was his sudden calmness an act? And what if he snapped again at her touch? Or if armed police officers came pounding in? Anything could set him off because he was unpredictable.

He reached down a little farther, his eyes challenging her to grab hold.

Trusting Andrews was a gamble.

Another flurry of thoughts went through Maggie's head in a matter of seconds. First she remembered Woodrow and his expression of pain.

Then Charlie's sweet smile that looked so much like his dad's, always making her heart shift and flutter. Her little piece of Colby that she clung to desperately. She imagined Charlie in their bed, his head on her pillow, innocent in his sleep, sometimes even laughing out loud in a dream world that only knew good things.

Her little boy had no idea that his entire future could be changed the next time he opened his eyes. And why should he have to face the possibility of not having a mom in his life? What gave Andrews the right to take that from her son? She had never encouraged him. Never led him on.

She didn't deserve it, and her son damn sure didn't deserve it.

No, Andrews hadn't snapped yet, but who could say what he'd do if a SWAT team busted through? He was unstable. Angry at her one moment, then contrite. He was calm now, but anything could happen in the last moments. Was she really going to leave it up to him?

Maggie felt her pulse racing faster.

She breathed.

Andrews was mistaken if he thought she'd allow some whiny lowlife like him to come between her and the things she loved. The anger began to boil inside her, causing her entire body to quake as she thought about how much power he'd taken from her before.

But he didn't see it. She wouldn't let him.

Not yet.

"Are you coming?" he said, irritation entering his tone.

She didn't know what he had in mind, but when her eldest brother's face flashed before her, she knew what she had to do. She actually had all her brothers to thank for the instincts she suddenly found. At one time or another, they'd all made sure that by the time she entered junior high, she had some smooth moves tucked away in her pocket in case she ever needed them. They took turns helping her perfect those moves all the way up to the time she left for college.

She didn't meet Andrews's eyes. She didn't want him to see what was brewing there.

It might get ugly, but if he didn't think she could take a punch or a roll around the floor, he sure hadn't studied her enough. He should've thought that one through, because it was time to show him what a Dalton was made of.

Maggie took his hand and let him use his equilibrium to pull her into a standing position, but at the same time, she brought her knee up and straight into his groin. She didn't take it easy on him either—not like she had with her brothers—and she literally felt him cringe from the flash of agony as it entered his body.

He folded forward like an accordion, dropping her hand to cradle himself and leaving his face wide open.

Quickly, Maggie hooked two fingers into his nostrils and pulled up with all her might until the palm of her hand collided forcefully with the bridge of his nose.

A flurry of profanity left his mouth, and he fell to his knees.

"You bitch—what are you doing?" he screamed, one hand on his privates and the other on his nose.

Maggie didn't hesitate.

When he curled into a protective ball, she pulled the syringe from her back pocket, yanked the top off with her teeth, then bent down and jabbed it into the side of his neck.

He flounced around and tried to block her, but she hit the target.

"Asshole," she finished, pushing the syringe all the way down and draining it completely.

He twitched a few times and then was still.

Maggie didn't wait to see if it was enough to keep him immobile. She pulled the syringe from his neck, leaped up, and ran into the hall and to the back door.

"I'm coming out," she shouted from beside the frame. "Don't shoot!"

She heard a loud sobbing and then was embarrassed when she realized it was coming from herself. She gathered her courage and moved into the open doorframe. The night sky opened up before her as she vulnerably faced the line of cars and uniforms below it, squinting at the beams of light shining directly into her eyes.

"Drop your weapon!" a faceless someone shouted.

She looked down at the bent needle in her hand.

Her weapon.

She dropped it and let out a long, ragged sigh.

"Where is Andrews?" someone else shouted, his voice authoritative.

"Incapacitated," she shouted back. "Just through there and on the floor, but you'd better hurry before he wakes up."

A uniformed officer ran to her, and as Maggie moved closer, she saw Colby behind him.

He reached her just as her knees felt weak and the adrenaline drained from her body.

"I've got you, baby," he said, his arms wrapping around. "That's my girl. Just relax. You're safe."

Their embrace only lasted a minute before she felt a pull on her arm and looked to find Quinn waiting, somewhat impatiently. Liam was beside her. The torrent of tears competed with the fear in her best friend's eyes, pushing Maggie to wiggle loose.

Quinn's arms were around her instantly, and she whispered through her hair.

"You scared me senseless."

Maggie took a deep, heaving breath. "I think I did the same to myself. But, Quinn, you should've seen me take him out. My brothers would be proud."

"Thank God you'll be around to tell them," Quinn said. "I can't imagine if I'd lost you, Maggie."

Maggie's heart swelled. If felt good to be so loved.

But it didn't quell the earthquake of adrenaline that still had her visibly shaking.

"Let us have her," the cop said, trying to separate them. "We need to move her to safety so we can take Andrews into custody."

"I'll move her to safety," Colby said, stepping in front of the officer. With one swoop, he lifted Maggie into his arms and carried her through the band of lights to just beyond the line of cars.

She wanted to struggle. She needed to walk on her own. But it felt so good in his arms. So safe. And so damn right.

"You did it, Maggie," he murmured into her hair. "You absolutely did it, you badass fiery woman. I knew you would."

He knew she would.

That told her he had faith that she could stand up for herself. That she was independent and strong. That he didn't doubt her.

And for Maggie, that was enough. She could finally lay her armor down.

"Take me home to Charlie," she said.

"Damn right I will, Mags."

She heard the ragged sob in his voice and let her body relax against his, laying her head on his shoulder and breathing in the familiar intoxicating smell that was her Colby. This time she accepted his strength and acknowledged that for once, she needed him. Ironically, with that concession finally embraced, it was the strongest she'd ever felt.

Chapter Thirty

Maggie accepted the glass of champagne from Colby. He hadn't left her side during the last eighteen hours. He hadn't even put up a fuss when she told him he had to change into some nice pants and a button-down shirt for the event at the inn if he was tagging along.

He looked handsome as hell in it too.

But she still preferred his jeans and boots. He was a Georgia country boy through and through—and best of all, he was *her* country boy.

Woodrow flanked her other side, and Maggie felt completely protected but thoroughly drained. While Quinn and some of her employees ran around to finish putting the last touches on everything for the vow renewal, Maggie got to reenact her evening of trauma repeatedly. Everyone wanted all the juicy details, and she hoped this was the last time she had to tell them.

"And then what did he do?" Kira asked.

Maggie was surprised to see Quinn's sister there, especially without her husband. Hopefully it meant her anger at her parents had subsided.

"Not what you think," Juniper said, winking at Maggie.

"He held his hand down to help me up, and I thought about Charlie," she said, then instantly blinked back tears at the mention of her son. She looked over to where he was sitting at a table with Kira's children, happily adding another block to a precarious-looking tower.

"Then she kicked his ass up one side and down the other," Juniper said, nodding proudly as though she'd been Maggie's manager in the corner of the ring, cheering her on.

Kira laughed. "I so wish I could've seen that."

"Oh, me too," Colby said. "But I got to see his face when they brought him out. Remind me not to start any more arguments with her. Charlie and I don't want to see her in motion."

Maggie smiled. Thankfully her traumatic evening wouldn't be a memory that Charlie would have to deal with. By the time he'd woken up the next morning, Maggie was there to be the first person he saw, and he never had any idea what had transpired or how close he'd come to losing his mama.

"Good thing for your brothers, Maggie," Kira said. "But I don't recall Quinn saying she learned any self-defense from them."

Maggie laughed. Someday soon she'd tell her brothers everything and give them the accolades they deserved—once she was sure that Andrews was secure so they couldn't kill him.

"They thought Quinn was too girlie to teach. But as it turns out, accountants aren't really fighters either. Maybe a few years behind bars will teach him some moves."

The Hawaiian trio of singers started in to a new, mellow song, and Colby swayed to the music as though he was enjoying it. It was a far cry from the country and western stations he listened to at home, so she found his interest amusing.

"You weren't scared walking out there to a full brigade?" Lani asked.

Maggie nodded and laughed. "You bet your ass I was scared! I screamed that I was coming out and not to shoot."

"But you shot Andrews up!" Kira said.

"She sure did. Straight into his neck," Juniper said.

"Wow," Lani said. "You could've killed him."

Maggie shook her head. "No, the big stuff is behind lock and key. Dexdomitor is kept on the crash cart and used for a short sedation.

Enough of it was perfect for the few minutes I needed to get away. He had a nice little nap and didn't wake up until he was in the ambulance already cuffed."

"It's good you thought of it," Lani said.

Maggie shrugged. "Honestly, I was kind of hoping I'd give him enough of the drug that he would never wake up. But one, we don't keep that much on the cart, and two, deep down I didn't want to kill him. I don't need someone's death on my conscience."

"I hope he rots in there," Colby said, suddenly angry again.

Maggie touched his arm and he settled.

"Oh, he will. Just the escape will add on ten years, not to mention kidnapping," Juniper said. "And a charge of animal cruelty."

They'd all heard about how Andrews had sprayed Woodrow in the face with bleach and then nearly strangled him. Luckily the sweet pup was fine and seemed no worse for wear.

Maggie nodded, but she didn't feel angry at Andrews any longer. She'd kept nothing but fear and bitterness in her heart since she'd met him and wasn't going to give him any more of her headspace. She'd chosen to forgive, because that's what her mama taught her and what she knew would bring about her own peace. The penal system would make him pay enough.

Kira and Lani began telling a story of someone they grew up with who was stalked. Maggie zoned out, not really caring to hear any more on the subject for a while. Across the way, she noticed Quinn's parents. They stood together, nearly attached at the hip they were so close. They were definitely what she'd consider relationship goals. The way that Noah looked at Jules was something every woman dreamed of and hoped for. And Jules was still gorgeous, even in her fifties.

Maggie envied Quinn and her genes because she was going to look just like her mother when she reached that age.

Jonah caught Maggie's eye and smiled. He looked so different in this setting, all slicked up, that she barely recognized him. She gave him a little wave and wondered who his guest was. It was a pretty young woman, and Maggie envied the boho bag that sat at her feet, a vibrant pattern covered in frogs that contradicted the elegant dress she wore.

Helen was there too. Other than the black pug, Cinder, that she had agreed to foster, she sat alone. She kept one hand on the dog's neck, her fingers rubbing gently as she watched everyone interact around her, especially Jules.

Maggie felt sorry for her. She'd been a wicked old lady in the past, but you could see that she wished she could be more a part of her daughter's life.

Jules was one of the kindest people Maggie had ever met, and she wasn't exactly cold to Helen, but you could tell that they still hadn't completely mended their mother-daughter relationship. Maggie doubted they ever would, honestly. Helen had played the biggest part in separating Jules from her first daughter, and although they were getting a second chance now, they'd lost thirty years. How could that ever be truly forgiven?

Maggie's thoughts were diverted when she saw Joe coming toward them. He saw her, too, and smiled big.

"Maggie. Colby. You both look great," he said, leaning in to kiss Maggie on the cheek.

Juniper came in closer to stand beside Joe.

"Joe," Maggie said, "I'm so glad you came. I wanted to tell you again how sorry I am that hiring me brought you so much trouble."

"No, Maggie," he replied. "Don't say that. It's not your fault, and hey—I wanted to remodel anyway. The back area is going to be state of the art when I get the insurance to pay out. I'm just so glad you weren't hurt."

"Except for my tailbone," Maggie said, laughing.

During the crisis, she hadn't felt the pain of being jerked down to the concrete floor, but it settled in afterward. Since then Colby had teased her relentlessly about the soft pillow she carried everywhere. But other than that, she'd walked away fairly intact—a miracle considering the shape that Andrews woke up in.

"Don't think that's going to get you workers' comp," Joe teased.

Colby was being quiet and when Maggie looked at him, he stuck out his hand to Joe. "Can we do this again? The last time I was a real shit, and my dad always told me to not shake a man's hand unless I meant it."

Maggie hadn't heard that Colby had been anything less than a gentleman to Joe, but she was proud of him now for making it right.

They both laughed, and Joe took Colby's hand. "No worries," he said, giving it a firm shake before dropping it. "I can understand where your head was. A good man can't think straight when someone he loves is in imminent danger."

"No, it's not okay," Colby said, suddenly humble. "I also want to thank you for giving Maggie a job. And for being her friend."

Joe nodded and met Maggie's eyes for a split second before answering Colby.

"My pleasure. She brings a lot of energy to the clinic. And hey—I heard you've never surfed? If you'd like a few lessons, I'll be glad to take you out. Unless, of course, Maggie wants to teach you. She did pretty well herself first time up."

Colby smiled, and a silent message seemed to travel between the two of them. "I'd like that. Charlie can't stop talking about you either. He's showed me that shark's tooth you gave him at least a thousand times already."

"Ha!" Joe barked. "Well, you keep Maggie nailed down until she's fully ready to come back. Her job will be waiting. Now if you'll excuse me, I'd better do some schmoozing—get my name out there and all that, you know. Build some new business."

Juniper nudged him with her elbow. "I'll join you. With your charm and my good looks, I'm sure we can drum up some new customers."

"It's beautiful out here, isn't it?" Colby leaned in and whispered.

Maggie felt a jolt of electricity go through her when his lips grazed her earlobe. She shivered.

"Cold?" he asked.

"No, I'm fine. And yes, Quinn's done an amazing job turning this into a romantic spot for David and Julianne."

Everywhere you looked there were candles lit, their flicker a lovely backdrop for the exquisite flowers placed throughout the venue. Arrangements were on the tables, and petals were strewn down the white carpet. Quinn had even had a special arbor set up at the end of the carpet with soft pink-and-white plumeria woven around it.

"My stomach is going to sue me for nonsupport if I don't get something in it," Colby said, rubbing his belly.

Maggie heard it growling and laughed. "I'm hungry too. The smells coming from the kitchen are killing me. I can't wait to dig in."

Woodrow thumped his tail, picking up on their conversation.

Maggie saw David come from inside the inn and look around. Maggie knew he must be searching for Quinn, so she caught his eye and pointed toward the café entrance.

He nodded and headed that way.

"I think they're getting ready to come out," she said. "Maybe we should all sit down."

They scattered, finding their seats. Maggie noticed that Kira sat with her parents and sister, her husband nowhere in sight. Quinn had told her that Michael had admitted to contacting the media and planting the seed about her being the lost girl. All because he'd felt slighted that his business with Helen had become a family discussion. He'd asked for forgiveness and agreed to counseling.

Colby put his hand on Maggie's waist and guided her toward the front row, next to the reserved seats for Quinn and Liam. Charlie joined them, and they sat down. Woodrow made himself comfortable at their feet.

Maggie leaned toward Colby. "Have you seen Liam?" She could see his mother and brothers, but he was absent.

"No, not for a while. He's probably helping Quinn out, don't you think?"

Maggie shrugged. "I wish we'd get started. I just want to go home and decompress."

He leaned back and put his arm around her. "I agree. This will be nice, but we're still making up for lost time. Doing nothing with you and Charlie would mean everything to me right now." He smiled and squeezed her closer. For the first time in a while, she didn't want to be let go.

~

Quinn was getting a lot of thinking done as she helped prepare another pupu tray for the snack table. Before she'd come to Maui, she'd only had herself and her ex-fiancé to worry about. Now with the discovery of her big family, there were so many different threads of things going on all the time. Keeping up with all of it was hard to do.

She'd talked to her mother earlier about Kira. Her sister had apologized for the way she and her husband, Michael, had acted. She'd confided that their grandmother had said no to the loan, but even if she'd said yes, Kira claimed she'd had a change of heart. Michael, however, was going to take a little longer to come around, as he'd had stars in his eyes about their possible business venture, and he felt ganged up on by the family.

Jules said he'd be fine in a week or two because he had to be; they were all he had. His own family was on the mainland, and visits between them were rare. Michael had a lot of weird quirks, but Kira said he was smart enough to know that his children needed grandparents and other relatives. He'd been in Hawaii long enough to know that *ohana* was everything, and he wouldn't let them suffer over the loss of a business dream.

Quinn was impressed with the compassionate way that her mom talked about Michael, as though he, too, were one of her adult children and just needed some extra time and understanding.

She finished stabbing the prosciutto-and-cheddar apple slices with toothpicks when she looked up and saw David. He looked very handsome in a pair of white beach slacks and a baby-blue button-down shirt.

"Hi, is Julianne about ready?"

"She wants to talk to you, actually. Can you come to our room?"

"Of course. Is everything okay?"

He faltered. "Well, yes. But I'll let her tell you."

Quinn turned to Maria. "Can you finish up without me?"

"I'll be fine. I've got the little mermaid to help me too," Maria said. "Pali already set up all the chairs and is supposed to be here to carry out the food."

Maria's daughter beamed up at them. "Pali's bringing his girlfriend."

They laughed.

"Don't embarrass your brother, Alani," Quinn said. She pulled off the apron she was wearing over her new dress. Liam had helped her pick it out from one of Maui's finest boutiques that morning, and it was the prettiest thing she'd ever owned. The long wrap dress was made from the lightest chiffon, and the pale-pink orchids crawling over the cream background gave it just the right amount of softness in a muted color that wouldn't take attention away from whatever dress that Julianne wore.

Quinn's shoulders were bare under the thin straps, and the skirt swooshed in the most divine way around her legs when she walked, making her feel pretty.

She followed him to his room, and when she went through the door, she could see Julianne was on their private terrace. She was surprised to see Liam there, sitting across from her and holding her hand, as he appeared to be listening to her.

"Liam?" Quinn said.

He stood and waved for them to come out.

Quinn walked through the room, taking note of how neat it was despite their lengthy stay. Someone had been to the library, and a stack of books at least two feet high was beside the bed, the only thing really out of place.

Liam stood and pulled out a chair for Quinn, and she sat down. David stood behind Julianne, his hands on her shoulders. She looked lovely, having picked a warm color of rose to complement her usually pale face. Her hair was done differently, pulled back in an elegant chignon that made Quinn wonder if someone had come to style it for her. She mentally kicked herself for not having thought of it first.

"Julianne, you look beautiful," she said. "Are you just about ready?"

Julianne reached out and took Quinn's hands, holding them between her own. She smiled serenely.

"I had the most wonderful experience last night, Quinn. I think it was meant for me to share, and I'd like to tell you about it."

She looked questioningly at Quinn.

Quinn hid a sudden flash of anxiety. Everyone was on the terrace, waiting for the ceremony to begin.

"Of course," she said, resisting the urge to look at her watch.

David pulled up another chair and sat beside Julianne.

"First," she said, "I need to tell you that I was blessed in this life to have two gifts. One was my ability to dance. From the time I took my first steps, I could feel the music in my soul, and my body reacted easily to it, giving me grace and stamina that some might envy."

Quinn nodded. "David said you're an amazing dancer."

"I was," Julianne said. "Now I still hear the music, but the dancing is in my soul, only visible to me. And that's okay. I've done enough dancing for one lifetime. But the other gift I have is one that not too many would be envious of."

Quinn was curious now.

"I have mantic dreams," she said.

"I don't understand," Quinn said, confused now.

"If you go back in history, even centuries ago, people have looked to the stars or visionaries to predict the future, right?"

Quinn nodded.

"Well, since I was a young woman, I realized that many of my dreams were prophetic. Not all of them, mind you, but over the years I began to be able to tell which ones were simply my mind downloading fantasies and memories, and which were messages. I rarely share them with anyone but David. However, I've been careful to keep a journal, and to later mark the ones that occur in reality."

Quinn couldn't imagine what she was getting at. Was she afraid of the ceremony? Had she seen a storm brewing? What?

David cleared his throat. "She's become very accurate. It's there in black and white, with dates and details. But it's something that we've kept between us. Just because she's seen the future doesn't mean she has the power to change it."

Quinn thought of Liam's father. It wasn't exactly the same, but dreams had led him to his life's work too. She believed in the power of dreams and intuition. But listening to David talk about something so unusual felt strange in itself. From what Quinn knew of David, he was a very straightforward and methodical man. Not one who you'd guess would believe in such things.

"I'm lucky that my dreams tend to stay on the personal side. Just to be clear, I could never predict a natural disaster or tragedy that would affect a mass crowd. I'm thankful for that, as well. I'm happy just to live in my own little world without taking on the burdens of strangers or the impending destruction of our earth."

"Tell her what you saw," said Liam, his tone encouraging.

Julianne smiled again. "The first dream was last week, and I saw Liam's father coming to you, his heart on his sleeve."

Quinn nodded, but she wasn't sold yet. It wasn't impossible that Julianne or David could've seen Ano leaving her suite. But then, how would they know he was Liam's father?

"The second dream I had was last night, and in it, I saw you and Liam."

Now Liam was smiling. She must've already told him.

Julianne stared serenely ahead as though seeing the dream in her mind again. "You were wearing a ring, and you both were very happy. It was obvious to me that you had given your dedication to each other and sealed your future as one."

"Was it here, in Hawaii? Or somewhere else?" Quinn asked, curious if there were mountains and a spread of land in the background.

Julianne nodded. "It was definitely Maui. The ocean was roaring behind you, and the wind was blowing your hair in the sea breeze. And Quinn." She leaned in closer. "There were children. At least two."

Quinn sat up abruptly, taking her hands from Julianne. Now it was getting to be too much. She was sensitive about not being a mother. It wasn't a subject to play with.

"I don't understand what you're trying to tell me, and Julianne, we have guests waiting. We really need to go."

"She's trying to tell you that she already saw this," Liam said, then got out of his chair and went down on one knee. He pulled a box from his pocket and opened it.

Quinn was speechless. It was the most exquisite ring that Quinn had ever seen. It sparkled against the black box—a diamond that was delicate, nothing too big or grandiose—and it was obviously antique. It fit Quinn's personality exactly, as though she'd picked it out herself.

Liam was calm. "I was going to wait until after the ceremony when I got you alone. But Julianne convinced me my timing would be off."

She felt overwhelmed with emotion, and her heart beat so loudly, surely they could hear it too. The timing was still off, for she'd already made her plans, and unfortunately, as much as it broke her heart, they didn't include Liam.

"Quinn, I know that you always strive to protect those around you. Because of that, you've planned to leave this island and walk away from the relationship we built in order to ease the pressures on your family's reputation. To save your grandmother. You're selfless. Loving. Loyal. All the things that I want in a partner. But this time, I want you to be selfish. I want you to stay and we'll face whatever may come. Together."

She couldn't think of a single word of response. Whatever option she chose would hurt someone, and that's what she didn't want to do.

"I've figured out how to tell your story without throwing your grandmother under the bus," David said. "You were so traumatized when you were found washed up that your parents didn't want a media circus. You needed therapy. The kind that Maui doesn't offer, so they sent you to stay on the mainland. You did well there and stayed, with their permission. That's not against the law."

Quinn wanted to let out the ragged sob that she held back. Was it really possible unraveling her story for the public could be that simple? She wouldn't have to leave Maui? Her parents? Helen wouldn't face further punishment than that she'd already set out for herself?

And, of course, Quinn didn't want to leave Liam. He was everything she'd ever wanted in a partner. Seeing his face made her day better. If ever she had a problem or needed advice, he was the one she turned to. The one she trusted. They just fit together physically and emotionally, all their broken pieces coming together to make her feel whole.

"Quinn, I want you to be my wife," Liam said. "Please marry me. Tonight."

"Tonight?" Quinn looked at Julianne.

"Yes, tonight. You can take care of the legalities tomorrow, but the ceremony can be done. Right now, with everyone you love already gathered round," Julianne said.

"But you and David—"

She held her hand up to stop Quinn's words. "David and I don't need to renew our vows." She reached up and took his hand. "We are as strong now as we were the day we met. In my dream, I didn't see me up there in front of friends and family. I saw you. And Liam."

Quinn looked into Liam's eyes and saw nothing but love. And hope. She thought of his father, who had praised his son for giving so much to his family, always putting aside his own needs. Suddenly all the hurt and betrayal from her past relationship just faded away and she knew, Liam would never hurt her. And never try to change her. He wanted her for who she was, not for who he wanted her to be.

"I love you, Quinn. Please say yes," Liam said. "Stay with me."

She nodded, and he broke out in a huge smile.

"Is that a yes?" he asked.

Finally the sobs erupted, but they were happy tears. She was going to continue to be the strong woman that the magic of Maui had taught her to be. She'd face her troubles just like Maggie had faced her tormenter. This was her life, and no one was going to make her give up what she had with Liam.

"Yes," she said. "Yes, yes, yes."

Liam stood and pulled her out of her chair, straight into his arms. He held her so close that it felt like they were one.

"Are you ready?" he whispered.

It was time to fulfill Julianne's prophecy, no matter how crazy it sounded.

Quinn heard Julianne sniffling and peeked to see David embracing her. Maybe the woman had a real gift and maybe not, but it really didn't matter now because her dream was the catalyst to Quinn following her heart. She looked up at Liam, the man who was about to be her future.

She'd made a lot of bad decisions in her life, but this one—this would not be one of them.

"Let's do this," she agreed.

~

Maggie was doing her best to pat down Charlie's cowlick, but she looked up when the band paused, then started playing the soft wedding song.

"Okay, Charlie, be still. This will be over in ten minutes or less and we can eat dinner. There's cake too."

He obliged, leaning into her, and Maggie once again thanked the universe that she was still able to be a mother to the most awesome little boy in the world, even if he had insisted on wearing Superman socks with his dress shorts. Before this week, she might've been embarrassed, but now she felt proud that he knew his own style and did his thing. She promised herself that she wouldn't stress over the little things anymore, but would instead celebrate them.

She turned to look and saw David pushing Julianne's chair. Instead of coming to the place where the Hawaiian elder stood, the Bible in his hands, David parked Julianne in the front row and took a seat next to her.

"What's going on?" Maggie said.

Colby shrugged, as clueless as she was. She looked down the row at Juniper, but her attention was narrowed to watching who would come next.

The music escalated a notch.

Moving up the aisle next was Liam. His elbow was linked with Quinn's, who was holding the bouquet that she'd made for Julianne. Liam had his arm looped through hers and wore the proudest smile Maggie had ever seen.

Quinn caught Maggie's eye and held up a hand, showing off a ring that hadn't been there before.

"Oh Mary, Mother of God," Maggie muttered. "They're getting married."

She knew this had to be impromptu. Otherwise Quinn would've told her. They shared everything. Maggie could barely contain her shock that Quinn was going against her usual tendency to overthink, then plan everything out to the last detail.

Who was this woman, and what had she done with Maggie's best friend?

Around them everyone stood, and there was a murmur of surprise that spread like a wave around the terrace.

Maggie struggled to her feet and watched as Quinn and Liam first paused at the row where his family stood. He reached out and took the hand of an older man who, judging by their likeness to each other, had to be his father.

Liam kissed his mother and they moved on, stopping where Jules and Noah were.

Jules was crying, the tears streaming down her face visible to everyone as she leaned in to Quinn, hugging her close. Noah shook Liam's hand and then put his arm around his wife and daughter. Beside them, Quinn's sisters exchanged astonished looks and whispered to each other.

Maggie turned to Colby. He wasn't even looking at Quinn and Liam. His eyes were set on her. She knew she was lucky to have him. And even luckier that she'd finally come to her senses. Now she knew that one of her greatest fallacies was her tendency to confuse independence with stubbornness. She'd learned over the last few days that it was okay to need someone, and it's not weakness to accept help from those who love you. It's simply letting them show they care in the ways that they can handle.

She could've saved herself a lot of heartache if she'd only figured that out sooner.

"Have I told you that you look ravishing in that dress?" he whispered.

"Shh . . . ," Maggie said. "And yes, you've already said that. A few times." She blushed. The dress was a little more feminine than her usual taste. A pale pink to offset the shade of her hair, with a hem that grazed the ground. Her feet peeked out, and Colby couldn't stop looking at the little turquoise ring around her toe.

He said it was sexy.

Quinn and Liam reached the front, and everyone else sat down.

Colby moved his chair closer to her. Their legs touched now, and the sparks were palpable. She poked him in the ribs with her elbow, but that only made him slide closer.

A breeze picked up, and she burrowed under his arm until she could feel the heat of him.

It was simple. Colby made her feel alive. He always had. She'd denied every good thing about them as a couple, but the truth was, there was never going to be anyone else. Not for Maggie.

She thought back to the night before, when she'd come out of the clinic. He was the one she'd looked for first—the only one she'd wanted.

Colby had cried and held her for so long, then swore she'd never get rid of him again. And that was a good thing because Maggie wasn't going to waste another moment of another day living in this lifetime without him.

The detective and a few other officers had followed her over, and they'd stood back, respecting the reunion.

Now a hush fell over the crowd as the music stopped. Maggie could see Quinn's face from where she sat and had never seen her look so happy.

Quinn turned, just slightly, and found Maggie. She smiled and nodded, a silent message between them, an acknowledgment that Maggie was next. Then she turned back to Liam, all his for the next moments.

Colby saw it too.

"What was that about?" he whispered, his head touching hers and his breath warm on her cheek.

Maggie laughed softly. "Nothing. But Colby, I have something to say. I never thanked you for overcoming your fear of flying to come here. I still can barely believe that you did it. For me."

Over their heads, she heard Liam agree to have Quinn as his wife. A murmur went through the crowd, then Quinn began her vows.

Colby smiled down at Maggie. "Oh, Mags, you just don't get it, do you? I'd follow you anywhere. There's no place too far."

Acknowledgments

To the readers in my online book club, My Book Tribe, thank you for making the last two years more fun as we gather together to banter about books. To those who aren't members, please drop by and visit. We are just one click away! To all my readers far and wide, thank you for continuing to read my work and recommending it to others. If you enjoyed *No Place too Far*, I would be very grateful if you could post an honest review on Amazon and/or Goodreads to help the book gain visibility and new readers.

Mahalo to the people of Maui again in this second book set on your lovely island. Your history is full of stories and legends, and I've enjoyed learning more through the research for this series.

To Amanda, I'm still living vicariously through your adventures on Maui, and many of them you will find within these pages. Maggie is a lot like you: strong and capable with a fiery and passionate spirit. Learn from this story: don't ever be afraid to ask for help, and never let anyone put out your flame.

Many thanks to my Ben for putting up with me when I was in the homestretch of writing this book and at the same time working with builders to finalize our new home. You've stepped in and done more than your share. It's this teamwork that makes our marriage so special, and what has made the last twenty-six years together so full of love.

Kelly Crake Ozgunduz and other Facebook friends in animal care, thank you for letting me pick your brains on animal clinic logistics and drugs. To those of you who are in my circle and on Kay's Krew, you are responsible for a big part of the success of my books, and I can't thank you enough. To Danielle, Gabe, and the rest of the team at Lake Union Publishing, thank you for continuing to help my words reach readers. Your hard work is acknowledged and appreciated. To Alicia Clancy, thank you for believing in this series enough to acquire it and to see it through. To Sarah Murphy and Alicia Clancy (again), you are both great editors who were instrumental in the developmental passes to get Maggie's and Quinn's story to be the best that it could be.

Last, there are so many people in my life whom I've never met that I can say I care about. I have such a strong online community of support, and though I probably share too much of myself, I don't regret a single bit of it. That you can reach through the screen and make me feel better with your words of affirmation says a lot about you. Raymond Loewy says, "People will turn to you, follow you, support you only as long as they are confident that you are doing your best."

Well, I'm doing my best, y'all. I really am. Thank you for seeing that.

From the Author

The town of Hana on Maui is often referred to by its residents as the "last Hawaiian place," and I can attest that a day spent driving there will soothe your soul and heighten your senses. The famous Road to Hana winds its way through a timeless, untamed rain forest paradise of lush flora, grand waterfalls, and a myriad of quaint—and sometimes startling narrow—bridges. Some say the drive is not for the faint of heart, but I say you don't want to miss it! Be sure to bring good hiking shoes, a swimsuit, and plenty of bottled water and snacks. Start your journey with a full tank of gas, a humble attitude, and a heavy dose of respect. If you are just visiting, remember you are a guest and the Hawaiians are gracious enough to share their treasure with you.

In the tiny town of Hana, you will find a strong sense of protectiveness from the people about their land, called the *'aina*, which has been passed down from generation to generation. Hana's long history boasts many legends of battles and heroes. As I've been experiencing more and more of Maui, I felt that Hana was the perfect place for Quinn to start her new life, among the ghostly shadows of the brave who came before her.

I also hope you enjoyed Maggie and Charlie. Maggie Dalton was a fun character to create, considering she has a fiery sense of independence that I've always admired but never attained. I think there are many women like Maggie who can mistake needing someone for being needy. Never be afraid to share your burdens with those who love you, for that is why they are on your life path.

As for Maggie's story line, the subject of stalking is a personal one for me. By definition, stalking is a pattern of behavior that includes harassment and intimidation and may cause fear or concern for the person who is the focus of the behavior.

Decades ago, I survived my own traumatic stalking ordeal. I use that memory, and more of my life experiences, to bring authenticity to my work. In turn, I feel that sharing the stories of my soul helps my healing process.

I hope all of you will continue to follow along in the By the Sea series. In book three, you'll see familiar characters and get to know Jules in more depth. You'll discover how strong of a wife and mother she really is when yet another of life's punches hits her full-on. Mothers are usually the glue that holds everything together. Through the years I've learned that some of the best moms grew up with tumultuous child-hoods, causing them to rebel as teens. How they overcame those lessons and learned from them is what separates the good from the great moms.

If you have survived a difficult childhood, background, or have experienced a toxic family relationship, I think you'll especially connect with the next book in the By the Sea series.

With gratitude,
Kay

READERS DISCUSSION GUIDE

1. Maggie has an issue with her pride, and because of it, she doesn't allow those who love her to encircle and help protect her. Are you like Maggie, keeping your troubles close, or do you utilize the bonds of family and let them intervene when you need help?

2. Maggie's pride also made her push Colby away because she thought he resented having a family. Have you ever felt resented by a family member? How did you move past it?

3. In this story, we explore Maui from the opposite point of view of a tourist. If you ever go to Hawaii, will you see it in a different light? If so, why?

4. Many single parents can relate to Maggie because of her living paycheck to paycheck and her modest housing and car conditions. When you started out, did you have to struggle to make ends meet, or was it different for you? If Colby hadn't come back into the picture, what are some ways Maggie could have gotten ahead in an area like Maui, with such a high cost of living?

5. Quinn did a great job renovating the inn and starting the business, but do you think she has done as well in forging bonds with her newly discovered family?

6. It's an admirable trait to put your family first, but Quinn pushes it to the extreme, tending to set her own dreams and desires aside. Many women are wired the same, but do you feel that once you turn a certain age, you're more inclined to put yourself first?

7. Maggie and Quinn have opposite personalities. Discuss how they are different. Do you have any friendships with opposite-minded people? If so, what draws you to them?

8. Family is important, but some people are closest to those who are not blood relations. Do you have someone in your life that is family by choice, not by blood?

About the Author

Photo © 2013 Eclipse Photography

Kay Bratt learned to lean on writing while she navigated a tumultuous childhood and then a decade of domestic abuse in adulthood. After working her way through the hard years to come out a survivor and a pursuer of peace, she finally found the courage to use her experiences throughout her novels, most recently *Wish Me Home* and *True to Me*. She lives with the love of her life and a pack of rescue dogs on the banks of Lake Hartwell in Georgia. For more information, visit www.kaybratt.com.